I0537349

SHIFTING SELVES

MIA MARSHALL

An Elements Novel

Match
Books

This one's for my mother, who was not the inspiration for any of the parents in this book.

You didn't just give me life. Through your love and unflagging support, you gave me wings.

CHAPTER 1

There are benefits to living without friends. Not many, but a few. For instance, during the decade I lived alone, I never wanted to strangle someone I loved.

"I hate you all." The words came out in a grunt. I was incapable of anything louder, needing all my air just to remain in my current contorted position.

"Breathe, Aidan." Vivian took my hips in her hands and twisted them slightly to the side, increasing the stretch. My thighs threatened to crumple beneath me. "You're seeking balance, remember?"

I turned my head to glare at her, and that small movement was enough to destroy the little equilibrium I possessed. I toppled over, landing soundly on my yoga-pants clad butt. A small black cat strolled past me, pausing just long enough to drop into a perfect downward-facing dog and prove the inaccuracy of that position's name. "Nobody likes a show off, Simon." I stretched out a hand to yank his tail, but it vanished a moment before I could grab it. The cat transformed easily into an attractive, black-haired, and buck naked man in his early twenties. He strolled to one of the deck chairs and sat next to Sera, seemingly unconcerned about the possibility of splinters.

"You do not seem to be embracing the spirit of this exercise," he observed.

I wiped my face, finding an actual drop of sweat had

beaded on my forehead. That was unacceptable. Though winter had finally surrendered its grip on the mountains, allowing spring its slow, triumphal return, the day wasn't nearly warm enough to produce sweat. It appeared I was, despite all my efforts to avoid such torture, exercising. I glanced toward the back deck, where my so-called friends were finding great amusement in my pain.

"I'm thinking insanity might be an acceptable alternative. If I promise not to kill any of you when I go mad, can I drop back into child's pose?"

Sera flicked a small fireball toward me, her version of cracking the whip. "Get back into warrior. Now." I grimaced and rolled away from the flame, letting it land harmlessly in the dirt.

Once, Sera wouldn't have been so cavalier. We might both be elementals, but I was water, and waters could burn as easily as any human. Of course, that was before we learned Sera and I had the same father, thus making me an absolute freak. I was the offspring of two full-blooded elementals, the only way any living creature could control two elements.

On the plus side, it meant I never had to worry about third degree burns. The only downside, really, was an unfortunate tendency to develop a fractured personality and go batshit crazy, as I'd seen happen with two other dual magic elementals. It turned out incredibly powerful and insane elementals were considered poor ambassadors for our race, so there was the constant threat of my death if the others ever learned what I was.

We'd spent the last month coming to terms with my possible future and looking for ways to avoid that fate. I'd opted for the comforting embrace of denial. The others were a bit more proactive in their efforts to keep me from going mad. Unfortunately, the only solution we knew at the moment was for me to never use fire, which meant I needed to avoid getting angry. Hence the yoga, intended to help me find my zen center. It might be more effective if I wasn't so annoyed they'd decided exercise was the best solution.

I eased myself into a lunge, cursing the entire time. I swung my arms skyward, and for a single moment I felt my body perfectly aligned. Hell, I almost felt healthy. The sensation lasted only so long as it took for my thigh muscles to cramp, announcing their displeasure with Vivian's plan for my mental health. "Corpse pose," I announced, throwing myself flat on the ground, eyes closed tight.

I heard Vivian sigh heavily and move away from me. I cracked my eyes just enough to watch her run through a series of stretches requiring an improbable amount of strength and flexibility. It was impressive, in the same way I felt impressed when watching Olympic sprinters from the comfort of my couch, preferably while eating a large piece of cake.

Sera's phone buzzed, and she checked the incoming message. "You're spared, Ade. Carmichael has finally seen fit to grant us an audience. He and Johnson want us in their office this afternoon."

I was glad my eyes were closed, giving me at least half a chance of hiding my annoyance at this news. Unlike Sera, I quite liked Carmichael. He and his partner Johnson were both good agents, and the fact that neither of them had attempted to arrest us and lock us in a government lab upon learning what we were was a definite point in their favor.

However, the FBI office was well over an hour away. This meeting would take the better part of the day, and I'd hoped to catch Mac when he returned in a couple hours.

A month had passed since I'd made the decision to

return to Lake Tahoe and live in the cabin we rented from Mac, and in that time I'd yet to find a single moment alone with the man, despite a concerted effort on my part. Every time I tried, he seemed to slip away. I'd gotten used to seeing the tail pipe of his Bronco as it sped away or the locked door of his Airstream trailer.

I knew he was avoiding me, and I had no idea why. Now, it looked like another day was going to pass without providing any answers.

"Do they want Vivian, too?"

Sera started to answer, but Vivian was already shaking her head, her long black dreads swaying with the force of the movement. "I have plans," she said. Considering that Vivian had sufficient hacking skills to break into the CIA database, I suspected she had good reason to avoid our friends at the FBI. Sera didn't argue, but she looked unhappy.

"Vivian," she began.

"Leave it." Vivian tended to be calm and grounded, and I'd never seen her angry. The look she gave Sera suggested there was a first time for everything. "It's not your call."

I spoke quickly, trying to break the tension. "So long as this means I've done my yoga for the week, I don't care who goes." Sera and Vivian ignored me.

Simon had a more effective method of redirecting their attention. "When you return, could someone please drive me to the train station? I packed this morning."

Vivian and I turned immediately toward him. "No!" Our protests were simultaneous and heartfelt.

He looked surprised by our reaction. "But the case is resolved. That was the reason Sera asked me to join you. I am no longer needed, and festival auditions begin this month."

Outwardly, Sera appeared calm. She nodded, her face

expressionless. But her right hand tapped rapidly against her thigh, and I knew she was already formulating a plan to change his mind. "I don't think today will work. Maybe tomorrow? I'll let you know." Her vague tone was deliberate, because Sera was never vague. She turned toward the house, tabling any further discussion of Simon's return to Oregon, and I wasn't eager to bring it up again.

"You know," said Sera, looking around the room, "For someone who tries to avoid law enforcement, I'm spending way too much time in this office."

"It's because you have a crush on Carmichael," I suggested. "I heard you call him the pretty one, you know."

She cast me a withering glance. "Yes, but that was before I spoke to him."

I grinned at her, not even attempting to hide my amusement. Before Carmichael, I'd been the only person who dared to argue with Sera, and even that usually fell into the bickering category. Long before we knew we were sisters, we were acting the part.

Apparently, Carmichael never got the memo informing him that Sera was usually right. When he'd learned about elementals, he struggled to come to terms with the knowledge, and part of that struggle involved a heated dispute with Sera about whether Brian or Vivian might have homicidal tendencies. She still hadn't forgiven him, particularly when she learned he'd been right. While I knew Carmichael was a hard-working agent who just really believed in catching the bad guys, Sera thought he might be her personal nemesis.

The two men entered the room together. In theory, they should have been a study in contrasts. Carmichael was the golden boy, the sort of man who modeled men's clothing in upscale catalogs, whereas Johnson was rougher around the edges. One was blond, the other dark. Carmichael offered a tight smile, while Johnson gave us a fifty-watt grin. And yet, despite all the contrasts, they felt like two sides of the whole. They wore nearly identical dark suits, and the sunglasses tucked into their jacket pockets looked to be the same brand. Both walked with confidence and absolute certainty in their mission, and when they sat down, both gazed at us with the same expectant look.

Several seconds passed. "So... we're here," I finally said. I could practically hear Sera roll her eyes. She could sit in silence for hours, waiting for the other person to talk first. When confronted with a stoic face, I was more likely to become verbally incontinent.

The corner of Carmichael's mouth twitched, suggesting he was well aware of this quirk. He ought to be. The two men had spent many hours interrogating me when they thought I was connected to Brian's murders. To be fair, I had been connected—just not in a way anyone had anticipated.

"It's good to see you, Ms. Brook." He turned his attention to Sera. "Ms. Blais." Johnson continued to smile happily at us both. While Carmichael was still trying to fit our existence into his version of reality, Johnson was thrilled to discover an entirely new world, and I thought he might like to move there full time. It didn't hurt that he had the barest strain of earth blood running through his veins. It gave him no power beyond some impressive gardening skills, but it still caused him to feel connected to us in a way Carmichael clearly did not.

Once, Johnson believed we were psychotic killers. Now, he smiled broadly every time he saw us. "We've been transferred," he announced.

"You're leaving?" I asked, confused.

He shook his head. "Not at all. It turns out my partner

here wasn't quite as circumspect as he could have been when writing the report."

Sera stared at Carmichael, her black eyes hard and unforgiving. I suspected she was wondering how much of his body she could set on fire and still get away with it.

I spoke hesitantly. "You know our people expect secrecy from us. A report like that, it'll cause trouble for us, Johnson."

"That's the best part! The FBI already cleaned it up for us. No one will ever see it."

Sera couldn't remain silent any longer. "Not seeing how FBI involvement is good news, Johnson."

He was downright giddy. I began to feel a level of dread directly proportionate to his excitement. "It turns out some at the Bureau already knew about you. And other things. They keep it quiet, of course, for obvious reasons, but the secret's already out. And now that we know, we've been transferred. Did you know there are shifters in the mountains? Shifters!" He was practically bouncing in his chair from excitement.

I looked between the two of them, filling in the blanks slowly. "If there's some secret branch of the FBI that knows about us, where the hell were they when Brian was shoveling earth into people's lungs?"

Carmichael stared back at me, his face calm but impassive. "As you well know, secrecy is only possible when few people know the secret. This is a tiny, off the books section of the Bureau, with limited manpower. They had task forces in the Appalachians and in Phoenix, but no permanent one on the west coast. Until now."

I considered his words. "You're telling us you're the freaking X-Files, aren't you?"

Sera appeared to enjoy that far too much. I had a feeling Carmichael would be known as "Scully" from that moment on.

"Something like that. It has a different title, of course. When you have a higher level of security clearance, you'll learn it." Carmichael slid two thick piles of papers across the desk. "Read and sign, please."

I sat deliberately back in my chair, arms crossed. "Sign what, exactly?"

"A non-disclosure agreement and an employment contract, Ms. Brook. We'd like you to work for us, starting today."

AN HOUR LATER, we sat in Sera's ancient Mustang, parked on the side of the road. Ahead of us, about a hundred feet down the road, sat a large wooden home that backed up to the edge of the Tahoe National Forest. We'd been staring at the house for several minutes, considering our options.

"We're not actually doing this, are we?" I asked. The fact that we were already parked in front of our first assignment didn't dim my hope that Carmichael and Johnson were playing an elaborate prank.

"I think we are." The words were contemplative, as if she wasn't sure what we were doing there, either. "Besides, imagine the novelty of being gainfully employed. Considering that you're in your 60s and I'm not much younger, perhaps it's time we stopped mooching off our parents."

We let that hang in the air. We weren't speaking to our parents at the moment. Neither of us had spoken to our father since the day we learned we were related, and I was steadfastly refusing to call my mother. On a good day, I only had to ignore three phone calls and half a dozen texts from the two of them. Other days, I needed to turn off my phone to have a moment's peace. As determined as I was to ignore them, they were equally determined to have their say.

I just wasn't ready to listen to their excuses, their reasons for denying me the truth of what I was my entire life. For now, avoiding my lying, overprotective parents seemed a logical step in the "keep Aidan calm and sane" plan we were subscribing to these days. I was happy to pretend I was an orphan for the foreseeable future, or possibly that I'd been hatched.

"So we'd be, what, adults?" I asked, pulling myself back to the conversation.

"Let's not get carried away."

"Does this mean we're supposed to wear black suits and matching sunglasses?" I looked down at my worn blue jeans and long-sleeved white tee. Sera already tended to wear lots of black, but she spiked hers with bursts of color, bright reds or deep royal blues. Neither of us looked particularly official.

Sera shook her head sadly. "We don't even get a badge or the chance to rough people up. I think we'll be lucky to have business cards. What would our title be? Liaison to the supernatural community? We can't exactly drop that into the 'win a free lunch' basket at the local deli."

"Whatever. We should still get the sunglasses, though."

"Agreed."

"But seriously, shouldn't we have been vetted first? Or trained? At some point, someone would have figured out we have absolutely no idea what we're doing and decided this was a ridiculous idea."

I was happy to be deemed incompetent if it meant we avoided the responsibility of working an FBI case. Gainful employment had sounded like a good idea when we were in the agents' office. An hour's drive later, with an unknown shifter's house sitting before us and absolutely no clue what we were supposed to do, I thought we should have been assigned something a bit more entry-level to start.

Sera turned to me, one dark eyebrow raised. "We're off

the books, Ade. They don't need to train employees who don't officially exist. And you think they haven't thoroughly checked us out already? Really, this is your fault. If you hadn't told Carmichael we solved those murders, you'd still be at the cabin, doing yoga."

When she put it like that, this didn't sound like such a bad option.

Of course, we hadn't so much solved the case as tripped and stumbled over the murderer who'd been hiding directly under our noses. It didn't really say much for our investigative prowess, but I'd neglected to mention that to Carmichael. It would have interfered with our bragging rights.

"We're just supposed to talk to them, right? That's it?" Sera nodded, looking dubious. I shared her doubt. If there were two people alive who should know how inept we were at tactfully interviewing someone, it was Johnson and Carmichael.

She tapped her fingers against the steering wheel. "Hey, at least this saves us from having to hide the shifters' existence any longer, since apparently some secret FBI cabal already filled them in."

"True. But even overlooking our complete lack of training or skill in the art of interrogation, what makes them think the shifters will talk to us?" I asked, watching the house. There was still no sign of movement, not even a squirrel darting among the fir trees.

Sera laughed. "You know Carmichael wouldn't give me any authority if he had another option. We're all they've got, cause they sure as hell know the shifters won't talk to human agents. They must think there's a chance they'll talk to us, what with the whole shared magical heritage thing. I guess we're better than nothing."

"Awesome. If we do get business cards, can that be our

tagline? Utterly clueless, but better than nothing."

She glanced at me, a quick sidelong glance, and her mouth quirked up in a smile. It was a tiny moment, but I instantly felt an answering smile pull at my lips. We were still finding our footing after years of estrangement, still adjusting to being sisters as well as friends. We were getting there, one bad joke at a time, and I treasured every sign that the bad years were behind us.

Sera fidgeted in her seat. Unlike me, Sera never could sit still for long, and few things bothered her so much as long periods of inactivity. It was a typical fire characteristic, one that had passed me by completely, along with all the physical traits. Sera looked like a classic fire, short, dark, and powerful, a compact ball of energy ready to explode at the slightest provocation. Even her hair was wild, a curly mass that refused to be tamed. I was tall, blond, lanky, and unrepentantly lazy.

I was also impetuous and quick to anger, qualities I'd long chalked up to what I'd thought was my human half. I now knew they were a manifestation of my fire side, a truth I still had difficulty accepting. Sometimes, I felt like a stranger to myself, with half my genetic code an unknown force just waiting to betray me. I'd only consciously accessed my fire magic once, but that had been enough. It had changed something within me, in that core where the magic lived.

Now, I always felt the fire inside me, demanding my attention. I didn't know how to acknowledge it and stay sane, but I also didn't know how to live as half a person. Lacking any answers, I was sticking with my favorite coping mechanism: denial. It might not be the healthiest strategy, but it sure beat going nuts.

Sera jerked into motion, swinging her door open. "Fuck this. Let's go see what those furry bastards have to say. And try to let me do the talking, okay?"

I followed behind her, wondering just how long it would take us to get fired.

CHAPTER 2

The front door was opened by the most enormous man I'd ever seen. His shoulders filled the doorway, and his head grazed the top of the doorframe. Though I was far from an expert on shifters, I would have bet my first paycheck that this man was, like Mac, a bear.

He didn't speak. He stared at us, dark eyes glaring beneath a heavy brow. The message didn't require words. We were not welcome.

A quick glance at Sera suggested her plan was to match him glare for glare. Entertaining, perhaps, and I imagined a battle between the two would be a contender for magical pay-per-view, but it was unlikely to get us in the door any faster.

"Sorry to bother you. This is Sera Blais and I'm Aidan..."

He cut me off. "I know what you are." The words were a growl, rough and deep in his throat.

"You do? That's, ah, wonderful." I attempted to make my expression match my words but likely failed. I hadn't even known shifters existed until I met Simon, but every shifter I ran into seemed to know exactly what I was. With the exception of Mac and Simon, none of them seemed inclined to like me, either.

I couldn't entirely fault them for their enmity. I was an elemental, born and raised among the old ones, and even I occasionally found our attitude a bit elitist. We were

descended from the earth's original creatures, the product of those first magical beings and humans, and we were
damned proud of that history.

Shifters were also descended from those original creatures, but they were the result of matings with animals.
The elementals who'd raised me refused to admit shifters
even existed, so horrified were they by the thought that
our ancestors dabbled in what they considered bestiality.
Those that did speak of them tended to do so with a sneer,
an upturned nose, and the unshakeable belief that elementals were far superior beings.

For some reason, shifters found that attitude offensive.

I forged ahead, forgoing tact altogether in a desperate
need to just get this over with, already. "We're here because
the local FBI thought we might be able to assist you."

Incredulity darkened his features. I wasn't certain
whether he was more angered by FBI involvement or elemental presumption, but considering that I was the walking, talking symbol of both those things, I realized tact
might have been a better strategy.

The man spoke slowly and carefully, enunciating every
word, ensuring there was no possibility of miscommunica-
tion. "The FBI thought you could help us? The local FBI
who doesn't know we exist?"

"Um, yeah. That one. If it helps, we weren't the ones
who told them about you. They already knew. We just told
them about elementals, which was our right and which we
had no way of knowing would lead them to you or cause
them to set up a permanent task force in the region. So...
surprise?"

I finally had the common sense to stop talking. I looked
at Sera, indicating this might be an excellent time for her to
jump in. She rolled her eyes at me once but finally decided
to help. "Are you familiar with the Department of Obvious

Paranormal Evidence Suppression? They're responsible for keeping magical races hidden from human knowledge, and some shifter activity has recently been less secretive than they would like."

Sera spoke these blatant lies without even blinking. All we knew was the agents had a source who'd indicated there were problems among the shifters, and this was the place to start asking questions. Also, to the best of my knowledge, no division of the Bureau used the acronym DOPES.

But the man before us knew none of this, and we'd obviously hit a nerve. "We take care of our own problems." He spoke to Sera only, obviously having dismissed me and my bright empty smile. He turned slightly to face her, providing me with a view of the living room. Several people huddled on a sofa, waiting expectantly for us to leave. Tension emanated from the room, fear and worry coating the air.

"Look," I said, stepping forward until mere inches separated me from this walking barrier between me and people I might be able to help. He turned to me in surprise, obviously expecting me to accept my dismissal. "I understand. You know what we are, and we also like to solve our own problems. In fact, Sera and I are the ones who solved the recent elemental murders. I know you heard about those. But shifters helped us, and we would have been foolish to turn them away. We're offering you our help. I suggest you refrain from being foolish, yourself."

It was a bold speech, and he looked torn between respect and a strong desire to slam the door in my face. Before he could decide what to do about the abrasive elementals on his doorstep, a figure appeared behind him, and the choice was made.

"Aidan?" Mac stepped into the doorway, nudging the older man out of the way. "What are you doing here?"

My heart stuttered and a familiar heat spread through

my body. Usually, Mac was where I expected to find him, and I could brace for my body's inevitable response. This time, I was unprepared, and the shock rippled through me.

I kept telling myself that this reaction was the result of years of self-imposed solitude and celibacy, an assertion that would carry more weight if I reacted like this to any other man. Perhaps it was that Mac was roughly the size of a small truck and considerably better built. Perhaps it was the way I always felt a little safer when he was around. Perhaps it was just the result of a kiss we'd shared a couple weeks before.

It was, I knew, all those things. Unfortunately, he'd given no indication that he wanted to repeat that kiss, while the memory often sent me into a slack-jawed stupor.

"Aidan?" He was staring at me, brown eyes focused intently on my face. I always had the feeling he saw me just a little more clearly than anyone else did. It was simultaneously exhilarating and terrifying.

Eventually, I remembered I was supposed to speak. "Why are you here?"

He smiled, the smallest uptick of his lips that only hinted at the humor buried within. "I asked you first."

I shrugged. "FBI."

He copied my movement. "Family."

"Oh." We all stood for another moment, no one bothering to move from the doorway. "So, can we come in, or what?"

He watched me for several more seconds, then wordlessly moved to the side, creating a small space through which Sera and I could enter the house. It was a narrow gap, and I deliberately let my arm brush his as I entered. I took a quiet breath, absorbing his warmth and scent. I suspected my libido was not behaving in accordance with FBI regulations for home visits.

The house opened into a high-ceilinged foyer, with rooms on either side and a staircase directly ahead. The home appeared to have been built sometime in the sixties, if the wood paneling that lined every wall was any indication. Wooden beams ran along the ceiling, and hardwood floors covered with throw rugs woven from natural fibers were beneath our feet. A stone fireplace, currently unlit, completed the effect of a perfect mountain cabin. It felt like the owners had done all they could to bring nature into their home.

A dining room dominated by a heavy wooden table was to our right. The living room I'd spotted earlier opened on our left, and I now had a better view of its inhabitants. In addition to the two women sitting on the sofa, a teenage boy, maybe fifteen years old, sat in an armchair. They all stared at Sera and me with blank expressions. They would not be outright rude, but they weren't ready to welcome us into their home.

I felt Sera move to one side, Mac to the other. "This is my Uncle Will and Aunt Celeste." He indicated the man we'd spoken to earlier and one of the women on the couch. "Their son Brandon, and Celeste's sister Eleanor." I nodded at all of them, trying not to stare at Mac's family with too much curiosity. With the fearful vibe emanating from that room, it wasn't the best time to look for a family resemblance. In truth, now that I was inside the house, I had absolutely no idea what to do next. I'd attended funerals with a more upbeat crowd.

"How can we help?" I knew I was supposed to question them in a calm and professional manner, but the words popped out. It seemed the only question worth asking.

Besides, for Carmichael to expect calm and professional from me and Sera, he'd need to show the kind of blind optimism rarely seen outside hippie communes. He knew what we were, and he'd sent us in regardless. I thought that gave us free rein to be ourselves. That's the logic I was going with, at least.

My offer was met with a resounding silence. The two women on the couch stared at me, their faces sullen and unwelcoming.

My defense came, surprisingly, from the man who'd been avoiding me for the last month. "They can be trusted, Will."

Will met his nephew's eyes and tried one final time. "They're outsiders."

Brandon spoke for the first time, his words quiet and pointed. "Some would say the same of me, dad." I studied the teenager, noticing that while the boy had his family's brown hair, his eyes were a pure blue. Unlike the others in the room, who all had the dark brown eyes of a bear, he was human.

Unlike elementals, shifter powers don't weaken if they mate with humans, so one is never a half-human or a weaker shifter. A child is simply a shifter or a human, depending on which genes they receive, and many shifters had human children or spouses.

I felt Mac shift slightly until he was standing behind me, literally backing me up. "It's okay, Will. I know them, and they're not like the others."

I was so grateful for his support that I opted to overlook the implied insult to my race. Sure, the old ones needed several long months of sensitivity training, but they mainly lived inside the elemental enclaves. Outside the enclaves, we were like any other group of people, with some far more tolerant than others.

Unfortunately, even saying that some of us were more tolerant than others meant there was a lot of intolerance most elementals never bothered to acknowledge.

As if on cue, I felt my phone vibrate. Without even checking, I knew it was my mother. She hadn't texted in hours, and she was overdue on her daily harassment. I ignored her.

Sera pointed at Mac. "What he's trying to say is we're not assholes. At least not most of the time."

I nodded, trying to look sober and trustworthy. Will was unimpressed. He looked over my head, meeting Mac's gaze. An undeniable aura of power surrounded Mac's uncle, suggesting depths of strength far beyond his physical prowess. "If you vouch for them, they're your responsibility."

Mac made no audible reply, but when Will nodded and turned away, I assumed the matter was settled.

Remembering our purpose, I addressed the entire room. "I'm afraid we need more information."

Eleanor spoke with barely concealed scorn. "Didn't the FBI give you everything you needed?"

I nodded sagely and searched for a response vague enough to hide the depths of our ignorance. "Yes, but we need to hear your version. This is the FBI, after all. You know they don't have all their facts straight."

Will snorted, indicating agreement with that statement, if nothing else. "It's James. My son's gone missing." He seemed to think that explanation enough.

"Has he done this before?" He shook his head slowly, as if he needed to think about the answer. I mentally changed his "no" to a "maybe."

"Did he leave a note? Pack a bag?" This time, the head shake was immediate. In the corner, Brandon squirmed in his chair and refused to meet my eyes.

Sera also noticed. "Care to share with the rest of the class, Brandon?"

His father's eyes narrowed on him, and Brandon found a loose thread on his shirt especially interesting. He was skinny and long-limbed, a boy still growing into his body.

"It was cold yesterday, so he was wearing his heavy coat. But today I went to borrow the other one, the lighter one, and it was gone. He had it with him."

It was possible that once, in the course of history, a teenage boy had thought far enough ahead to plan for variations in the weather and take both his coats on a day trip. I wasn't going to count on that happening this time, however. When James had left, he'd planned on being gone for a while.

"Any idea where he went?" I asked. Brandon shook his head miserably, and his father expelled a disappointed breath.

"We already looked for him," he said, "and if you think for one moment that you and that useless facial decoration you call a nose have a chance of finding an eighteen-year-old boy when a household of shifters failed, then you are welcome to try, little water."

In bare feet, I was only an inch or so shy of six feet. Granted, Will still towered above me, and was probably twice as wide, but I found I didn't much care. I was decidedly unused to being dismissed as a little anything, and I had no intention of starting now. "Nah, you're right. I'm sure me and my decorative nostrils would be no help at all. Sera, can you do anything to find this kid?"

As always, she easily caught her cue and answered without missing a beat. The fact that our audience might not appreciate our routine was irrelevant. "I could light a fire, maybe. Smoke him out?"

"That assumes he's in the forest somewhere. And really, with all the water around here, a fire could be easily stopped. It was a wet winter, you know."

"Fair point." She nodded, appearing deep in thought. "We really ought to find someone with a connection to the forest. You know, they could communicate with the earth, see who's walked over it lately."

"That's an excellent idea. Or maybe we should find someone who can talk to the water, see who's been crossing all those lakes and rivers, going where even the best shifter nose can't follow?" I took a step toward Will, a smug smile tugging at my lips. I stood up to my full height and looked him directly in the eye. I still had to tilt my head, but I was close enough to prove there was nothing little about me. "I wonder where we could find anyone like that?"

He stared back at me. His eyes, I realized, were a shade darker than Mac's chocolate brown ones, but he had the same broad, honest face. Even in the midst of our stand-off, I found myself inclined to trust this man, though I reminded myself that didn't mean much. Lately, I'd been trusting all the wrong people.

Finally, Will shook his head, breaking our stare. "Are they always like this?" he asked Mac.

Mac shrugged. "You get used to it."

"Right." He turned back to the living room and began issuing commands. "Eleanor, you stay here with Celeste in case he returns or anyone phones. Brandon, you're with us. Let's take the FBI's finest to where you last saw James." The sneer that returned to his voice when he spoke of the FBI made me rather glad we didn't have business cards or badges. "All right, little water. Let's see what you can do."

FORTUNATELY, WILL DISPLAYED the same fondness for over-sized vehicles that his nephew did, and the five of us easily fit in his Explorer. It was an older model, with plenty of scrapes and a few rust spots threatening the green paint, but it was roomy enough for two shifters, a gangly teenager, and their guests. The two older men took the front seats and Brandon hopped in the rear, leaving the middle seats for me and Sera. We were surrounded, and I suspected that was no accident.

We headed northwest through the trees. Spring had come late that year. Snow still covered the mountain peaks, which glimmered under the early May sun, but it had melted from the forest floor, revealing warm brown dirt and the early signs of spring growth.

My spirit couldn't help but lift at the sight. Sure, my life was kind of a mess right now, with one problem jumping on top of another without politely waiting for the first problem to be solved. I had a father I feared, powers I didn't understand, a potential future as a madwoman, the constant fear of being found out by other elementals, and a new job for which I was completely unqualified. Even worse, my friends were forcing me to exercise. But, hey, at least it was a beautiful spring day, and I planned to enjoy it.

The car was silent. The three men stared out their windows, lost in thought. They gave no indication they would provide information before it was absolutely necessary. Sera considered each man in turn, a stubborn set to her jaw.

Eventually, she settled on Brandon as the most susceptible and began to stare at him, her gaze determined and unwavering. He managed to ignore her for at least five seconds. To be fair, that was more than I'd ever managed.

"What?" he asked. He was surly and belligerent, the perfect juvenile delinquent.

"Tell us what you know," she said.

I caught Will's eyes in the rearview mirror, watching us intently.

"I don't know anything," he muttered. She continued to stare. I almost felt sorry for Brandon.

"I don't think she believes you," I said. He shifted in his seat, trying to escape her gaze.

A low growl came from the front of the car. I didn't know whether the warning was intended for us or Brandon, but I was certain Papa Bear wasn't happy at the moment. Brandon cast a nervous glance toward his father, then blatantly attempted to change the subject.

"Are you really half water?" he asked, sounding skeptical. Most of the stronger elementals—quarter-blooded and above—still lived in the enclaves, so it was likely he'd never met any truly powerful ones.

I nodded, and jerked my head toward Sera. "She's three-quarters fire." I figured it couldn't hurt to remind them that we were bad motherfuckers in our own right. Brandon glanced between us, and I thought he was working hard not to look a little impressed.

That was the wise reaction. We might act like buffoons on occasion, but Sera could set everyone in this car on fire and casually roast marshmallows at the same time, if she were so inclined. Hell, I probably could, too, if I didn't mind losing a little bit of my mind in the process.

I glanced at Mac. He was still facing forward, but I felt a rush of tenderness for the back of his head. He must have told them a little about me, for them to know how strong a water I was, but that was all Brandon knew. Mac hadn't told his family about my fire side. He knew the cost of the elementals learning I was a dual magic would be my life. The council would make sure of that.

It was a welcome reminder that, in this case, I'd trusted the right people. Sera, Mac, Simon, and Vivian, they held my life in their hands, and they were keeping it safe.

"Do you know many elementals?" I asked Brandon.

He shook his head. "No, but I was home schooled with kids from other shifter families until recently. We only mainstream for high school, even the human kids. They want to wait till we're old enough not to blab family secrets." He muttered the words into his chest, avoiding our eyes.

Having come from a similarly sheltered background, I

understood, and I felt a small pang of sympathy for the kid. No one wanted to admit to being socially maladjusted. "So, what can you do?" Brandon asked. "Can you make it rain and stuff?"

I nodded. "I can, if there's enough water in the air, but I have to be cautious. It ends up on YouTube if someone notices the storm is limited to a small area."

I don't think he heard anything beyond my first two words. "Could you do that sometime? Could I watch?" Despite himself, he was curious, and his interest caused the detached teen facade to drop for a moment.

I tried to take advantage. "When did you last see James?" I hoped that the sudden change of topic would catch him off guard.

He didn't fall for it, choosing instead to stare out the window and ignore me. I felt my earlier sympathy dissipate.

Will answered instead. "Brandon says they met up after dinner and went to the lake, but James wandered off after shifting. That was the last time anyone saw him."

"You didn't see anything?" Brandon shook his head, looking more than a little guilty.

"We'll see what the water tells us," I murmured, as much to him as to myself.

CHAPTER 3

Despite living in the area for years during college, I'd never been to Independence Lake, but after a few minutes in the area, I was considering buying a local home.

It was smaller than Lake Tahoe, but the water was every bit as clear, and it was surrounded by acres of old growth forest. It didn't suffer from the throngs of tourists that plagued its better known cousin, and at this time of year only the most dedicated kayakers paddled through its icy water. It was the sort of place that allowed you to picture what the mountains were like hundreds of years ago, when, paradoxically, uncontrolled wilderness offered peace in a way a tamed mountain never could.

If I lived in a place like this, I might never need to worry about my fire half manifesting.

Brandon showed us where they'd been the night before. I spotted several footprints in the area, both human and animal, possibly from where shifters had already searched.

I prowled around the lake edge, examining the area. "Brandon, where did James shift?" He pointed, and I walked to the spot. There were too many footprints to follow a trail, though I still tried. The paths led further into the woods and provided no clues as to James's whereabouts. When I returned to the others, Will looked amused by my failure. It was no more than he expected.

"Give me the shirt." I held out my hand, and Will passed

me a sweatshirt James had worn the day before. The shifters had used it to learn his scent for tracking. I had my own
plans for it.

"You think you'll have more luck with his smell than
we did, little water?" Will looked greatly amused by the
thought.

I might be naturally inclined to trust this man, thanks
to his resemblance to Mac, but that didn't mean I wasn't
equally inclined to drench him in a six-foot wave if he kept
patronizing me. I reached behind me, getting to know the
water. Just in case.

"Were you home schooled too, Will? Don't know how
else to explain you knowing so little about us." To my surprise, he laughed. He deliberately stepped away from me
and leaned against the SUV, giving me the freedom to do
what I needed. Though his pose was relaxed, his eyes were
sharp, studying my every move.

Before I could begin, Vivian and Simon appeared
silently before us. Between his cat nature and her affinity
for the earth, no two people could sneak around a forest the
way those two could. On the whole, it was a fairly useless
skill, but I enjoyed watching the shifters jump when they
arrived.

Sera had phoned them on the ride over, asking them to
join us. We filled them in quickly, blatantly ignoring any
confidentiality guidelines the agents might have expected
us to adhere to. I'd already chosen to trust these people
with my life. After that, what were a few national secrets
between friends?

"Just so you know, I am not getting drawn into another
mystery in need of solving as part of some master plan
to keep me in Tahoe," Simon informed us. His objection
noted for the record, he promptly shifted and ran up the
nearest tree. It was quite a bit taller than the average house

cat would be comfortable climbing, but Simon showed no such reservations. A moment later, he was jumping from branch to branch, able to examine the trails in a way no human or bear ever could.

"Brandon, where were you when he vanished?" He pointed to a large boulder, part of an outcropping of rocks that rose from the lake. It had a smooth, flat surface, and I imagined it was a favorite fishing spot for locals.

I perched on the rock and studied the shoreline. The water to the right was wide open, and Brandon would have seen anyone leaving the area that way. To my left, about two hundred feet away, the shoreline curved gently into a promontory that created a sizable blind spot.

I walked to that section of the lake and knelt at the water's edge. The water immediately rushed to me, wrapping around my Converse-clad feet in greeting. I ran my fingers through it, sharing its joy at finding an old friend. We'd been born from the same source, from the magic that long ago created every landscape on earth, and though millennia had passed, we still felt an unshakeable kinship. I might feel I lived in a state of constant chaos these days, but at least one thing never changed. When I touched the water, I knew peace.

Gently, I moved my hand over James's sweatshirt, picking up the residue from his sweat the day before. It wasn't much, and if he hadn't worn it while exercising, I doubted I'd be able to sense a thing. There was merely the hint of the water that formed his sweat, the tiniest suggestion of the being who'd worn this shirt.

It wasn't enough. I grabbed a bottle of filtered water from my bag and poured several drops onto the sweatshirt, letting it mingle with the dried sweat and revive it, until the water could tell me the story of the young man who'd worn the shirt. I wouldn't be able to read it as clearly as if the sweat had never dried, but it was better than nothing.

I let his essence fold into the tiny ridges of my finger-prints, become one with my own magic. I let it build slowly. It wouldn't tell me what James looked like, what he'd been thinking or doing or even feeling at the time. All I could achieve, with a tremendous amount of concentration, was a vague sense of his self, that quality that made him unique despite living in a world of seven billion people.

I waited, simultaneously breathing in the water and the scent, until I felt James's essence form in my mind, com-pletely separate from my own self.

I dipped my hand in the water, sending my new knowl-edge through the water along the shore, looking for a match, the spot where he might have entered the lake.

Though much smaller than Tahoe, this was still a large lake, and there was a tremendous amount of water to explore. I kept my eyes closed, refusing to allow for dis-tractions, and I focused wholly on the secrets the water revealed. The magic encountered dozens of people, fish-ermen who'd dipped their hands in the water or kayakers who'd stepped rapidly through the chilly shallows, but not as many as it would have found in summer. It was still a manageable amount.

At last, I found him, further away than I expected and weak. Still, it was enough. With eyes closed, I pointed to the spot. "There. Check there, Vivian." I heard her move away toward the spot I indicated. If there were any recent disturbances to the soil, she'd find them.

While she did that, I stretched the magic further through the water, looking for more evidence of James's presence. There was a clear path from the shore, but only for about five feet. There, it ended abruptly.

"Someone was here," called Vivian. "Last night. This whole area is disturbed, though."

"Like there were a bunch of shifters tromping through, looking for a lost cub?" asked Sera, sounding irate. I couldn't blame her. She was ridiculously powerful, but until we needed something set on fire, she was useless.

My eyes were still closed, avoiding unnecessary distractions while following the trail, but Simon's voice let me know he'd shifted back to human. "The prints are the same. It was one bear and one human in, I believe, size eleven shoes. Or just one shifter in both forms."

"James." Will sounded pained, and I made a mental note to cut him a little slack, at least until he started calling me little water again.

"Only one person went into the water," I agreed. I opened my eyes at last and looked directly at James's father. "Will, I think he did this deliberately. He set a false trail along the shore, then waded into the water, where he knew your noses would be useless."

A weight appeared to lift from Will's shoulders. While a runaway teen was no cause for celebration, it still beat the other explanations for why his son was missing.

I moved my magic through the water that undulated at the end of James's trail, seeking an explanation for its abrupt disappearance.

There it was. It was the smallest hint, the quickest dip of human flesh reaching out to help another. "He got into a boat, and he wasn't alone."

Will nodded at me once, a short acknowledgement of gratitude, then rounded on his other son. "Brandon, let's have some words." He stalked far away from the rest of us, leaving his son to follow dismally behind him.

Above me, I caught a flicker of movement as Simon shifted back into cat form and raced silently along the branches, looking for a good spot downwind to eavesdrop. He might lack any skill with weaponry beyond his own sharp claws, but there was a reason we called him our ninja.

I sat on the shore and waited. Mac, I realized, was watching me, might have been watching me the entire time. "I didn't know you could do that," he said quietly.

I should have ignored him. I should have offered a polite answer. I should have done a whole lot of things other than flirt with the man who'd spent the last several weeks avoiding the crazy half-fire chick. I should have accepted that he didn't want me and my bonfire full of baggage, and it was time to move on.

I've never been very good with shoulds.

Instead of letting him go, I smiled and let my eyes fill with vague, silent promises. "There's a lot you don't know about me."

I swore his breath hitched in his chest for just a moment. It was enough. I felt warmth thread through my body, heating my cheeks, dropping through the core where the magic lived and heading even lower.

"Aidan." Brandon's voice snapped me back to the present. He walked toward us slowly, his father's disappointed gaze on him the entire time. Brandon looked dejected and, for a moment, far younger than his years. I imagined that whatever his father had wanted to know, the interrogation hadn't been pleasant. "There's no one around. Could you make it rain now?"

I was unable to resist his pathetic expression, the face of a kid who just wanted something pleasant to wash away his doubt and pain. I quickly wrapped my magic around the water hovering in the air and, for good measure, pulled some from the lake as well. I let it circle above us before dropping slowly, drenching the three of us in a cold shower I knew at least one of us desperately needed.

———

It was a cozy ride back. Neither Vivian nor Simon had their own car, so they'd been dropped at the lake by a friend of Vivian's. Being the shortest, Sera squeezed into the back and immediately resumed her silent interrogation of Brandon. Eventually, the poor kid was going to confess to kidnapping the Lindbergh baby if it meant Sera would stop staring at him. Will hadn't shared with us the details of his conversation with his son, but I wasn't too bothered. Simon would fill us in later.

Vivian was squished between me and Simon in the middle. She was quiet, as she usually was, but it wasn't her normal silence, that of an introvert more interested in studying the world than talking about it. This time, her silence was heavy and draped in sadness.

"What's wrong?" I kept my voice low. I don't know why I hoped for privacy while surrounded by shifters, but I couldn't stay quiet and ignore her misery. Vivian had spent hours listening to my various woes. It was her turn.

"It's nothing," she muttered. A moment later, she changed her mind, whatever she'd been holding inside all day breaking free in a rush. "Olivia says we might be able to be friends. That's it. I've been trying, and I thought, now that the killings were over, we could, you know. She says she doesn't give second chances. And I can't even tell her I left to protect her." She ended her disjointed rant with a small grunt of frustration.

Simon lightly stroked her arm, an easy, comforting gesture. He already knew, I realized. So did Sera.

That far-too-familiar sense of being an outsider crept over me, and I forced it down. I knew where that led. Frustration, anger, fire. Madness. I needed to be zen if it fucking killed me. It wasn't their fault they were more observant than I was.

I'd been a hermit for ten years. I'd lost a few people

skills during that decade, and if I was honest I'd never had too many to begin with. If I'd taken even a moment to think about what Vivian was going through, I'd have seen it coming.

When we thought the murderer was killing human partners of elementals, Vivian split with her girlfriend. Now that her ex wasn't in danger, of course she'd try to repair the relationship—but she needed to do so without admitting they broke up to save Olivia from a homicidal magic man who didn't exist in her version of reality.

Relationships between humans and elementals were always fraught. It was hard to keep the secret when we lived so much longer than they did and needed regular access to our element. Telling the secret carried its own risks.

Vivian lifted her shoulders, a single, helpless shrug. "She says she doesn't trust me."

"Give it time." Mac was quiet, but he'd obviously heard every word. "It takes a while to build that sort of thing again."

Vivian nodded. "So, you're saying I shouldn't hack her Facebook account just yet?" I worried she wasn't joking.

Sera shook her head. "It would probably be easier just to date someone new, Viv. You're hot. Move on."

I noticed Brandon had snapped out of his sullen teenage reverie and was looking at Vivian with renewed interest. "You have a girlfriend?" he asked a little too eagerly.

Six pairs of eyes rolled simultaneously, and the rest of the drive to Will's house was silent.

Though Will had become progressively more civil over the course of the afternoon, we were still summarily dismissed at his front door. Mac cast an apologetic glance our way, but he still followed his uncle inside. In the past I'd heard him speak of his family in less than flattering terms, but I saw none of that animosity here. Though I planned to corner him at the cabin for more information, I couldn't be sure where his loyalties truly lay.

Fortunately, we had a spy. Unfortunately, it was Simon, who often prolonged his grand reveals until he felt the response would be sufficiently dramatic. And so we were all surprised when he starting speaking the moment the doors closed on Sera's Mustang.

"Vivian, tablet." She pulled the ever present device from her bag. So far as I could tell, it was her security blanket. "We need to find a girl named Pamela. No last name, I fear. She attends the local high school and is most likely around James's age, so probably a junior or senior." While he spoke, Vivian swiped her hand across the screen, her movements rapid and confident. If the information existed anywhere online, she would find it. "I suspect we do not have much time. The large man was quite insistent. If not for our presence, he would have demanded more details from his son. That is almost certainly what he is doing now."

"I found three," said Vivian. "Any more information?"

"Brandon thought they might have run off together, so we should assume they were dating."

"There is no indication of that with any of these girls," Vivian said. I could hear the annoyance in her voice that came when a problem resisted being solved.

"Only because you don't think like a teenage boy," said Sera. She pulled over and held out her hand for the tablet. "If James is anything like the rest of his family, he's a decent-looking kid, and his sweatshirt suggested he's pretty mainstream, at least in the way he dresses. Let's assume the hardcore goth is out, as is the mathlete who looks utterly terrified in her school photo." She passed it back. "Door number three it is. Get me the address, and we just might beat Big Will there." She grinned at me, delighted to have a purpose and to be one step ahead of the man who'd dared to disrespect our authority.

"Are you seriously making me be the voice of reason?" I asked.

"You could only be the voice of reason if I learned ventriloquism."

I ignored her, as any effective voice of reason should. "This goes beyond the parameters of our job, doesn't it? We were just supposed to talk to the shifters. We talked. If Pamela's human, that's the agents' job."

She swung a sharp u-turn when Vivian gave us the address, taking us back toward Truckee. "You're making assumptions. We don't know what she is. And I didn't notice you questioning our parameters at the lake."

"Well, that was different. Will was pissing me off, and I wanted to prove him wrong. Totally professional, obviously."

"Obviously." She nodded soberly and continued to drive at an extremely unlawful speed toward Pamela's house.

"So, what exactly do we hope to learn from this girl, Simon? Did you get anything other than her name?"

Simon smiled, a smug, close-lipped smile. "You can learn whatever you want, though based on your collective interviewing prowess, I will manage my expectations in that regard. Just keep her distracted for a few minutes, please."

PAMELA'S FAMILY LIVED just northeast of town, not far from the Nevada border. Their home was the sort of over-sized, under-designed monstrosity I was used to seeing in planned suburban developments, where it made a strange sort of sense. Here, it stood out from the smaller wooden homes, an ostentatious display of the owner's wealth and general disregard for neighborhood harmony. The lawn was an impeccably maintained sea of green, and a Range Rover sat in the driveway. I guessed that the car hadn't gone off road once in its pristine life.

"Well, this will be fun," I observed. "Who here speaks Stepford?"

"Vivian does. She was raised in Connecticut. That's your native tongue, right?"

Vivian rolled her eyes at both of us and pointed wordlessly at herself. Seen through her eyes, perhaps a dreadlocked woman currently wearing steel-toed boots and a t-shirt that read "talk nerdy to me" wasn't our most harmless-looking ambassador.

"I'm sure they're perfectly lovely, open-minded people. Still, you might want to stay in the car, Vivian." I glanced at Sera, currently wearing head-to-toe black with an impressive amount of eyeliner. "Maybe you should, too." I stepped quickly out of the car before Sera's conjured fireball could test whether my newfound resistance to fire extended to my eyebrows. Simon hopped out in his four-footed form and took off around the side of the house.

I strode up the path. Sera was right behind me, though Vivian remained firmly planted in the backseat. When I rang the doorbell, the chimes reminded their dog he was supposed to be on guard duty. A series of frenzied yips carried through the door, along with the exasperated tones of a woman who'd long since given up any hope of owning a quiet animal.

At first, the woman who opened the door seemed to be about my age. Well, the age I appeared to be, at least, since that whole longevity thing really worked in our favor. She was as fit as any twenty-five-year-old, with the kind of lean muscle tone that came from hours in a Pilates studio, but a closer look revealed a few thin lines around her eyes, and she carried more knowledge in those eyes than most twenty-five-year-olds could claim. I quickly moved my estimate upward, putting her well into her forties.

Her look was one of contrasts. Her clothes were neat and tailored, and though my interest in fashion didn't extend far beyond jeans and various items made of cotton, she seemed to favor classic American designers, the sort that would produce commercials with young blonds frolicking in a meadow. She balanced that with heavy eye makeup and thick sand-colored hair that swirled around her shoulders, and she possessed unsettling amber eyes that didn't seem to blink nearly enough. This had to be Pamela's mother. A small corgi danced around her ankles, happily waiting its turn.

"Hello," I said, before Sera could begin her "stare and wait" routine. This woman's eyes had the kind of strength one sees in people used to getting their way, and I had a feeling she wouldn't cow before two young women at her door. "We were hoping to talk to your daughter for a moment."

She looked us up and down, and I was certain she was about to subject us to a lengthy series of questions. Just as I made a mental note to steal either Johnson's or Carmichael's badge the next time we saw them, she leaned back and hollered, "Dana!" Turning to us with a smile that went nowhere near her eyes, she said, "Wait here, please." The door shut firmly in our faces.

"I think this is going well," said Sera.

"We're getting promoted any day now," I agreed. "We probably should have specified which daughter we wanted."

The door swung open, and the girl standing in the doorway was so different from her mother that she might have been adopted. She was blond and quietly pretty, with just enough extra weight for soft, gentle curves. I imagined adults told her she was lovely all the time, but it was the sort of beauty most boys would overlook for a few more years. I wanted to hug her and assure her it would get better someday soon. She looked like she wanted to disappear into the floor.

"Can I help you?" Her voice drifted off on the final word, as if she was unused to speaking sentences of more than a word or two.

"I think there's been a misunderstanding. We were hoping to speak to your sister." I kept my voice soft and even. I felt like I was speaking to a skittish deer.

She shook her head and addressed her reply toward her shoes. "She's not here."

"When do you expect her back?" I only got a shrug in reply.

"Maybe you can help us. We're here on behalf of the FBI," I told the top of her head. Fortunately, she showed no interest in seeing any physical evidence that would support our claim. "James MacMahon hasn't been seen since last night. I understand Pamela knew him?"

"James is missing?" That was news to her. She temporarily forgot her deep desire to not exist and looked at us, her eyes round and horrified. "Where is he?"

Sera closed her eyes tightly, obviously resisting the urge to make an inappropriate joke at this girl's expense. "We don't know. That's why he's missing."

Dana's head bobbed up and down several times. "Of course. Sorry."

"You knew him?" I asked.

"Only a little. He was two years above me, but he always came to the football games. Sometimes, he sat near my family. We talked a little." Blood rushed to her cheeks, and she quickly bowed her head, letting her hair swing forward to cover the telltale flush. She'd enjoyed those chats more than she was supposed to, and she knew it.

"We heard he was dating your sister," I nudged gently.

She shook her head again, more decisively than she had before. "No. They were dating, but they broke up a couple weeks ago." She spoke loudly, and even turned her head slightly toward the inside of her home, as if she wanted the words to be overheard by her mother.

Pamela, I gathered, wasn't supposed to be dating James. I was sure that was an interesting fact, though I couldn't say why.

Before I could follow up on that line of thought, several frantic barks resonated through the house. The dog I'd seen earlier dashed down the hallway, nails clicking against the wooden floor and short legs churning wildly in an attempt to catch the small black cat racing three feet ahead of it, carrying several articles of clothing in his mouth.

We immediately created a cat-sized opening between our legs, allowing Simon just enough room to escape, and promptly moved back into place, preventing the dog from following. I wobbled back and forth a few times to block Dana from seeing the cat who'd just stolen several pieces of her family's wardrobe. With any luck, she'd assume I was drunk rather than an accomplice. A moment later, I heard the car door slam and figured that was our cue.

"Thank you for your time. Please let Pamela know we'd like to speak to her, and call us if you hear anything about James." I looked to Sera, who held up two empty hands. I quickly scrawled my name and number on the back of a grocery receipt. Dana looked unimpressed. You know you're not doing well when a teenager questions your professionalism.

We walked toward the car with stiff spines, trying to appear at least a little competent. Inside, Simon was just pulling on his jeans, a thoughtful look on his face.

Sera wasn't in the car a full second before she began her torment. "Dude. You were chased by a corgi. You will never live this down."

"I did not plan to go downstairs, but these people keep a spotless house. There were no dirty clothes to be found other than in the laundry hamper." He handed the stack up to me. "I wasn't sure which were Pamela's, so I grabbed everything it looked like a teenager might wear." I nodded and quickly felt my way through several shirts.

There was little residue to be found. This family didn't seem to sweat much. "Hand me that water bottle, Viv?" I poured a small amount on a couple of shirts, trying to revive whatever essence still lingered.

"A corgi. A dog with only half the legs of an actual dog, and it was right on your tail. Quite literally, in fact."

Simon attempted to look dignified. "They are much faster than they look, those dogs."

I blocked them out and concentrated on the shirt, looking for any sign of that second person who'd been at the lake. I had little hope of finding anything and was stunned to encounter a perfect match on the second article of clothing.

"It's her. The woman at the lake."

Sera abruptly stopped teasing Simon. "Who?"

"Don't know." I looked closer at the shirt on my lap. It was cap-sleeved and bright pink, and I thought Dana would wear a size larger. "Pamela, I'd guess. Or her mother." We both looked quickly toward the house, just in time to see a curtain fall back into place from an upstairs window. "Well, that's not suspicious at all."

Sera grunted her agreement, then started the car. As we made our way slowly down the street, loud music blaring from the open windows, we passed a green Ford Explorer heading the opposite direction. I smiled and waved cheerily at the two large, grumpy men in the front seat.

CHAPTER 4

After speaking to Dana, I wanted to return to the cabin, situate myself on one of the living room cushions, and patiently await Mac while practicing my best smug expressions. I made it through the first step of that plan. The second two were derailed when Sera and I found our father waiting for us.

Josiah Blais stood in the living room with a bemused expression. Seen through his eyes, it was a rather unconventional room. When a fire destroyed the furniture, drapes, and wallpaper, we'd replaced it all with oversized floor pillows, orange curtains that had likely been on sale since 1977, and swathes of teddy bear wallpaper, of which several panels had accidentally been hung upside down. Considering Josiah was the reason we'd needed to redecorate in the first place, I found his scrutiny of the teddy bear fortress inappropriate, to say the least.

If his presence hadn't been disconcerting enough, seeing my mother waiting next to him was enough to convince me I'd skipped right to the hallucination stage of mental instability.

"Hello, Aidan." She nodded at me and roundly ignored my three friends.

"I'll be upstairs," murmured Vivian, heading toward the spiral staircase in the middle of the room. She tugged lightly on Simon's sleeve when he showed no inclination to follow her, and he reluctantly left the room.

Finally, the four of us stood alone, my twisted little family.

There were so many things I wanted to say, so many reasons to scream at them. They'd hidden the truth of my existence my entire life, and my ignorance had caused unspeakable harm to myself and others. They'd forced me to live a more sheltered life than a harem bride for the first fifty years of my existence and achieved nothing in the process. I was still in danger of going mad, still in danger of being killed by my own people, but now I coped with those risks while occasionally demonstrating the emotional intelligence of a banana slug.

I'd been born a little broken. Their insistence on denying what I might become ensured I stayed that way.

All these thoughts crashed together in my head, a senseless cacophony of noise and instant anger, and I did the only thing I could. I forced it down, imagining the rage folding into smaller and smaller squares until it was just a tiny speck.

Some people rushed to their parents in times of stress, seeking comfort for their worries and fears. I did not have those parents. I had parents so determined to protect me they sought to control every aspect of my life. Any anger I revealed would become a weapon, justification for wrapping me in cotton wool and hiding me from the world once again.

"Why are you here?" My voice was steady. If I wasn't using every bit of my emotional control to maintain that measured response, I'd have been quite proud of myself.

Josiah opened his mouth to respond, but my mother answered before he could. He looked at her in astonishment, unused to being interrupted.

"I was worried about you. You haven't been answering

our calls."

I turned to her, this woman I loved as much as I loved anyone on this planet, and briefly wished the earth might swallow her whole. "Worried about what? That I might be furious you tried to hide what I was? That I might not want to speak to you after a lifetime of lies? Or maybe just that you never warned me that, the first time I met my father, he might try to kidnap me for observation?"

Josiah rolled his eyes. "Really, Aidan, such exaggeration accomplishes nothing. You know everything I did was for your safety. This visit is no different. If you won't live with me and Serafina in Hawaii, then please consider returning to your island with Fiona." I glanced at Sera, who gave a tiny shake of her head. She hadn't signed off on that plan. "We know so little about dual magics, and until we understand how your powers will develop, you really must live in isolation, in a state of contentment. Fiona and I will work to determine the best course of action." He smiled easily, believing his point so obvious there was no room for argument.

There is always room for argument.

"That presumes I find peace around either of you at this point." I looked at Josiah and let the rage briefly fill my grey eyes, then I deliberately let the fire die. Whether he acknowledged it or not, I had control, damn it.

"I've been more content in the last two weeks than I've been in ages. I was alone for years, hating myself and hating Sera for things that weren't our fault, because you never told me what I was. I lost a decade to your lies, hiding from truths I didn't understand, and now you're asking me to hide again. If you hear nothing else I say, hear this. I am done hiding." I stood up straight, quite impressed with my own speech.

Josiah was harder to impress. He threw up his arms at

my refusal, just another father exasperated by his errant, unreasonable daughter. He began to pace the room, so much like Sera that, for a moment, I almost wanted to trust him. "Serafina, you know this isn't the best solution. Getting drawn back into another FBI case? It's only a matter of time before something upsets her and she accesses her fire side again." I didn't bother to ask how he knew about the FBI. It sometimes seemed Josiah had a spy network to rival the CIA.

It also didn't seem worth mentioning that Josiah once helped me access that fire side. His logic shifted and changed as necessary to support his beliefs and maintain control. It was as erratic and unpredictable as any flame.

"How the hell did you end up relatively normal?" I muttered to my best friend.

She smiled at me. It was quick, a simple, open smile, but it was answer enough. She'd survived being raised by Josiah because, somehow, Sera had always known exactly who she was.

"I trust her, father." The words were quiet, the barest whisper, but it was the first time I'd ever seen Sera openly defy her father. Everyone else, sure. She barreled through life, doing exactly as she pleased and demanding the rest of the world conform to her specifications. While her father might have seen her angry, even angry at him, she'd never before refused him.

"Serafina," he cajoled, confident she would change her mind. She only shook her head and held his gaze, a little nervous but still determined.

"Aidan," my mother said, "come home. There's no reason for you to remain here, and I'm sure I can convince the aunts not to shun you for telling the FBI about us. You really had no choice, thanks to Josiah and his pet." Her glare was icy, more anger than one usually saw in a water. I really did have a way of bringing out her best.

It didn't matter what she said. It didn't even matter how much anger I felt for my parents. None of that had anything to do with my decision. There was one fact of which I was certain, and that made my choice easy. "I am home, mother."

My mother offered no reply, once again as calm and placid as any water. Her face was the funhouse mirror version of my own. We were so much alike we could pass for sisters among humans, but she was pure water, fluid and adaptable, whereas I was stubborn and focused.

Even so, I wasn't fooled. She was calm now because she believed I could still be convinced, and she was already considering each argument I offered and devising counter-strategies. Smiling serenely, she nodded her head and strode to the door, leaving without another word.

Josiah started to follow, then stopped abruptly. "I can't just ignore this situation and watch you go utterly mad. You are still my daughter."

I shook my head. "It doesn't matter how often you say it. It doesn't make it true. You provided some genetic material, but you've never been my father." I didn't wait to hear his response or see how my words might wound. I walked quickly up the staircase, leaving him behind.

Even so, I heard his final words to Sera. "Please. Try to talk some sense into her."

There was a low murmur, words I was unable to pick out, but her final reply was unmistakable. "Leave, father. Leave while you still have one daughter left." The door shut quietly behind him.

THE NEXT MORNING, I awoke to a silent house. I crept downstairs and fixed myself a cup of tea. It was one ritual I'd reclaimed from my days of solitude. I'd wake with the sunrise and sit at the breakfast bar with my mug and journal and see what my subconscious felt like writing about that day. It was still the best therapy I knew.

Some days, Vivian would join me before catching a ride to the university for her graduate classes. A week prior, she'd officially given up her apartment on campus, choosing to move into the cabin permanently and bringing along a small mountain of computer equipment. She gave no reason for her choice, but I thought I understood. After everything that happened, it would be a long time before any of us really felt safe alone.

Today, it was just me at the breakfast bar. I wrote for a long time, attempting to sort through my various parental angst. When my personal life remained an unsolvable mess, I outlined what little we knew about the missing shifter boy, looking for connections we overlooked the day before. I knew the agents would want me to update them, but that didn't sound nearly as interesting as figuring it out myself. Besides, it wasn't even eight o'clock. They wouldn't be in the office yet. I was only being helpful by taking the initiative, surely.

Sera's laptop rested on the breakfast bar. Hesitantly, I opened it and began searching James's and Pamela's names with no real idea what I was looking for. Vivian might be a computer genius, but she was hardly typical of our race. Most elementals weren't renowned for their technical proficiency. We lived too long to hop on every new fad that appeared, and many of us had assumed that computers were just a passing trend.

I hadn't shared that belief, but I'd disappeared during a decade when technology moved from something that was pretty cool to something that used to only exist in science fiction movies. I still had almost no idea what I was doing.

By the time Simon and Vivian appeared, I'd learned

nothing of note about James, Pamela, or her mother but had somehow lost an hour on a website I'd never seen before. I looked up absently as they entered the room. "Where have you been? You have to see this site I found. It's amazing."

Vivian stood behind me to get a better view. "Wikipedia?" Her voice was strangled, the sound of someone trying desperately not to laugh.

I sighed. Apparently, my discovery was only thrilling to me. "Whatever. While you were out, I learned about every country music award from the last ten years, and none of you can take that away from me."

"Find anything about the case?" This was from Sera, wandering into the room with a large yawn and heading directly for the coffee pot.

Somehow, the magical combination of blue links and honky tonk had pushed any sense of urgency from my brain. "Um, only if James is now living in Nashville." She sent me a dry look that I cheerfully ignored. She couldn't be too superior, considering she'd been in bed while I'd been hard at work. Well, intending to be hard at work.

Vivian grabbed the laptop and quickly typed an address, causing the wondrous Wikipedia to disappear. It was replaced quickly by a map of the Lake Tahoe basin. "Fortunately, some of us have been working this morning. Those of us the FBI isn't paying, I might point out."

"Free rent isn't enough for you, Viv?" Sera filled a mug and hopped up on the breakfast bar, craning her neck to get a view of the screen.

"You know how much a hacker on the FBI payroll would make?" Vivian replied evenly, bringing up a small blinking dot on the screen.

Sera's eyes narrowed, the expression of a woman formulating a plan. Machiavellian tendencies seemed to run in my family. "If I paid you, I'd have to pay Simon, too." She turned to Simon. "But you're still packed, aren't you?"

Simon stepped away from the toaster, where he appeared to have been admiring his own reflection. "Yes, I still plan to return north. While I enjoy your company a surprising amount, I miss performing."

"We could clap every time you shift." I thought it was a helpful suggestion, but I only received a baleful stare in reply.

"Okay, got her." Vivian tilted the laptop slightly, making it easier for everyone to see. "It looks like Carmen is currently at the gym. I'm guessing James isn't with her."

"Carmen?" I asked.

"Carmen Avila. Pamela's mom, potential wearer of incriminating clothing and owner of an easily hacked cell-phone GPS system. She's all yours, ladies."

Sera grabbed Vivian's shoulders in a one-armed hug and squeezed lightly. "Never leave us, Vivian."

Before Vivian left for class, she programmed my phone's map application to show the blinking blue dot. Simon refused to accompany us, insisting we needed to learn to function without his brains and charm, and there was no answer when I knocked on Mac's trailer. His Bronco wasn't in the driveway, and I wasn't certain he'd returned the night before.

When my phone rang two hours later, Sera and I were sitting in her Mustang half a block from a nail salon, attempting stealth in a car that steadfastly refused to blend. I answered on the first ring.

"What, exactly, are you hoping to learn by following Carmen?" If a growl could sound amused, that was the tone of Mac's question.

"You know, grooming tips. I wanted some guidance about whether I should get the French manicure or just a natural buff. Why are you here?" I craned around in my seat, looking for a sign of the Bronco.

There were several moments of silence, during which I suspected he was counting slowly to five. "And if I asked you to leave?"

"I'd ask why you were following Pamela's mother, because I doubt your presence here is mere coincidence, and I'd inquire whether you planned to share what you learned."

"Aidan, I'd help if I could, but this is shifter business. There are limits to what I can share with you."

I considered being understanding for a moment or two, then decided being reasonable seemed like too much effort. "You once had no problem being involved in elemental business."

"That was different."

"How?" Another long silence, though I suspected this was due to his lack of an answer. Without warning, my frustration at his recent avoidance techniques came to the surface, and my reply came out sharper than I intended. "Look, Mac, find out what you're allowed to share, then get back to us. Because we were one step ahead of you last night, and we plan to stay one step ahead of you until we find James. You know we can be trusted, and you know you want us on your side. You can tell the rest of your furry brethren I said so." I hung up while he was still attempting to sputter a comeback. I didn't definitively get the last word, but it was close enough.

Sera gave me a contemplative look. "What?" I asked.

She just shook her head. "We're the best liaisons ever."

Carmichael chose that particular moment to phone us. Fortunately, he called Sera, leaving me free to track Carmen on my phone.

I couldn't hear Carmichael's end of the conversation, but Sera's was more than articulate enough for the both of them. "Report?" she asked, as if she'd never heard the word before and needed him to define it.

Muffled yelling came through the other end, and she grinned, enjoying his outrage. "Today? I don't think that will work for us." The blue dot began to move. I showed the screen to Sera, and she nodded and put the car into drive.

"I'm pretty sure it's against state law to drive while on the phone. An FBI agent wouldn't want you to break the law." I spoke loudly enough for Carmichael to hear me.

"You're absolutely right, Aidan. I'll call you later, Carmichael." Though I still couldn't make out any of his words, Carmichael's tone was plenty expressive. "What's that? Sorry, sta...tic. Can't...hear." She threw me the phone, and I pressed the end button. "It might be worth finding a backup employment plan, Ade."

I indicated she should turn left at an upcoming intersection. "I'm sure my English degree and your art history one prepared us for rewarding careers filing TPS reports."

She grimaced. We both had plenty of money, and always would. We were from old families, powerful lines that had existed since the birth of our race and had the bank accounts one would expect from people who'd relied on compound interest since the days of the Holy Roman Empire. We could easily live on just the dividends from our trust funds for the rest of our days, but neither of us were too keen on taking money from our parents right now. It might have only been a token effort at individuating ourselves, but even a token felt better than nothing.

"Turn right at the light. It looks like she's heading toward the freeway."

At the light, Sera came to a full stop. There was no traffic, and she could have easily made the turn, but instead she lingered, eyes fixed on the rearview mirror and a small smile playing on her mouth. I twisted around to see the rear window completely covered by a large grill, the sort that might belong to an SUV. Like, say, a Bronco. "Where is she now?"

I looked at the screen. "Wait." The light turned green, and still she sat, unfazed by the enormous vehicle inching its way toward her or the honks of the cars waiting behind the Bronco. I watched the blue dot slowly merge onto I-80. "She's gone. Go for it."

She turned slowly into the right lane. Mac tried to pull around her, eager to reach Carmen. Sera drifted into the left lane, blocking his way. "You've still got her?"

"Yep. She's on 80, heading east."

She drifted back to the right lane, easily cutting him off again. "Think he can find her from here?"

"Only if the shifters have a Vivian on staff. Otherwise, he's just guessing."

She grinned. "No one else has a Vivian." She stuck in a tape and turned the volume up loud, raising her voice to be heard above the Pixies. "You know, I've always wanted to lose someone in a car chase."

"Is that so?" I kept my voice calm while checking that my seat belt was secure and gathering some water from the air, just in case I needed it to repair injuries sustained in a car crash.

"Ade, I think today's the day we strike that one from the bucket list." With no further warning, she swung the wheel hard to the left, turning from the far right lane and crossing three lanes of traffic. Mac was right behind us, making the same treacherous turn.

"Good news is, we just got confirmation they don't have a Vivian," I said. "Bad news..."

"Bad news is Mac's as damned stubborn as you are," she finished. She made a sharp turn into an alley, and my entire body swayed in my seat, fighting for equilibrium. She barely slowed at the end of the alley, just long enough to confirm we wouldn't die instantly if we pulled into traffic at that moment. The car hurtled across the street and darted into the next alley. Mac was forced to slow down to allow a truck to pass, but a moment later he was across the road and gaining on us with unexpected speed. Sera cursed. Her eyes scanned the approaching street, planning her next maneuver.

"Do try to remember that longevity isn't the same as immortality, please."

"How the hell is he making these turns? He drives a box on wheels." A light bulb appeared to go off. She slowed down, driving almost like a normal person, and took a left at the next light, heading out of town and away from the freeway. She watched Mac follow us in the rearview mirror, grinning the whole time. "You know, it's a good thing I know this area as well as I do." Ten minutes later, we were well into the trees, driving along a twisting two-lane road with the Bronco following closely, expecting us to lead him toward the woman we were both tracking. "And a good thing we went to so many parties in college. Mac's not much of a party guy, is he?"

"No, he's not." I smiled, quickly grasping her plan. Sure enough, a moment later she turned onto a dirt road, one many high school and university students had traversed in the years before they turned twenty-one and could legally hit the bars. At the end of this road was a clearing where countless kegs had been tapped and many a young party-goer had lost their virginity, the contents of their stomachs, or their dignity.

The place was famous both for its isolation and because it provided an exit strategy if a party was busted by the cops. This side of the clearing was blocked by an enormous fallen tree trunk, which was slightly raised on one end about a meter and a half off the ground. It wasn't enough space for a cop car loaded with sirens or, for that matter, a large Bronco, but it provided plenty of room for a '66 Ford Mustang. Sera cruised underneath and sailed to the opposite side of the clearing, but Mac was forced to draw to a stop. For just a moment, he was close enough that I could see his face. I couldn't be sure, but I thought he might be laughing.

Sera was already on the only other road out. It was just a tiny strip of dirt, too small for the Bronco. Even the Mustang barely fit. I pushed a button on my phone, and Mac answered immediately.

"Yes?"

"One step ahead, big guy," I said, enjoying the cocky tone I heard in my own voice. "We're always gonna be one step ahead. Let us know when you're ready to talk." With that, I hung up, confident I'd gotten the last word this time.

CHAPTER 5

"I don't care if you duct tape him and trap him in the house. Simon stays." I whispered, but my vehemence was perfectly clear.

Sera adjusted her position, giving herself a slightly better view of the room below. "Is this because of how much you've come to appreciate his company?"

I felt myself slipping and clutched the tiles more tightly. "What other reason could I have?" Cautiously, I inched forward. My body scraped across the tiles, and I winced, certain those below could hear. A moment passed, and then another, but no one looked upwards to find two elementals gazing curiously through the skylight.

"For the record, this wasn't on the bucket list." She was smiling, though, and it seemed likely she was rewriting the list to include "climb stranger's roof for the hell of it" even as we spoke.

"Spying on a bored housewife because she might have some connection to a missing teenage bear shifter? I can't imagine why not." The object of our pursuit sat below us, reclining elegantly in a white armchair and surrounded by several more women on equally white sofas. They all held copies of the same book on their lap. "Let's agree that, no matter what happens from here, we never admit we successfully ditched Mac only to observe a book club meeting in a planned community outside Reno."

"Hell, let's agree to never admit to being in a planned community and call it good."

I nodded my enthusiastic agreement. "And agree to drug Simon, lock him in the closet, and leave all future roof-climbing expeditions to him."

"I'm in. Our karma's solid these days. I'm pretty sure we're due at least one excessive display of power."

Any retort I might have made died on my lips. My karma might be somewhat more flawed than Sera's, given the bodies I'd left in my wake. Even the memory of those deaths was enough to cause something in my core to stir. I felt it stretch and grin, that fiery side of myself. It was eager, and it wanted an outlet.

Several deep breaths later, I forced it down and mentally locked it away, scared of how easily it kept springing to life. I reached for the only magic I wanted to call my own, looking for the water that defined me. There was less of it in the air here than in Tahoe, but I still found enough.

Sera watched the entire process, obviously drawing her own, accurate conclusions about my sudden distraction. "You with me?" she asked.

I blew out a gust of air, imagining the tension leaving my body with it. It was a technique Vivian had taught me, and while most of the time it felt like New Age nonsense, it still beat exercise.

"I'm here."

She nodded, watching me carefully. "He might be wrong, you know. Or lying. You must have considered it, cause I have."

She meant Josiah, the man so certain I was a ticking time bomb. "Of course. You think that wasn't my first impulse? Life would be so simple if he were just lying. But it's him, and my mother, and Brian and Trent Pond. More than any of that, there's me. I don't know how to explain it, but something's changed since I discovered my fire side. All the time, I feel a little unbalanced. Something is a tiny bit off, and I don't know how to fix it."

Her face was thoughtful. She believed me, but she wasn't giving up, not yet.

"Tell me, what's it like?" I asked. "Accessing fire, I mean. I find physical water and talk to it, manipulate it. There's no fire around right now, but you could still burn down this entire neighborhood."

She sat up carefully and looked around, at row after row of identical pale houses. She grimaced. "Don't tempt me." She pulled a small orb of fire from the air. She juggled it lightly between her hands, then brought it to her mouth, swallowing it whole and smiling.

"So, when Carmichael sacks us, the circus is still our backup plan?"

"Hell, yeah. I'll look good in one of those leotards. You can be the bear tamer." She cast a sly glance my way, one I studiously ignored. Sera had been surprisingly quiet on the subject of Mac's and my thwarted flirtation. I'd known it couldn't last.

Luckily, she moved on. "You've made fire. Maybe not intentionally, but you know how to do it. Do you remember what it was like?"

I remembered rage, pure rage coursing through me and obliterating everything good in its path, everything that might care what was right and wrong. I eased myself onto my back till I was staring up at the cloudless blue sky. "Yeah, but I don't remember how the fire started."

"It's not that different from what you do. You find the components of water and pull them to you." I demonstrated easily, letting a stream of water encircle her head. "What are the components of fire? Oxygen, heat, and fuel. Well..." She waved her hand, indicating the air surrounding us. "Oxygen is rarely a problem." She took my hand and held it to her forehead. "Heat never is, either. We run hot, though we still tend to feel cold when the temperature drops too much." Eyebrows knit together, she quickly felt my forehead. "Not as warm as me, but yeah. You're warmer than average."

I felt my own forehead and wondered how I'd never noticed it before. Elementals don't often go to doctors, since no modern medicine was as effective as exposure to our element, but I'd been in contact with many other elementals, must have felt their skin and heat.

But I hadn't, not really. I remembered my mother, always hovering, always keeping my aunts from giving me extended hugs or sitting too close to me on the sofa. In college, I'd dated, but never another elemental who might interpret my heat as indicative of an illicit fiery heritage. Hell, a month ago I hadn't even known it was possible to be what I was. There was no reason for someone to think I was anything other than the water I'd been raised to be.

"And the fuel," I asked, seeing the final piece clearly. "That's the anger, isn't it?"

She nodded. "It's always there, in all of us. Just a small, constantly burning flame of rage. We don't even notice it most of the time, until we want to access it. And then..." She held out both fists, indicating first one, then the other. "Rage, plus magic." She brought her fists together, and fire burst forth as they met.

"Can I learn to do that? To only access it when I want to?" She turned a concerned face to me, and I continued hurriedly, "And then use that control to never, ever call it."

Her face was solemn, her voice quiet. "I don't know, Aidan. I don't know."

"Don't move."

It took a moment to realize the voice was coming from

the yard below and was directed at us. It took a fraction of a second longer to identify the sound of a shotgun being racked. I assumed that was also aimed in our direction.

Despite the command, we both deemed it wise to raise our hands slowly into the air. "Because I think it bears repeating," I muttered, "one, longevity's still not the same as immortality, and two, we really fucking need to keep Simon around."

A FEW MINUTES later, we were in a cool garage, perched on a pair of beat-up metal folding chairs. We were not physically restrained in any way, because it wasn't necessary. The large gun pointed at us was sufficient deterrent, should we feel the desire to sit somewhere else.

I'd debated our options during our awkward climb from the roof down to the backyard, and again during the short march through the side yard into the cool garage attached to the main house. I had nothing.

Sera's fire was absolutely useless in close proximity to gunpowder. I could fill the gun barrel with water, but as my entire knowledge of firearms came from 80s action films, I had no idea what that would achieve. For the moment, I had to trust that a couple of fit, carefully made-up suburban wives would explore tidier options before resorting to homicide.

"Who sent you?" Sera's head jerked toward the woman asking the questions. She was a bronzed Amazon goddess, her body seeming to consist of nothing but long red hair, lean muscles, and spray tan, her beauty as carefully constructed as Carmen's was wild and natural. Carmen stood behind this unfamiliar woman with her arms crossed. The remainder of the book club had been asked to wait inside, which might be a bad sign. When people started removing potential witnesses, there was reason to be nervous.

Sera, of course, refused to answer, leaving a gaping silence I rushed to fill. "You know, it seems like the first question a harmless book club would ask might be 'who are you,' or perhaps 'why the hell were you on my roof'?" I barely had time to appreciate my own retort before my head snapped back and pain shot through my jaw.

Fire came instantly to attention, hissing and crackling, demanding release. It shot upwards along my spine, warming my flesh and bone with its touch and coiling tightly around my mind. My vision narrowed until I only saw a woman standing before me, begging to be set alight. My palms tingled, and heat worked its way into my fingers, seeking release. For a moment, I vanished completely, and the other self took over. I felt fire's grin spread across my face, its sharp gaze peer through my eyes.

It was pure, joyous power, and it was terrifying.

The woman standing before me took a small step backwards, and Carmen tensed. No one ever seemed to fear my water side, but the first glimpse of fire brought these women to attention, even if they didn't understand why.

The pain in my jaw subsided to a dull throb, and I began to remember myself. I could almost hear Vivian's voice, whispering that I needed to find balance. With great concentration, I forced the seething mass into submission before my fingers could start sparking and give me away. It resisted, whimpering and demanding freedom, and I took several slow breaths before it reluctantly quieted. The fire withdrew slowly, whispering promises for our future the whole way.

I knew I should worry about this, but at the moment I had a good reason for avoidance. I figured I'd deal with the shotgun and current crazy bitch first, dual magics and future crazy bitch second.

"That wasn't necessary." I rubbed my still-sore jaw and

suspected I'd need to spend some time in the water to avoid an impressive bruise.

She spoke carefully, watching me the whole time. "You were trespassing on my property. I had every right to shoot you. Be grateful I'm a reasonable woman."

"Let me have a moment, Diane." Carmen's voice was quiet, not intended for our ears, but it was also calm and altogether lacking any hint of menace. "I don't believe they're here for you." Diane met her eyes, and a long, silent conversation passed between the two women.

Diane stepped back, the gun still trained on us. Carmen turned another metal chair and straddled it backwards, folding her arms across the top. It was a strange juxtaposition, her tidy sweater set and chinos against the informal pose. "Alone," she clarified. "They're two young women, Diane. What do you think they could do to me?" She placed a tiny emphasis on that last word.

Again, that look passed between them. Carmen appeared confident and certain, while Diane looked almost bitter. I didn't understand it, but I didn't expect to feel much empathy for the woman who punched me in the mouth. She left the garage slowly, walking backwards the entire way, daring us to give her any excuse to empty the shotgun. We remained still until she was in the house, then turned to Carmen. With gunpowder removed from the immediate equation, Sera's powers were back in play, but it seemed polite to at least hear Carmen out before we burned down her friend's house.

"Did Will ask you to follow me?" she asked. Her voice was level and calm, revealing no emotion. She was neither friendly nor antagonistic. Hell, she barely seemed curious. She let her eyelids drop just a fraction, giving them a hooded look that she fixed on us, unblinking.

"You know Will?" I stalled.

She merely tilted her head and watched me. She blinked once, twice, and her pupils constricted and expanded in the space of a heartbeat. I glanced at Sera, staring at Carmen with recognition in her eyes. She'd seen it, too.

"You're a shifter," I said. She'd only shown us the barest hint of a slit pupil, but I knew those eyes. I saw them every time I looked at Simon. I wondered whether he was unable or unwilling to disguise all his feline traits, because in the space of a moment Carmen once again looked completely human. Of course, now that I knew what she was, it was obvious she moved with the grace and efficiency of movement I'd only seen among shifters. "Does Will know?"

She said nothing, but her look suggested she thought I was at least six different kinds of stupid.

I could only think of one animal that had those eyes. "You're a cat."

She sniffed and sat up straighter. I'd seen Simon do the same thing whenever he felt we were underestimating him. "In the most general sense."

I looked at her perfectly maintained body and carefully applied eyeliner and swore I wouldn't say it. It was offensive and stupid and unnecessary. I bit my tongue and repeated the vow. It did no good. "Please, please tell me you're a cougar."

Beside me, Sera made a series of sputtering noises that indicated she either really wanted to laugh or really wanted to smack me.

Carmen's look suggested I'd been promoted from stupid to stupid and irritating. I was on a roll. "Mountain lion." Her tone was disdainful. I knew better than to ask a shifter what animal they were—it was considered a significant breach of etiquette—but, as usual, the faulty filter between my brain and mouth trumped manners. I suspected Carmen only answered me out of a sense of pride.

"But you have a dog."

"As a pet."

On behalf of dog lovers the world over, I chose not to follow that line of inquiry any further. "Is everyone...?" I vaguely waved toward the door.

She shook her head. "Diane is my sister, but she didn't get the gene. It's how she can stand to live in this place." Her sneer seemed to encompass the entirety of the planned community.

I thought of her home, every bit the suburban monstrosity as the one we currently occupied. She guessed the direction of my thoughts. "I married a man with more money than taste. But it does back up to the forest, so it was worth fighting for in the divorce. And I admit, I quite enjoy the spa bathtub and walk-in closets."

I nodded, unsure where to go from there. I glanced at Sera, letting her know I was done babbling and she was free to step in any time. She rolled her eyes at me, but took her cue. "We're looking for the missing MacMahon boy," she said.

Carmen nodded. "Will said as much when he visited last night. Seemed to think my daughter might know something. I guess you thought the same thing. I don't know what Brandon said or why, but Pamela's not dating James anymore. I thought it best for the relationship to end."

"Well," Sera said, "it's a good thing children always do what their parents tell them to do." She delivered this line without a hint of sarcasm, but Carmen got the underlying message. Her gaze snapped to Sera, the one person in the world who could easily beat a cat in a staring contest.

"Nothing you've said so far explains why you were on my sister's roof." Carmen's voice was low and menacing. She was running out of patience.

I hurried to intervene. "Someone from your house was

at the lake the last time James was seen."

Her look was contemplative, and she put the pieces together faster than I'd expected. "The clothes," she said slowly. "I knew that cat had to be a shifter. A clever one, too. And working with an elemental? That is... unusual." Her tone suggested she was thinking a different, less flattering adjective. "You must have read the sweat. I've heard of that, but never seen it. Interesting." She studied me, her cat eyes cataloging my every physical trait, and I feared she was debating how my earlier loss of control fit into her knowledge of water elementals.

I gazed blandly back at her. I might not want to talk to my mother again this century, but I was still grateful I looked so much like her. Physically, I didn't bear a single stamp of my fire side. Other than that brief moment when my eyes turned to flint and chaos flickered across my face, there was no reason for her to guess what I really was.

"You know a lot about elemental powers," I said.

"I know a lot in general." Her distracted tone kept the words from sounding arrogant. "But it wasn't me at the lake. Thank you for sharing this information with me. May I have a day to discuss this with my daughters? I'll inform Will if I learn anything relevant." It was a formal request, made for the sake of politeness, and not one she expected us to refuse. We nodded, seeing no other option.

"Good." She stood, and we began to do the same. The meeting, or whatever it was, appeared to be over. "I did not say you could leave. Diane will want words with you. You intruded on her house, after all."

I briefly considered making a break for it, but a quick glance at Carmen's quads convinced me I'd be caught instantly. Plus, she had claws and an extremely cunning look on her face. We sat down slowly, choosing to play this scene out.

"Of course, I am sure I could smooth things over with Diane. If..." She let her voice trail off.

"What do you want?" Sera's question was blunt, her face annoyed.

"That shifter who visited my home. I would like to speak to him."

I snuck a look at Sera. I wasn't much in the habit of using my friends as bargaining chips, but neither did I fancy confronting Diane and her large gun again. "Why?"

She waved off my suspicious tone. "He's not in any trouble, and I have no desire to hurt him. I simply want to meet this new cat in town."

"We can't speak for him," I said carefully.

"You don't need to. Simply convey the message. He's free to make his own choices. Of course he is. He's a cat. I only want you to give him that choice."

It seemed a harmless enough trade, but something in her narrowed gaze caused my stomach to feel like lead. "We'll give him the choice."

"And strongly suggest he choose to ignore it," Sera added.

"Fair enough." Carmen smiled, a tight, close-lipped smile. "Then we are done here." Without another word, she walked into the house, likely to explain why she'd freed the hostages and then to vote on next month's book selection.

"Out of here?" I muttered.

Sera didn't reply. She was too busy bolting for the side door. I wasted no time following, and moments later we were a few hundred feet down the road and jumping into the Mustang. She gazed around her at rows of perfect houses and even lawns, and grinned a small, evil grin. She rolled down the windows, stuck The Clash in her stereo, and cranked the volume up to eleven as we made our noisy escape from suburbia.

CHAPTER 6

We stopped for lunch at a roadside diner on our way back to Truckee. It had torn, vinyl booths from which yellow stuffing sprang exuberantly and waitresses who stopped adapting to current fashion trends in the mid 70s.

Even more importantly, it served pancakes all day long. It was the perfect palate cleanser after the sterile, controlled suburbs, and Sera and I both relaxed into our seats. A thick stack of carbohydrates dripping with fat and sugar has a magic all its own, a mystical power that allowed us to forget our cares for an hour.

While we waited for our food, I pulled water from the air. Holding it out of sight under the table, I quietly healed the bruise developing on my face, hiding all evidence of Diane's earlier assault. I saw no reason for anyone to know just how easily Sera and I'd been rendered mostly helpless.

It wasn't until we felt sated and finally free of all suburban cooties that we returned to thoughts of the missing shifter. Sera checked her phone, reminding me to do the same.

I'd lived ten years without any portable electronic devices, and I'd yet to settle into the modern trend of consulting them on an hourly basis. I was surprised to see I'd missed several calls while being held hostage by the world's most insane book club hostess, most of them from Mac. "Eenie meenie miney mo," I muttered. At Sera's questioning eyebrow, I explained, "I'm trying to figure out who should yell at me first. Mac or Carmichael."

"Oh, let me call Carmichael. Please." That settled it. I called the agent directly.

"What part of 'liaison' requires you to climb roofs in Reno?" he said by way of greeting.

"Are you tracking us?" I did my best to sound indignant. When you have no actual defense, there's no choice but to apologize or go on the offensive. The second option involved less groveling.

"I don't need to. I have an alert set up for Sera's car, and it seems that, wherever the Mustang appears, some helpful neighbor phones in a crime. Today, we had reports of reckless driving in Truckee and the aforementioned roof climbing. The second call was quickly canceled by the homeowners, by the way."

"Of course it was. We were liaising. They realized that and opted not to have us arrested." I sounded so reasonable. I'd become a convincing actress any day now, I was sure.

"You liaise from the roof?" Or perhaps it was still a work in progress.

"Would you believe they were slate elementals?" Sera held out her hand, demanding the phone. I swatted it away, repeatedly. "Anyway, everything's fine. We got some information, and no one's threatened to sue the FBI on our behalf once today. We'll drop by the office later. Or tomorrow. Maybe the day after."

There was a long, ominous pause. "We really need to draft a job description for you two."

"Can't," I said cheerily. "Off the books, remember? Hey, Sera wants to speak with you." He muttered several incomprehensible words that sounded less than flattering, then hung up. "Looks like he got disconnected."

The corners of her mouth slid a fraction upward. Whatever she might say, she was enjoying the game with Carmichael. "Where now?"

Our options were limited. "Back to Carmen's? She might still be in Reno, and Pamela ought to be home from school soon. We could talk to her before her mom tells her what she's supposed to say."

She nodded toward my phone. "You going to call Mac first?"

I thought of all the times he'd ignored me lately and decided turnabout was fair play. "He can wait to yell at me." I turned off my phone, ensuring I stuck to my plan. I knew that if I saw his number on my caller ID, I wouldn't be able to resist answering.

We drove at a casual pace back to Carmen's home, which in Sera's case meant only ten miles above the stated speed limit. She even allowed me to turn down her music, so we were both relaxed and at ease when we pulled to a stop outside Carmen's behemoth of a house.

Our calm state came to a screeching halt when we saw a Bronco and an Explorer parked in the driveway. Two large bear shifters stood between them, conferring. They watched us walk toward them, their faces dark and serious.

"You should answer your phone," said Mac by way of greeting.

I muttered some vague combination of excuse and apology.

"What's going on?" asked Sera, studying the front of the house. From our vantage point, the house looked exactly as it did the day before.

Will answered evenly, his matter-of-fact tone a marked contrast to his cloudy expression. "It's possible Pamela's been missing for two days. Two nights ago, she told her mother she was staying with a human friend while that girl's mother was out of town. That friend just called, looking for her. She had no idea Pamela was supposed to be with her."

"What about school?" I asked.

Mac shook his head. "Not for the last two days."

"Carmen hasn't heard from her daughter in two days, and she's just now getting worried?" I tried to hide my judgment of such a relaxed parenting style and failed. I was sure my overprotective mother would appreciate the irony.

"She texted, but we have no way of knowing who actually sent those."

"Is Carmen here?" We'd lingered long enough at the diner she could have easily beaten us home, particularly if she answered her phone. I couldn't believe we'd been Mac's or Will's first call.

"She's tracking." Will didn't sound like he expected her to have much luck.

"Trail stops at the river?" It was an easy guess. I doubted the shifters would have requested outside involvement if it weren't absolutely necessary. I thought of the other person who'd been with James at the lake. All signs pointed to it being Pamela. "I think I can say, with near certainty, that Pamela was running away with James two nights ago. Hell, she's probably with him now. You're not looking for two kidnapped kids. You're looking for two shifters who ran off together and knew how to lay false trails and cover their own tracks. Any chance the bears and cats went all Montague and Capulet on them?" We already knew Carmen wasn't a fan of the relationship, and I took Will's stony expression as confirmation he felt the same. "They're holed up together somewhere, trust me."

I felt pretty proud of myself. Case solved. Okay, solvedish, considering we didn't know where they actually were. Even so, I'd figured it out. For a moment, I allowed myself to entertain the fantasy that I might be able to keep this job for longer than a week.

"Are you done?" Will's words were even, but I still sensed waves of anger rolling off him. I took one surreptitious step back, remembering what happened to Mac the one time he nearly lost control. It wasn't necessary. Will kept himself tightly contained, and I didn't see even a single claw extend or an unwanted strand of hair grow on his face. "See if the other girl knows anything," he told Mac, who nodded and turned toward the front door. Will stared at me for one long second, then nodded, appearing to come to a decision. "Follow me."

Sera indicated she'd go with Mac, and I trailed after his uncle. He led me to the backyard, stepping carefully on the paving stones to avoid disrupting the soil. He stopped and pointed.

I followed his finger to several small dark spots. It took a moment for my brain to acknowledge what my eyes were seeing. I quickly stepped back, disregarding the evidence I might be trampling in my haste to get away from the blood congealing on the back patio. I wasn't squeamish, not the way Vivian was. It wasn't the blood itself that bothered me, but what it signified.

"It's Pamela's?" I asked from several feet away. Their noses could tell not only whose it was but when it had been spilled.

Will nodded. "It's been here about two hours. She must have returned home after her mother left for the gym and while Dana was at school." His hand clenched into a fist, and he closed his eyes. I suspected he was willing something to appear that he could pummel into a heap of dust. I was feeling much the same urge, and I didn't have the muscles to do a fraction of the damage he could.

I quickly imagined several scenarios. In the first one,

Pamela had been with James, but they separated for some reason. When she returned home, someone grabbed her. Maybe it was the same person who grabbed James, but the smart money, the money that knew how common domestic violence was, even among teenagers, would say she'd gotten away from an abusive boyfriend, only to have James return for her. I looked nervously at Will. I doubted he'd be willing to entertain that theory.

The other choice made no sense. Someone who lived in this house had been in the lake, and if it wasn't Pamela, it looked like Mama Cat had a lot of questions to answer. Again, I hesitated to tell Will, fearing the bear's version of a fair trial involved several blows to the head and bellowed demands to know where his son was. Nothing in that scenario explained why Pamela was now missing, either.

For now, it seemed like those with the least emotional investment should be handling this. How I'd become the calmest person in the room was a question for the ages, but it was the current reality.

"We'll get her back, Will. Her and James both." The words should have been empty. I had no idea how to find two teenagers, and no real investigative experience to rely on. But I spoke them with utter certainty. I'd seen enough bad stuff lately, seen too many innocent people lose their lives. I wasn't going to sit by and let something else happen if I could do anything to stop it—and if James turned out to be one of the bad guys, I'd figure that out, too.

I swallowed my pride, my bravado, and my quick retorts, and looked Will directly in the eye. "How can I help?"

He met my gaze, seeming to accept my genuine offer with grace. A reluctant grace, but grace nonetheless. "My nephew will take you to the river. Maybe you'll find something. God knows any information would be a help."

I left Will staring at the blood, looking for answers where

none existed.

I found Mac in Carmen's immaculate living room, perched on a luxurious brown leather sofa. He was whispering quiet words to a miserable Dana, trying to offer comfort she wasn't ready to accept.

Sera watched impassively, deep in her own thoughts. I imagined she was constructing scenarios similar to those I'd already worked up, and I could only hope she was finding more answers.

Mac looked completely out of place in that room, large and rough. His blue jeans were worn and his flannel shirt faded, and his hands, resting lightly on his muscled thighs, were strong and callused.

Yet, somehow, he made his surroundings look tasteless, wan and overdone and false when placed against the simple, warm life that pulsed from him. I wanted to walk to him and place my hands on his tense shoulders, but I had no idea if he would welcome my touch. Instead, I opted for a quiet, "Hey."

He already knew I was there, of course. But he waited until I spoke, and turned around slowly. "Will showed you?" I nodded. There was nothing else to say. "Let's go to the water, then." He stood and walked slowly past me.

Mac drove us to the river, passing trees slowly regaining their leaves after the harsh winter. Snowplants and delphinium burst through the ground, their nubs of green and red and purple only hinting at the riot of color that would decorate the land in another month or two. It seemed ludicrous, such beauty and rebirth in the face of our fear and worry and, though no one wanted to say it aloud, the all too real possibility of the shifters' deaths.

We were silent when we reached the river, the other two waiting for me to speak to the water. I only hoped it had answers. I sat on the shore and dipped my hands in the chilly water. Even in the shallows, it held none of the warmth of the springtime sun, the runoff from the mountain snow moving too quickly downstream to bother taking the time to heat itself.

It didn't matter. My fire heritage might mean I liked to bundle up in sweaters and scarves, but water could dip near freezing and make no difference to me. It didn't feel cold. It felt like part of me.

Unfortunately, that's all I felt. Unlike the static lake, the river had already changed many times since Pamela had gone missing, and I felt no hint of life beyond the usual fish and plants that populated the water. There was something warm-blooded, too. A beaver, maybe. As I watched, I thought I saw a few brown heads break through the water, but they disappeared so quickly I wondered if I'd imagined it.

Seeing nothing else, I shook my head at Mac and Sera. The river was a dead end.

Mac looked like he'd been expecting that news. He phoned his uncle and relayed my findings, then returned us to Carmen's house. In our absence, someone had cleaned up the blood. Once everyone who needed to had caught the trail, I supposed there was no need to keep it. It wasn't like anyone would be calling the local forensics team to come out and provide an analysis. The house was eerily quiet, and it appeared our welcome was at an end.

Lacking any better options, it was time to return home. Mac and Sera moved to the driver's side of their respective cars, leaving me to choose my ride back. I took several steps toward the Mustang, certain that, based on his recent behavior, Mac had no great desire for my company.

A second later, I decided I didn't really care. I deliberately turned around, just catching Sera's amused expression in my peripheral vision. I pulled myself into the passenger seat of the Bronco and smiled at Mac. "I'm riding with you," I said unnecessarily.

He held my gaze for a long moment, his brown eyes filled with complicated emotions I could barely begin to understand, then he simply nodded and turned the key.

The ride home was quiet. I'd noticed that, while Mac and Simon never protested when Sera or I played music, they never put it on themselves. The human part of them might like it, but it seemed the animal side avoided anything that interfered with their senses. And so the cab was filled with a heavy silence, only the sound of the engine and the wind rushing past the windows providing any accompaniment to the thoughts ricocheting around my brain.

I was desperately aware of his proximity, that warm body less than a foot from mine. It would be so easy to simply pick up my hand and lay it on his thigh, or to scoot across the bench seat and curl into him, resting my head in that perfect hollow between his shoulder and chest. I felt my hand lift, seemingly of its own volition, wanting to act on that impulse before my conscious mind could reason with it.

I'd thought we had something. Or, at least, I'd thought we could have something.

We were nearly to the cabin. I finally had him alone, and I was about to lose my only chance to talk to him. Soon, the others would be around, and he'd disappear back into his Airstream trailer, and I'd be fighting to get a single moment alone with him. This was it.

"So... we kissed." Well, that was one way to start the conversation.

His entire body stilled for a moment, then his eyes slid slowly toward me. It only lasted a second, and then he returned them to the road, but it was enough to feel scorched from head to toe.

"I remember," he said simply. He face was impassive, giving nothing away.

"Okay, then. Just wanted to be sure I hadn't imagined it." I paused, giving him the chance to respond. He said nothing. I turned my face to the window, wondering if he'd notice if I flung the door open and made my escape. Right now, a bit of road burn seemed preferable to sitting in the Bronco another minute, wanting to climb into the lap of a man who clearly didn't want me there.

The quiet stretched between us again, and somehow my mouth was breaking that silence before my brain had a chance to approve its words. "So, what? It was just a thing? It didn't mean anything? Or is this because of the whole doomed-to-be-crazy thing?" Hey, I might need to work on my eloquence, but at least I got to the point.

He gripped the steering wheel in a perfect ten-two position and continued to watch the road. Just when I thought he wasn't going to respond, he quietly said, "It meant something."

My heart stuttered and seemed to stop altogether, then joyously launched into double time. Part of me wanted to leave it there, knowing that whatever may have happened or might happen in the future, we'd shared one kiss that meant something. It almost felt like enough.

Unfortunately, Earth's insistence on continuing to spin through space meant few things ever stopped exactly where you wanted them to. Though he didn't release his grip on the wheel or lift his eyes from the road, Mac wasn't done speaking.

"I remember kissing you. I remember thinking I was holding someone remarkable in my arms, and being fairly certain I didn't want to let her go. I remember that."

I was about to find out how long an elemental could live without oxygen. His words stole my breath, and I could do nothing but stare at him, my eyes roaming over his profile. His straight nose and high, broad cheekbones. His thick brown hair, a little too long. His jawline, locked in place. It was a face I found beautiful, but it wasn't a relaxed, romantic face. The words might sound like a declaration, but the face was locked and closed.

Our time was up. He turned right, pulling into the long road that led to the cabin. I desperately racked my brain, looking for the words I needed to say to make him turn to me with soft eyes that matched his words. For once, I was speechless. Declarations of my own swam just below the surface, vague words and promises I'd never spoken before and didn't know how to articulate. I wasn't even sure what they meant. I only knew I wasn't ready for this ride to be over.

He drew to a stop in the driveway, next to the beat-up Chevy compact I'd driven down from Oregon and ignored ever since. Sera wasn't back yet, but the living room was lit. Real life waited for us, just a few feet away. Mac turned the engine off and unbuckled his seat belt, turning to face me.

"I also remember that you left that night. You took off without a word to anyone, and headed straight into a dangerous situation you didn't need to be in. You didn't trust me to help you, and you definitely didn't trust me to believe in you, though I would have done both. I know you're still coming back to the world after a long time away, and I know you have a lot to deal with. This isn't about the half-fire thing. I can deal with that, but I can't deal with you running away, not again. Honestly, I'm not sure you're ready to be kissing anyone, not yet."

I opened my mouth once, twice, looking for a rebuttal that didn't exist. Mac tended to be the strong, silent type until he had something to say, and it appeared he currently had a lot to say—and all of it was true. I was the one who'd acted like the kiss meant nothing. I was the one who'd left. "But I came back." I spoke in a whisper, my throat closing around the words.

He reached out one hand to cup my cheek. The calluses I'd noticed earlier scraped lightly against my skin, and I welcomed the rough touch. Without even thinking, I leaned into his hand. I pressed against his warm skin and let him hold me, if only in that small way. I watched for the moment those chocolate brown eyes softened. It didn't take long. He seemed content to simply sit like that, and I began to think he had nothing else to say. Finally, he answered. "I guess that's a start."

I looked at him, at that broad, tanned face that was quickly becoming one of my favorite sights in the world, and began to prepare long, reasoned arguments why waiting was entirely unnecessary. Before I had a chance to deliver any of them, his eyes moved to the rearview mirror. He instantly removed his hand from my cheek, his demeanor becoming impersonal and almost business-like. "Your friends are here." A moment later, he was outside the car and moving toward his trailer, leaving me alone to deal with the black sedan easing its way down the driveway.

CHAPTER 7

Sera wasn't far behind the agents, having made a quick stop for some food and beer. We'd all been drinking a lot less since Brian revealed his true self, somehow associating cocktails and late nights with his boozehound ways.

Even more than the rest, I avoided crossing the line from relaxed into tipsy. We still didn't know what had pushed Brian from fun-loving college student into murder-loving psychopath, but I figured it couldn't hurt to walk a different path than he had whenever possible. Even so, with the sun beginning to show its face on a regular basis, many days found us lounging on the back deck, bottles of beer firmly in hand. After all, if I gave up alcohol altogether, I was pretty sure that meant the terrorists had won.

It was almost warm enough to be outside, and we had sufficient deck chairs for everyone to sit. However, doing so would allow Carmichael to keep his dignity, so Sera insisted we all talk in the living room. He scanned the floor for the most likely chair in a pile of floor pillows. I cheerfully patted a lumpy one next to me that featured some form of mutant ninja turtle. He gingerly lowered himself to the floor, carefully adjusting his suit and looking like he wanted to make an emergency call to his dry cleaner.

Sera walked into the room, cold six-pack in hand. "Beer, Scully?" she asked.

Carmichael shook his head. "We're working."

Johnson was already reclining against the wall, a panel of upside down teddy bears surrounding his relaxed face. "I'll take one," he said, holding out a hand.

"Johnson! It's like I don't even know you," I said, reaching for my own bottle. He'd come a long way since we'd met. A few months ago, he'd been a serious, uptight agent intent on imprisoning me for several human lifetimes. I was sure he could still summon that agent at a moment's notice, but at some point he'd let us see the man underneath, and I'd discovered I was quite fond of the Johnson that didn't want to lock me up and throw the key deep into the fires of Mordor.

"Off the books means off the clock, right?" He grinned and took a long swig from the bottle.

Sera nodded. "Exactly. Though I should warn you, not everyone appreciates our flawless logic."

Johnson didn't bother to respond. He was too busy watching Vivian play with earth. We still had plastic bins full of soil scattered throughout the living room, a remnant of our old security system. Vivian had spent the last few weeks filling them with her favorite plants, but they still provided a bit of defense for our resident earth. We weren't ready to disarm the teddy bear fortress yet, but we'd made it prettier.

Vivian closed her eyes and slowly fed the earth's nutrients into the latest seedlings. As we watched, the plants sprouted a full half inch. She was a weak elemental, but that didn't stop Johnson from watching her with an expression of awe in his eyes.

Fortunately, she was also a patient elemental. "Place your hand on the surface," she told him. He quickly obeyed. "What do you feel?"

His face wrinkled in concentration. "Nothing."

She picked up his hand and moved it to another section

of soil. "Try here." Once again, his face tensed. "Not like that. Breathe. You can't force something to happen. Just root yourself to the earth, become part of it."

He cracked one eye open, uncertain about the use of such blatant hippie language, but he tried again. With each long, slow breath, I could see the tension exit his shoulders and the muscles in his face relax, leaving him calm and open. "I feel... is that a worm?"

Vivian nodded. "A big one about an inch below the surface." Johnson laughed openly. I was glad for him, but I also hoped Vivian was managing his expectations. With practice, he might learn to read the earth a bit, but that was all he could achieve. He was too weak to manipulate it, and his tiny drop of elemental blood was unlikely to provide anything other than a few blue ribbons in the county fair's vegetable competitions.

Carmichael abruptly decided we'd socialized long enough. "What can you tell us about the shifters?"

I glanced toward Sera. Mac was still in his trailer, and while Simon was in the room, the agents hadn't noticed the black cat perched in the beams. Their absence spoke volumes: leave them out of it.

"Well..." I stretched out the word, searching for an answer that sounded terribly informative while divulging no real information. I knew the shifters would continue to include us in the search for the missing teens only if they believed we weren't then feeding their information to the FBI.

Fortunately, Sera knew better than to leave me in charge of keeping secrets. "What do you want to know?"

Carmichael turned to her, his body tensing at the sound of her voice. "Everything you learned in the course of doing your job." There was an unmistakable emphasis on the last word.

"Shouldn't a job come with benefits and paychecks? I'm not sure we actually have a job." Her look was as innocent as Sera could manage.

He sputtered. "It's been two days. We need processing time. We need to know this is going to work out."

She shook her head. "See, that's the problem. You keep acting like you're doing us a favor, when I'm fairly sure it's the other way around. It's not like you two could wander into a shifter home and get answers."

A red flush creeped into his cheeks, a flush I'd only ever seen Sera cause. The woman had a gift. "We could always find other elementals."

"You think so?" Her doubtful tone made it clear how likely she considered that possibility. "Maybe. They wouldn't be as powerful as we are, though. Not as pretty to look at, either." She smiled at him, an easy, harmless smile, and took a pull of her beer.

"What do you want?" He spoke through gritted teeth.

She waited a long time to respond, taking several more swigs and appearing to think carefully about her answer. I knew she'd decided what to say before she even started this conversation. She might have been planning it since we left Reno. "I want you to understand that this is our world, not yours. Not yours either, Johnson, I'm sorry to say. We want to help you, but we're going to deal with our world the best way we know how, and sometimes that will involve keeping its secrets. And you, well, you're going to accept that and keep your whining to a minimum. Also, you guys do direct deposit, right?"

I admired how she failed to mention that shifters didn't remotely consider us part of their world.

The red flush spread and darkened, and I was pretty sure his body vibrated slightly. I had to give him points for control, though. His hand didn't twitch once toward his firearm. "Daily updates on all supernatural occurrences," Carmichael insisted.

"Weekly. And we prefer the term magical."

"Though our powers are steeped in nature and, we are, obviously, quite super." I couldn't resist contributing. Sera shot a conspiratorial smile my way. Carmichael chose to ignore me.

"Every other day." Johnson watched Carmichael haggle, though he showed no sign of jumping in.

"Twice a week or none at all. Final offer."

He studied her, weighing the strength of his position and seeing all its weaknesses. "Twice a week reports on all magical issues and daily reports on any human involvement, and your pay will be docked instantly if we find out you are withholding information we needed. That's our final offer."

Sera and I both nodded. It was a fair compromise, all things considered, though I feared we'd lose a fair bit of our pay if Carmichael followed through on his threat.

Carmichael exhaled, his relief tempered somewhat by his obvious annoyance. "Now, can you please fill us in on the basic points of the case?"

She gazed off into the distance, considering. "The shifters are having a couple of bad days." Considering that update enough, she stopped talking and waited for him to explode.

Somehow, he held it together. "Are elementals involved in any way?"

"Other than you asking me and Aidan to butt in? No."

He leaned forward, looking earnest and determined. I suspected this was a ploy. "You trusted us once with your secrets," he implored.

The foolish man couldn't know that a woman raised by Josiah Blais was completely immune to emotional manipulation. She'd been taught by the master, and no one else had a chance. If anything, she looked amused. "And word still managed to get out within the FBI. Neither of us are exactly welcome at home these days."

This time, she neglected to mention that neither of us felt any desire to return home. Few people could tell partial truths with greater conviction than Sera.

Carmichael was running out of arguments. I wanted to save him, since he had no real chance of winning against Sera, and the longer he tried, the more foolish she'd make him feel.

"We can't," I said. "These aren't our secrets to tell. You need to understand that. We'll wear the white hats and help however we can, but we're not going to betray the magical community more than we already have. I know you think you have a right to this information because of your new job, but that's just not true. You're still an outsider. The best we can do is tell you when there's information we're not allowed to share. Let us keep some loyalties, Carmichael."

I thought loyalty was a language Carmichael would understand. He sighed heavily. "Let me see if I've got this right. We asked you to liaise on a case and communicate your findings to the FBI. We sent you to work on a case you would never have known about without us. Now, you are asking us to continue to employ you, despite the fact that your version of liaising involves telling us almost nothing about the case to which we assigned you unless it suits you and your friends."

Sera and I looked at each other. "That's about it, yeah." I nodded and gave him a bright smile.

Carmichael rubbed his hand over his face, scrubbing his own skin in frustration. "Any human involvement?"

It was one small thing we could give him. "One of the

shifters lied and said she was staying with a human friend. I'm not sure the girl knows anything, but you can talk to her."

Sera nodded and gave them the name she'd learned from Dana. "Other than that, it's all shifter families." She offered Carmichael a small apologetic smile, one honest enough to catch him off guard. Sure, she was happy to bust his balls just for the fun of it, but we were also telling the truth. There were things we couldn't tell these men without the shifters' permission, and it took a rare sincere moment from Sera for Carmichael to finally understand that.

He nodded at her. "Thank you. And, considering that we don't appear to be doing any work this evening, I'll take one of those beers now." He smiled a weak, tired smile, and with it the agent melted away, leaving a man in his place. It was the first time I'd ever seen Carmichael as anything other than the determined, focused agent. It made me think I should call him by his first name, if I had any idea what that was.

Instead, I walked to the kitchen to grab his beer from the fridge, wishing the whole time that Mac and Simon would join us and there was one less secret I had to keep.

DAYS PASSED, EACH hour creeping slowly by as absolutely nothing happened. The phone remained silent. I knew Will and his family were continuing to pursue every lead they could find, questioning James's and Pamela's friends. I assumed Carmen was doing the same, but no one updated me or Sera.

We knocked on both their front doors at least once a day, but no one opened them. Maybe Mac had told them we were in contact with the agents. Maybe they just didn't like us.

I wasn't sure what we'd have done if someone had

answered. An abusive boyfriend or crazy mother still seemed the most likely scenarios, and I had no idea how to simultaneously help and investigate the two families.

The agents checked in regularly, and they confirmed what we already suspected. Pamela's friend knew nothing. She'd merely been an excuse, a distraction while Pamela snuck away with James. She had no more idea where they'd gone than we did.

We had little information to offer them in turn, a fact of which they were grudgingly accepting.

Vivian spent hours on the computer, digging up every bit of information we could find on our key suspects. She learned that James got his driver's license the moment he turned sixteen, earned Bs and Cs in school despite strong test scores, took regular guitar lessons in Tahoe City, and was a menace on a snowboard. Nothing in his history hinted at violence.

Carmen's story was more complicated. Vivian's research indicated a wild past, the kind of life that felt more appropriate to a big cat than the preppy trappings that now surrounded her. In high school, she'd been the sort of student who, if she'd spent half the energy on her studies that she spent attempting to skip class and outsmart the teachers, she'd have been valedictorian. She'd skipped college, preferring to educate herself in the San Francisco nightlife. She only stayed in the city a few years before returning north with a few dollars to her name.

Somehow, I knew it wasn't the lack of money that brought her back. The evidence suggested that Carmen was a resourceful woman, the kind who knew how to separate men from their money. No, San Francisco was beautiful, with manicured parks and tourist-friendly forests along the coast, but it wasn't the mountains. She was here because this was her home.

Only a week after returning, she met Mark Avila in a Sacramento bar frequented by well-heeled political types. She convinced him to marry her within a week and divorced him less than a year later, taking full advantage of California being a community property state. A month later, she found a man more than happy to take on a beautiful divorcee and her infant daughter. He lasted almost three years. The second husband had visitation rights to see Dana, but the first hadn't been heard from since the divorce.

It might be suspicious, if it bore any resemblance to the current case. Carmen liked gullible older men with money who made her life easier. Kidnapping her daughter and her boyfriend simply made no sense.

Sera and I spent a lot of time on the throw pillows, tossing theories back and forth and trying to find an avenue worth exploring. One we knew how to explore, more to the point. We knew we were in over our heads, though neither of us wanted to admit it. We had no training in this kind of work, no idea where to begin, and no clue how to open those doors that remained steadfastly closed.

I hadn't seen Mac since the night the agents interrupted us. I didn't know if he was avoiding me or working the case separately, but it didn't matter. The message was clear: I wasn't welcome in parts of his life.

Vivian was rarely home, spending all her time either in the library or with her ex-girlfriend. She continued to scowl and mutter whenever I asked for details, so I assumed it wasn't going well.

Simon was still with us, though didn't know for how long. Reluctantly, we'd passed Carmen's message on to him, along with a slew of reasons he could ignore her request. He nodded once, confirming he heard us, but said nothing in response. No one wanted to remind him of his talk of leaving, and we walked on eggshells around him, hoping that if we never mentioned it, he might just forget. Cats aren't renowned for their long memories, after all.

Sera and I waited, feeling more useless by the hour. By the third morning, I felt ready to climb outside my own skin. The agitation pulled at my center, at that ball of energy that rested quietly in my core, just waiting for a chance to spring to life. It demanded release. I hoped ignoring it would cause it to quiet and atrophy, but I feared the opposite was true. I suspected it would only grow louder until I sated it with action.

And so, when Sera exploded from her room on that third morning, hair wild from sleep and eyes bleary from lack of caffeine but still a bundle of pure energy, I understood the force that motivated her when she announced, "Screw this. We're doing something today." It was the same force coiled within me, familiar and foreign at the same time.

"Back to the lake or the river?" I suggested, with little hope that we'd find anything in either spot.

She shook her head, clearly sharing my doubt. "I think we exhausted those. Think if we camp on their doorsteps, the families will finally open their doors?"

"We could maybe stop at a costume shop for some bear or cat ears. Might make them more accepting of our presence."

She was amused by the thought. "While my sexy cat has served me well at more than one Halloween party, I don't think it'll work quite as well on Carmen."

"You know, if it ever comes down to a fight between you two, I'm not sure who I'd put money on. I mean, you, obviously, cause of the whole loyalty thing and the way you could set her on fire, but otherwise it would be a hard call. That woman scares me."

"It's the claws. She'd be hell in a slap fight."

"Fair point." The conversation tapered off into comfortable silence, both of us trying to come up with a plan that was only somewhat ridiculous. I got there first. My idea was still mostly ridiculous, but it was the only one we had.

"Get dressed, Sera. Something casual and, er, hot." She simply looked at me, her scornful expression suggesting she was always hot, regardless of her outfit. "We're going back to school."

CHAPTER 8

"I assume your plan is more complex than we sit outside a public school until someone arrests us for loitering in a suspicious manner? Cause I had plans today that didn't involve ending up on a sex offender registry."

We were parked across from the square mass of brick and concrete that formed the local high school. It was the sort of utilitarian building built for function rather than design, the city planners unwilling to shell out any money for unnecessary architecture. At the moment, it was silent, and we could only wait impatiently for the lunch bell to ring.

"I thought we might be able to get Brandon to open up a bit more if we got him on his own, away from his family. From what I've heard, siblings know secrets that would horrify parents, so we need to know what he knows. And I'm hoping he'll be more forthcoming if he's talking to an attractive woman."

Sera nodded slowly. "You remember I did my best to scare the actual bejeesus out of him when we met, right?"

I was unconcerned. "He's a teenage boy. Fear and attraction go hand in hand."

"I just want to be clear about this. Am I wearing my extra tight jeans to seduce Mac's teenaged cousin?"

"Seduce is such a strong word. I was thinking charm. Cajole, perhaps."

"Why did I get assigned this particular task?"

I shrugged. "Hey, you always say you're the hot one. If you're willing to relinquish that title..."

"Please. I've seen your recent attempts at flirtation. If we want the kid to fall down laughing, you're our go-to girl." She sighed, a big, dramatic exhalation that let me know how put-upon she felt. "Until you get your mojo back, call me Mrs. Robinson."

"Hey. My mojo is working just fine."

"Really? How's Mac?"

I muttered several comebacks under my breath, most of which involved creative combinations of profanity, then settled for a simple, "Shut up."

She grinned, knowing she'd won that round. Her victory allowed her to be magnanimous. "Give it time. I mean, you are kind of a freak. People need to warm to that. But you have your good points. Okay, sure, you have boring taste in music, and you drive like someone's cataracts-ridden grandma. You wake up at a completely ridiculous hour each morning. You could win an Olympic medal in stubbornness."

"I assume the good points are coming eventually?"

"Sorry," she said, sounding not sorry in the least. "I got sidetracked."

"Don't forget the part where I'm slowly becoming insane. That's got to be a selling point for someone."

Her smile fell instantly, and when she next spoke, her voice held no hint of laughter. Apparently, I'd found the one subject she didn't want to joke about. "That is not going to happen, Ade. It's just not. You hear me?"

"How can you be so sure? I mean, yeah, we only have Josiah's word that madness is inevitable, and normally I'd say his word is about as valuable as Monopoly money. But my mother said the same thing, and you saw what Brian became. I know you didn't meet Trent Pond, but trust me, he wasn't living in the same reality we do. Whatever I am, whatever I might become, it's not good."

"But Trent was just a little nuts, right? I mean, he was in a regular mental hospital, not one for the criminally insane. So there've got to be different levels of crazy. We just need to figure out how to keep you on the low setting."

I'd already considered this option and had a working, if highly depressing, theory. "Yes, but Trent was ice and water, right? Similar elements. Brian was ice and earth, very different ones. And me, well..." I let the silence speak for me. Water and fire were polar opposites. If I was right, I wasn't just looking at a ride on the crazy train. I could be its conductor.

I looked at Sera, at this friend I'd only just gotten back. It was too soon to lose each other again. "Besides, if the elementals ever learn what I am, I won't even have a chance to go crazy. The council will order, well, you know." I stopped, unwilling to speak the words aloud.

She knew. "Not going to happen, Ade," Sera repeated. "I've thought about what you said on the roof, that something feels unbalanced now. That might be true, but I've gotta say, I see no evidence of that. You're the same pain in the ass you always were. So I'm choosing to believe there is a way around this, around all of it, and we will find it." The words were heavy, a proclamation of fact rather than one woman's opinion. When she spoke with such confidence, I had no choice but to believe her. "Besides," she added. "When do I ever not get my way?"

"Never," I admitted. She nodded, satisfied I was finally seeing reason.

A clanging bell cut through the air, and a moment later the school's heavy doors flew open. Teenagers spilled from the depths of the building, their voices loud and energetic, releasing tension built up from sitting quietly for hours on end, absorbing knowledge most of them didn't want. They called to each other noisily, running to their cars and pulling quickly away from the curb, off to the nearest fast food restaurant where they could enjoy their short-lived freedom with a side of trans fats.

We studied the students carefully, looking for any sign of the sullen, brown-haired teenager we'd met a few days ago. Just as we were about to give up, we saw a group of students slink around the side of the building and move toward the trees that surrounded the school. In the center of the group, his slouch and slow gait the international body language of the bored teenager, walked Brandon.

We followed. Their trail was so obvious even a human could have found them. Heavy footfalls left clear shoe imprints on the ground, and the trampled grass pointed the way as clearly as an arrow. If I hadn't already figured out Brandon was human, the fact that he didn't notice us approaching would have been a clear indication he didn't get the shifter gene.

In addition to Brandon, there were three other teenagers, two boys and a girl. The other boys were both skinny, their gangly limbs and lean faces suggesting they weren't done growing yet. They wore oversized clothes likely intended to conceal their lack of muscle tone but which only served to highlight how thin they were. One had bleached hair, clearly done at home with a peroxide bottle, and the other had piercings in his left eyebrow and beneath his lower lip.

The girl was small, quiet, and almost painfully adorable, nothing but enormous brown eyes and soft cheeks. She was trying to balance being so damn cute with harder clothes. She wore all black with lots of silver jewelry, and streaks of purple hair framed her face. Everything about this group suggested bored teenagers who thought they were far more trouble than they actually were.

My sheltered upbringing meant I'd never met this kind of student growing up, let alone become one myself. Sera, who'd attended a public high school as part of Josiah's efforts at limited assimilation, grinned as we approached. She'd spent a few years sneaking off into the trees with her own school's bad boys, and this was familiar ground for her.

"Brandon!" she called. They turned immediately, and I noticed cigarette packs being surreptitiously returned to pockets. "Don't mind us. We won't tell." In a heartbeat, her sardonic expression vanished. Her eyes softened, and she let her full lips tip into a soft, conspiratorial smile. She leaned casually against a tree, a pose that allowed her to jut one hip to the side and emphasize the curve from her waist to her thigh. Sera had an impressive curve to display, and Brandon's male companions noticed.

"Oh yeah?" said Bleached. "Why should we trust you? You don't go to the school, do you?" He sounded more hopeful than worried, as if he thought Sera might be a very mature senior. With a bit of extra swagger, he withdrew the cigarettes again, doing his best to show that he was old enough to smoke, or for anything else Sera might have in mind.

"Nah. We just know Brandon. Don't we?" She gazed at him, letting her eyes suggest all sorts of potentially inappropriate connections. Brandon looked on the verge of utter panic, trying to figure out what had changed between Sera tormenting him in his dad's car and flirting with him in Smokers' Woods. I couldn't help him, either. I was too busy trying not to laugh.

Bleached glanced between Brandon and Sera, trying to read the situation and his own chances. He flicked the lighter and brought it toward his face, only to have the flame disappear every time it got close. "Dude, this thing's broken. Give me yours." He grabbed his friend's, only to encounter the same problem. Sera's face was impassive, but Brandon looked amused. He knew what Sera was but felt no desire to clue the others in, making me think the rest were human.

"What do you want?" he asked. Surprisingly, Sera's little trick with the fire made him marginally more helpful. I didn't know whether this was due to the reminder of our magical connection or just his fear that we'd give something away, but he was slightly less sullen than he'd been before. He'd been upgraded to merely snippy now.

Still, he spoke the words confidently, making eye contact in a way he hadn't in the car. I was happy to see I'd been right. He was the big man among his friends, and he needed to impress them.

"So direct." She stood up straight and wandered closer to Brandon. His two friends watched every step, but I kept my eyes on the lone girl. She appeared to be slowly disappearing into herself, as if her already uncertain existence dimmed further once the boys stopped noticing her.

I'd known girls like that at university, shy and quiet, unable to demand the attention they craved. You never asked that girl where the weekend's parties would be held, or what the latest fashions were. She was never the first one to know such quickly changing information, but she made up for it by observing, always observing, and no one had a better grasp on who was hooking up, who was nursing a crush, and who'd actually found the type of love she desperately wanted for herself. In other words, she was the perfect one to ask about James and Pamela.

Sera was still talking to Brandon and his friends. She'd lowered her voice to suggest secrets and intimacy, and the boys continued to behave like hormones on legs. It was good to know that, in a world where everything was horribly unstable, I could count on teenage boys to make fools of themselves over an attractive woman. Brandon himself looked immune to Sera's charms, but not the adulation of his friends, and I swore his chest puffed up and he stood at least two inches taller while they spoke. I picked out a couple words from the conversation and knew they were discussing James.

Divide and conquer, then. I sidled over to the girl, who was watching Sera work her magic with something between envy and despair. "Hey," I said. "What's your name?"

She looked at me in surprise, as if she'd given up on someone at this school addressing her directly.

"Mary," she murmured. She lifted her chin slightly, trying confidence on for size. It was an uneasy fit, but I suspected she'd grow into it over the years.

"Good, solid name," I assured her. "My mom decided to get creative and named me Aidan, which caused no end of confusion at college. They put me in the boy's dorm, and it took weeks to sort it out. Not that I really minded." I hadn't. Before college, I'd never seen a naked man in person, and it was quite an education to share a bathroom with fifteen of them.

Mary smiled slightly, but I couldn't tell if she was merely trying to be polite. I forged ahead. "Sera and I are trying to get some answers. As soon as we have them, we'll leave you alone."

She turned to me, interest definitely piqued. I didn't think she felt any great animosity toward us, but neither could she warm to us. As long as we were there, she lost the benefit of being the sole girl in the group, with all the attention that provided her. I suspected she hung with these boys because even their awkward attempts to treat her like a guy who just happened to have breasts were still better than trying to fit in with the other girls. While Sera and I remained, that balance would be off.

"What do you want to know?" she asked.

"We're trying to learn a bit more about Pamela. Her family is worried about her." Mentioning that some of Pamela's blood had been found on the wrong side of her skin felt like unnecessary information.

"Cause of James?" She asked. I nodded knowingly, as if I was already in on whatever secrets she was about to share with me. "I don't know why they're stressed about him. James is cool." Her eyes drifted to Bleached and Pierced, mentally comparing her companions to the missing shifter and finding them lacking. "I mean, I know he got in trouble sometimes. He was always in detention for being late. But he wasn't ever rude. He never made fun of me."

I felt a sudden urge to yank this girl away from the teenage boys, who didn't seem nearly as harmless as they had a moment ago, and deposit her in a nice safe chess club where she'd possibly be treated with respect and reverence. Building themselves up by preying on this girl's fragile self-esteem wasn't something I could easily ignore. For the moment, though, I shook it off.

"You never saw him yell at her? Did they fight?"

Mary shook her head vehemently. "Never. They were that couple, you know? The one joined at the hips and lips. He looked at her like she was every dream that ever came true."

When she put it like that, it sounded pretty nice. Unfortunately, it also decreased the likelihood that James was the one we should be chasing. I took a moment to consider how disturbed my life was, that I was hoping to find an abusive teenaged bear shifter.

"I heard they broke up weeks ago," I said, remembering Dana's loud proclamation intended for her mother's ears.

Mary shook her head quickly. "No way. If anything, they

seemed to be together more than ever, always whispering about something." And Dana covered up for her, as I'd suspected.

"What was Pamela like?"

"She was one of those girls. You know. Homecoming court. Played volleyball and even looked good in those tiny shorts. Good grades. Nice to everyone. I mean, I wanted to hate her, but I couldn't. She always seemed so real, you know?"

I nodded slowly, trying to put the pieces together in a new way. A bear and a cat fell in love, which was enough for their families to want them separated. Add in an old-fashioned "good girl falls for bad boy" plot, and we not only had the ingredients for an awesome romantic comedy but a compelling reason for Carmen to want to separate the teenagers, especially if she found out their breakup was a scam.

Unfortunately, while that might explain why James had vanished, it didn't help at all with Pamela—unless Carmen had hidden her own daughter as a decoy.

"Did you ever hear any rumors about them running off together? Any sign they were planning something?"

She shook her head, and I held in a sigh. It wasn't her fault the two lovebirds had actually managed to keep a secret in the rumor mill that is high school. But her next words stopped me cold, and made me thank the gossip gods that shy teenage girls who paid way too much attention to others' business existed in the world.

"In study hall last week, I overheard her on the phone, making plans to meet someone. She told her friends this person was making all her dreams come true." I gave her my best encouraging look, urging her to share every bit of unsubstantiated gossip. "I didn't know Pamela well, but everyone knew she only had two dreams. James, and getting the hell out of Tahoe. She's not here, so I guess she got one of her dreams. Maybe both, I guess, if James is with her."

"Did she say anything else about this person?"

She shook her head. "Just that she was so excited, because she never expected this person to be on her side. That's all I know."

It was more than we'd had an hour ago. Pamela and James hadn't merely been the victims of an escape attempt gone awry. Someone had helped them plan it, and it was someone she knew. And just for fun, it was someone unexpected, because otherwise it would have been too damn easy.

I glanced toward Sera, standing in the middle of a teenage boy triangle. She caught my look and offered a generous eye roll, indicating she was at the end of her patience with those particular fools. Fortunately, the bell rang, the distant noise echoing quietly through the trees.

"Damn," muttered Pierced. "We never even got a smoke, either."

"It's for the best," I said brightly. Their heads snapped toward me, so distracted by Sera they'd completely forgotten I was there. "Smoking causes low sperm count. Impotence sometimes, too."

They scoffed, but I saw a hint of worry flicker in their eyes.

"No, really. It can take a while, but it happens." I began to walk away, then remembered Mary's earlier words. They weren't getting off quite that easily. "It's worse with bleach, I've heard. Like, the hydrogen peroxide soaks into your brain, through the skull, interacts with the nicotine and boom, constant limp dick."

"No way," said Bleached, all false bravado. Even so, I saw his eyes roll upwards, trying to see his own impotence-causing hair.

"Dude! You're fucked," laughed Pierced, exactly as empathetic as I expected him to be.

"Same with titanium. That's what your piercings are, right? It can leach into the skin over time and just mess everything up, you know, below the belt." It was utter nonsense, but at least it would force these idiots to do a bit of research. They might actually learn something.

Sera couldn't resist joining in. "You're right. I read something about that. By the time they're twenty-five, their dicks will be completely useless, won't they?"

I watched panic fill both their eyes. Pierced's hands were twitching, looking like he wanted to rip the metal from his face that instant.

It was like shooting fish in a barrel. Really, really stupid fish. "Twenty-five? You're optimistic. I bet he bleaches once a week, and he has at least two piercings. And they smoke, what, half a pack a day? I give them a year. Two, tops. Enjoy 'em while you got 'em, boys!" I placed a soft emphasis on that final word, subtly reminding them they were too young to enjoy anything with us, ever.

The teenagers ran back to the school, possibly in search of the first device with internet access. I noticed Mary smiling quietly as she trailed behind them and felt an answering grin cross my own face. No matter how much information we'd actually retrieved from this lot, I decided it had been a productive lunch.

"So," I muttered, as we made our slower way back to the car. "Learn anything interesting?"

"James had an accomplice in his escape."

"So did Pamela. You know who it was?"

She jumped easily over a tree root blocking the path. "Nope. But James talked about leaving for years, even before he met the girl. Moron One told me this, and based on the look Brandon gave him, I don't think that was information we were meant to have."

I mulled that over. "Considering that everything we're not supposed to know seems to be shifter related, I'm going to posit that James wanted to escape his family and/or shifter culture."

"You're positing?"

"I think Carmichael might have touched me the other night. I'm blaming him, somehow."

"Fair enough. I'm always happy to blame Carmichael." She paused to consider everything she could lay at Carmichael's feet, then got back on track. "So we talk to Mac?"

My sigh was a lot louder than it needed to be. I wanted to talk to Mac. I wanted to see him and hear his voice and accidentally on purpose rub against him, but I also wanted to keep a tiny shred of dignity. I didn't need to keep giving him chances to reject me. "I guess," I said, with a noticeable lack of enthusiasm. "And if he doesn't want to tell us more about shifters?"

"We find another way. You hungry?"

I nodded.

We reached the car and stopped plotting ways to learn about shifters when we became more interested in fighting over music. Normally, I let her play her tapes in the Mustang—after all, her car, her rules—but the local Americana station was playing Dolly Parton. Some things in life were sacred.

"Leave it," I placed both hands over the radio's face and dug my fingers into the plastic. She made a half-hearted attempt to pry them away, but the need to keep at least one hand on the steering wheel put her at a marked disadvantage. "It's a classic."

She turned toward town, heading for a coffee shop still serving breakfast. "So is *Citizen Kane*, but that doesn't mean I want him in my car." She was going through the motions, but she wasn't particularly invested in the argument. She was too busy craning her head, trying to see the reason for the cars unexpectedly coming to a stop in front of us. Sera did not do well in traffic. "You see a problem?" Her fingers tapped at double speed along the steering wheel, frustrated at the delay.

I leaned out the window, trying to see past the SUV in front of us. At first, I saw nothing. The cars were all slowing, but the problem wasn't just in the road. Pedestrians, as well, had stopped moving, and everyone was gazing at a spot about a hundred feet up the road. Some faces were outraged, some were concerned, and a few simply looked amused. It wasn't until two people moved slightly that I spotted the object of everyone's attention.

"Sera, you're going to want to park." I already had my seatbelt undone and the door open. Without giving Sera time to respond, I sprinted down the street, heading for the tall, brown-haired, and very naked teenager wandering around the sidewalk with a look of equal parts confusion and pure terror.

CHAPTER 9

"James!" I had no doubt we'd found the missing shifter. He had the same coloring as his uncle and cousin, the same broad face with high cheekbones. While he lacked the bulk of his relatives, I knew that was only a matter of time. He already had the broad shoulders and strong arms I knew to expect in bears—and at that moment, I was seeing those body parts, and all others, a little too clearly.

He was surrounded by locals, none of whom had expected their day to be interrupted in this way. Some were showing enough common sense to stand back from the large, terrified teenager. Others demonstrated compassion, trying to calm him with soothing words that had no effect. Many more simply stared.

I none too gently pushed past those standing in my way until I was only a few feet away from the boy. "James!" I called again. He slowly turned to face me, uncertainty written across his face. He had no idea who I was, but unlike the others, I at least knew his name and approached him with a small amount of confidence. I had to hope that was enough.

"Your parents will be here soon. Will and Celeste. I'll call them. But we need to get you inside, somewhere safe and warm, okay?" I tried to use a gentle tone without sounding as if I was speaking to a small child. Sometimes, the line between comforting and condescending is annoyingly thin.

Whatever I did, it worked. He nodded once, then simply turned and entered the store behind him.

"Kids," I announced to the throng of witnesses. "You know, with their streaking and planking and other... things. What are you gonna do?" While I babbled, I reached for the door handle and followed James inside, offering the unconvinced faces on the sidewalk one final, earnest nod.

I closed the door behind me and leaned against it for a moment, blocking anyone inclined to follow. We were in an upscale women's clothing store, and fortunately it was still early enough on a weekday to have no shoppers. The only woman present worked there, and she hadn't noticed my entrance. She was too busy staring at the naked eighteen-year-old standing in the middle of her shop.

"James, have a seat," I suggested. He didn't look at me, but he found a pink, spindly-legged chair outside a dressing room and sat quietly. I grabbed an oversized shawl from a nearby rack and, eyes averted, draped it over his lap. That was as much for my comfort as his.

"Who are...? You can't..." The poor salesperson stuttered, uncertain of the proper etiquette for this situation.

The door banged open and Sera strode in. She was already on the phone, rattling off our address to the person on the other end. "Will?" I mouthed. She gave a curt nod. Finishing the conversation, she hung up, flipped the deadbolt on the front door, and loosened the window and door curtains, giving us as much privacy as the gauzy pink drapes allowed.

That was too much for the salesperson, who finally managed to complete a sentence. "You cannot do that," she announced, pulling herself up to her full height. Her three inch heels helped with that.

Sera glanced at her and made no attempt to look impressed. "You've just closed the store for us. In return, we will buy one of everything you have in stock." She looked around and amended her answer. "Well, one of everything that's not pink."

I looked at James, who appeared dazed. He displayed no interest in his surroundings, neither the place nor the people. He stared at the floor, his gaze unwavering, unconcerned that he was naked in front of three strange women. "We'll take the shawl and the chair, too," I offered, thinking that the woman might find a sweaty shifter butt print an unwanted improvement. We might not want to touch our trust funds for ourselves, but I felt a certain joy using our parents' money to help the shifters.

While Sera made arrangements with the salesperson, I phoned Carmichael, ensuring that no 911 calls about a lost naked teenager would lead to law enforcement descending on the shop. I kept an eye on James, but other than the occasional blink, he never moved.

Impromptu shopping spree completed, Sera walked up to me. "She'll be in the back for the foreseeable future. I hope you like pashminas. You now own thirty of them."

"Well, that takes care of Christmas, at least. Did you recommend she stay back there?"

Sera nodded. "Until someone comes and gets her. She has my black AmEx and permission to use it as necessary."

"In case a bear in a clothing store does as much damage as a bull in china shop?"

"Exactly."

On cue, the store darkened slightly, the light streaming through the delicate curtains blocked by a very large man. I quickly unlocked the door, letting in one family member after another. Will, Celeste, Mac, and Eleanor all stepped inside.

James's parents rushed to their son's side. He looked up once, acknowledging their existence, then returned to staring at the floor.

"What happened?" I can't say Celeste spoke those words. She growled them, a low and deranged sound, and I saw a desperate beast staring at me behind her eyes. I was reminded of every story I'd heard about enraged mama bears in the wild, harmless and shy until their cub was threatened. Even then, I couldn't say she looked dangerous, exactly. Unhinged would be more accurate. I filled her and Will in quickly with the little we knew.

"He's been like this since we found him," I said. "He hasn't said a word."

Will and Celeste stood next to their son and buried their noses in his neck and hair. It was a strangely clinical movement, with none of the intimacy I'd have expected with such an action. They were simply trying to acquire information.

"I'm going to see if there's a trail," said Eleanor, stepping outside. Five minutes later, she returned, shaking her head. "The scent just appears two blocks from here. I'm guessing he was dropped off in a car."

Will and Celeste stood up, having learned all they could. "He's lost weight." Celeste spoke in a heavy whisper. "He needs food. Does anyone have...?" Her voice drifted off, forgetting her thought halfway through the sentence. She rummaged in her purse, and a moment later she popped a small round pill into her mouth. I doubted it was aspirin.

"There's a saleswoman in the back currently alternating between fear and greed," I told the room. "She might have something. If she protests, tell her we'll buy another scarf." Mac nodded and stepped away.

He returned a moment later with a small insulated lunch bag filled with a fruit salad. He placed this before his cousin and stepped back. James glanced at the fruit, then ignored it altogether. We all watched him, uncertain what to do next.

"I thought you were mostly carnivores," I said, unable to stand the pained silence.

Mac glanced at me, and for a fraction of a second I saw the sly smile I'd missed these past few weeks. "There's a lot you don't know about me."

I recognized my own words from the lake thrown back at me. I made a mental note to thoroughly read the Wikipedia entry on black bears, then returned my attention to his cousin.

"Did you pick up anything?" I asked his parents.

Celeste just stared at me with glazed eyes, already retreating into her own little world. Will's expression was a strange combination of relief and pain. James was safe, but he definitely wasn't okay. "Listen, little water. I appreciate you finding him, more than you'll ever know. But I don't see any water around here, nor any clothes you can read. Unless you have something to contribute, perhaps it is time you and your friend left and let my family take care of its own."

I was going to start a drinking game for every time Will implied he didn't really need my help. I looked at Sera. "Can you find the thermostat? Let's crank it up to ninety in here." She nodded. Everyone else looked confused. "For the record, Will, someday you're going to like me and Sera. We grow on people."

"So do tumors," he noted mildly.

"You'll learn eventually, big bear. Now, what did you smell?"

Will looked uncertain, then gave in. He had nothing to lose. "There's something odd. I don't recognize the scent at all. It's coming from his pores, something inside his body." That was exactly what I wanted to hear.

Sera had found the thermostat, and the room was already

heating up. James's chair was close to one of the heating vents, and I watched him closely, waiting for my chance. "It will take another minute," I said.

Will turned to me, and his tone was resigned and even a little apologetic. "I admit it. I'm not used to asking outsiders for help, but maybe that's just me being stubborn. If you can help in any way, I would be... I would be grateful." It took him two tries to get that sentence out, but when he finally managed it, the words were strong and his gaze steady.

A single bead of sweat formed on James's brow. It was time.

I walked carefully toward James, as I would to an agitated dog, giving him every opportunity to skitter away if he perceived me as a threat. He turned toward me once, observing me with quiet, dead eyes, then returned his stare to the floor, completely dismissing my threat potential. Let's hear it for being a skinny blonde. Sometimes, being underestimated actually helped.

I moved my hand slowly toward James's face. I remained in his field of vision at all times, not wanting to startle him. With the index finger of my right hand, I plucked that single drop of sweat and held it lightly on my fingertip.

Next, I recalled that unique sense of James I'd felt at the lake. It was fading a bit in my memory, becoming blurry around the edges, but I still remembered enough.

I stretched my magic toward that that tiny drop of sweat. It filled every molecule, eager to hear the many voices of the water. Eyes closed in concentration, I listened to every story, and from those I separated James's essence from everything else, seeking anything unfamiliar.

The room was silent. Everyone watched me, their breath held. No one moved.

I let that all go. I tried to let the entire room disappear.

I had so little to work with, just the tiniest drop of water. I paused. "I found something." I couldn't identify it, but it triggered an unexpected sense of familiarity. I'd known something like it before. "It might be related to the scent Will described. I'm not sure what it is, either." I turned it over, tried to pull it into my consciousness, but it skittered away, the memory just out of reach.

Just as I began to pull the magic back into myself, I felt a hint of someone else, someone who'd pressed herself so closely against James that her very essence entered his skin. It was a familiar smell, and one I was certain Will knew. I'd been with him when he'd picked up the scent of her blood.

I looked at Will and Celeste accusingly. They were willing to accept my help, and Will might even be somewhat apologetic, but they still weren't volunteering information I might need. My patience for the shifter's isolationist attitude was definitely wearing thin. "He was with Pamela," I told them in a cold voice, letting them know I knew.

There was no warning. One moment, James was sitting quietly in the chair. The next, he stood in a half-crouch between two racks of party dresses, eyes darting frantically in every direction. He held the defensive posture, looking for threats in every corner. One hand extended to the side, palm facing backwards, as if he was holding someone behind him—or protecting them.

No one moved. No one glanced away. We all watched James, afraid to even breathe.

Mac took one slow step forward, then another. James's eyes were wild and unreasoning, prey cornered and desperate. Mac would be able to take him, but there was no telling what effect that might have on James's delicate mental state.

Will did the same on the other side. "You think this might be why we didn't say her name, little water?" His tone was dry, even as he closely watched his son's movement.

About three feet from James, Mac stopped. "No one is going to hurt you," he said in a calm, soothing voice that didn't hold even a hint of condescension. If Mac was in need of a new job, I suspected he'd make an excellent hostage negotiator. "You're safe now."

James's brows knit together as he processed the words. He looked around the room, appearing to register his family one member at a time. Awareness seeped into his eyes, and he spun in a slow circle. For the first time, I thought he might actually be seeing what was in front of him.

When James completed his study of the room, his face didn't fall. It crumpled. His mouth went slack, and his chin pulled in and quivered once, twice. His eyelids lowered, and the muscles in his cheeks seemed to vanish, leaving a face that looked incapable of supporting itself. This only lasted for a second, maybe two, before his control reasserted itself. With one long breath, he schooled his features into a flat, expressionless mask.

"She's not here. Pamela isn't here."

Mutely, Mac shook his head.

Will stepped toward his son, hands out in a calming gesture. They appeared to be trying to soothe a wild animal, which wasn't far from the truth.

I had a bad habit of forgetting how close the beast always was to the surface, how much the animal shared space with the man. I tended to see what was in front of me and forget the rest, and this was a good reminder that I was standing mere inches from a potentially lethal bear.

I decided it was a good time to move several steps away and ended up standing behind Sera. Apparently, I had no qualms about asking my best friend to serve as a barrier between myself and potential threats. I added that to my mental list of things to never mention to the FBI.

"Where is she? She was here." His words sounded twisted and confused, as if the sentences weren't quite emerging the way his brain expected them to.

"Pamela hasn't been here, James." Mac and Will both moved a step closer. They were surrounding him, I saw, preparing to act quickly if he shifted.

It was a cautionary measure only, as James showed no sign of anger. He merely looked bewildered. "No, no, she's never been here. It was…" His face stilled into a look of tremendous concentration. I saw his eyes move up and to the left, then quickly side to side before they stilled, unable to find the memory they sought. "I can't remember." Misery colored every word.

"But where were you?" Celeste asked. Even in her pill-enhanced haze, her mother's instincts wanted an explanation for her son's disappearance. If she knew what had occurred, she could prevent it ever happening again.

"I don't remember," he repeated.

"Did you run off with that girl? Did someone take you? Who were you with?" The questions fell from Celeste's mouth, sloppy and rushed.

"I don't remember," he said, the dull despair from earlier giving way to anger. It wasn't directed outward, however. James kept all his rage for himself. "I don't remember anything. I remember getting in the car with Brandon to go to the lake, and that's it until I found myself wandering naked through downtown Truckee. That's all I know."

"It's okay, James." Mac moved one step closer. "You don't need to remember right away. You're home now, and safe. That's what matters."

James met his eyes, and I watched him noticeably relax under the power of Mac's reassuring words and demeanor. For someone with a penchant for destroying inanimate objects when pissed off, Mac was surprisingly good at calming others down. "I want to remember," James said in a whisper.

Of course, every family has that member who can't read a room, and it appeared Eleanor was this family's version of the drunk uncle. "But what about Pamela?" She persisted. "If he can't remember anything, how are we supposed to help her?"

James's agitation returned instantly, and he began to shake. He looked much as Mac had the night he'd fought off an uncontrolled shift, ready to explode out of his own skin. Will and Mac sent matching death glares Eleanor's way.

Mac looked at me, now huddled near the cash register, and I saw his concern, clear as day. He knew exactly what it might cost me to defend myself, if it came to that. "You need to leave now," he said. "I'll meet you at the cabin."

I knew he was capable and strong and didn't need my help. Even so, I was reluctant to leave him in the middle of the crisis if there was any chance I could help. James was still shaking uncontrollably, and there was no way of telling when or if he'd regain control.

Mac must have seen something of this in my face, because that look of amused exasperation he seemed to reserve just for me crossed his face. "I'm not protecting you. I know better than to try. But this is something we know how to do. Don't distract me, okay?"

I couldn't argue, and Sera urged me toward the back door. My last view of the shop was of Mac and Will standing on either side of James, whispering slow gentle words to a young man who looked ready to break into a million pieces.

CHAPTER 10

We exited through the back room, leaving an address where our new clothes could be delivered and a strong suggestion that the woman avoid the front of the shop for at least another hour, maybe two. That cost us another three hundred dollars worth of accessories, but at least we wouldn't be responsible for a mauled shop girl on that particular day.

We arrived home just as full night was settling across the mountains. Finding the brightly lit cabin waiting for us was a welcome reminder that safe places still existed in the world. Sure, safe places that were occasionally set on fire or invaded by my demented parents, but it was still my home. After the unexpected parental visit the other day, Sera and I'd decided to keep the blinds open, allowing us to view the interior of the cabin and know, in advance, who was waiting for us. If my parents showed up again, I'd be prepared. Prepared to run and hide until they went away.

At that moment, however, it was just Vivian and Simon sitting quietly in the living room. There was a chill in the air, and they'd lit a fire. Simon lay before it in feline form, belly wantonly exposed to the flames. Vivian worked next to him, casual in a pair of yoga pants and a white t-shirt that advised people to adopt a direwolf.

As I watched, she absently gave his belly a quick rub, an intimacy I'd never expected Simon to tolerate. Instead, he arched his back a little, and I could almost hear him purring from the driveway. I'd known the two of them had become close friends, and I smiled to see it, but I also felt a bit sad at what Sera and I were missing while we ran around chasing shifters that didn't want us in their business in the first place. Looking in at their peaceful tableau, I decided a quiet evening at home was exactly what we needed.

The peaceful vibe continued when we opened the front door and were met by the strains of dreamy music carried along by delicate vocals, so different from the raucous punk favored by Sera or the country I preferred. We hadn't had much music in the house, partly because it seemed out of place amidst the tension and uncertainty that had recently defined our lives but mostly because it was damn near impossible for me and Sera to agree on music. She might control the stereo in her car, but there was no way I was conceding the house so easily.

It appeared Sera wasn't in the mood for conflict that night. Rather than change the music or even comment on its lack of a backbeat, she stretched across a couple of throw pillows, eyes closed, and appeared to actually relax.

I looked around for the stereo and CD case, wanting to know what we were listening to, and found nothing. Instead, I saw Vivian's laptop, connected by a single cable to a pair of small speakers.

"So, this is an mp3, right?" I asked, fairly certain I had this one right. I kept thinking I was caught up on current technology, and then I caught the looks my friends occasionally gave me, looks that contained a mix of surprise and amusement. I was doing my best to not sound like someone's elderly aunt inquiring about "the google," but I knew I succeeded less often than I'd like.

Vivian shook her head. "It's a Pandora station. It's playing Feist right now," she told me.

"What's a Pandora?" I asked. Damn. There was that look again.

Sera was already stretched across several pillows, and she didn't move or open her eyes. "If you tell her, Vivian, I'm going to double your rent."

Vivian was unmoved by this threat. Considering she paid nothing, that wasn't surprising. She patted the cushion next to her, and when I sat down, she tilted the monitor so I could see the screen. Quietly, she described the website to me, then ran through a series of other music apps, reminding me again how much I'd missed during my time away.

I refrained from saying, "Gimme," and grabbing the laptop from her hands, but only just. My excitement must have been palpable, as she finally handed the computer to me, leaving me to it. A moment later, I was lost in a mad series of keystrokes and clicks, looking for music I hadn't even known existed that morning.

"Steve Earle has a son making music and you didn't even tell me? Someone's getting fired."

Sera cracked one eye open and briefly considered responding, then decided her world-weary expression was answer enough. Happily ignoring her, I started a new station based on "Harlem River Blues," then stretched out next to Simon, enjoying the fire alongside him.

"Why country?" Vivian asked. "I mean, you grew up on an isolated island in the pacific northwest. That's not a place I'd associate with country music."

I shook my head. "It wasn't. Most of them preferred classical. Of course, most of them are so old, that was their version of pop music. I have one aunt, though, the youngest and craziest of the bunch. She loved human stuff, and she had a bunch of old records, Loretta Lynn and Johnny Cash and Dolly Parton."

I paused, uncertain how to finish. Only Sera knew this story. "I didn't have a lot of friends growing up. You know the old ones don't have many children, so there weren't other kids on the island. I read and watched a lot of TV and movies, and those characters kind of became my friends, but it wasn't enough. I wanted to know more about the world I was missing, about the emotion behind it, and there's no music in the world that can tell a story better than country music."

Though I'd spoken in an even voice, I worried they'd view me with pity after hearing that story. I didn't want them to guess how lonely I'd truly been. It was over now, and that was what mattered.

Simon rolled across the floor until his head was even with my knee, and he silently head butted my leg. Remembering his moment with Vivian earlier, I gently reached out a hand to scratch his head. He looked at me, and for a moment I thought I'd crossed a line, then he rubbed his cheek firmly against my hand, purring.

"You know he's just marking you, right? You're now owned by Simon." I swore his small cat smile grew at Sera's words. I kind of wanted to kiss her for knowing to change the subject.

I tugged lightly on Simon's ear, then turned my own belly toward the fireplace, mimicking his pose. Unfortunately, the relaxed movements weren't reflected in my next words. "What he'd want with such an unpredictable pet, I've no idea. If they knew what I was, my own people would put me down as a danger to society. That's not doing wonders for my self-esteem." I forced a laugh, trying to lighten the impact of my words.

I didn't want my friends to fixate on my instability, and even I did my best not to think about it. Denial and I weren't as close as we used to be, but we were still more than passing acquaintances. But between the peaceful vibe, the warm room, and the gentle guitars playing, my control had slipped and I'd aired my fears. I'd accidentally spoken the truth.

I felt my fire magic stir, reminding me how easy it would be to pull the flames to me, to warm and recharge myself in a way I'd never done before. I could be complete.

I determinedly avoided eye contact with the others, terrified of what I might see there. Support. Concern. Fear.

Sera pulled herself to a sitting position. "No," she said.

I looked at her, eyebrows up.

"You're not an animal. No offense, Simon." If it was possible for a cat to shrug, that was his response. "You're a thinking creature, in control of your actions. Well, most of the time. Or sometimes. Okay, on occasion you take the time to think before you act. Once or twice a year, at least."

I knew the words were intended to comfort, but they were also intended to draw me away from the self-pity canyon I was threatening to fling myself into. It worked.

"You're just pissed because I'm actually useful in this investigation, whereas you haven't had the chance to set a single thing on fire."

"I haven't ruled out the Reno book club just yet," she said. "Hope springs eternal."

I laughed, and I was myself again, the fire within me once again as quiet as it had been all the previous decades of my life. We returned to our quiet evening at home. As the minutes passed and I didn't feel the fire beckon again, I could almost convince myself I'd imagined its siren song.

A couple of hours later, just when I was ready to stop waiting, the door opened, and Mac walked slowly into the room. Normally, everything about his presence felt larger than life. Even more than his physical size, there was an aura that extended far beyond his bulk. When he was around, he seemed to take over any room in which he stood.

For the first time, Mac looked small. Sure, he was still approximately the same size as one of the local mountains, but his shoulders were pressed down and hunched, as if a series of weights were forcing him toward the ground. His strides weren't long and confident. Rather, he shuffled into the room, head down.

When he saw us all gathered together, his eyes moved quickly to me. For a moment, longing flashed across his features, and I knew he wanted comfort as much as I wanted to give it. The moment passed, his face shuttering quickly, and he sat on the opposite side of the room. He pressed his back against the wall and tilted his head upwards, eyes closed. I thought he was trying to absorb some of the room's peace for himself.

Simon shifted quietly and pulled on a pair of jeans. I appreciated the gesture. While I was growing increasingly accustomed to Simon's nudist tendencies, it was a lot harder to have a serious conversation while steadfastly averting my eyes from Simon's genitalia.

I didn't want to rush Mac or interrupt his moment of calm in any way, despite being desperate to hear what news was bad enough to cause Mac to look weak. Fortunately, Sera had no such compunction. "Spill," she demanded.

He rubbed his large hands roughly over his face, tugging at his skin and pulling at his hair until parts of it stood on end. It might have been comical, were it not for the heart-wrenching expression he wore.

"Is James okay?" I asked.

He shook his head, once, twice, then let out a harsh bark of laughter. "He's calm again, if that's what you mean. He's talking. He can't remember anything from the last couple days, but he's eating and answering questions. We got him home, and he finally went to sleep a little while ago. The poor kid's exhausted."

The memory loss was worrying, and didn't help us in our search whatsoever, but otherwise it all sounded like good news. There was nothing in his words to explain Mac's attitude.

"What else?" I pushed.

He looked again toward the ceiling, perhaps hoping some new truth would descend from on high. He was not so lucky. Finally, he spoke. "James can't shift."

Simon went perfectly still. Even his eyes froze, and for a moment he seemed to disappear within himself, as if he was seeking his own magic that allowed the change, confirming it was still present. Slowly, his expression evolved into one of pure horror. "That is not possible," he stated, as if to convince himself. "The animal is a part of us. It cannot be removed."

Mac nodded, agreeing with Simon's words, if not his conclusion. "I know."

"He cannot even partially shift?"

Mac shook his head. "He feels the desire. He feels like he's going to lose control. That's what happened earlier. And then nothing happens."

I watched the two shifters. I could only imagine what it meant to them. If I learned that my connection to water could be removed, I suspected I would look every bit as terrified as my friends did now.

Mac and Simon held eye contact for a long time, having a long, wordless conversation full of fear and confusion. This wasn't something that was supposed to happen.

"I've never heard of this happening before," said Mac, confirming my thoughts. "I've never even heard that it was possible."

Simon shook his head. "Neither have I. You know more than I do, of course, having grown up with shifters, but I sought out a fair number of them in university. This is..." Simon tapered off, unable to finish. I'd never known Simon not to be perfectly precise and exact in his words.

"So, does this mean he's human?" Vivian asked doubt-fully. I was shaking my head even before Mac. Losing the magic that separated us from humans wouldn't make us more like them. It would make us incomplete, unable to fully function.

Incomplete like I was, unable to access all of my magic.

I violently squashed that thought, refusing to pay it any attention, not now. Not ever. I was as I'd always been. That was more than complete enough for me, and right now, it really wasn't about me.

"What happens if you don't shift?" I asked. If elementals didn't regularly access our element, we withered, much as a human would from lack of food or water. The magic is what connected us to the land, what recharged and repaired us. Without it, we were disconnected and weak. I hated the thought of that strong young man made powerless so early in his life. "Is his magic just gone?"

I felt a connection hover tauntingly out of reach, an answer I knew I possessed but was unable to grasp. I reached for it, but it flittered away.

Mac's voice called me back to the present. "He doesn't think so. James says he feels it, weak but still present. He just can't access it. And no one can answer your first ques-tion, because there's no evidence of this ever happening before. The most we can do is make an educated guess, based on the times shifters have deliberately refused to shift."

Vivian was already putting the pieces together. "If you don't shift, does that mean the beast has no release?"

Simon nodded. "We must give our animal halves free rein on occasion. It is what we are, and it should not be denied."

Mac took a long breath and expelled it slowly. He met my eyes, and though I knew he didn't want to ask for comfort, I tried to give it to him, tried to provide whatever support I could from across the room. "We know that, if we deny the animal, it only gains in strength. Hypothetically, it will become so strong it takes over. We think, if James is unable to shift, it's only a matter of time before he becomes a wild animal that just happens to look like a human being."

THAT NIGHT, SLEEP eluded me. My window faced the rear of the house, and the coursing river that ran behind the cabin, thick and heavy with melted snow, usually offered a source of peace and helped me find an easy oblivion. After the events of that day, however, I found no solace in the water's gentle power. Every time my eyes drifted shut, they popped open again, as if the answers might be found on my bedroom ceiling.

When my eyes did manage to remain shut for longer than a moment, images of James projected against the lids. Not James as I saw him tonight, but as he would likely become. Mac had described the fierce battle that would wage within his cousin, as his human half fought desperately to maintain a foothold on James's conscious mind, to repel the beast by pure force of will—a battle it was impossible to win.

One day at a time, the human intelligence would dim in his eyes. The upright body would hunch, seeking a return to the animal's four-legged stance. He would become uncontrollable and irrational, eventually unable to form words. His speech would devolve into a series of growls or grunts. He would have all the desires of the bear and none of the physical strength or defenses. He could not be let out of the house, where he could harm others or find harm himself. James would live the rest of his life, trapped in his home. Caged.

It was a horrible image, made all the worse by the certainty that I could do something to prevent it. There was an answer hovering just outside my consciousness. I chased it, over and over again, trying to identify the smell I'd caught on James's shirt, trying to match it with something that was scratching at my mind, urging me to put the pieces together.

Finally, a few hours before dawn, my anxious, exhausted mind finally gave up the fight, and I felt myself drift slowly toward sleep. In that space between the conscious and unconscious mind, that moment of drifting without purpose produced the answer I'd been actively searching for all night, a memory sharp and clear, though it was from a night I longed to forget.

The essence I'd found didn't belong to a person. It belonged to a drug, one used on me the night Brian tied me to my bed and promised we'd be together soon. He'd called it a cocktail, and it was partly intended to knock me out and make me more docile. Given the circumstances, of course, nothing short of repeated blows to the head with a large mallet would have made me docile, but I had to give him points for effort. And somewhere in that cocktail, there was something I hadn't consciously noticed at the time, so distracted was I with the more pressing issue of the madman at my bedside.

My subconscious, fortunately, had been paying attention, and it remembered the cocktail and its other purpose. Yes, it had made me sleepy and confused, but Brian had also used it to block my access to my magic.

I let myself breathe a quick sigh of relief. The drug's effects weren't long-lasting. In fact, they'd worn off within a matter of hours. With any luck, James would be fine in a day or two.

And yet, Brian had developed the drug for an elemental. Though our magic derived from the same source, it might work differently on shifters. It was too great a risk to ignore.

Also, Brian was dead. Someone else was using his concoction, and I could only think of one person who'd worked closely with Brian and also displayed a marked enmity for shifters.

I lay in bed and cursed loudly at the ceiling for several more minutes. Because, as much as I might wish otherwise, I knew of only one way to get more information about this drug, and to possibly learn more about the abductor himself.

I had to talk to my father.

CHAPTER 11

Once I made the disturbing connection between Brian's cocktail and the shifter abductions, I was unable to sleep. In that final hour before dawn returned light to the world, I crept out of bed and made my way to the river.

Elementals slept and ate as humans did, and to a certain extent we needed it for survival. We were born from the union of magic and humans, and so we bore a human shape and possessed some human needs. And yet, our survival was far less reliant on those needs. We could easily go days, even weeks, without food or sleep, so long as we had access to our element.

And so I stood by the river for that last hour before daybreak, quietly pulling its power into me, letting it interact with the magic that resided in my core. I sought the peace I'd been unable to find in the hours I'd tossed and turned in my bed

His approach was so quiet, I shouldn't have known he was there, but I sensed his presence the moment he neared. He said nothing, merely stood with me, watching the water rush by. The river wasn't as full as it would be in another month or two, when the majority of the snowpack melted and the summer sun had yet to claim the water for its own, but it was already stronger than it had been when I first arrived in Tahoe. We watched it rush by, the water growing lighter and less opaque as the sun slowly raised itself above the horizon.

For a long time, I was content to stand next to him, the warmth of his body nearly tangible, and the scent that belonged only to him drifting toward me on the morning air.

I saw a few rocks appear downriver, dark and smooth. I was feeling so calm that it took me a moment longer than it probably should have to remember that rocks weren't supposed to move. They were familiar, too. I'd seen them before, in the river near Carmen's house.

"They're river otters." Mac's voice was low and gentle, doing his best to retain the peaceful mood.

I struggled a bit to do the same, because I kind of wanted to squeal like a hyperactive five-year-old upon learning there were otters living behind my house. The nature I loved could be immense and awe-inspiring—and I was glad to be surrounded by such majesty—but sometimes nature could just be downright cute, and that was every bit as wonderful.

The otters dipped below the water and vanished as easily as they'd appeared, leaving me feeling a tiny bit happier than I'd been before their visit.

"You can't sleep, either?" I asked.

He gave a non-committal shrug, and then he let out a long breath, as if he'd come to a decision. "I heard you come down here." It wasn't a declaration, by any means, but it was still more than I'd dared to hope for. I turned to him in surprise. "Shifter ears," he explained, misunderstanding my expression. With a small smile, he pointed to the body part in question. "They work great when there isn't a thunderstorm interfering." As quickly as it appeared, the smile vanished, lost in memories of the night Brian attacked me and Sera while he'd been only a hundred feet away, wholly oblivious.

I knew he blamed himself for not recognizing what Brian was. I blamed myself too, though it was neither of our faults. "You got there in the end," I reminded him.

"Yeah. I have a bad habit of showing up after the worst of the danger's already passed." There was an edge to his voice, a mocking tone directed squarely at himself. I thought he was remembering far more than that one night.

"Hey." Before I had time to think about what I was doing, my hand was on his upper arm, wrapped loosely around his bicep. My instant awareness of the touch was reflected in his eyes, and I awkwardly released my grip, letting my hand drift to my side. "I thought you said you know better than to try and protect me."

His snort conveyed both his exasperation and amusement. "Well, I know better than to eat a fourth serving of pie, too, but I still do that every Thanksgiving."

Blowing out my breath in an exaggerated sigh, I easily pulled the river to me and circled it around the two of us until we stood in a cyclone of water powerful enough to yank us both into the river and hold us below the surface if I asked it to do so. I tried to offer Mac a serene smile, but I'm pretty certain it veered into smug. "I can handle myself."

"Fair enough," he conceded. "Do you plan on carrying a river with you wherever you go?" He wasn't joking.

I didn't know where this version of Mac was coming from. He'd never been anything but quietly supportive before. "What's going on?" I asked, my voice sharper than intended.

I kept the water spinning around us, our own private cocoon where the rules of the outside world might not apply. I could feel tension and frustration pouring off him. I'd felt something similar before, when we'd first met and he'd shown me what it looked like when an enormous adult male had a temper tantrum. He wanted to rage, I thought, to release the poison crawling through his mind.

I thickened the water, trapping him with me. "Tell me."

His eyes met mine, and for a moment I knew the beast was looking at me. He blinked, and he was just Mac again. Agitated and angry, but Mac. "Seeing James like that, it was a reminder of how little control we really have. How easy it is to be hurt. Aidan, I look at you and I see so many ways I could lose you. To your insane parents. To the elementals if they ever find out what you are. To your—" He stopped abruptly. To yourself, he'd wanted to say.

Everything he said was true, which was why it was so irritating. I felt something begin to break, and I stopped playing fair. "What do you mean, 'lose you'? You didn't want me, remember? So you don't get to stand here now and act like I'm yours."

He was practically vibrating with suppressed emotion now. It was anger and hurt and, above all, a fear I didn't understand. "Don't be stupid, Aidan. I never said that."

I felt the water slip, for just a moment, and I fought to hold it steady. I had to prove him wrong. He had to know I was in control.

"No, you said I wasn't ready to be kissing anyone. And now you're telling me you don't think I can protect myself. You really don't think highly of my ability to decide for myself, do you?" Even as I spoke the words, I knew I was distorting his meaning on purpose, trying to hurt him the way I was hurting. I'd thought I was okay with him wanting distance. I was wrong.

He threw up his hands in exasperation. "I never said that, either! You know I want you. You know I think you're amazing. You know that."

I did know that, but it seemed to make no difference. "Then why?" I wanted to sound in control, but I couldn't.

When you're asking the man you want more than any other why he won't be with you, control isn't easy to come by.

He shook his head, a sharp gesture intended to remove the anguish creeping across his features. "Let's forget, for a moment, that you ran away to Oregon." I began to protest, but he ignored me, determined to finish. "How can we be together? We're fighting, and I'm terrified to yell at you. I thought I was okay with the half-fire thing, but I will not be the one who pushes you over the edge. I'm not always a calm man, Aidan, and you can't be around that. You can't be angry or frustrated or anything that might trigger the fire."

I knew he meant well, but his intention didn't matter. I'd spent most of my life with other people making decisions for me, and I couldn't accept Mac being one of them. Of all the people in the world, I needed him to think I could take care of myself, and learning that he didn't think that turned my irritation into the very anger he was trying to prevent.

I took one deliberate step toward him until we were nose to nose. Well, nose to clavicle. I tilted my head up and met his worried brown eyes. "So, to be clear, I'm the delicate china doll that needs to be wrapped in bubble wrap and carried around, lest someone break her?" There was iron in my voice. Iron and fire.

"Will you stop twisting my words? I'm not worried about someone breaking you!" That time, he wasn't able to find his quiet voice, and the words were shouted directly in my face. My own rage rose in response. Part of me wanted to scream at him. Another part wanted to push against him, to force this enormous man to bend to my will. And a final part, larger than it had any right to be, just wanted to claw at him, to press my lips to his and devour him until we were both lost.

I did none of those. My anger did what it always did,

and the rage from my fire side blocked my connection to the water. The cone of river water, freed from my control, crashed around us, soaking us both. Neither of us moved or even seemed to notice.

"I'm worried you'll break yourself," he whispered. "And there's nothing I can do to stop it." Without another word, he returned to his trailer, leaving me on the river bank, shivering for reasons that had nothing to do with the cold.

MAC JOINED THE rest of the cabin for breakfast, and we both did our best to pretend nothing had happened.

When I finally remembered to tell him my nighttime realization and my plan to visit my father, he immediately phoned his family with the new information and let them know he'd be busy all that day.

It didn't matter if we were fighting. There was no way he was going to let me face my father without the support of friends. It really wasn't easy to stay angry at the man.

He wasn't alone. While my friends had confidence in my ability to function day-to-day without going crazy, they apparently didn't view a visit to Josiah, during which I asked whether he'd started abducting shifter children, as a day-to-day activity. They collectively decided I needed supervision.

A lot of supervision, in fact. We took Mac's Bronco, because it was difficult to fit three elementals and two shifters into Sera's much smaller car. In case I wasn't secure enough with four babysitters, they'd placed me in the back seat, with Simon and Vivian bracing me on either side.

I suspected the company had much to do with that morning's loss of control. The kitchen window overlooked the river, and anyone watching my confrontation with Mac would have seen the rage briefly consume me. My friends knew that every time I accidentally tapped into the fire magic, I was slowly creating a schism between the two halves of my psyche. This morning, that short loss of control had likely pushed me one step closer to insanity, a fact I really wanted to ignore. I didn't feel any crazier than normal. Not yet, at least.

Even so, I needed to stay calm. It was just that simple. Calm and controlled at all times, just as I'd been raised. It sounded peaceful and mind-numbingly dull.

I looked to my right. Vivian was looking out the window, her face serene as she quietly observed the passing scenery. "Do you ever get angry?" I asked.

She turned to me surprised. "Of course I do."

"Really? When?"

Sera twisted in her seat to listen in. Mac had refused to let her take over his stereo, and she needed some form of entertainment for the drive. "Seriously, Viv, when?"

Vivian fidgeted under our dual scrutiny. "Last week. You were both there. Remember when I couldn't break into the MI-6 database?"

I looked at her, dumbfounded. "You mean the night you cursed twice and ate a large bowl of ice cream?"

Vivian nodded. "I dislike being thwarted."

That I could believe. So far as I could tell, Vivian had no intention of selling national secrets to terrorist factions or blackmailing high ranking government officials. She simply wanted to know everything there was to know, and she viewed a government firewall the same way the rest of us viewed a somewhat challenging Sudoku. It was nothing more than a puzzle to be solved.

"But..." I could tell Sera was trying to figure out how to phrase her next words without sounding condescending. Finally, she gave up. "You'd make a lousy fire, Viv."

"Thank goodness for that," said Simon. "We have enough hotheads in this car. I can't be the only one in favor of a calm, reasonable approach to life's problems."

"Hey!" I protested. "When I'm not setting things on fire, I'm totally reasonable." I decided to change the subject before anyone began a rebuttal. "So, Vivian, how did you manage to calm yourself down from that shocking fit of rage?"

A small, self-satisfied smile crossed her face. "I broke into the MI-5 archives. They were redacted files, though," she added modestly.

Sera whistled, impressed. "If you ever decide to take over the world, can I be your consultant? I can think of a few changes I'd like to make."

"Pancakes on every restaurant menu," I suggested. "And none of those weird-ass fruit-flavored syrups, either."

"I was thinking we give in to global warming for a while. You cold weather-loving freaks have had your day," said Sera.

"A koi pond in every yard," said Simon. The distant, dreamy look in his eyes suggested he wasn't entirely joking.

"Reunite The Clash," added Sera. "We can reanimate Joe Strummer, right?"

"Do you listen to any bands in which all the members still live, Sera?" I asked.

She shrugged. "Hey, the good ones always go young while the boy bands live forever. What about you, Mac? What would you change?"

His eyes met mine in the rearview mirror, his somber gaze reflecting none of the others' levity. "I'll get back to you."

He swung the wheel, turning us into the parking lot of Truckee's lone luxury hotel, the building Josiah owned and lived in when in town. The place he intended to call home until I finally saw his version of reason and returned with him to Hawaii. "I'd like to have fewer crazy relatives," I said quietly. I glanced at Sera, staring at me with more compassion than I could handle. "Present company excluded, of course. You'll always be nuts."

She grinned, and the expression vanished from her face. "Gotta keep up with you. Sisters are supposed to be competitive, you know."

As we walked to the lobby, my friends quietly surrounded me, forming a protective barrier. Though I hated being treated as weak in any way, I found the support touching, even knowing how ineffective it was. Josiah could incinerate them in an instant if he felt so inclined. He also had to know that if he did so, Sera and I would be lost to him forever. I suspected he had a few more cards to play before resorting to such extreme measures.

"Ms. Blais. Ms. Brook. I'm Jonathan, Mr. Blais's new personal assistant." A young man rushed up to us. His dark eyes and hair and bronze skin identified him as being almost certainly a fire, and a reasonably strong one to still have the traditional coloring. Though he looked eighteen, he could have easily been well into his 30s or even 40s, depending on how much elemental blood coursed through his veins.

He was handsome, with a carefully tailored suit and tidy haircut he'd likely paid too much money for. Josiah always did like to surround himself with signs of wealth and control, creating the sort of environment that relaxed him while causing everyone around him to tense up.

Jonathan clearly was not expecting us, and our presence had him panicking. "Mr. Blais did not tell me you were coming. He's not here at the moment, but I'm certain he'd want you to wait." He attempted to herd Sera and me toward the elevators while determinedly ignoring our friends.

I planted my feet. "When do you expect him back?"

"Oh, any time, any time. Please, you can wait upstairs." I watched him carefully as he spoke the airy words, and I saw the hard flint in his eyes. He knew Josiah was eager for his daughters to return to him, and Jonathan was determined to keep us at the hotel until his boss returned.

Naturally, this made me even more determined to leave.

"Where is he? We can go to him." I smiled, a big, harmless smile I didn't mean in the slightest.

"He's looking at a new piece of property on the south shore. Really, he'll be back any minute." Once again, he tried to push us toward the elevator. He made the mistake of placing a hand on Sera's and my backs. Sera, of course, would not be pushed anywhere, and she firmly planted her feet. My absolute lack of muscle tone gave him some advantage, and he'd have been able to move me closer to the elevator if he hadn't been stopped cold by the low growls coming from two of my companions' throats.

Vivian watched the entire scene, more entertained than concerned. I knew she disliked lingering in the hotel lobby—her dreads, combat boots, and well-worn *Doctor Who* t-shirt made her stand out in this five-star hotel—but for the moment, she appeared to be enjoying herself fully. I realized it was a long time since I'd seen her smiling so easily, and I hoped it meant the distracted Vivian of the last few weeks was a thing of the past.

Jonathan was having considerably less fun. He hastily dropped his arms to the side and held his hands out, palms up, trying to show us how innocent his intentions truly were.

"Mr. Blais only wishes to speak to you. I know he'd want you to wait." I couldn't shake the suspicion that, if we chose to wait in the penthouse, we'd find ourselves trapped until Josiah returned, or possibly teleported to the volcano compound. If anyone on earth knew how to teleport people, it would be Josiah.

I tilted my head and tried to soften my expression, looking innocent. Jonathan took a step backward.

Someday, my face was actually going to make the expression I asked it to make, but today was not that day. I gave up, and laid it out for him. "We are going to leave now, Jonathan. You can either tell us where Josiah is, so we can go directly to him and he can speak to us, as he wishes," I placed no small amount of emphasis on that final word. "Or we can leave, and wander around for a bit. Maybe go out of town for a few days. Maybe check into a hotel where he can't find us. And then, you'd get to explain to him just why you were so determined not to divulge his location."

All the blood drained from Jonathan's face, causing him to look at least a decade or two older. "Of course, Ms. Brook." He quickly scrawled the address on a piece of hotel stationery, handed it to us, and scurried away.

"Should I feel bad about abusing that lackey?" I asked curiously. After all, the poor man was just doing his job. It wasn't his fault that job required him to do my father's evil bidding.

"No," said Sera, plucking the paper from my hands. "He needs to be tougher than that to work for our father. You did him a favor."

I turned around and promptly pulled up short to avoid crashing into Carmen. I had no idea how long she'd been standing there. None of us had sensed her arrival, so quietly had she approached. Damn cat feet.

Mac was scowling, and even Simon looked a bit miffed. I suspected they really didn't like anyone getting the drop on them, particularly another shifter. The self-satisfied smile hovering around her lips let me know she was well aware of this fact.

"Where is he?" Carmen asked Sera, glancing pointedly at the slip of paper in her hand.

Sera's scowl mirrored Mac's, and for a moment I thought she might swallow the evidence, simply to prevent Carmen from getting something she wanted. Instead, she tucked it neatly into the front pocket of her black jeans and held the woman's gaze, Sera's blank expression more than a match for Carmen's smug one. "He'll be back soon. You can wait."

Instead, Carmen took a single step forward, until she took up Sera's entire frame of vision. She was a couple of inches taller, and Sera was forced to tilt her head to maintain the stare. Sera maintained the expressionless mask she wore when she was the most volatile, but I saw tiny sparks coming from her fingers, the magic close to the surface. Worryingly, I noticed that Carmen's nails were extending, hinting at the deadly claws she carried in her alternate form.

I wanted to believe they were just posturing, but I couldn't be sure. If it came down to it, Sera should win any battle. With her magic, she could set Carmen on fire in the blink of an eye. Carmen might be intimidating, but I suspected even she needed a moment to recover from third degree burns.

However, there'd be no room in such a fight for even a moment of hesitation. Carmen could shift in the space of a heartbeat and rake a long claw across Sera's throat, slicing the jugular before Sera was even able to singe her eyebrows. Death tended to bring an abrupt halt to any magical offense.

Regardless of who would win, I knew we didn't want the battle to occur in the busy lobby of a luxury hotel.

"Why do you want to see him?" I asked. I had a fairly good idea, but I hoped such a harmless question would defuse the situation, at least temporarily.

She tilted her head toward me, considering me with

large, unblinking eyes. It was strange to watch her movements, so similar to Simon's and yet so foreign. She was a predator in a twin set. It didn't seem to matter to her how much power we could wield. Until we proved otherwise, we were prey. I forced myself to hold her stare, knowing she'd interpret it as a challenge. To be fair, it was easy to be brave when defended on all sides and when at least one of those bodyguards had claws that made hers look downright dainty.

Carmen appeared to realize this as well. She stepped away from Sera, though I didn't make the mistake of confusing her strategic retreat with our victory. Her eyes remained sharp and tense. "I understand he might know something about what happened to James, which means he might know something about Pamela. Why else would I be here?"

I nodded, deflating. I even resisted making some smart-ass comment about being there for the hotel's fabulous spa, though such restraint pained me. Because nothing about Carmen suggested she ever felt like a victim, I'd forgotten how much pain she was likely feeling. Her daughter was still missing, and her only leads were the same ones the rest of us had. The fact that she was here, seeking the same answers we were, suggested she wasn't involved with the abductions.

James wasn't violent, Carmen was clueless, and we were back at square one.

Mac wasn't quite ready to trust her, however. "May I ask how you learned about this?" His voice was calm and polite, but his gaze was dark and his body seemed to expand, taking up even more room.

Carmen looked at him, her eyes calculating and thoughtful. Perhaps she hadn't scrapped enough with elementals to know how dangerous our powers could be. She might respect our powers in an abstract way, but she didn't view us as a threat. She had no such confusion about Mac. Bears might not be pure predators in the way of mountain lions, but they were much, much bigger. She didn't stand a chance in a straight fight, and she knew it.

That didn't stop her from taunting him slightly, feeling safe in such a public place. "I have good ears," she said, with such a pleased expression I decided the phrase "cat who ate the cream" was inspired by a shifter.

If possible, Mac tensed further, and his face grew darker. Carmen was basically admitting to spying on the cabin and overhearing his earlier phone call to his family.

Simon's response was entirely different. He showed no such anger. In fact, he looked intrigued. For once, he was not the one skulking along rooftops and crouching under windows, hearing things the speaker never intended him to learn. And though I couldn't explain why, I wanted to keep Simon far away from this woman.

"It doesn't matter what you know, or think you know," I said, bringing her attention back to me. "Josiah will never talk to you. You do realize he's an old one, right? A full-blooded fire centuries older than the forest you call home?" The way her eyes widened momentarily told me this was, in fact, new information. "You can show up hissing, with bared fangs and freshly sharpened claws, and he'll pet you lightly on the head and call you a bad kitty. Do feel free to try, though."

I saw the fight slither from her body. However, while she might have conceded this battle, she had yet to surrender the war. She gracefully lowered herself into one of the lobby's sumptuous armchairs and made herself comfortable, neatly curling her legs beneath her, as I'd seen Simon do countless times over the last months. Based on his close attention to her movements, I knew Simon noticed, too.

"You might be right, water girl." I did my best to hide the grimace of distaste, knowing that was exactly what she was aiming for. "But if there's even a chance he knows something about my girl, I can't give up. He'll walk through this lobby eventually." She positioned herself so she had a clear view of both the front doors and the elevator banks and prepared to wait.

I shrugged. She could stay in the lobby as long as she wanted. That just made her Josiah's problem, and I was more than petty enough to wish further problems on my father.

I turned to go and felt the others do the same. All except one, that is.

"I believe I will stay here." Simon's somber green eyes met each of ours, briefly, and then he eased into an armchair next to Carmen's. "Someone will need to inform you if Josiah returns while you are in transit."

It was a perfectly reasonable explanation, but looking between him and a self-satisfied Carmen, I knew it had nothing to do with his decision to stay.

Unable to find any words to articulate my unease, I nodded once, then headed toward the door, trying to ignore the doubt that gnawed at me every step of the way.

CHAPTER 12

We drove in near silence toward the address Jonathan gave us, over an hour away in South Lake Tahoe. It was a beautiful drive, with the road skirting the western side of the lake the entire way. Campsites, cabins, and resorts lined the road, and in another month or two it would be crawling with vacationers tooling along on their rented bikes or entire families crossing the road with full picnic baskets and oversized inflatable rafts.

Until then, the locals still owned the road, and traffic was relatively light. We eased our way around the turns, the lake on our left. As we neared Emerald Bay, the ground rose gently, pulling us higher into the mountains. The lake stretched below us, shockingly blue and enclosed on all sides by the mountains. Some days, I marveled that I was lucky enough to call such a magnificent, peaceful spot my home.

And yet, at that moment, I found little of that peace in myself. I couldn't fully articulate it, but something simply felt off. This did not feel like the same group of people who'd spent months working together to find an elemental killer, slowly becoming a family in its own right. Today was the first day Vivian wasn't dashing off somewhere, trying to repair her relationship with a woman we'd never met. Simon was currently hanging out with a woman who set off all my alarm bells, but whose occasional whiskers gave her charms the rest of us lacked. And Mac... well, Mac and I couldn't seem to be alone for five minutes without finding something new to disagree about.

It felt like things were falling apart, and I had no idea how to stop them.

We were high enough up that I couldn't even touch the water for comfort, my magic unable to reach that far. Mac was now navigating the most nerve-wracking section of highway 89. High above the lake, there's a section of road where the mountain drops away, leaving a two-lane road with no barriers and a drop of several hundred feet on each side. We'd driven up and down this ridge dozens of times over the years, but it still made me consider taking up prayer for a minute or two. To my right, I noticed Vivian grip her own handle tightly, and even Sera stopped fidgeting for the minute it took us to cross and once again have the comforting wall of the mountain on our right.

Sera's phone rang, the sudden noise breaking the silence. The tension that coursed through her body let me know it wasn't someone offering to sell her a fabulous time share in Las Vegas. Mac, who could easily hear both sides of the conversation, turned left at the next campsite, pulling into a parking lot overlooking the lake and turning the car around.

"She wants to talk to you," Sera held out the phone. "Carmen," she mouthed. I shrugged and took the phone.

"I know I can be a bitch," said Carmen by way of greeting. I saw no reason to disagree. "Then again, so can you."

"I prefer to think of myself as charmingly irreverent," I informed her.

"I'm not apologizing."

"Neither am I."

"Good. So long as we understand each other." She took a long pause. "Will you help us, then?"

We seemed to have skipped several steps necessary for this conversation to make any sense, but Mac was already turning right onto the highway, preparing to take us back north. I smacked the back of his seat and offered my best series of "Dude, what the fuck?" gestures, but he simply shook his head and continued driving.

"Carmen, I need a bit more information," I told her, since Mac obviously had no plans to clue me in. All I knew, based on the speed with which he was taking the turns, was that he was in a much greater hurry to get back than he'd been to reach our original destination.

"Pamela's back. According to Dana, she walked in the front door twenty minutes ago, sat down at the dining table, and hasn't moved since. I just got back from the hotel, and the bears met me at the front door. They're hoping to learn more information to help James. We need you to do whatever you do with the clothes or sweat."

"Carmen, there's no guarantee I'll find anything new. I might be able to pick up another person's essence on her clothes, but only if they were sweating when they touched her. And if it was done recently." It seemed a good idea to manage expectations when dealing with a pissed-off mama cat with long, sharp claws.

"But you'll try." Carmen stated. It wasn't a request, but it didn't need to be. Of course I'd help.

"Keep her away from all heat sources for now," I told her. "And inside, out of the wind. Anything that might speed her clothes drying." Even I was impressed by the authority in my voice. "It's okay to take off her clothes and get her into some clean ones, but put them in a fresh plastic bag and store it in the refrigerator. Also, make sure she doesn't sweat until I get there, so if she starts, lower the thermostat. We're just leaving Emerald Bay now, so we won't be there for another fifty—"

I didn't get to complete the thought. A loud popping sound shook the car, and the Bronco jerked violently to the right. Mac never even had time to swerve before we were falling down the side of the mountain.

TIME REINVENTS ITSELF during crises, rejecting linear strictures in favor of a more chaotic existence. No longer does one second follow another, or one minute lead to the next. Time claims to be rigid, but the moment it thinks no one is paying attention, it grasps the opportunity to rewrite its own rules. Time only pretends to make sense.

And so, as we tumbled down the mountain, I existed in two completely different worlds. In one, the crash happened in a heartbeat. The Bronco crashed into a tree, but that didn't slow our fall. We simply spun out and continued to plummet. I was aware of uncontrolled movement, of Vivian's and my limbs intertwined as we were yanked unceremoniously upwards before being jolted back down. Our seat belts likely saved our lives, but at the time all I felt was a searing pain as our chests were gripped mercilessly. I quickly lost track of which way was up, only recognizing various degrees of pain as we were tossed about the Bronco, unable to find any purchase when nothing stayed constant.

In the other world, I saw everything. I saw Sera brace herself against the dashboard, and a distant, clinical voice in my head told me that was wrong, because she had a better chance of survival if she allowed herself to go limp. Mac's hands were glued to the steering wheel, his grip so tight I saw the plastic warp and bend under his fingers. He was still desperately trying to bring the Bronco back under his control, forcing the wheel enough to the left to avoid the trees directly ahead of us. Vivian's face was ashen, her mouth tight and eyes panicked, but her attention was all outside the car. I knew she was calling the earth, trying to raise it and slow our rapid descent, but she lacked sufficient power for that level of manipulation.

We careened down the mountain with nothing to slow our fall but the pines. Each time we scraped against a tree, the metal groaned, and the car would lurch in a new direction, seeking out the next barrier the mountain wanted to throw between us and the lake below. Our bodies became more broken with each jolt and revolution the SUV made. Without access to our elements, we wouldn't last much longer. I couldn't bear to think what shape Mac would be in when we reached the bottom. If we reached it.

At last, we were close enough to the lake for my magic to reach, and I shoved it from my body, demanding it attach to the water and feed me its life.

Mac swung the Bronco hard to one side to evade one tree, only to find another in our path. The left side of the SUV crashed into it, and the Bronco's side crumpled, the tree forcing a sharp dent into the metal only inches from the driver's seat. I had no time for relief, as the entire vehicle swung into a clearing and tilted harshly toward the ground, executing a gut-churning roll down the steep slope.

Mac and Sera were viciously shaken with every movement, but somehow they were still alive. The Bronco might have a voracious appetite for fuel, but it was also the product of the 1970s American automotive manufacturing ethos, when it was perfectly reasonable to expect a vehicle to double as a tank. I saw countless dents in the roof and sides, but for the moment the general structure was miraculously intact.

The same could not be said for the windows, all of which had shattered as we fell. Several pieces had torn through my sweater and were imbedded in my arms, small pools of red forming around the tears. Blood oozed down Vivian's face. One of her legs didn't seem to be positioned quite right, and her right arm flopped loosely against her body. I felt liquid on my own face and arms, and distantly wondered whether it was all my own blood.

The SUV showed no signs of slowing. Rather, gravity was eagerly jumping into the mix, tugging on the Bronco and luring it into a second revolution. We still had at least fifty feet until we crashed into the water. It was too far to survive.

We were, I dimly realized, going to die. I was a full-blooded elemental, capable of living thousands of years, and I was about to die from being tossed around the back of a rusted-out SUV. I'd never given much thought to the way I'd die, since I didn't expect it to happen before we all had flying cars and jetpacks, but this particular method never even made it onto the short list.

To have any hope of surviving, I needed to immerse myself in water, and Vivian needed to place her hands on earth. Even then, she'd likely need a fair bit of time in a human hospital. There was only one possible way I saw to accomplish this. It was a long shot, and it risked exposing us to all humans in the area, but when the choice was between exposure and death, my internal debate resolved itself pretty damn fast.

My magic was still deep in the lake, pulling whatever energy I could to counteract the damage caused by the fall. Now, I summoned it, whispering to the molecules that they needed to come to me, and come quickly. Their movement was sluggish at first, the water reluctant to follow an unfamiliar path, but it could not resist for long. It recognized me from the years I spent swimming in its depths. More importantly, it recognized the magic as its old friend. As the memory of its own birth alongside the earth's primordial magic returned, it came willingly, eager to reunite.

I widened my reach and continued to tug, even as the Bronco completed another full rotation. Once again, it showed no signs of slowing. I wasn't certain Vivian could survive another turn. Her body already looked like a rag doll, and the blood on her face was flowing freely.

I felt a wet stickiness on my own legs and looked down to see my leg twisted unnaturally, and what appeared be my own shin bone poking out of my jeans. I was beginning to wonder if I could survive another turn, as well.

I no longer asked the water to come to me. I begged it. I wasn't even certain I controlled the magic any longer. I thought it might be controlling me, rushing to bring my element to me, to save me from the human weaknesses all elementals shared, regardless of how much magic raced through our veins.

Water poured through the broken windows. "Hold your breath and unhook your seat belt," I ordered, but it was unnecessary. Sera was already free and pulling her small body through the window.

By now, the lake had risen a full thirty feet, at least in Emerald Bay. In other parts of Lake Tahoe, I knew kayakers and boaters would find the water inexplicably dropping several inches. The Bronco was on its side, resting against the slope and surrounded by water, its frantic descent halted at last. I felt no relief yet. It took every ounce of concentration I possessed for the water to hold the vehicle in place, and I couldn't maintain it for long. Soon, I'd need to let go, and the Bronco would either resume its fall or sink to the bottom of the newly risen lake—or both. In either case, the others wouldn't survive.

Sera was standing on the passenger side, the only part of the car now clear of the water. She yanked hard on the rear door handle. It was stuck. "Not me," I shouted. "Mac first."

The face he turned to me was livid, his jaw locked in a

stubborn set I knew meant he had no intention of agreeing with me. Water now filled the entire driver's side of the Bronco.

I stuck my head above the waterline so he could hear me clearly. "We don't have time to argue," I said, forestalling whatever arguments he was preparing to make. "If we end up under water, Vivian and I can fit easily through a window, and I won't drown. You can't fit, and you *will* drown. Go!"

I looked at Sera and worried our argument was moot. She was fighting desperately to open the front passenger door, which had been crumpled and broken by the fall. The locking mechanism was stuck.

I saw rage cross Sera's face and felt the answering emotion rise inside me, my personal fire-starter once again proving it had no sense of timing. I closed my eyes against the sight, refusing to tempt my other side, but it still chafed against its reins when it felt the warmth of Sera's fire.

She was melting the door handle, I realized. She kept one hand on the door the entire time, completely immune to the searing heat. The moment the metal softened enough to release the locking mechanism, the door wrenched open in her hand, providing a single exit.

Mac cast one more look toward us, but my jaw was set every bit as stubbornly as his was. "Don't even start. Either you play the hero and we all die, or you get out and help us. Now, get your oversized ass out of the car while you still can." I reached out one hand, trying to ignore how bruised and bloodied it looked, and gave him one weak shove against the shoulder. He nodded, then moved quickly toward the door and pulled himself out, instantly reaching a hand back in for Vivian.

She was barely conscious, and it wasn't easy to maneuver her into the front seat. Fortunately, she was able to float across the top of the bucket seats. Mac gripped her wrist, and a moment later he was pulling her out. "Get her to ground!" I yelled up. He nodded, already handing her to Sera, who was in the lake. The last I saw, she had Vivian under one arm and was awkwardly paddling uphill, moving above the water and toward the earth Vivian desperately needed to begin the healing process.

"Now you," ordered Mac, reaching his hand back into the cab. I nodded and eased into the front seat, but I'd waited too long and exerted myself too much. The water still surrounded the SUV, but it struggled to hold it in place. I lost concentration for a moment, and that was enough. The Bronco completed its final rotation, coming to a stop upside down.

Mac dipped below the surface and stared at me through the jagged remnants of the window. I was now trapped in the water, and his expression was one of pure panic. It was oddly comforting to see that he sometimes forgot about my other side, the same way I forgot about his. "I'm okay," I mouthed at him. He nodded, looking uncertain.

For the most part, I really was okay. The water surrounding me was already improving my most superficial injuries, but I still had plenty of deep ones that needed time to heal. My movements were stiff and painful, and I pretty much hurt everywhere, but I could still move.

I pushed myself toward the open door, where Mac waited for me. As I watched, several small bubbles of air escaped his lips. I doubted he had long. I floated toward him, or tried to. My ripped jeans leg caught on the gearshift, trapping me inside the Bronco.

I gave my leg a tug, but I was too weak, and the fabric refused to give. I twisted to reach the gearshift but was forced to stop when the contortion reminded my body of its many wounds. Mac swam toward me, and I happily gave up some of my air to swear at him in great detail, though the water stole the words and saved him from hearing the more creative names. I thought he got the general gist, though.

With exaggerated gestures, I pantomimed that he should head to the surface, a suggestion he refused with an equally exaggerated head shake, apparently choosing to ignore that I was a freaking water who could not drown, whereas he was extremely mortal.

"Idiot," I mouthed. He smiled, clearly catching that one. I took a deep breath, just to prove I could, and he finally gave in, darting to the surface for air. A moment later, he was back, sliding into the cab. His body floated lightly above mine. With nimble fingers, he quickly freed me, then pushed himself backwards, grabbing my wrists as he slid past. He pulled me lightly from the vehicle, and a moment later our heads burst through the surface of the lake.

He gulped the air, and I knew that later I'd need to deliver a lecture on the right time and place for big dumb heroics, but at that moment I didn't care. He was alive. We all were.

Mac studied me carefully, looking for wounds, and I did the same in return. Somehow, against all odds, he was still whole. He gently touched my scalp, where I knew blood continued to flow from many wounds. "I'm fine," I said. It was an obvious lie, but I figured the fact that I was capable of telling it was a point in my favor.

He released one long ragged breath, and I felt the worst of the tension ease from his body. "Let's get behind the car so you can let the lake go without it falling on our heads," he said, already trying to pull me up the slope in the same direction Sera and Vivian had headed earlier.

The water had other plans. It wasn't letting me go anywhere, not so long as I remained hurt. It wrapped itself around me and held fast, refusing to let Mac pull me onto dry land.

"I can't," I told him. "I need to stay in the water, to heal."

He assessed the situation quickly, then grabbed me, pulling me toward where the lake should actually be and putting a fair bit of space between us and the banged up Bronco. Once we were safely away from the vehicle, I asked the water to withdraw, to return to its home. It eagerly obeyed, and we coasted downhill on a rush of water, stopping at last in the bay. A moment later, the Bronco made a final roll down the hill, coming to rest in the shallows of the lake.

It was over. Somehow, we were all still alive. But I remembered the noise I'd heard, and I remembered seeing the most conscientious driver I knew lose complete control of his vehicle.

We were alive, but someone hadn't intended us to remain that way.

CHAPTER 13

The moment we were safe, I sought out the others. Sera and Vivian were perched high above us, braced against a couple of rocks to keep from sliding further down the mountain.

Mac followed my gaze. "Will they be all right?"

I studied my two elemental friends closely. Sera had already set fire to a newly created tree stump, using its energy to repair the damage she suffered. She looked shaken, but mostly unhurt, and she was walking. Even as I watched, a slight limp in her left leg disappeared, healed by the fire.

Vivian was a different story. She'd spread herself across the ground and dug her fists into the soil, seeking as much of the earth's power as she could access. She looked broken, but alive, and the earth would have already started repairing the worst of the damage. Sera crouched above her, and even as I watched, a smile split her face. Relief poured through me at the sight. People accused Sera and me of behaving inappropriately all the time, but even we wouldn't crack jokes while our friends fought to stay alive. Vivian was going to need a fair bit of care, but I knew she would live.

"Yes," I said, slowly. If we'd been human, unable to pull healing power from our elements, we wouldn't be alive. I felt shock settle across me like a delicate shawl, a whisper-thin barrier between my conscious mind and reality. We'd come so close to not being here, and I hadn't the faintest idea how to begin processing that knowledge. "They're going to live." He exhaled, his own relief written clearly across his face.

I could already hear sirens in the distance, emergency vehicles likely called as soon as the other drivers saw us swerve off the road.

Mac still held me gently, treading water. I quickly scanned his body, for once with no lust in my heart. He had no element to restore him, and yet he looked surprisingly intact. "How are you unhurt?" I asked, confused.

He performed the same check on me, making a quick account of my many injuries. My leg was easily the worst, and the water was clear enough for him to see the full extent of the injury. He pulled me toward him, my body feather light in the water, and wrapped himself around my torso, my back to his front. This left my legs free to float before me, unhindered and easily accessible by the water. Even as I watched, the bone seemed to be withdrawing, returning to its rightful place inside my body.

"My mother told me always to wear my seat belt." He seemed to consider that answer enough. He tightened his arms around me, as if determined to eliminate all distance between us. It was painful, especially where the seat belt had cut into my skin, but I didn't mind. I craved the same closeness he did, and his hands embracing my sore flesh were simply a reminder we were still alive. After the ugly words by the river just hours ago and a crash that could have torn us apart permanently, we were both still here. Right now, that was all I needed to know.

And, so, even though his explanation didn't make sense—he should be at least as badly hurt as Vivian, but I saw nothing beyond a few cuts and some rapidly swelling bruises—I felt no need to look beyond the simple miracle that he was still with me.

In the water, we found some semblance of peace, but around us, chaos reigned. Kayakers' heads whipped about in a panic, trying to understand why they'd just been raised nearly thirty feet and then returned unceremoniously to their original position. A few had been overturned and were clinging to their kayaks, working to right themselves and find their way out of the freezing water. A handful of day-trippers ran around the beach, soaked from their impromptu swim, gathering their dripping belongings and chattering urgently, all the while casting nervous glances toward the lake, scared it would once again forget it was supposed to be a placid tourist destination rather than an actual force of nature.

"Oops." I watched the unintended results of my actions with growing concern. Elementals might have looked the other way when I privately informed a couple of discreet federal agents of our existence. They were unlikely to be quite so understanding when we landed on the evening news—though a twisted part of me looked forward to watching the freakishly cheerful meteorologists explain this one.

While the campers' and day-trippers' phones were water-logged and useless, the kayakers were more pre-pared, with their possessions in waterproof bags. They were already pulling them out and snapping photos, and I expected they'd find their way online within the next thirty seconds. "Hey, if you could terrorize everyone with a Twitter account, that would be awesome. You don't need to full on shift or anything. Just a growl or two should do it."

I felt his chuckle, the slight vibration through my body and the warm exhalation of breath on my neck, and I wel-comed the distraction. I didn't want to think about what we'd just survived—or how my own people would react to the very public way I'd saved us.

Mac and I were too exposed, floating in plain sight of anyone with questions about what had just happened—which would be pretty much everyone. This seemed to be one of those times when hiding was the better part of valor, and I thought it was caution rather than cowardice that urged us toward the shallows and into the shadows cast by the towering trees. The fact that caution coincided with my deep longing to not deal with what had just happened was mere coincidence, I was sure.

We were tucked away in one of the bay's many nooks, close enough to the shore that Mac was able sit down and stretch his legs along the bottom of the lake. He still held me close, tucked securely against him, as the water moved around me, finding bruises and cuts and slowly feeding them the magic necessary to be whole again. The sooner I could heal myself, the less cost there would be to my mortal life. If I was forced to exit the water now, I would live, but I'd need to heal as a human, a process that could take years off my lifespan. As long as Vivian and Sera were safe, I wasn't going anywhere.

And, I thought, feeling Mac's chest press against my back, I had other reasons for wanting to stay put.

"It's going to take a while," I said. "I have a lot to heal. Are you going to be okay in the water?"

The lake never warmed up before mid-summer, and even then few would call it balmy. It was warmer in the shallows, but not by much, not in May. It didn't bother me in the slightest, but he had to feel it.

"You know I'm still a bear, right?" I was glad I was facing away, so he missed my blush. I did keep forgetting that. He was so warm and human that it was hard to picture him standing in a freezing Alaskan stream, catching any unlucky salmon that swam past.

I glanced down to see the water slowly darkening, a pool of blood that didn't belong to me forming in the water.

"You're hurt, you idiot." I struggled in his arms, trying to free myself enough to learn the extent of his injuries. He didn't budge.

"I'm fine," he said.

"There is nothing fine about that amount of blood being outside your body." I ran my hand gently along his leg, feeling for the wound. It was high on his leg, and though his calm voice made me think it hadn't hit any vital blood vessels, I couldn't be certain. So long as his blood was spilling into the lake, I needed to do something. "I can try to heal you." Even as I spoke the words, I was shocked to hear them coming from my mouth.

Any strong water possesses the ability to heal, if they're so inclined. The body is, after all, ninety percent water, and a practiced water can manipulate cells with ease. It requires training, since the healer is basically working blind, but I had enough rudimentary knowledge to heal a simple wound. My mother was an expert, and on more than one occasion I'd worked at her side as she attempted to train me.

It hadn't stuck. I'd hated the entire process. If one can use magic to heal, one can also use it to harm, and I'd never been comfortable holding another's life in my hands. Long ago, I'd chosen to forget I had the ability, so much so that I hadn't thought to use it, even when my life was threatened by others. It was too much power, and I instinctively knew I should not have it. I hadn't thought about that ability in years.

That was before Mac was in pain.

He squeezed me lightly. "It's okay. I have my own magic, you know. I may not heal the way you do, but I'll still heal.

Save your strength for yourself."

"You sure?"

"Look." He was right. The pool of blood was dispersing, and little was flowing forward to take its place. The wound was slowly closing.

"Would it help to shift?"

I felt the slight movement of his head shake. "The bear's always there. It's just a matter of which skin I'm wearing at the time."

"That goes both ways, right? The human is always there, too? If you shifted now, you'd know me, right? I wouldn't want to find myself in the grip of some mad attack bear." When I put it like that, I had to wonder if I was insane to be so close to him and feel so little fear. In fact, I wanted to snuggle in a bit more.

"I'd always know you, Aidan." It was a whisper, but I heard him clearly. The words sent a shiver through me that had nothing to do with the temperature of the lake.

I had no reply to that, so we sat in silence for a long time, watching my bone return to its proper place. It was a slow process, with the water dulling the pain as well as healing the broken leg, and the dual effort slowed everything down.

"Tell me about your mother," I finally said, remembering his earlier comment about the seat belt.

Though he didn't move, I felt tension coil through his body. A moment later, he released it with a heavy breath, and his words were teasing, though the tone was somewhat forced. "Are you trying to get me on your couch, Dr. Brook?"

"If you were on my couch," I began, then abruptly stopped. My mouth had begun that sentence without consulting anything but my libido, and I wasn't prepared to tell him what I'd do to him on a sofa, therapeutic or otherwise. I rapidly changed the subject, rushing through the next words in an effort to distract him. The vibration of his suppressed laughter told me I wasn't as successful as I'd have liked.

"You mentioned your mom a minute ago. You never talk about her, or anyone in your family, really. I thought, from what you once said, your family had all kinds of issues, but Will seems great. I mean, in an overbearing, occasionally condescending sort of way, but I'm Josiah's daughter. Will's an amateur by comparison."

"Will is great," he agreed. "But Will did not raise me."

For once, I remained silent, refusing to fill the space with my ramblings and allow him a distraction.

He sighed, recognizing that I wasn't letting him off the hook, and he finally settled on giving me the Cliff Notes version. "I was raised by my father and mother, though she died years ago. Let's just say he wouldn't have won any parent of the year awards. He wouldn't have won any parent of the hour awards, for that matter. He kept us—me and my brothers—away from Will's side of the family for years."

"Why?" I asked.

"Because they choose to live as humans."

Such a simple sentence, and yet in that moment I learned more about Mac than I had in the last month. "You mean you stayed in bear form? But I thought two of your brothers were human? How many brothers do you have?" I recalled a conversation we'd had many weeks ago.

He shook his head. "There were four of us total, two humans, two bears. And no, we weren't always in bear form, though we often were. We simply lived as bears, even my human brothers. No houses. No indoor plumbing. No cooked food. Not for any of us."

I managed a weak smile, though I knew he couldn't see

it. "So I'm guessing you're not a big fan of sushi now."

He said nothing, didn't even acknowledge my pathetic attempt at humor. It seemed he had oceans of words that wanted to spill forth, and perhaps the only way he knew to remain sane was to hold them all in.

I knew what that was like. I'd been there. Some days, I still was.

"What happened?" I didn't want to pry, but neither did I want to leave those words hovering on the tip of his tongue, slowly poisoning him. I knew the damage such words did when left unspoken for years.

I waited a long time, and when he spoke, his voice was controlled, the voice of a man who'd just practiced the speech in his own head, testing it for weaknesses and its potential to cause pain.

"My father, older brother, and I were scavenging for food one day. It was early spring, so we were famished, having just finished hibernating. We smelled a feast and ran to it, too hungry or stupid to remember why we needed caution. We found a large RV parked in the middle of the forest, and an older couple, probably retired, sitting down to eat. As soon as I saw the humans, I pulled back, and my dad did the same. My brother was too eager."

He stopped speaking, and for a moment I thought he was finished. When he began again, the waver in his voice was unmistakable. "The man had a gun, and he shot the bear he thought was threatening his wife. The bullet was right between his eyes. My brother died instantly."

There were no words, but I wrapped my hands around his and pulled them to me, tightening his hold. He did not fight me, and a moment later his face was buried in my neck. He was shaking, fighting for control, and I felt a wetness that did not come from the lake. His next words were muffled. "My father made him live as a bear, and so he died as one. We don't switch back after death, Aidan. The couple called the forest service, and his body was burnt. I never saw him again."

I reached one hand back and threaded it through his hair, holding him gently against me. I didn't say a word, and I didn't need to. The words he'd withheld for years spilled from him, whispered into my skin. "You know they call me Mac cause of my last name, right? For years, it was my only name. My father couldn't lose the family name he'd been born into, but neither would he give us our own names. Animals don't have names, you know. It wasn't until I moved in with my uncle that I was given a first name, so that I could begin to move in the human world."

"Did you leave after your brother's death?"

I felt his nod. Slowly, he lifted his head, forcing himself to relax. "I left that night, walking on two legs for the first time in years. I had no clothes, and so arrived at my uncle's cabin completely naked. He took me in, a wild thirteen-year-old boy, and he educated me, taught me how to be human as well as beast. I owe him everything."

I didn't want to ask, but the story wasn't yet complete. "And your father? Your brothers?"

He shook his head. "I don't know. God help me, I don't know. I just left them, Aidan. I tried finding them once, but they'd already moved on to another location. I couldn't track them. And though I stayed at Will's for years, they never found me, either."

My leg, I noticed, had healed while we spoke. It was still a bit sore, but the bone was mended and the skin was mostly closed. I twisted slightly, spinning in the water until we were face to face. I was cautious of his leg, but it no longer bled and the wound appeared closed.

I placed my hand to his cheek, and he leaned into it slightly, a mirror of my actions the night he'd told me we couldn't be together. At that moment, I didn't care about that, or that he was determined to keep some emotional distance. I didn't care that he was trying to make decisions for both of us. I didn't care about anything except removing some of the pain from his eyes.

"Everyone carries burdens," I told him. "Once, you told me to remember the things I've done, but to forgive myself, too. How's that going for you?"

It wasn't a smile. His mouth barely moved. And yet, I felt a hint of humor infuse his body and the slightest weight lift from his shoulders. It was just enough for him to keep going for a little while longer. "I think it's a work in progress," he told me.

"Fair enough." I gave him the time he needed to return to himself, to stow his past away so he could once again be the man I knew in the present.

Everything in me strained toward him. Even as I watched him recover from the painful memories, I wanted to press my body full-length against his, to grasp his face and meet his lips with my own, to melt into him. I wanted to know him completely. His body, yes, but also his past, his burdens, his terrors. Him.

Whoever Mac was, I wanted him, and the certainty behind that thought proved as terrifying as the other events of the day. These emotions were just another kind of cliff, and even as I sat quietly in the water, I felt myself hurtling over the edge.

I tried to appear casual as I pushed myself backwards, using his chest as a brace and not letting my fingers linger overlong against his body. He was right, I realized. It wasn't enough to want to kiss him. I needed to be ready, and the thought of the unrestrained free-fall that awaited me if I gave in to these feelings caused something inside me to lock up in terror.

Mac's breathing slowed and he appeared calm, but when he met my eyes, his were still open and raw. He saw every fear coursing through me and he sent his own back, fears of abandonment and loss. This man, I knew, had the power to heal or destroy me, perhaps at the same time, and I might have the same power over him. It was terrifying—and I also knew it didn't matter. I would keep falling.

We stayed like that for a long time, letting silence speak what we could not say with words. At last, it became too much, and I broke away, looking up the slope. Sera and Vivian were long gone in the ambulance, and it was time for us to join them.

But first, there was one thing I absolutely had to know. "So, what name did your uncle give you?" I grinned, hoping against hope I was speaking to an Alfred or an Ichabod.

He laughed, and it felt like the first honest laugh I'd heard in hours. "A man's got to have some secrets, Aidan." He stood and pulled me from the water. I stood easily on the healed leg, and we inched toward the shore, preparing to face the fallout from the day. "Let's go see what chaos you've wrought this time."

WE TOOK A more conventional path up the slope than we had on the way down, walking slowly uphill while various news vehicles passed us in the opposite direction. With the steady traffic, we couldn't walk side by side, so I walked slightly ahead of him.

I was aware of his presence the entire way, though a fair bit of my attention was focused on pulling water from the air and using its power as an energy source, providing me with enough strength to make it up the steep slope without panting like a marathon runner on the twenty-fifth mile. I wanted to think I was low on energy because of my recent need to heal and the summoning of the lake, but I suspected I was just that out of shape.

Mac, of course, took long easy steps, as if he was strolling casually down the street. I made a half-hearted mental note to attempt cardio at some point in the distant future, a plan I forgot the moment I reached the top.

For once, this wasn't due to my refusal to ever do anything that could be interpreted as exercise. This time, I abandoned all other thoughts the moment I saw Josiah waiting by the side of the road.

Of course he'd be there. Of course he would. Josiah always knew everything that happened before anyone else did, and all of Lake Tahoe tilting slightly toward Emerald Bay was the sort of thing that would catch his attention. Even so, he didn't look annoyed or worried. He looked, if anything, pleased. That concerned me.

His gaze raked over Mac, then dismissed him entirely, all in a single moment. He directed his words to me only, as if the enormous shifter towering above him was merely part of the landscape. An unusually shaped tree, perhaps.

"Well, this is problematic," he said, with a broad gesture that encompassed the rescue crews, news vans, and excitable campers. "Do you still claim you have control over your magic?"

Though I'd only known he was my father for a short time, he already had the ability to piss me off as only a parent can.

"It's not like I set anything on fire. I just fancied a bit of a swim."

He groaned and rolled his eyes. "Are you determined to draw the interest of the council? There are limits to what I can cover up."

I tensed, finally acknowledging the fear I'd held at bay since we landed in the lake. The water council's stated goal was keeping our presence hidden from humans, but like most bodies with a bit of power, they'd come to enjoy its taste. Now, they were the waters' only form of self-regulation. Drawing their attention was the equivalent of driving for several miles with a cop car in the rearview mirror.

"I had to," I said, dropping the attitude. "It was that or die. And what happens if they do have issues with me? They have no way of knowing what I am. I didn't even know."

"Old ones know many things. If they saw you lose control of your water magic, they'd likely know why. It is safer to avoid their eye." His face darkened for a moment, then smoothed quickly back into a mask of detached amusement. I didn't even think he was covering up anger. He simply moved through emotions that quickly. Mercurial, thy name is Josiah.

"I'm sure you'll agree this is not something we can ignore."

I snorted, thinking of his unexpected visit and frequent phone calls over the last several weeks. If that was his version of ignoring, I shuddered to think what he'd be like when he was paying attention to me.

It was time to change the subject. "Where's Vivian?" I asked.

"She was taken to Barton Memorial," he answered. "Serafina accompanied her."

"How was she?" I tried to hide the worry in my voice. I wanted to give this man no weapon to use against me, no further knowledge of my emotional weaknesses. He already knew how much I cared for my friends, and that knowledge was dangerous enough. If he believed they made me unstable, I feared he'd have no qualms about eliminating them altogether.

"She'll live." His tone was, at best, disinterested, but immediately sharpened for his next question. He cast an accusing look in Mac's direction. "Can I assume there was a reason Mr. MacMahon chose to drive you over the cliff?"

Beside me, Mac tensed, the way he always did in Josiah's presence. I couldn't blame him, considering my father treated him like an oversized nuisance when he even bothered to acknowledge his existence.

I spoke quickly, pulling my father's attention back to me. "We were going north to... do something," I ended weakly, unsure how much shifter business I should reveal to Josiah. His raised eyebrows let me know how unsuccessful my diversion had been. I continued quickly, trying to gloss over my vague answer. "Well, first we were coming to see you, actually, but then we needed to turn around and go back, and then there was a pop, and a flat tire, and then, you know, we plummeted down the mountain." I finished with a firm nod, hoping my babbling and the thought of his daughter's near death by Bronco would distract Josiah from the things he wasn't meant to notice.

It was effective, certainly. He stared hard at me for a while, then did the same to Mac, then he paced restlessly for a long minute, his movements short and loaded with excess energy. An aura of rage surrounded him, its power crackling and hungry, and part of me leapt in joyful recognition. I closed my eyes tightly, desperately seeking my water center. When I opened them, the fire aura was gone.

"Are you saying someone tried to kill you?" He rushed toward me as he spoke, hands wrapping around my upper arms as he peered closely into my face.

"I'm saying loud pop, flat tire, deathward plummet. That's all I know."

He stared at me again, processing my words, then flew into a lengthy tirade. I didn't know the language. This being Josiah, it was possible no one alive still knew the language. The gist of it, however, was unmistakable. If translated into contemporary English, I suspected his rantings would include several variations on "motherfucker."

While Josiah continued to rage, I whispered to Mac. "Is there any hope of getting to Pamela? There's still the chance I could read her clothes."

Josiah abruptly stopped speaking in tongues, and said calmly, as if telling me that day's weather report, "Your mother's with her. Serafina phoned her as soon as she was able. She didn't want to risk losing fresh evidence. Fiona then brought the girl to the bear's home, as she thought she might be able to heal both Pamela and the boy. Why did you not phone her as soon as the boy returned?"

I decided "because I was a stubborn idiot" wasn't a confession I was ready to make to my father.

Also, so much for keeping shifter secrets. I stared at Josiah, searching for any indication of unease or concern about what my mother might learn. After all, in addition to being a control freak of an old one with dubious plans for my future, he was still one of our best suspects in the kidnappings, due to his knowledge of Brian's cocktail.

Though it was possible the worry that scored his face related to the case, I doubted it. He was already on his phone, arranging for the Bronco to be delivered to his private mechanic and insisting on a full investigation of the engine and all four tires.

Immediately after, he phoned someone regarding the news footage currently being captured below. I was unable to hear every word, but I did clearly catch "magnets" and "erase" repeated several times. He didn't appear to spare a thought for the shifter teenagers. It's what I'd expect from the man who considered them a lower life form, but it also suggested he wasn't involved. Either that, or my utter lack of acting ability didn't come from his side of the family.

I really wanted to get to the hospital and check on Vivian, but I knew I could do little good standing at her bedside with a worried look on my face. Right now, the best thing I could do was reach Pamela and help read whatever evidence remained, so that I might have some good news to share when I finally saw Vivian.

Of course, there was a marked downside to this plan. To get back to Truckee, we'd need to ride with my father. Sure, I'd needed to speak to him anyway, but I'd anticipated having Sera as a buffer. I hadn't planned on a fifty-minute car ride squished between two men who patently disliked each other.

And, if that wasn't enough, my mother waited at the end of the journey.

I cast a longing look over my shoulder, wondering if throwing myself over the cliff was still an option.

CHAPTER 14

We expected Josiah to drive us to the cabin, where my old Chevy sat, patiently waiting for me to remember it existed. No one else would lower themselves enough to drive the twenty-year-old compact, and while I refused to believe I was the grandma-esque driver Sera accused me of being, I did prefer to let others drive whenever possible.

Josiah appeared to have other plans, of which he'd already informed his driver. We cruised past the turnoff for the cabin without slowing and headed directly toward Will and Celeste's home. There was no hesitation and no uncertainty in the movement. The man knew exactly where we were going.

Being Josiah, it was possible he had a dossier on every magical being in the region, including their addresses, but I still made a mental note to ask Simon to sweep Sera's car for a tracking device. Considering we shared a father with no appreciation for personal boundaries, that really ought to be a weekly ritual.

He showed no inclination to drop us off and continue on his merry way. Instead, he followed us to the front door, his steps light and cheerful. I swore I caught him whistling at one point.

"You can go now," I suggested. "I can't imagine Will and Celeste will be happy to find you on their doorstep."

His upbeat demeanor vanished in an instant, and he

turned hard, black eyes to me. "Until you see fit to tell me the extent of your involvement with these shifters, I will learn for myself what sort of dangerous situation you have placed yourself in. I'm certain the home's residents will understand a father's concern." He paused briefly before saying "shifters," making me wonder just what he'd prefer to call them. The reminder of his prejudice lessened any pleasure I might have felt at the thought that, for once, Josiah didn't appear to know everything.

We were on the steps leading to the house when Carmen strode through the front door and blocked our path, determination written in capital letters across her face.

She and Josiah were roughly the same height, and she had no problem placing herself directly in his path, forcing him to make eye contact. While Josiah's eyes were cold and hard as granite, hers were predatory. Her slit pupil fixed on his face, looking for weaknesses I doubted he possessed. I'd say this for Carmen: she might be arrogant and secretive, but she sure as hell wasn't a coward.

Against my will, I felt myself beginning to like the woman, especially if she wanted to keep giving Josiah grief. There weren't enough people in the world willing to do that.

"What do you know?" Carmen demanded. I noticed she was clenching and unclenching her hands, stretching out invisible claws.

To an outsider, Josiah's face did not move in the slightest. I, however, had been friends with Sera for years, and I knew a thing or two about reading a fire's inscrutable expression. A single blink was all it took, and that tiny indication of surprise told me he had no idea what Carmen was talking about.

"I haven't asked him yet," I told her. She turned to me with a growl, and I swore I saw those perfectly manicured nails sharpening into points. "Hey, we were a little distracted." I held my hands up in mock defense and gave her a moment to take in my and Mac's appearance. Our clothes were torn and stained, and I suspected the current state of my hair would cause a beautician to fan herself.

To be fair, even after calling the hospital for an update on Vivian, using Josiah's non-waterlogged phone, we'd had time to ask about the drugs. I simply hadn't been in any mood to deal with his answers.

"What happened to you?" Carmen asked. "Never mind. I don't care." She turned back to Josiah. "Tell me about the drugs."

At first, Josiah nodded sagely, so accustomed to having all the answers it seemed to be his default response, at least until he bothered to process Carmen's words. He threw a comically bewildered glance my way. "Aidan, what is this crazy woman talking about?" While I knew he was exaggerating for effect, I also thought he was utterly clueless.

I felt something release in me, a worry I hadn't known I was holding dissipating in the face of his apparent innocence. Well, innocence on this charge, at least. I feared he was still a borderline sociopath whose questionable motives had caused him to overlook the death of far too many innocent humans and shifters, but somehow I still thought there was a line between being complicit in another's horrible actions and causing his own. It was one thing to have a father who was merely passively awful on occasion. It was something else altogether to be the spawn of an actual, comic-book villain.

He might not like shifters, but he wasn't responsible for their abductions. That much, I had to believe.

"The other shifter who was returned, he couldn't shift," I explained.

"Can't," corrected Carmen. "He still can't. And he's getting worse."

I glanced at her, startled. Based on how long Brian's concoction affected me, James should have improved by now. "It was the same drug cocktail Brian gave me," I told Josiah. "I recognized it."

This time, he didn't even attempt to appear impassive. The muscles in his jaw locked, and his fingers tapped out a rapid-fire beat against his leg. The movement was so like Sera I felt a burst of affection for the man, a feeling that simultaneously shocked and horrified me. Josiah was many things, but he was not my friend.

Except he and Sera shared an equally strong determination to protect me. This reminder of Brian's abuse, an action Josiah had notably not approved, animated his face and caused him to sputter for several long moments. Finally, he grabbed my arm and pulled me away where the others couldn't hear. He would defend himself to me, but not to Carmen. "I knew nothing about that," he said to me, his face as earnest as I'd ever seen it. "You know I didn't."

"And now?"

He shrugged, a helpless "Who me?" gesture that wouldn't fool the most gullible child. "After he was removed—" It seemed his attempts at protection extended to protecting me from my own actions.

"After I roasted him like an oversized marshmallow," I corrected, not allowing the euphemism. I might be an unstable, unpredictable bundle of future homicidal psychosis, but at least I was an honest one.

"Yes, that. I had his apartment cleaned of any questionable evidence. They found nothing you wouldn't expect to find in the apartment of a young man with a predilection for inebriation."

"It's the new millennium. Just say he liked getting drunk." I didn't even know where the words came from.

Never before would I have considered being irreverent with Josiah. Long before I'd known he was my father, he'd still terrified me.

Somehow, over the past month, I'd stopped fearing this man. He was still far more powerful than I was, but I also knew he wanted one thing no amount of power could provide. He wanted my acceptance. In my own way, I held the reins, and that lessened the fear I'd once felt for him.

The raised brow he turned toward me suggested he was well aware of the change of tone, though I had no idea what he made of it.

"So we have no idea who has access to the drugs that are keeping our children from changing?" Carmen called to us, drawing our focus back to her.

"Pamela can't shift, either?" I asked.

She shook her head, and I saw that her predatory gleam wasn't simply that of a woman seeking answers. It was the look of a mother determined to do whatever she needed to protect her daughter. Though I knew, realistically, that she hadn't a chance of taking on Josiah and winning, at that moment I wasn't sure I'd bet against her.

"Is she in the same state as James?" I asked her.

She shook her head, a slow, mournful movement. "No," she said. "It's worse. So much worse."

It was a full house. James's entire family gathered in the living room. Will and Celeste whispered together in the corner, their faces drawn and somber. Will looked deep in thought, and his wife appeared to have aged ten years in the last week. They cast worried looks at Carmen, entering behind us. More than anyone, they knew what she was feeling now. Mac joined them and began speaking in the same low tones, learning all he could about what had transpired while we were crashing into the lake.

Brandon slumped into the sofa, studiously ignoring everyone around him. This included Dana, who sat next to him, casting the occasional nervous glance my way. The poor thing looked overwhelmed by the tension that infused the room. Several times she almost appeared to think of something worth saying, then changed her mind at the last minute and let silence continue to reign.

Eleanor sat alone. From the armchair in the corner, she watched my mother's attempts to heal Pamela with a combination of interest and distrust. I imagined her efforts looked like a ridiculous form of faith healing to those unfamiliar with the abilities of waters. My mother, for her part, roundly ignored Mac's aunt. While Eleanor had reluctantly accepted Sera's and my help, that didn't mean she trusted all elementals—and given elementals' general attitude toward shifters, perhaps rightly so.

I'd never heard my mother speak ill of shifters, because I'd never heard her say a word about them. Until today, I'd assumed she'd been, like me, ignorant of their existence, but she looked pretty damn comfortable sitting in their cabin now, working on one of their daughters. It was just one more lie, one more way she'd kept me ignorant about just how large this world truly was.

I couldn't blame Eleanor for not trusting her when I was also unable to do so.

Unexpectedly, Simon was also present, having hitched a ride with Carmen. He sat easily in one of the side chairs, legs curled beneath him while he deliberately cleaned his nails, seemingly immune to the tension surrounding him on all sides. His eyes widened when he took in my disheveled state, and I realized no one had told him about the accident—or about Vivian.

"Everyone's okay," I told him immediately, before he could panic. "Vivian's in surgery now for some internal bleeding, but the doctors aren't concerned. Sera's phone's out of commission, but I spoke to the hospital directly."

Simon looked unconvinced. With a terse nod, he pulled out his own phone and escaped to the relative privacy of the front porch, needing to confirm my report.

I turned to watch my mother work on Pamela. At first glance, she didn't appear to be doing anything. Her eyes were closed, and one could be forgiven for thinking she was taking a power nap. I knew better. I tentatively sent out my magic, letting the tendrils ease toward her, finding where her power danced across Pamela's skin. She then reached deeper, sending the threads into Pamela herself, gently touching the water that ran in her blood and animated every cell of her body. She was reading the girl's entire history.

The act was simultaneously intimate and dangerous, and exactly the sort of thing that had caused me to reject my own healing ability. After I'd ceased training with my mother, I'd only attempted it one other time, when there'd been nothing to lose. The last time I'd reached into someone's body, I'd tried to force life back into the corpse of a newly dead woman. It hadn't worked, and I hadn't tried it since—but I still carried the memory of that woman's dying blood. I had enough ghosts in my head. I didn't want any more.

My mother, however, was a full water, and she was an artist. I'd never known her to have any emotional difficulties with patients—or with anyone, for that matter. She opened her eyes when she felt my magic whisper against hers and nodded once in acknowledgement. "I'm glad you are here. I would like your opinion."

I walked toward her and the teenage girl laid out on the living room rug. I took a moment to appreciate that it was fluffy, white, and made of fake fur. Those bears, I decided, just pretended to be tough. Inside, they were a bunch of softies who ate fruit and decorated with synthetic fur.

To look at her, Pamela was at peace. Her eyes were closed, and her breathing, while shallow, was regular. She had the same glowing skin as her mother, and there was no hint of pallor beneath its rich tones. She was dressed in a clean pair of pajamas and a heavy robe, and one would never guess the trauma she'd likely experienced over the last couple of days.

"Did you make her sleep?" I murmured.

She nodded, absently. "She was quite agitated when she arrived. This seemed the best solution."

"Did you read her clothes already?"

"They'd done as you asked and kept the clothes in a plastic bag in the refrigerator, but I found nothing, not even a hint of Pamela. It was almost as if they'd been washed right before she was released."

I grumbled at our lost chance. She might as well have been returned naked, as James was. "Have you found anything unusual in the sweat? Anything chemical?" It was as difficult to describe my memory of Brian's mixture as it was to describe a scent, though I asked the question more as a matter of form than anything else. If she couldn't shift, it was a safe bet she'd been given the same thing as James.

My mother placed her hand at the hollow of Pamela's throat and carefully drew one small drop of water through the skin. She handed it to me gently and waited.

"It's the same," I confirmed.

"Her body's been put through the wringer," she said quietly, her words meant only for my ears.

"Any idea where the blood loss came from?" I asked.

"Here." She pointed to a cut several inches long behind Pamela's left ear. She hesitated, and I thought it had less to do with me and more to do with a living room full of shifters. "I think someone hit her on the head to knock her out, and it opened this cut. Nothing bleeds like a head wound, so it would explain the blood you found at her house. And this," she indicated a pinprick on Pamela's neck, "is where they inserted a needle to drug her."

I opened my mouth to ask who could sneak up on a shifter and closed it just as quickly. It had to be either someone she knew or another shifter. No wonder my mother didn't want to speak of it openly.

"She has bruises and cuts over her entire body, and something in her neurological system feels off. It feels like it's still struggling to adapt to some new, invasive presence."

"Like a virus?" I asked.

"I wish I could tell you what it was, but I do not understand these shifter brains. They're so messy." She spoke the final word with a whisper of distaste. My mother did like things to be tidy. It really was a wonder she managed to not only tolerate my chaos, but love me in spite of it.

I felt an unexpected softening toward her, which I quickly beat back. I knew I loved her, and I didn't expect that to change in the foreseeable future. That didn't mean I was ready to forgive her.

"Do you need a control, Fiona?" I started visibly and let out an undignified squeak. Once again, Carmen had appeared seemingly out of thin air.

"There's a reason some cats wear bells, you know," I muttered.

Carmen wisely chose to ignore me. "A control brain," she repeated. "I'll have similar neural pathways as my daughter. Would that help you identify what's been changed?"

"It will," my mother said, her face thoughtful. "I'll have to put you to sleep, as well."

Carmen shook her head vehemently. She was putting a lot of faith in my mother, but even her trust had its limits.

"I'll be fine," she insisted.

My mother looked skeptical, and somewhat unimpressed by the woman's stubbornness. "We're discussing the equivalent of non-invasive exploratory brain surgery on a conscious patient. It could be unpleasant."

In answer, Carmen stretched herself out beside Pamela. She flicked her amber eyes toward my mother. "She's my daughter." My mother nodded, understanding, and I felt that damn rush of affection again.

My mother sat at both women's heads, somehow appearing regal despite her casual, cross-legged pose. She placed one hand on the back of each woman's neck, fingers pointing gracefully down the spine. She closed her eyes, and the entire room waited.

I, for one, used that time to feel like an absolute ass. I'd known my mother was in town when I'd learned James couldn't shift. If I'd simply called her at the time, she might have been able to fix him already. I'd been so determined to ignore her that I completely overlooked the help she could provide—and now James and Pamela were paying the price for my obstinance.

Sitting in the house didn't provide nearly enough opportunity to wallow in my self-loathing, so I quietly excused myself and headed to the front porch. I sat down gracelessly on the steps, in no mood to attempt anything requiring delicacy or lightness of movement.

"Vivian is out of surgery." I hadn't noticed Simon already sitting on the porch, but even so, I didn't jump at the sound of his voice as I did with Carmen. Then again, I never did for Simon. Whenever he appeared, it felt like he was in exactly the right place at the right moment. There was no need to be surprised. "I convinced the nurses to put Sera on the phone, and she assures me Vivian will be fine, and so long as she can immerse her hands in pots of earth, she will be discharged in a matter of days."

I exhaled, releasing at least some of the fear and anxiety that had been building since the Bronco went over the cliff. "That's good. That's really, really good news."

"It is. And yet you still look miserable."

"Shut up. I'm happy. There's just a lot of other stuff going on in there." I gestured behind us. "I made a pretty big mistake."

It was a good thing I wasn't expecting any sympathy, because that wasn't Simon's way. "If a mistake was made, do what you can to repair it, then let it go. Or are you berating yourself for that which you cannot change?"

"Hey, this is changeable. I could stop being so stubborn. It's within the realm of possibility."

"So is a winning lottery ticket, but I do not suggest you rely on that as a feasible life plan," he said. "There is always room for improvement, but I imagine your basic nature is what it is. You do know the fable about the cat and the frog, right? In which it is the cat's nature to kill the frog?"

That didn't sound quite right. "You mean the scorpion and the frog?"

He shook his head, exasperated. "Do not be ridiculous. A scorpion would be an inferior character to a cat. My version is much better."

"But doesn't the scorpion cross the river on the frog's back? How does that even work in your version?"

He shrugged. "It was a large frog. The point is, while you are unlikely to kill any frogs, you are equally unlikely to stop being unnecessarily stubborn. Plus, you had a good reason this time. Your mother failed you. It is entirely reasonable to hold a grudge, at least for a month or two. After that, it becomes self-indulgent, but for now you are safely in the window of allowed sulking."

I looked at him, and fought the familiar urge to ruffle

his hair and scratch behind his ear. "You do have a way of knowing what to say, Simon. Maybe you should talk to Viv's mom about becoming a therapist."

He sniffed. "Listen to strangers moan about their problems all day? Hours of talking in which we discuss things that have nothing to do with me? How tedious."

"Fair enough." I let him pretend to be selfish, though I knew otherwise. For those he considered his people, Simon was as loyal and kind as any human or animal I'd ever met, which had made his announced exit all the more unexpected. I'd made the mistake of assuming, now that I'd found friends I wanted to stay with forever and ever, they'd feel the same.

"Are you really going to leave?" I asked. I hadn't planned on mentioning it, but I found myself unable to stay quiet.

Simon, however, didn't have that problem. He sat in silence for a long time, long enough that I began to think he was consciously avoiding giving me an answer.

"I do not know," he finally admitted. "Though I am glad to be here, I never planned on this becoming my permanent home. It felt like the choice was being made for me."

I knew there was more and quietly waited. "I've never known any other cats," he said at last. "Though my mother has been understanding and supportive—far more than yours, I might add—I was still adopted, and she is still human. I did not even know other shifters existed until the day I ran into a group of coyotes mid-shift. I was in cat form at the time. It was an unfortunate introduction to my kind, and it taught me a whole new appreciation for my ability to climb trees. After that, I started to seek shifters out, but I never found as many as I would have liked, at least until I moved here. Tahoe appears to be crawling with shifters."

I nodded. I still felt like a blooming idiot for not knowing shifters even existed during my previous time in the area. The damn furballs were everywhere.

"Carmen and her family might be my only chance to learn more about who I am. Certainly, they are far larger than I am, but the basic anatomy remains the same. She has offered to introduce me to the local cat community. Now, I feel like I have a reason to stay for myself, and not simply because I like my roommates. I am making the choice to stay."

"Are you moving out? Will you live with the cats?" With those words, I finally named the dread I'd felt ever since Carmen had expressed an interest in my friend.

I'd thought it was because I feared the intimidating mountain lion, but that was never it. I'd feared Simon was drifting away from me, that if he met the cat, he'd have less interest in being my friend. Shame at my own selfishness lay heavy in my chest and brought heat to my cheeks. I didn't want to be that kind of person.

At least this was a mistake I could still correct. "It's okay if you do. Really. Just visit us often, okay?" The words were slightly awkward, a forced lightness covering my underlying dismay, but Simon nodded, seeming to accept them at face value.

The door behind us opened, and Eleanor stepped out. She took several gulps of air, then shook herself from head to toe, releasing whatever nerves she was still holding. When she noticed us watching her, she quickly calmed herself and tried to pretend she hadn't stepped outside to have a low-level freakout.

"Fiona—your mom—she is not normal," she said.

"I'm guessing she just withdrew blood without a syringe?"

"Yes! What the hell is that about?"

I laughed. I couldn't help it. Out here, away from the Parlor of Despair that Will's living room had become, Eleanor looked both lighter and younger. She was, I realized, only in her early thirties, at least a decade younger than her sister.

"She takes a drop or two from several organs and compares them. It's a way of learning what the kidney and liver are filtering out." I'd never made it that far in my training, mainly because I'd had much the same reaction as Eleanor to drops of blood floating above the patient's skin.

"And she can't do that inside the body?"

"She says it's easier if she isolates the blood." I shrugged. "She learn anything yet?"

"She just finished. All she did was shake her head at Carmen and lay down herself. I think she's napping."

I knew she wasn't sleeping, but my mother often needed a few minutes to recharge immediately after a procedure. I nodded and felt an awkward silence descend. I really didn't know this woman well and had no idea what to say to her while we waited for my mother's report. Simon showed no desire to help me out, either.

"Have you lived in Tahoe long?" I asked. Small talk, that was the ticket. Especially if the small talk told me whether she might have known Brian and therefore had access to his drugs. My suspects kept refusing to be guilty, and I really needed to find another possibility. Plus, someone had helped James and Pamela escape. It might as well be Eleanor.

Eleanor looked at the towering pines that surrounded her with something akin to gratitude. "I was born and raised here, but I left the minute I graduated high school. Lots of us do that. We think we can get away from the mountains, from the forest. See the world."

Like Carmen, I remembered. And Pamela, who dreamed of getting out of Tahoe, and James, who wanted to leave his shifter life behind. "Where did you go?"

"Every university in every city I could find. I racked up one degree after another, trying to make a home in libraries instead of the woods. It didn't work. I lasted as long as I could, but we can never stay away. It's our blessing and our curse. We belong to the land. I was already heading back when Celeste called me. James was talking about leaving Tahoe, and she wanted me to talk some sense into him, to explain why it could never work. I tried, but there's no talking sense into a teenage boy."

I nodded. I understood what it was to have that connection to the land. "Wasn't it worth it, though? You got to see some of the world, meet other people." I was hardly a world traveler, but my insistence on leaving the island was the best choice I'd ever made.

Eleanor didn't look convinced. "I saw a world intent on destroying the nature it needs to live. The few places where nature was revered, where I might have found some peace, I was scorned by those that lived there. Some even denied my very existence." She didn't elaborate, but I knew she spoke of elementals. I fought the pointless desire to apologize on behalf of every narrow-minded old one in existence.

"Celeste tried to tell me, but I didn't listen. What younger sister wants to acknowledge the wisdom of her sibling? Long ago, she told me we had no choice. As long as we were bears, we would return to the forest, over and over again. Our human face may allow us to walk in the outside world, but it doesn't allow us to live there. She was right, of course. It just took me a little longer to figure out."

And strike one more suspect from the list. This didn't sound like a woman who would help others escape, not when she considered it a futile effort.

I was completely out of ideas. It was, I decided, time to hit the refresh button and try to put the pieces together in a new way. Also, pancakes. It was always time for pancakes.

My mother finally exited the cabin, followed by Mac, Will, and Josiah. Somehow, even while surrounded by shifters, my father was able to ignore them. He made eye contact with me and my mother and simply paid no attention to any of the others.

I'd forgotten Josiah was even still there, and that concerned me. If my father was choosing to be quiet and unobtrusive, I assumed he had some ulterior motive for doing so.

Eleanor and Will cast barely-concealed looks of loathing his way. They might slowly be accepting my presence, but it helped that I wasn't a prejudiced asshole. My father couldn't make the same claim. He was exactly the kind of old one the shifters resented, and with good reason.

Even my mother received little more than civility from the two bears. They would accept her help because they had no other choice, but they would not forget she was a full-blooded elemental.

In return, she wasn't rude, but her bland politeness never veered into anything that could be mistaken for warmth.

At that moment, I was certain that, had it not been for Mac vouching for me and Sera, we'd never have been invited into their home.

I couldn't worry about any of that now, however. My mother looked worn and thin. For once, I saw the weight of the centuries in her eyes, and the tiniest lines of stress threatened to crack her perfect skin. She'd be heading directly to a water source once she shared her news, of that I was certain. "The women are resting," she said. "They will need peace for several days. I had to explore much deeper than I anticipated."

"Were you able to heal her so she could shift? What about James?" The pained silence that greeted my question was answer enough. "We need to find the person who did this, don't we? They must know how to reverse this. What did you learn? Did Pamela remember anything about being captured?" The questions poured forth, one desperate hope piling onto another.

I was really tired of not knowing anything.

Sadness scored my mother's face. "I think pure instinct brought Pamela home," she said. "She knows nothing, Aidan. She remembers nothing."

"Not her attacker? Not where she stayed?"

Will shook his head. "Pamela remembers nothing. Not even her own name."

I looked around the circle, the other faces reflecting the shock I knew was on my own. "Amnesia?" It didn't even sound real. It was the sort of thing that only happened in soap operas.

"I'm afraid so, little water." Josiah's face snapped toward Will when he used the diminutive term. It appeared he wasn't comfortable with any paternal figure granting me a nickname. Because I was petty, that made me like Will even more. "She doesn't know a thing. James knows his own family, but he remembers nothing about where he was, who took him, or what they did to him—and he's only getting worse as the beast takes over. It's been a full week since he shifted." Will's anger built steadily as he spoke. The only reason he wasn't dismembering someone right now was he had no idea where to begin.

"That's not all," said my mother. "Something has changed in Pamela's nervous system. I wish I could tell you more than that, but that's all I know. I performed a careful comparison of her and Carmen's pathways, and I found a sort of block in Pamela's brain. Her brain is sending her body a message to shift, but it's not being received."

"Could that explain why she can't access her memories?" I asked.

"I don't know. It really doesn't make sense. If it's as you told us, that it's a drug that wears off, the effect should be fading, but it is not. The obstruction is consistent. I have no answers, I'm afraid." I could count on one hand the number of times I'd heard her admit that, and her helplessness made everything so much worse. No matter how mad I was at her, I still expected my mother to have all the answers during a time of crisis. "I will try again later, after we've all rested a bit."

I looked at Josiah, standing perfectly still and taking in as much information as he possibly could. I expected he was storing it away for future use in his big, scary brain. "And our only lead," I said pointedly, staring him down, "is you. Whatever you say, you knew about Brian's concoction, and you don't have a great history of being an innocent bystander. You have to know something." I felt anger bubbling inside me, that constant reminder of what he'd done, what he'd allowed to happen. I didn't need a mirror to know my eyes were sharpening, filling with the intensity that always accompanied the beginnings of a fire.

Simon moved quietly to one side, offering silent support. On the other side, Mac lightly touched my hand, reminding me who I was.

My mother saw all of this, and a quickly hidden concern flitted across her face. She didn't want me to know how worried she was, but it was there. It was always there, I suspected, and likely had been from the day I was born. "You know that's not what happened. Think, Aidan," she told me.

I didn't want to. I didn't want to be logical. Life would be so much easier if I could just blame Josiah for everything that went wrong, then return to my warm cabin. Except she was right. This one couldn't be blamed on my father.

He was many things, but he wasn't stealthy. He couldn't get close enough to a cat shifter to smack her on the head without her permission. Set her on fire, sure, but that's not what we were dealing with.

"Damn it," I muttered. It was the most gracious defeat I could manage. I turned and walked far away from the circle. If I needed to, I would walk all the way to the cabin, until the rage boiling within me eased and I stopped wanting to set my entire world on fire.

CHAPTER 15

We weren't able to see Vivian that night, or even the next morning. Sera spent the night at the hospital, watching over Vivian's sedated form. She phoned the cabin in the morning to tell us there was no rush. The doctors had ordered a full series of diagnostic tests, looking for an explanation for her rapid healing. While the MRI and CT scan wouldn't reveal the potted plant at her bedside, they would take long enough that we wouldn't be able to see her until well past noon.

With the Bronco firmly out of commission and Mac unwilling to ride in my tiny car, I borrowed the Mustang for the hour's drive back to South Lake Tahoe. It was a nerve-wracking trip. This was partly because it required us to pass the scene of our accident, a feat I only managed by slowing to ten miles per hour, taking many deep breaths, and offering fervent prayers to any deity willing to hear them.

It was also nerve-wracking because, while the Mustang was larger than my Chevy, Mac still barely fit. His knees pressed against the dash, his head brushed the roof, and his shoulder nearly brushed mine as I drove. For an entire hour, I was painfully aware of his body one easy touch away, and only Simon's presence in the back seat and our concern for Vivian kept me from pulling over and embarrassing myself in some new and desperate way.

We found Sera sitting in the waiting room, fidgeting so much I was surprised she hadn't managed to set her chair on fire. Even from ten feet away, I felt the spark of her magic, felt the way it reached across the room, hungrily seeking an outlet. A distracted fire was worrying enough. That I was agitated enough for my own magic to wake and find hers was far worse.

I no longer needed to be enraged to wake up my fire side. That merely fed the magic, strengthened it so that even weak, cold emotions had the same effect. At that moment, I felt no anger, but I still wanted to set something on fire.

Simon sat quietly beside Sera and lightly rested one hand on her forearm, letting the simple touch calm her. "She will heal," he said, with utter certainty.

She nodded. "She will. She was in surgery longer than expected, but the doctor is astounded by her progress." She allowed a small smile. I wondered how many bags of soil she'd snuck into the room. "She had some internal bleeding, and her left leg and right arm are broken. The arm was fractured in three places, he said." The words were spoken with a careful distance I knew she didn't feel. "Olivia, her ex—or maybe not so ex, considering—is in there."

I attempted a weak smile. "She tried to work things out, and all she had to do was throw herself over the side of the mountain and nearly die. We could turn that into the latest relationship self-help book." I carefully avoided looking at Mac, not wanting him to think I was talking about anything other than Vivian and her ex-girlfriend.

"Crash Into Love?" suggested Sera.

"I was thinking more along the lines of I Love You, You're a Selfish Cow Who Ignored Me Until I Nearly Died. Yours is probably more marketable, though." It was possible I felt some animosity toward this unknown woman who'd caused one of my good friends pain.

"You must be Aidan. Vivian told me I'd recognize you by the completely inappropriate words coming out of your mouth." I froze at the words spoken directly behind me. Apparently, the ex wasn't going to remain an unknown woman for any longer than it took for me to turn around.

"You couldn't have warned me?" I muttered.

Sera shrugged, unconcerned. Simon fixed his sharp green gaze just over my shoulder and said, quite clearly, "Why would we stop you from speaking the truth?"

Hey, if it was going to be awkward, at least I had company. I turned to catch my first look at the woman I'd been freely insulting a moment ago and almost wanted to apologize. Everything about this woman suggested she was sweet and harmless. Everything except her eyes, that is.

She wasn't especially tall, and she had the body of someone who regularly walked but couldn't be bothered to restrain her diet, muscled and soft at the same time. Her hair was a yellow blond, and her pale skin was dotted with freckles unobscured by any makeup. A pair of cat's eye glasses rested atop a button nose and magnified her pale blue eyes. She wore cotton pants and a striped button-down shirt, and a messenger bag was slung across her body. Inside the bag, I could see several skeins of yarn and a pair of knitting needles loaded up with stitches.

In short, she looked like a cross between a graduate student, a librarian, and someone's grandmother. The effect was only marred by her eyes, sharp and angry. In her version of reality, Vivian had broken up with her to be with us, and she showed no signs of forgetting that fact.

"You do know she dumped me, right?" Olivia pointed out. Her tone was dry and irritated, and far more superior than I would have liked. I felt my earlier urge to apologize shrivel up.

I had many retorts to her comment, the most dominant one being the need to defend Vivian, who'd only broken up with Olivia to save her life. There are many reasons I tire of the secrecy that surrounds what we are, but at that moment, my inability to have the last word and put this woman in her place were at the top of the list.

"She's our friend," I said instead, and really, that was all that mattered.

She looked unimpressed. "She's awake now. I'm getting a coffee."

She pointed us down the sterile white hall toward the recovery rooms, then moved in the opposite direction. I'd never visited anyone in the hospital before. The strong elementals with whom I'd been raised had no need of human medicine, and during my relatively brief time in the human world, I'd been lucky enough to have no need for such a visit.

My only reference for such visits were images from movies and television shows, in which a carefully made-up patient smiled wanly, bravely facing her fate from a clean and tidy bed.

The reality wasn't so neat. Vivian's face was swollen and purpling from the multiple contusions she'd suffered in the fall, and her arm and leg were both held from her body at an awkward angle. The bed sheets were already wet with sweat and wrapped around her in odd ways to accommodate the broken limbs. Plastic tubes poked out everywhere, IVs and catheters and breathing tubes, a sickening roadmap of bodily fluids and medicines. It was the sort of thing that would normally cause my squeamish friend to grimace and avert her eyes. Now, she barely seemed to notice it.

Her eyes were heavy and glazed, holding little of the intelligence I associated with Vivian. Her skin, normally a rich cocoa tone, looked sallow and thin. More than anything, she looked tired, the sort of exhaustion that went well beyond the physical body.

And this was after a night of exposure to her element. While I'd been flirting with Mac and resenting my father and feeling guilty about not helping enough on the case, she'd been here, fighting against a small world of pain.

For the second time in minutes, that spark deep within flared to life, along with a voice insisting this was no accident. The Bronco had been sabotaged, and while I was damn certain Vivian hadn't been the target, here she was, suffering because of us.

I distantly heard a low growl and was only moderately surprised to discover it came from my throat. I looked down at my fingers and noticed, curiously, that they were beginning to spark.

A sharp pain snapped me back into my body. "Ow," I said, rubbing my upper arm and looking toward Sera, who was more than ready to deliver a second blow. "Thanks." I didn't know what else to say.

"Hold it together, Ade. I can only worry about one of you at a time, and it's Vivian's turn."

She was right, of course. I gave a short, terse nod.

Sera pushed the sliding glass door open and walked softly into the room, followed by Mac. I knew there was no way he could have prevented the accident, but watching his guilt-torn face when he saw Vivian, I wondered if he knew that.

These days, it seemed there was plenty of guilt to go around. We were all getting our share.

Simon and I followed, and Simon moved directly to the room's chair and curled up in it, making it clear he had no plans to go anywhere until Vivian was healthy again.

I tentatively held her hand, or at least the part of the hand sticking out of her cast. "You know we're going to figure out what happened, right?"

She turned to face me, and the look on her face broke my heart. She looked like she'd given up. "It doesn't matter," she said.

"I'm just going to assume that's the drugs talking, Vivian," Sera said.

I forced a weak smile. "You know we won't let this go. Sera will get all determined, and Mac will intimidate someone, and I'll annoy the villain so much they'll announce themselves just to shut me up. We still need to work out the kinks, obviously, but on the whole I think it's a solid plan."

Vivian winced, unamused. "It doesn't matter," she repeated. "So you find this guy. There will be another. And another. There's always another." She attempted to turn to face the other wall, but Simon was in her line of sight. Sighing, she closed her eyes, blocking us all out. "This shit never happened in Connecticut, you know."

"If you're thinking about moving back to Connecticut, we need to lower your dose." Sera's words were light, but her face was hard as stone.

Vivian opened her eyes once more, taking in each of us in turn. It seemed she was committing us to memory. "I can't do it anymore. Give me a boring life with my computers and girlfriend and the occasional Buffy marathon. If I stay with you guys, it will be my death. It's over for me." She sounded regretful, but not at all uncertain of her choice.

And there was nothing we could say to argue. Four helpless faces watched as she closed her eyes and drifted away. Her breathing slowed and deepened, and we knew she was asleep. I hoped her dreams were better than her reality had become.

The door behind me slid open, and Olivia stepped into

the room. "I'm staying with her," she announced.

Simon studied her curiously, as if she were an especially large mouse. "No," he finally said. He proceeded to ignore her completely.

"She's my girlfriend," Olivia told him. He offered no response.

"Ex-girlfriend," I pointed out. "She's our friend. No prefix required."

"It's just a word. It means nothing." She grabbed another chair from the corner and placed it on the side of the bed opposite Simon, pushing me firmly out of the way. She sat down and cast a look his way that clearly said, "So there."

"Are we having a competition to see who loves her more?" I asked. "Considering that you ignored her for the last month, I'd put long odds on you if we're betting."

She said nothing, and Simon was working hard to pretend she wasn't there. I knew it wouldn't be long before a nurse urged several of us out of the crowded room, and I moved toward the door, leaving the two of them to duke it out.

"It doesn't stop, you know." The words were spoken so quietly I wasn't sure they were intended for my ears. Even so, I paused by the door, waiting to see if she would continue.

She did. "You don't stop loving someone just because they go away, or because they hurt you. You don't stop even when you don't trust them anymore. Give me whatever title you want, but I was never her ex, not really."

Simon didn't look at her, but I knew he was listening. I could almost see his ears twitch in her direction.

"You couldn't have said this to her before?" I asked.

"I didn't say I was without regrets. I said I loved her. I imagine those things aren't often mutually exclusive."

I wanted to dislike her, just on principle. I wanted to

be harsh and cruel to this woman who'd caused Vivian, kind and gentle Vivian who'd only sought to protect her, a moment of pain. And yet, I sometimes felt like I'd been formed from a mix of magic and regret, and I could not fault her for admitting her own weaknesses.

"I wish it didn't take something like this to make us realize what matters." Her eyes were on Vivian's face, traveling slowly over her bruised features, and the glow that lit her face told me she saw nothing but Vivian's beauty.

"Maybe the odds are more even than I thought," I whispered. I followed Sera and Mac outside and slid the door closed, leaving Simon and Olivia to sort out the rest themselves.

SERA AND I walked in silence down the hospital's long, white corridors. It was already late afternoon, and most visitors had gone home. The only people that passed us were nurses and orderlies, all walking with purpose, their rubber-soled shoes providing the only whisper of sound. We stopped at the nurses' station for an update, and they confirmed what we already knew. Vivian was healing quickly enough to surprise the doctors, but not so fast that they'd attempt to make her their next case study.

Mac waited for us downstairs, not wanting to linger in the building after seeing Vivian. Sera thought the sterile world of the hospital was simply more than his bear could handle, and I could believe it. I'd already noticed he started twitching if he was in a room without windows, or too high above the ground floor. Vivian was much the same way. They functioned, but they didn't like it.

"Does she have enough soil?" I asked, thinking of her second floor room. "I know they say love's the greatest cure, but I'm not sure even Olivia and Simon can manage that. Plus, with the glances they keep giving each other, their animosity might cancel out the love."

"She has an entire garden underneath her bed. And isn't laughter supposed to be the best medicine? I thought love made us sick."

"That's just you, you cynical creature. And Vivian didn't look like she was in much mood to laugh. I think..." I paused, reluctant to articulate my concern. "I think she meant what she said."

"She did." Sera's face transformed, hardening into that expression of pure determination I knew and loved. "Good thing people change their minds, isn't it?"

I reached out a hand and gave hers a quick squeeze. We didn't touch often. I couldn't remember the last time we'd shown overt affection. But she was my best friend and my sister, and we'd nearly lost each other. She squeezed back, not offering a single quip in deflection of the honest moment.

We stepped into the stairwell and worked our way toward the lobby, both lost in our own thoughts. Vivian and Sera weren't the only ones I'd nearly lost. It was pure luck and the grace of his remarkably hearty bear constitution that had kept Mac here with us. I knew he was beaten and bruised, and he was walking stiffly, but he was still walking.

So easily, it could have been otherwise. A piece of glass piercing his heart, a tree trunk crushing him, metal sheets slicing through his skin, and I wouldn't be at the hospital. I'd be at the morgue or, more likely, I'd be curled up in a ball, feeling my entire world freeze with the knowledge of what I'd lost.

But I hadn't lost anything, not yet. I'd screwed things up, but as long as he was here, I could try again. Sure, I might screw things up in a whole new way, and the smart money would be on me doing just that, but I still had the chance. I couldn't waste it.

When we stepped into the hospital lobby, I saw Mac through the automatic glass doors. He waited by the car, leaning lightly against the hood. His weight was more than enough to cause the metal to droop toward the asphalt. There was a slight breeze in the air, and it whispered through his hair, causing the dark brown strands to dance in the wind. It was nearly nighttime now, and chilly enough that a family scurrying past were bundled in wool coats and scarves, but he wore only his usual untucked flannel shirt, red plaid this time, and a faded pair of jeans. He looked relaxed and unbothered by the weather, though his eyes were still sharp, constantly scanning and reading his surroundings.

He took my breath away, as no one had ever done before. I could use logic to explain my attraction to him. He was handsome and kind, determined and intelligent. He demonstrated a sense of honor rarely seen outside films featuring men at war. He liked me despite my faults and, in some cases, because of them.

And yet, that was only part of the truth. There was something else, something that logic and reason could never touch. I wanted him because some voice deep within was certain I belonged with him, though I could never say why, and because I thought he might belong with me, too.

He turned toward me and promptly stilled. I don't know what he saw in my face, but it was enough to bring heat to his eyes. He didn't move a muscle, and yet from a hundred feet away I felt him tense with awareness.

"Sera?"

"Hmmm?" Her tone was non-committal, but her mouth twitched with suppressed laughter.

"Stay here for five minutes, would you?"

"Just five? I know it's been a long time, Ade, but it usually takes longer than that." She smiled brightly at me, obviously giving up on the suppressed part.

"We're not going to... Well, not in the parking lot. I just need a moment."

She nodded and moved toward one of the lobby waiting chairs. One that, I noticed, faced the glass doors.

"Ahem." I indicated a seat facing the opposite direction, which she took without further protest.

"Go get him, tiger," she called over her shoulder.

I had no plan whatsoever. I only knew that whatever was between us, it wasn't going away. Whatever reasons and excuses we wanted to offer for why we shouldn't, whatever barriers he put up and whatever neuroses I needed to battle, whatever was between us was real.

I couldn't change the past. I couldn't alter my actions or his reaction to them, but I could damn sure stop pretending we were just friends and I was okay with that.

The doors slid open slowly, and I stepped through them. The cold night hit me instantly, the air sweeping over my exposed skin. I ignored it. I took long, deliberate steps toward him, never wavering. Mac rose slowly, a questioning look appearing on his face. I ignored that, too. I kept walking, one sure step after another, until the hundred feet that separated us disappeared.

"Aidan, I—" he began.

I didn't let him finish. Before I even came to a stop, I reached both hands to his face, feeling his rough cheeks beneath my fingers. I tugged gently, and he didn't fight me. He bent slightly and I met him, my body falling into his and my lips finding his own.

Our first kiss had been gentle, an exploration and query that barely hinted at the heat that could exist between us. This kiss was nothing like that.

This was a claiming. I used my lips and teeth and tongue to tell him I wanted him, that I could be his. I nipped at his bottom lip and ran my tongue against his, pulling him further into me, demanding. His surprise lasted only a moment before he met me in kind, wrapping his arms around me and pulling me against him. He lifted me off the ground until I stood on tiptoes, my face level with his.

He bit me back, then soothed the sting with his lips. We kissed with no slow finesse, no planned seduction. It was desperate and angry and possessive, both of us aware of how close we'd come to never having this moment. I threaded my fingers through his hair, holding him tightly. I needn't have worried. He was going nowhere. One arm wrapped around my waist, keeping me pressed against him, while the other slid under my shirt, his callused hand against the smooth skin of my back.

Everywhere he touched, he pressed me closer, until every inch of my body rested against his. I felt him everywhere. In my arms and legs, in my chest and core, I felt him, and warmth bloomed throughout my body, pulsing and hungry.

At last, we stopped using words to resolve our distance. We relied on lips and tongues and hands instead, telling long, timeless stories. With our bodies, we made fervent declarations and promises we'd not soon forget.

We broke apart reluctantly, and only a slowly-dawning awareness of our location kept us from undressing and continuing what we'd started on the hood of Sera's car. He moved his hands gently to my cheeks, holding me in place as I'd held him at first. We stared at each other, unable to look away while we found our breath again.

"In the future," I told him through heavy breaths, "I'm the one who decides when I'm ready to be kissing someone. Understood?"

"Understood." He spoke with mock solemnity, but he didn't fight the slow, unimaginably sexy smile spreading across his face.

"We still need to ride with Sera back to the cabin," I said, lest he was considering the same plan I was, which involved finding the nearest motel room, locking the door, and not reappearing for a week. He nodded.

"But I think it's time for you to take me home," I told him, thinking of the enormous bed in his Airstream trailer. If possible, his smile became even more devilish. He nodded again.

CHAPTER 16

There has never been a longer car ride. Road trips across the continental United States have taken less time than that single ride from South Lake Tahoe to the cabin. If possible, Mac might have grown in the time between our ride down and the one back. He now seemed to take up the entirety of the car, his presence expanding in every direction until I could think of nothing but his scent, his skin, the solid weight of his body against mine. Even the dangerous stretch of road where we'd had our accident failed to distract me for long.

Regardless of my parentage, most days I still felt partly human. Chalk it up to too many years believing I had a human father and my deep yearning to live a life beyond the elemental island on which I'd been raised. I still felt comfortable in the human world, despite what I now knew about my heritage.

At that moment, however, my perceived humanity was on holiday. All I felt was magic. It flew through my body and danced on my skin, charging everything it touched. It was strong and all-encompassing, and I feared my water side wasn't dominant enough to create such a powerful sensation of pure, unadulterated magic. Somewhere, deep in my rational brain, I felt a small voice attempt to assert itself, to warn me that something was off, that I was touching something unsafe.

I glanced toward Mac. He was in the front seat, so I could only see the back of his head and his shoulders, but that was enough. Even that sight called to me, their width and strength promising a safe haven. I couldn't lose that, not yet. I took a quick look within, checking for any wayward fire magic trying to sneak through, and I crammed everything I found in the deepest part of my core, imagining it trapped in a metal box with a thick padlock. It was all I knew to do.

Despite my fears and Sera's flat denials, everything I'd learned from Josiah and my mother, and from the actions of Brian and Trent, told me insanity was inevitable. If that's what my future held, then I was taking everything I could get while I still had the chance. Whatever happened, I would at least have this time with Mac.

So far, Sera had shown remarkable restraint. She'd given us the five minutes I'd asked for, plus a few more, and when she joined us, she'd somehow done so without comment. At one point, I thought I caught her humming a decidedly boom-chicka-wow-wow type melody, but when I met her eyes in the rearview mirror, she'd only offered me an innocent smile. Worryingly innocent.

The longer we drove, the more charged the silence became. I knew the others felt it too.

Finally, at the halfway mark, it was too much. "We need music," Sera announced. She leaned to her right, fumbling in the glove compartment while keeping her eyes on the road. The Mustang's stereo had received one upgrade in its life, to a radio-cassette player, and the glove compartment spilled over with cassettes you could no longer find anywhere but the deepest reaches of ebay. She pulled one tape after another from the mess, glanced at it and tossed it to the ground until she found the one she wanted.

The tape fell into place with a decisive click and she

promptly cranked up the volume. Sera did not believe music was good until it was destroying someone's eardrums.

She sat back in her seat, a satisfied smile on her face. A second later, the whine of electric guitars pierced the speakers and we were hit with the punk onslaught Sera so favored. It wasn't for me, but it was still a better option than awkward silence.

Then I realized which song she'd cued up. I met her eyes in the rearview mirror, trying to let her know with no words that I would kill her for this one, and I might even speed up my induction into the cult of the criminally insane just to bring that event about sooner.

She smiled back at me, this time with no attempt at innocence, while The Buzzcocks warned us of the perils of being an "Orgasm Addict."

IF THERE WAS one thing in this world I could count on, it was finding a dark sedan sitting in our driveway at the least opportune moment.

Mac saw the car at the same time I did. "No," he announced. "No, no, no."

While I appreciated that he was, for once, willing to join me in denial, his fierce rejection of their presence had little effect on the current reality. As Sera pulled her car to the far right side of the driveway, Carmichael and Johnson unfolded themselves from the front seat of their sedan.

"Damn," said Sera. "I forgot Carmichael was trying to reach us. With everything that's happened since yesterday, it completely slipped my mind. I'll try to distract him for you." I knew she meant it. She would tease me from now until the end of time about my love life, but she sure as hell wouldn't let anyone else interfere. She walked toward the agents with great purpose, fully intending to head them off at the pass.

I leaned forward, placing my head between the bucket seats so I could see his face. Mac was staring at the agents with an emotion weaker than hatred but still stronger than annoyance in his eyes. "Why is he always here?"

"That's rhetorical, right?"

He slid his eyes toward me. "All we need to do is run into those trees there. It's dark, they won't see a thing. We circle around, and we'll be at the trailer before they even know we're here. Far away from any and all overbearing pretty boy agents."

I was torn between the desire to do exactly as he suggested and the desire to mock. As usual, the lesser desire won out. "Why, Mr. MacMahon. I do believe you sound jealous." I batted my eyes at him for good measure.

"Why would I be jealous of them?" he said, almost sounding like he meant it. "What do they have to offer other than some well-tailored suits, expensive haircuts, years of education, and gainful employment?" He abruptly stopped speaking. I thought something had gone awry in the middle of that sentence.

There was a lot I could protest, but I began with the easiest to dispute. "You're gainfully employed," I argued.

"Construction work isn't exactly booming right now, Aidan," he told me.

"No, but you're on the ski patrol."

He snorted and then let out a short laugh. There was a joke here I was missing.

"How much time have you spent on ski slopes?" Mac asked.

"You mean, actually going down them while on skis? Exercising?" He knew how ridiculous that idea was.

"But you went to school with skiers. You know the basic body type, right? Several inches shorter than me and half as wide."

I thought I knew what he was telling me, but it didn't make any sense. Mac wasn't a liar.

"I'm not a skier, Aidan. Never have been. That's something Will and I came up with to tell people during the winter months."

"So, all those days you would head off to work, what were you doing, exactly?" I tried to keep the suspicion out of my voice.

"Napping," he said simply. "I was hibernating."

I stared at him, my jaw a full inch below its proper position. "You really are a freaking bear, aren't you?" He gave me an exasperated look I fully deserved.

"I work when the weather warms up, and pick up whatever odd jobs I can in winter. Mostly, though, I nap. I don't need to vanish for months at a time, but I do need to spend most of the day asleep."

"But this house. How do you afford it?" Real estate in Tahoe wasn't cheap, and a house like this, right on the river, was bound to be ridiculously expensive.

From the corner of my eye, I noticed Carmichael and Johnson watching us impatiently, likely wondering why we were still in the car. I didn't care in the slightest. They could wait.

"It was in my mom's family for years. I inherited it." He watched my face intently, as if he was looking for a sign that I regretted my earlier actions. "That's why I rent to Sera. It's the best way to make ends meet."

"So, just to be clear. I was about to sleep with a man who won't tell me his first name, who doesn't have a full-time job, and is a lazy bum who sleeps through several months of the year?"

He nodded, his face wary. "That's about right, yes."

I pointed to the trees he'd indicated a moment before. "So, race through there and meet at the trailer? Last one still wearing clothes loses."

I was out of the car in a heartbeat, but not before I saw the grin crawl across his face.

I made it two steps before I heard Carmichael calling my name. On the other side of the car, an undeniable growl emerged from Mac's throat, loud enough that I was certain the agents heard. "I think they saw us," I mock whispered to him and continued to head toward the trees.

"Aidan," called Carmichael again. I reluctantly turned around. He only called me by my first name when something was really wrong. "Would you mind telling me why, despite reports of a horrible accident involving a vehicle fitting the description of one your associate here drives, and despite reports that the lake actually tilted on its axis, all evidence of such events is being removed a second before Johnson or I can access it?"

"You're too slow?" Someday, Carmichael was going to smile at one of my jokes. Just not this day. "Look, the elementals and shifters have been hiding supernatural involvement for years. When it comes to discretion, we're all-stars while you guys, you're kind of on the bench."

Sera looked at me with equal parts amusement and shock. "I just used a sports metaphor, didn't I?" I shook my head, thoroughly ashamed of myself. "Anyway, one of ours has been doing some necessary clean-up work." I saw no reason to add that I was related to that person.

Sera's head snapped up as if she'd just remembered something important. "With everything going on, I forgot to tell you. He phoned this morning." She looked a bit embarrassed, as if worried I'd judge her for taking his calls. "There's no question someone tampered with the car. All the tires were rigged with small explosives."

Beside me, I felt Mac vibrate with anger. The agents had the opposite reaction, stilling until they resembled extremely serious wax figures.

"And it just happened to go off as we were crossing the most dangerous section of Emerald Bay Road?"

"There was a GPS device underneath the car. Whoever set it off knew exactly where we were." Her eyes met mine, and the anger I saw matched the rage rising in me. I squeezed my eyes tightly shut, forcing it back into my personal lock box. Several long, slow breaths later, I opened them to see Carmichael and Johnson staring at me with worry in their eyes.

"I feel like I'm always asking this when you're around, Ms. Brook, but what the hell is going on around here?"

I shook my head. "I really wish I knew. I only have a few pieces of the puzzle."

While we spoke, Mac separated from the group and returned to my car. He dropped easily to the ground and wiggled into position to view the tire well. When he emerged, he was carrying something dark and square in one of his hands. He chucked it in our direction before repeating the same procedure on Sera's Mustang.

I bent to pick it up gingerly. I might not be especially tech savvy these days, but I could still make an educated guess that I held a GPS tracker in my hand. As I studied it, the one attached to Sera's car landed at our feet.

The anger I'd tamped down a moment ago fought for release, and I was not alone. Sera was slowly losing herself, small spurts of fire popping from her body at random moments. Johnson merely looked at her in fascination, but at least Carmichael had the good sense to move out of range. Mac stepped into a thick grove of pine trees that ringed the house, and a series of loud crashing sounds followed.

Their loss of control, more than anything, drew me back to myself. Someone had to be the responsible one, and while I didn't want the job, it beat watching Sera light things on fire while Mac decimated our local forest on a tree-by-tree basis.

Unfortunately, that meant doing the responsible thing, which was figuring this freaking case out before another shifter disappeared or another car went sailing over a cliff. I cast one long, regretful look toward Mac, then said what needed saying. "All right then. You show us yours, we'll show you ours. Let's try putting this puzzle together."

ON DAYS THAT simply refuse to go the way they're supposed to, sometimes tea is the only possible solution. So far, this day had involved visiting a friend who lay broken in a hospital bed, hearing that same friend basically break up with me, learning that someone had tried to kill me, and coping with some painfully thwarted libidinal impulses.

This day might require the big mug.

I walked straight to the kitchen and put the kettle on, then dropped in a tea bag and waited, staring impatiently at the kettle. Behind me, I could hear the scrape of benches as the others settled at the rough trestle table in the dining area. "What do you want?" I called over my shoulder.

"Booze." Sera and Mac spoke in perfect unison. Smiling, I grabbed the tequila bottle for Sera and whiskey for Mac and carried both to the table, but not before adding a healthy dollop of the latter to my own mug. On days like this, even tea needed a bit of help to work its magic.

"Any more requests, you can help your own damn selves," I announced, plopping down on one of the benches. I deliberately sat away from Mac, fearing that even a soft brush of our thighs under the table would be too distracting.

Johnson stood abruptly and headed out the front door. He returned with a large roll of butcher paper, which he proceeded to unroll down the length of the table. He waved a thick marker around, looking for a taker. Sera grabbed it and pulled herself onto the table, crouching near the top. In strong block letters, she wrote "The Case of the Vanishing and Forgetful Shifters," then sat back, waiting for contributions.

"You just happen to carry butcher paper in the car?" I asked Johnson.

"I bought a new roll today," he explained. "I like to keep some in my office. It helps me to see things written out in full."

His words triggered a memory of sitting across the table while the former, serious version of this man thumbed through my private notebooks. I grumbled under my breath. He caught it, as I'd intended him to, and smiled at me apologetically. "I never did express regret for reading your journal, did I?"

"Nor for arresting me, I might note. Or Sera. When you think about it, it's really amazing we even talk to you, let alone allow you into our house."

Carmichael gestured expansively, encompassing the entire table in the movement. "But if we hadn't done that, we wouldn't be the big happy family we are now, would we?" Sera managed a derisive snort and began sketching in the corner. I could just make out the strong lines and exaggerated features of a caricature, and I suspected Carmichael was about to see an unflattering representation of himself. I figured it was best to interrupt her before she finished.

"Let's make a list of the involved parties." I looked at Mac, questioning, and he nodded in wordless agreement that the time for secrets was over. The GPS devices and exploding tire had made sure of that.

Sera stopped drawing long enough to write down the names and offer her own suggestions. "It's not that long, is it? Mainly Will and Carmen's families."

"I can't say I got any sort of teenaged criminal master-mind vibe from Dana," Mac said.

"Or Brandon," I agreed. "Not unless he's discovered some abduction-by-scowling method of which the FBI is unaware."

Carmichael cleared his throat, perhaps foolishly hoping to keep my brain more on track. "We should write them down anyways. There might be a connection we're missing."

"What do we know about the two women?" Johnson asked, pointing to Celeste and Eleanor's names.

"We know they're my family," Mac pointedly told him. He seemed to think that was answer enough.

"If we're including Dana, we have to at least consider them." I tried to keep my voice soothing, though the wry look he shot me made me think I'd crossed into condescending. I gave him an apologetic grin he seemed to accept, though he wasn't happy when Sera wrote "check out" next to their names.

"What about Carmen's ex-husbands?" asked Mac.

Sera paused in her work on the sketch to add their names. "They were rich and seemed to make marital decisions with their little head. We should probably look into it more." She wrote "alibi/motive?" next to their names.

Johnson flipped through his small notebook and began to recite. "Mark Avila is an environmental lobbyist in Sacramento. He attended California State University, Sacramento, where he earned a bachelor's degree in business. He met and married Carmen Hernandez eighteen years ago, divorced nine months later. Husband #2, Clay Reeves, owns a ski resort on the Nevada side. He has an MBA from Berkeley and has since moved onto his second wife, who appears to be younger and stupider than Carmen. Both men have solid alibis for the times the shifters went missing." Sera wrinkled her nose at him and silently crossed out "alibi."

"Is that it?" Mac sounded uncertain. It was a short list, and his family made up at least half of it.

"What about the Reno book club?" It was a stretch, but at the moment, stretches were still a better option than the near empty page currently facing us. Mac cast a questioning look my way, and I shrugged. With everything else going on, I'd forgotten to mention exactly where Sera and I had gone after we threw him off that day.

"You mean the people whose roof you climbed?" Carmichael was dubious. "What exactly are you accusing them of, beyond a desire for personal enrichment and possession of an easily accessible skylight?"

"We didn't like them," said Sera firmly, as if that should be enough to declare the matter settled.

The three men continued to look skeptical. They clearly were not taking my and Sera's gut instincts seriously enough. One little misdemeanor trespassing and you lose all credibility. "The homeowner had a big gun," I pointed out. Still nothing, since I was talking about someone in Reno. Big guns were considered a form of home decor. "One of them is related to Carmen, so if we're looking at her exes, it's only fair to look at the rest of the family."

They were starting to appear convinced, so I played my trump card. "And she hit me really damn hard," I finished.

That did the trick. Mac stared at me, and I didn't think it was worry I saw in his eyes. It was frustration that I hadn't told him sooner, combined with annoyance that someone as large as he should never hit a woman, no matter how much he might want to return the favor. "To be fair, I'd probably just said something tactless." The entire table snorted in unison.

"Add the Reno Book Club to the list. Innocent women don't often smack people in the face, even annoying trespassers," said Carmichael. Sera did so quickly, thrilled to include those women in our list of suspects.

"What are we really looking for here?" I asked. "A connection to the shifters? What about motive? Access?"

Carmichael shook his head. "Motive's a waste of time. There's no telling what goes on in someone's head. Go with facts. Evidence."

"Like the drugs." I was onto something. I knew it, and the others' interested faces told me they agreed. "We need to find out where they come from, which we've been trying to do, but we also need to figure out who's been buying syringes. Something is being done to them while they're missing. Maybe more drugs? Some sort of chemical lobotomy? We need to look into who might have access to that kind of equipment."

"Exactly," said Johnson. "We'll make an agent out of you yet." He smiled, but I noticed his eyes drifting over my shoulder toward Vivian's potted plants. He wasn't one hundred percent invested in his own agent work these days, I thought.

"Who else?" Sera asked, after writing "drugs" in capital letters, the straight line in the letter d forming a lit joint.

We sat in silence for a long minute, before Johnson finally spoke up. I think he'd been waiting to see if the rest of us shared his knowledge before spilling it. "There's the missing bobcat child."

Three heads snapped immediately toward him. Carmichael was in the loop, so he merely sat back and watched our reactions. "How do you know this?" Mac's voice wasn't exactly accusatory, but it was definitely a few notches past suspicious. The shifters were a tight-knit group, and if the abduction was common knowledge, he'd have heard about it by now.

Johnson met his gaze, his voice calm and level. He may only have the tiniest smidgen of earth blood, but he was as calm and grounded as any earth I'd ever met. "A mother took her eight-year-old son to the local playground. He disappeared, and her panicked reaction was quite public. For once, we were able to get to the scene before the shifters had a chance to hush it up. When we asked if the child was a shifter, the mother was distressed enough that she forgot to pretend she had no idea what we were talking about."

"Eight? That's so young." I forced myself not to think of the terrified young boy, wherever he might be. If the pattern held true, he'd be returned in a few days, worse for wear but alive. There was only one problem with that scenario. "It doesn't match the pattern. The others were in their teens."

"But the others were first-born," Sera noted. "Was he?"

Johnson nodded. "He's her only child."

"So, we're missing first-born children from the bears, mountain lions, and bobcat families," I summarized. "All predators. No, wait. Bears are omnivores, right? And mostly peaceful?" Let's hear it for Wikipedia, making me slightly less ignorant one day at a time.

"Yeah, but they're still the most dangerous animals in the area. Far more so than a bobcat. Any other common threads? Other than being shifters and first-born?" Sera looked around the table, looking for any possible explanation.

Mac shook his head, as clueless as the rest of us. "I'll talk to some of the other families tomorrow, see if they've lost anyone. Most of the non-predators are quieter and hard to find, and they avoid the bears and cats. Even shifters can be slaves to the circle of life. I know a few of them, though. I'll check with the marmots and otters, see what I can find."

"Marmots and otters?" I didn't mean to squeak that. I really didn't. "Those otters by the river, they were shifters?"

Mac ignored me, perhaps wisely. I might forget him in a heartbeat if I could hang out with otters on a regular basis.

"Focus, H2O," said Sera, despite the fact that she was working on a drawing that now claimed several feet of the paper. I looked closer, and realized it was us. All of us.

I stood dripping wet in a puddle of water, while Sera's hair crackled with flames. Mac was braced like a weight-lifter, the Airstream held proudly above his head. The two agents stood next to each other, a matched set of perfectly smooth suits and ties so tight they appeared to be cutting off their air. Simon leaned against a wall in human form, cool as could be, while his feline tail wrapped around Vivian's leg. And there was Vivian, tablet firmly in hand and four intact limbs. I could just make out "Missile Launch" written on the tablet screen and hoped the agents didn't think to question that too closely.

It was us, the way we should be, and yet we were falling apart.

"All this, it's barely a start." I ran both hands through my hair, tugging as I went. "It doesn't matter how many people go missing if we have no idea what's happening to them. We don't know why they're returning with their brains all messed up, why they have amnesia or are unable to shift. We have no idea why someone would ever want to do that, particularly another shifter. And we have no idea why we're involved enough that someone would want us dead, or even who in the car was the target. All of us? Just me or Sera or Mac?"

I stopped to catch my breath, but I wasn't done ranting. "You know what? I would really, really like to learn that answer, because I've had enough attempts on my and my friends' lives for one year. I'm pretty much over that. It's time we figure out what the hell's going on."

I spoke with authority, though it would have been more impressive if there were any answers to be found. Even so, we stayed up well into the night, swapping ideas, refining theories, trying to make sense of something that resolutely avoided a logical answer. Eventually, the liquor in the bottles dropped several inches, and everyone's eyelids were drooping and heavy. I glanced at Mac, and we both offered the other a weak, rueful smile, knowing we were both too worn out and exhausted to continue our earlier plans. Tonight would not be the night, after all.

Whoever he—or she—was, this kidnapper had a whole lot to answer for.

As the small hand of the clock crept toward the two, the agents finally decided they'd run out of ideas. They left, yawning the entire time, and Sera stumbled toward her bed, leaving the two of us alone. We stood a foot apart, preparing to go to our separate beds. Right now, I could think of no lonelier place than the warm queen-sized bed awaiting me upstairs, but I was simply too tired for tonight to be our first night together. "Tomorrow?" I asked.

He wrapped his hands around my waist and pulled me easily to him, placing a single soft kiss on my lips. "Tomorrow," he agreed, reluctantly disengaging. He moved to leave through the back door, but stopped abruptly, turning back to face me. "You know, you were right about one thing."

"Just the one?"

He smiled, slow and wicked. "You probably should know my first name before we sleep together." He leaned forward and placed his lips by my ear, so close I could feel the warmth of his breath, and he spoke a single word.

A moment later, he closed the back door behind him, leaving me standing alone in the room, an unabashedly dopey grin on my face.

CHAPTER 17

I awoke to a silent house the next day. Normally, Vivian's quiet rustlings pulled me from sleep, the everyday sounds of water rumbling through pipes or dresser drawers sliding open and closed. I'd hear her getting ready for her day at school and burrow into my cozy bed, appreciating the small joy of being warm, safe, and surrounded by people I loved.

That morning felt different. I slipped on my green robe and stepped lightly down the spiral staircase. Despite everything that had happened over the last few days, I half hoped to find Simon reclining in a sunbeam or Mac drinking his morning coffee, mystery novel firmly in hand. Instead, I found a profoundly quiet house. It was the kind of silence you only find in a truly empty space. The conscious mind can't explain it, but the subconscious picks up on the absence, the lack of even the tiniest movement or breath.

I knew I was alone, but I still padded quietly around the cabin. I opened the door to the downstairs master bedroom just a crack, to see Sera's bed rumpled and slept-in, but no Sera in sight. I crept back upstairs and opened Vivian's door, not sure what I expected to see. It was neat and organized, with only a little clutter on the desk from her computer odds and ends. Various Doctor Who action figures perched atop the monitors. A large spiral notebook sat open, as if she'd been interrupted in the middle of a project. It all looked like Vivian might return home any moment. I backed out slowly and closed the door.

Finally, I hauled myself up the ladder to the loft, though I knew Simon wouldn't have left the hospital. His space was as neat as Vivian's, though that was partly because he'd never unpacked from his earlier attempt to leave. His bag still sat on the twin bed. He might be planning to stay in Tahoe, but he didn't plan to remain with us. I barely resisted the urge to rip the bag open and hide all his clothes, thereby keeping him with us forever.

Giving up, I wandered downstairs and made some tea and buttered toast. When no one showed up by the time I'd finished eating, I took a quick shower and dressed for the day in a clean pair of jeans and a couple of layered knit tops, preparing myself for whatever weather the mountain chose to throw my way.

The air held a noticeable bite, and I wrapped my arms around myself during the short walk to Mac's trailer. Even outside, it remained quiet. The birds found little to sing about on such a cold morning, and the various forest critters had wisely chosen to hide until the weather consistently started to act like it was May. Snow was uncommon at this time of year but not unheard of. If the clouds overhead darkened any further, I suspected a spring snowstorm was on its way. I grumbled to myself and made a mental note to switch out my Converse for boots before I headed out for the day.

I banged on Mac's door, louder than I meant to. The silence was unnerving, and I found myself craving the comfort of another voice.

There was no answer. I knocked again, even louder this time. No one opened the door.

I glanced around the yard, checking for witnesses before

I brazenly entered Mac's house. The door swung open easily, but that wasn't unusual. I wasn't sure Mac ever locked it.

It was easy to see why. Mac's trailer held nothing of value. No electronics, no high-end decorations. All his furniture was bolted to the wall. I glanced around the room, figuring it only qualified as snooping if I opened any drawers or cabinets.

His kitchen counter was clear, the sink empty, and only salt and pepper shakers sat on the dining table. His closet was open a crack, but it was also empty. There were no hangers loaded with suits, no boxes stored at the bottom. Mac's comprehensive collection of jeans, white t-shirts and flannels didn't exactly need to be hung up.

The bedroom was equally empty, with just a dog-eared paperback resting on the desk, an old Dashiell Hammett. It was one I'd seen him reading before. I ran my fingers lightly over the well-loved cover, this single indication of his personality. I thought of the story he'd told me, of simply leaving his family and everything he'd ever known behind to start a new life. Glancing around the trailer, it looked like he was ready to do that all over again. If there was nothing he cared about, then there was nothing it would hurt to leave.

And yet, I knew he did care. He cared about other shifters. He cared about Sera, Vivian, and Simon. I'd seen it over and over again, in his warm eyes while we hung around the breakfast bar or stayed up late playing cards, chatting and teasing each other relentlessly. And I knew, beyond any shadow of a doubt, that he cared about me. How much, and how it might manifest in the future, I had no idea, but I knew he cared. I needed to believe he couldn't walk away from us without a backward glance.

The bed was neatly made, and I spared a brief thought

for how I'd hoped to spend this morning, waking up next to him in that king-sized bed. Perhaps I'd have opened my eyes to see him smiling at me, hatching wicked plans for how we could spend our morning.

As nice as the thought was, my general unease was more powerful than the image of rolling around with Mac. Everything was just too damned quiet—unnaturally so.

I spun around sharply and headed back to the house, ignoring the biting wind that whipped around me. In the kitchen, I headed straight to my phone, planning to call everyone and demand they return home immediately, preferably with hot chocolate in hand. My panic was brought to a screeching halt when I picked up my phone and found Sera's handwritten note stashed safely underneath. *Couldn't sleep. Gave up and decided to chase some bad guys. Talk later.*

She might have stopped using pronouns, but at least I felt a bit less like the only survivor in a zombie apocalypse. Everyone was fine. I was overreacting. I started to dial Sera from the land line, then promptly remembered her phone would also have been ruined during our unexpected swim in the lake. I had no way to contact Sera or Mac directly.

I wandered aimlessly for a few moments, but the silence of the cabin proved too much for me. I couldn't sit still for longer than a moment. I pulled out my journal and waited for that magic moment that always found me once I put pen to paper, the sense of clarity as the words spilled from my head onto carefully lined pages. It never came. I wrote one page, then another, and the words meant nothing. I didn't want to just sit around. I needed to do something.

We kept our spare keys lined up on hooks near the back door, and I noticed Sera's were missing. I grabbed the ones for the Chevy. My car might be a pile of junk, but it could definitely get me to Reno and back.

IT TOOK ME well over an hour to reach Diane's front door, a drive made immeasurably better by the absence of Sera's music. I used the time to zone out a bit and let The Devil Makes Three's cool vibe do its best to calm that morning's unexplained nerves. There were, I was certain, few moods an upright bass couldn't improve.

The first forty-five minutes of the drive were spent on the highway from Truckee to Reno. The final thirty minutes were spent driving aimlessly around the suburban development, turning from one identical cul-de-sac into the next and trying to find any characteristics that might distinguish one beige two-storied house from its neighbors. I finally recognized a tastefully painted satellite dish I'd had the opportunity to closely examine during our time on the roof. Unlike most of the other tastefully painted satellite dishes, this one was relatively close to the skylight.

When Diane opened the door, I relaxed, glad to have found the correct house. She, however, tensed visibly.

"What do you want?" She did her best to block the door completely, barring me entrance. This wasn't starting off well.

I pasted on my most winsome smile. She did not appear convinced. I held out my hands, palms up, the universal gesture for "I come in peace."

"I'm just here to talk. Calmly. Without guns or fists."

"And you thought to come to the front door this time? That is civil, indeed. Where's your fire friend?"

She knew, then. I assumed she must, despite being human. She'd been raised by a shifter family, and if she was at all like Carmen, she might know more about us than we knew about them.

The old ones felt no need to acknowledge the shifters' existence. Any strong elemental would find little to fear from a shifter, no matter how sharp the claws or rapid their movement. We had too many ways to defend ourselves and too many ways to heal.

Because elementals did not fear shifters, they did not respect them. Without respect, there was no reason to learn about them, to understand their ways or their motives. I wondered how many times that deliberate ignorance had bitten us on our collective asses.

The shifters were in a very different position. The elementals had placed them on the bottom of the magical totem pole and proceeded to sneer at them, to deny their close relation to our own magic and behaved, over and over again, as if shifters simply didn't matter. The shifters had good reason to know what we were, because we were the enemy. Everyone should know their enemies.

Diane might be human, but she saw my coloring and my build and knew I was a water, as she'd known Sera was a fire. I'd be a fool to underestimate her.

"It's just me this time," I said. "Can I come in for a few minutes? I would really like to talk to you. I'm sure we can both fake civility for a quarter of an hour."

She studied me, carefully looking for any threat. I thought calm, watery thoughts, making sure no anger lit my eyes, hardening them as they had at our first meeting. She tilted her head, still watching me. "I know why I don't like you. You skulk on my roof and spy on me and my family. What, exactly, have I done to you?"

"You did punch me in the face and threaten me with a firearm," I reminded her.

"Again, can I remind you of the spying on my family bit?"

She had a point. In the future, I should really only peep through the windows of families with no shifter blood and the kind of liberal politics that generally reject gun ownership. It would make my life much easier.

Diane watched me carefully, her eyes showing more agitation than she'd admit to feeling. She wasn't, I realized, just a version of Carmen without the shifter gene. She lacked Carmen's calm certainty and utter confidence. She'd been raised by cats, but she wasn't one, and I wondered how much that difference pained her. Everything she did was just a little too big, a little too showy. It felt like overcompensation, and I wondered how I'd missed that before.

"Start over?" I asked. I didn't hold out my hand, but neither did I attempt to threaten her with a ball of water. I considered that progress.

She nodded. We seemed to know where the other stood for the moment.

She turned, expected me to follow, and led me into a room that looked like the design love child of Ernest Hemingway and a deranged taxidermist. The color scheme was brown and blood red, the furniture was leather, and the overall theme was "Animal Zombie Apocalypse." On every wall, glassy eyes stared from the faces of surprised and quite dead deer. All herbivores, I noted. No cats or bears decorated the walls, so at least I wasn't looking at the dismembered heads of Mac's family.

"Are deers not shifters, then?"

"Of course they are," Diane said. She offered no further explanation. She sat in a dark red leather chair perched behind an immense mahogany desk.

Directly above her head, a rifle perched in its wall mount. I doubted the placement was accidental. The message was clear: if we were starting over, we were doing it on her terms. I resisted the urge to gather a ball of water, but only just.

Instead, I deliberately turned my back to her and perused the room's morbid decor, silently letting her know she wasn't that scary. I was feeling pretty cool until she spoke. "You realize I have absolutely no idea why you're here, right?"

It's a lot harder to be cool when the other person only finds you perplexing and odd.

I sat in one of the chairs facing the desk. Unable to find a convincing cover story to explain my presence, I opted to go with the truth.

"You know shifter kids are going missing and then being returned, right?"

She nodded slowly, her stare piercing. She may not be able to actually turn into a cat, but looking at her, I wondered if it was really so simple as Simon had explained to me once. He'd told me they either had the ability, or they didn't. Human, or shifter. Diane might not be able to turn into a furry, four-legged predator, but with her amber gaze so like Carmen's leveled directly at me, I had a hard time believing she entirely lacked feline DNA.

"I'm trying to figure out who's taking them, and I have few leads. You're one of the few shifter families I know."

"And?"

I shrugged, unwilling to say outright that I thought she might be involved. It must have been an articulate shrug, because she immediately understood.

"You're suggesting that, despite all evidence that you're an ignorant fool who only knows what my family is because Carmen chose to tell you, I'm a suspect simply because I come from a family of cats?"

When she put it like that, even I had to wonder what I was doing there. "Also, someone tried to kill me. Maybe."

"Just one person?" Her voice conveyed mild surprise that I didn't have several simultaneous hits out on my person, all of which carried sizable rewards.

"And here I was thinking you didn't like me that much and would be totally okay seeing me get crushed in a near-fatal car crash. How silly of me."

Diane leaned back in her chair and laced her fingers across her lean stomach.

"Did your mommy tell you how special you were? Did she say you were beautiful and everyone loved you and you could do anything you wanted to do? She must have, because I can't imagine why else you'd be so convinced it was all about you."

My mother had, in fact, told me that I should never really try to do much of anything, and should spend most of my life relaxing on the family island with her and my aunts. However, I doubted admitting to a life as a pampered trust fund baby would earn me any points with Diane.

I gritted my teeth and attempted to count to five. I made it to three. "I'm not accusing you. I'm trying to explain why I'm looking for answers any way I can get them. As for you, I still don't know what you would have done with that gun if Carmen hadn't pulled you off. So perhaps I have good reason to think you aren't one of the good guys."

She rolled her eyes so dramatically I'm pretty sure she got a good look at her own pituitary gland. "That was days ago. I'd have completely forgotten about it by now if you hadn't turned up at my door. And while I appreciate you ringing the bell this time, so far all you've done is question my moral fiber in my own house. You're making me wonder why I gave in to Carmen so easily."

She smiled widely, showing all her teeth. Even so, I didn't feel threatened. I was fairly certain she was posturing. Unfortunately, if she really was all bark and no bite, my reasons for being there were even flimsier than I'd originally thought.

I wasn't used to having the combative relationship I'd instantly developed with Carmen and her sister. These women riled me up, and I seemed to have the same effect on them. Whenever I was in their presence, I nearly felt like a cat myself, slowly circling them with hackles raised and claws extended. It was oddly satisfying, and yet it accomplished nothing.

"You're right. I have nothing to go on and no reason to think you're anything other than you appear to be." I said, speaking in a surprisingly calm tone. I was in the wrong, and I didn't see how denying that would help. "I'm trying to find answers, and I thought you might know something because of your connection to Pamela."

She studied me for a long moment, then released one long, deep sigh. I thought it was a bit overdramatic, but it did seem to indicate she'd stopped fighting me.

"What, exactly, do you think I know?"

"How close are you and Pamela? Did she confide in you?" Or perhaps ask for your help escaping with James? That last question might have been silent.

She held her hands before her, palms up. "She's my niece, but I can't say she ever had much need of a confidant. She's a popular girl with lots of friends, and her mother adores her. She had little need of someone else to talk to. Dana's the one who seeks me out. Let's just say she lacks the support network her sister enjoys."

This didn't surprise me. Everything about Dana suggested she neither sought nor received excess attention, though I doubted she was entirely okay with its lack. Everyone wanted to be noticed in some way, and I was glad she had at least one family member paying attention to her.

"Pamela never spoke to you about James? About how the families disapproved? I thought she might have trusted you, since you don't..." I awkwardly ended the sentence. I still understood so little about shifter etiquette, and I had no idea if I was poking a sore spot.

"Have whiskers? Hardly. If anything, it meant she'd

trust me less. Look, Aidan, we're family, and that means we'll always defend each other, but we're like any other family. We love each other, but we don't all get along or even like each other. And those who turn furry tend to believe those who don't can never really understand them. Maybe they're right." She didn't hide the bitterness in her voice, though I'd no idea if it came from her own lack of magical ability or the way the rest of the family treated her because of it.

"James and Pamela planned to run away, the night James was taken. Someone helped them with those plans."

Diane simply looked at me, her face open and questioning. She had no idea what I was talking about.

"I made a mistake coming here," I said, standing slowly. "I'm sorry. I really did think you might know something."

"You were hoping I was the bad guy and would confess," she corrected.

I shrugged. "It would have made my life a lot easier. Sure you won't do it anyway, just to simplify things?"

She laughed, though there was little humor in the sound. "I find myself torn. You're annoying and borderline incompetent, so I kind of hope you fail. At the same time, Pamela is my niece. I really do want to find out who took her."

She turned slightly, her gaze falling on the rifle on the wall. If there was anyone I wanted to get rid of in the next month or so, I suspected I only needed to tell Diane they were involved in Pamela's kidnapping, and they'd quickly disappear.

"I'll do whatever I can," I told her. "I'll see myself out." Before she could argue, I walked quickly from the room and through the house. It was, I realized, surprisingly homey. Away from the pristine living room we'd spied the other day and the animal rights' nightmare that was the study, the rest of the house was warm and even a bit cluttered.

In the hallway, I narrowly avoided stepping on a plastic yellow truck. Diane had children, I realized. Probably a husband. They must have been at school and work the times I'd visited. Diane was just another suburban woman who happened to be a card-carrying member of the NRA and spent the holidays with her shifter family. She didn't like me and had happily smacked me in the face, but if I was honest, I'd have wanted to do the same thing to someone caught crawling around on my roof. There really was no reason to distrust her.

I was ready to exonerate her. I had the door open and was ready to leave her and her family alone forever more, until I glanced at the shoe cupboard by the side of the door. It held all the family's footwear, sneakers and flip flops and men's hiking boots. A small pair of Mary Janes told me Diane had a daughter.

And, resting at the top of the stack, I saw a pair of comfortable, well-worn white shoes too large to be her daughter's and too small to be her husband's. They were the kind of shoes that belonged to only one profession, one that had access to the equipment that might have been used on the kidnapped teens.

Diane was a nurse.

CHAPTER 18

I wanted to sprint toward my car and immediately phone Sera, but neither of us had working cell phones. Instead, I walked with sure, steady steps across the wide, clean street. I opened the car door and climbed in slowly, and I waited a moment or two for the decrepit engine to warm up before I eased away from the curb and headed toward the entrance of the planned community. I followed the road away from the residential area, heading steadily toward the shopping district.

The sky was just starting to open up, dropping the light flakes that had been threatening all morning, though it was too warm for the snow to stick.

A large supermarket loomed before me, its enormous parking lot only partially filled at mid-morning. I drew into a compact spot tucked underneath a large maple whose leaves were just starting to return, far from all other shoppers. I turned the key, bringing the engine to a stuttering halt, made sure the windows were tightly closed, then proceeded to scream loudly while beating the steering wheel.

It wasn't anger. I was coming to know the difference in my own body, to feel the water magic I knew so well weaken and pull away as the fire claimed me. There was no such change this time, because it was frustration coursing through me, coupled with a healthy dose of self-loathing.

I'd believed her. I'd believed Diane was innocent, that

she couldn't be involved in these kidnappings. And no, a pair of white nursing shoes wasn't enough to convict her, but it sure as hell suggested she might not be entirely innocent.

I'd trusted Brian, too. I'd trusted my mother. I'd even trusted Josiah, as far as it was possible to trust an old one capable of destroying entire villages in a fit of pique. These were not people I'd ever expected to lie to me, and each one had, deliberately and repeatedly.

My mother and Brian had relied on my love for them, their belief that I would never closely examine their motivations. Diane was just relying on my gullible nature, my persistent desire to trust others and believe the best of them despite all evidence to the contrary.

I needed to toughen up. I'd spent the last several months surrounded by dead bodies and psychotic elementals, and now I was dealing with a mad scientist conducting experiments on shifter children. Believing the best of people wasn't an option anymore.

My fire side knew that. It had happily watched Brian burn, reveling in the death of a man I'd once loved. It was time for the rest of me to catch up.

I took a swig of water to soothe my raw throat and stepped from the car, heading toward a pay phone on the corner, one that miraculously even held a phone book. Tightening my coat against the chill, I fished several coins from my pocket and phoned the hospital, asking for Vivian's room.

Simon answered. He hadn't heard from anyone else, but he was able to provide an update on Vivian. She was stable, though she'd spent most of the morning asleep. Simon's voice was hesitant, the words heavy with exhaustion and concern, and he insisted she just needed to rest and be left alone for a few more days. I thought he might be trying to convince himself, as well.

I'd wanted to hear that a good night's sleep had revitalized her enough that she'd taken back her despairing words from the day before. I couldn't believe she would just walk away. Of course, that was the problem, wasn't it? She nearly hadn't walked away.

I arranged for flowers to be delivered, hoping a bunch of cheerful gerbera daisies said, "Sorry we almost got you killed again."

Next, I phoned the cabin. No one picked up, and each unanswered ring fed my anxiety. I left a message, telling them what I'd learned at Diane's, then hung up. There was nothing else I could do.

The concern I'd felt that morning threatened to overwhelm me, and I stubbornly beat it back. Sera might be small, but she was, almost literally, a walking firebomb. She could defend herself, and Mac wasn't some innocent shifter child. He was a grown man well aware of the current threats.

I was being silly, I insisted, and even a little paranoid. I needed to stop worrying about my friends who could defend themselves and start worrying about the shifter children who could not.

Even so, I didn't want to spend another hour out of contact with my friends. Across the street, I saw the bright logo of my cell phone service provider, and I crossed the road quickly, entering the pristine, warm shop. My purse was likely somewhere in the middle of Lake Tahoe by now, but I still had the cards connected to my trust fund. I'd been determined to avoid the temptation to use them, and so had kept them buried in a drawer for weeks now. For once, my stubbornness had worked in my favor.

As always, the American Express worked its magic. The store quickly arranged for a new phone with my old number.

While I waited, I weighed my options. There were still a few avenues we could explore. Mac was looking into the other shifters, and now we needed to research Diane's employment history. Beyond a basic internet search, I had no idea what that involved.

I felt a sudden pang at the loss of Vivian. She wasn't just a good friend. She was a vital member of our group. We might not have satin jackets with our names embroidered on the back—at least, not yet—but we were a team. They were my gang, the first one I'd ever really had.

With Vivian out of commission, Simon determined to remain at her bedside, and Sera and Mac incommunicado, I sharply felt the absence of those I'd grown to rely on.

I couldn't just sit and wait for my phone to ring. I supposed I could ask Josiah what he'd learned about Brian's Magic Deactivation cocktail, but that presumed I trusted a single word that came out of his mouth.

Someone knew about Brian's drug mixture and was using it on shifters. I had to assume that person knew Brian, and while Brian's work as a bartender ensured he had hundreds of acquaintances, I could maybe narrow it down through a Venn diagram of people he knew and our current list of suspects.

And the best way to figure out just who Brian had known was to hit the place where he'd spent most of his waking hours. Sure, it was barely noon, but it was time for a drink.

THE RAT TRAP was, without fear of exaggeration, the greatest dive bar in the history of the world. The fact that I'd spent most of my hours in that fine establishment a bit unsteady on my feet should not call that opinion into question. If anything, it should prove how truly awesome the place was, as I loved it despite the many hangovers I'd earned beneath its roof.

Located several hundred feet from the lake in Tahoe City, it had at one time been a classic dive bar, with a beat up jukebox in the corner, rickety wooden tables, and a scarred bar surrounded by stools with ripped faux leather upholstery.

In the 80s, the new owner decided that tiki bars were the wave of the future and introduced a tropical cocktail menu and a design scheme based on the Enchanted Tiki Room at Disneyland, all without removing any of the original decorations. Bamboo poles and snarling Tiki men were hung next to blinking neon beer signs, and piña coladas were served alongside generous glasses of bourbon.

When the Trap changed hands again in the 90s, the new owner displayed an unfortunate obsession with the indie film *Swingers* and installed a series of round booths covered in dark red vinyl, added a series of overpriced martinis to the drink menu, and filled the jukebox with rockabilly and swing music.

By the time Sera and I found our way through the door our third year of college, ownership had passed to Frank, a tiny and hirsute man in his forties who'd, remarkably, left well enough alone. He removed the designer martinis, but otherwise he was smart enough to realize he'd stumbled upon a charming sort of chaos that hipster bars around the country were desperately trying to replicate. He allowed the dive bar, tiki bar, and hipster swing bar to co-exist in unexpectedly perfect harmony.

Frank filled the jukebox with lesser known country and bluegrass from the past five decades to balance out the swing and classic rock left by the prior owners. If that hadn't been enough to earn my undying patronage, he'd also hired Christopher, the man who'd become my de facto big brother. He'd also hired Brian, the man who'd murdered Chris, but I couldn't fault Frank for that. Brian had fooled all of us.

The door closed behind me, shutting out the chill and leaving me in a different world. I stood in the doorway for a moment, letting my eyes adjust to the gloom and savoring the warmth.

A few die-hards ringed the bar, and a handful of college students filled a booth. I remembered those days and the glorious freedom of making our own rules for the first time in our lives. If we didn't have class and we wanted to go drinking, we damn well could, regardless of what the clock said. I didn't miss those carefree days—the party acquaintances I'd enjoyed in college had nothing on the friendships I now claimed—but I sometimes missed the easy certainty of being young and free of responsibility.

Even at noon, the place wasn't quiet. Loud drunken voices swapped stories, and the clacking of pool balls punctuated the music pouring from the jukebox. Whiskeytown sang "16 Days," a song that had been on the jukebox even before I left town. For a moment, I was convinced nothing had changed, and if I just stood there long enough, Chris would pop out with a big smile on his face, welcoming me back to town, and the last ten years would never have happened.

Instead, Frank looked up at me, and it was on his face that a slow, questioning smile appeared. "Aidan?" His uncertainty was damn near my undoing, and pulled me straight out of my reverie. I'd never seen Frank anything but confident and jovial, particularly when faced with a young woman. He was the sort of man for whom flirting was a joyous game, and he got away with it because everyone was in on the game, including his wife.

I hadn't planned to come back here. Sera was still a regular, and she'd been the one to tell Frank that Brian wouldn't be coming in again. Now that I was here, I was glad circumstances had led me through the door. The bar still felt like a tiny piece of home, the sort of place that could either solve or cause a whole slew of problems, depending on its mood at the time.

"Hey, Frank. It's been a while." It was weak, and I knew it, but too much time had passed for anything else. Frank nodded, seeming to understand. He might not know what had happened to Brian, but he was too sharp not to connect my sudden return to Chris's murder and Brian's disappearance. Sometimes, there's just too much to say, and it's better to gloss over it all.

Frank and I had never been close. I was a patron, and he was the charming bar owner who made everyone feel welcome. That meant caring about his customers while they were in the bar, but it also meant forgetting about them soon after they left his establishment. In a transient community like Tahoe, with a clientele prone to occasional binge drinking, it was probably best to maintain a certain amount of emotional distance.

Frank waved at one of the barstools, an expansive gesture that suggested he was offering me a seat on some treasured antique rather than on a bit of plastic. He grabbed a bottle and started pouring, not bothering to consult me. He still knew my drink, and a moment later he slid a glass full of whiskey toward me, lifting his own at the same time. "To old friends who magically appear out of nowhere, like the nymphs they so clearly are."

I sputtered on my drink and covered with an awkward coughing fit. Frank was just flirting, the way he did. Still, considering how poorly I'd been keeping the elementals' secret recently, he was hitting a little close for comfort. "How've you been, Frank?"

"Oh, you know. It's a good thing I always hear men get better with age, or else I'd just think I was getting old."

He paused for a moment, just long enough for my obligatory smile. "So, what brings you by after all this time, fair Aidan?" He was still upbeat, but his eyes were sharp, watching for the tiniest detail that might give away my purpose. Or maybe he was just wondering why the last ten years hadn't put a single line on my face.

"I understand Brian's gone missing," I said, telling the absolute truth. I did understand this. I also understood that he'd last been seen buried under the rubble that had once been my house, his spine broken and eyes vacant, but even I am sometimes capable of withholding information.

Worry scored Frank's rough features. "Yeah, Sera told me he'd taken off, but she didn't know where. He's never gone like this before, Aidan. He just vanished."

I looked down at the bar, letting my hair swing forward to cover my face. I hoped I looked overcome by concern, rather than like I was actively trying to hide my traitorous face.

Frank seemed convinced by my efforts, at least. "It's been a tough couple months around here, Aidan. I'm glad to see you, but I've gotta admit I'm wondering why you're here. Just felt like a midday drink, huh?"

I quickly found a story close enough to the truth that even my dubious acting talents might be able to pull it off. I tucked my hair behind my ears with one deliberately nervous gesture. "Brian... he was into some stuff." I left it open, giving Frank room to read into that what he wanted.

"This is a bar, Aidan. I imagine Brian was into a lot of things. He never caused any trouble though."

So much for keeping my face calm. The disconnect between Frank's words and the truth hit hard, and tears sprang to my eyes before I could stop them. "That's not true." The words were choked out, fighting their way past the lump forming in my throat.

Frank said nothing, but he filled up both our glasses. I took a moment to think of my car outside, and the need to remain sober enough to drive it, then decided that the drive home could wait.

I wrapped both hands carefully around the glass and pulled it to my lips, taking several long slow sips while I sculpted the truth into something Frank could handle. "He was giving drugs to girls." I met his eyes, letting him see the pain and the story behind my words. "At least, he gave them to me." Even as I spoke the words, a weight lifted from my shoulders.

I'd been trying to forget Brian's actions at my house, avoiding speaking of him in any way. I hadn't wanted to relive that day, and no one pushed me to talk about it. Once we returned to Tahoe, I'd only told the story once, letting Brian's uncle know that his nephew would not be returning. Stephen Grant heard a highly sanitized version, though—not the truth. I'd seen no reason for that good man to suffer with the knowledge of what his ward had become. The result was that I'd ended up protecting someone who deserved no protection. Maybe I couldn't tell the whole story, but I could damn sure tell part of it.

To my relief, Frank didn't look doubtful or angry. He wasn't a handsome man. He had a skinny build, heavy features, and eyebrows that put most mustaches to shame. He made up for it, though, with the permanent sparkle in his eyes and the way he had of looking at you as if you were the only woman in existence. With my words, that charm disappeared. He looked worn and empty, and when he finally met my eyes, he couldn't manage anything more than a dull, confused expression.

"You know how, whenever some calm suburban man goes around the bend, the neighbors talk about how nice and normal he seemed? It's kind of like that. I wish it wasn't the case, Frank. More than anything, I wish I could tell you something other than what I'm telling you."

He nodded, one terse nod, indicating I should go on.

"He held me against my will and drugged me. I'm okay," I said quickly, when I saw the heat rising in his face. "Nothing happened, but I had help. I think others are being drugged the way I was, and they need help, too."

"You want to know if I know anything about the drugs." He got right to the point. When you show up after not having seen someone in ten years, odds are good you want something.

"I don't think you know anything about the actual drugs," I clarified hastily. Frank might drink too much and smoke the occasional joint, and he definitely flirted with every woman who walked through the door, but that was as far as it ever went. "I thought you might know who Brian's been hanging out with the last couple months." I felt queasy speaking of Brian in the present tense, pretending he still lived.

Frank looked at the bottle, as if debating pouring himself a third drink, but he refrained. "I never saw him outside the bar, but he worked here for over a decade. I thought he was a nice guy, Aidan." I didn't point out that was what I'd told him he'd say. He needed time to get there.

His hand twitched several times, then he gave up and poured another drink. He topped mine off, though I'd yet to finish the second one. I was definitely going to need a taxi home. He leaned against the bar, his face heavy and weary. "You like to think you know someone."

"He was just your employee. He was my friend. I really should have known. I guess life is full of surprises, huh?"

Frank tapped his glass against mine, an ironic toast. "Ain't it just? I'm trying to think what to tell you. I don't remember much unusual going on. Brian served drinks to the college students and the locals. He poured strong and got big tips. He flirted with the women."

"He sounds like your mini-me," I said.

"But not as handsome, right?" Frank wasn't the sort to stay down for long.

"Of course not."

"You know, I did notice him hanging out a bit more with a woman I didn't know. She'd wait in that booth over there, the one closest to the back hallway. Pretty woman, though I only ever got a quick look at her. I might not even have noticed, except she was a redhead, and Brian had always shown a preference for blonds before." He tried hard not to give me a pointed look, and I did my best not to show how much being Brian's type had cost me.

I felt my heart jump. I'd only met one redhead during the last week. "Could you recognize her if you saw her again?"

Frank grinned, and the earlier weight all vanished from his shoulders. I didn't know if he was resilient or just really good at compartmentalization, but his grief about Brian already appeared to be a thing of the past. "Aidan, I may forget my anniversary, what I had for breakfast, and my own middle name, but I will never forget a pretty woman. Get me a picture, and I'll tell you if it was her."

I performed a quick image search on my new smart phone, but found no photos of Diane. Just my luck that our primary suspect was as averse to social media as I was. Even so, I felt an undeniable excitement and even happiness for the first time that day. I knew this was the answer. It was the only thing that made sense. She would have been an unexpected source of help to James and Pamela, she was a nurse, and she was a redhead. Still, it was best to be thorough.

"Was she...?" I held my hand off the floor, trying to indicate Diane's height. After two and a half drinks, my hand wavered somewhere between 5'5" and 6'. "With hair this long?" I put my hand to my shoulder.

Frank shook his head. "Don't remember seeing her stand up, and her hair was longer than that."

Of course, these meetings would have taken place weeks or even months ago, and Diane could have cut her hair since then. The pieces still fit.

At that moment, the jukebox shifted over, and Heart blasted through the speakers, Ann Wilson's powerful voice ripping through the room. Frank's head jerked up, something abruptly occurring to him. "You know how Brian always listened to that modern alternative shit? Boys in skinny jeans and girls with shaved heads. The sort of music I'll never let within a hundred feet of that juke-box?" I waited for him to continue. "I have no idea what this could possibly mean, but in the last couple months, he started putting on that Heart song all the time. 'Magic Man,' you know it? At least once a week, he'd play it. Just that one song, never anything else. Maybe he finally got some decent taste. No idea. But that's all I saw that was different."

A signal. I had absolutely no doubt that's what it was. Brian hated classic rock, but he'd had a twisted sense of humor, and he'd loved hiding his power in plain sight. He was telling someone else what he was—or what he had in stock. The drug that controlled magic.

I thanked him for his time and said my farewells, promising not to wait ten years before my next visit. I still needed to sober up, and I figured I should spend the next half hour or so down by the lake. I needed to recharge before calling the agents and suggesting they invite Diane into their interrogation room. After all, she was human. She belonged to them.

I made it one step toward the door before it opened, letting in a short, wild-haired fire elemental who, based upon her quickly concealed look of surprise, hadn't expected to find me here—and wasn't happy that she had.

"Felt like a drink?" I asked drily. We'd been doing a decent job of rebuilding our friendship, but we'd find ourselves experiencing a massive backslide if she wanted to pretend she wasn't avoiding me. I had enough people who claimed to love me but still opted not to tell me the truth.

Thankfully, Sera didn't pretend not to know what I was talking about. "I had a good reason."

I could only think of one thing that would cause Sera to risk our still delicate friendship. "If you're about to say you were protecting me, know that I will punch you." She said nothing, just stared at me. "Well?"

"I'm thinking of a way to phrase this so I won't get hit in the face."

I groaned, an exaggerated noise that involved a massive eye roll and a brief beseeching gesture directed in the general direction of the sky. I meant to play it as comedy, but it felt worryingly sincere. "What? What could it possibly be now?"

Rather than answer, Sera moved to the bar. "Hey, sexy. I'm gonna need a bottle, I think." She pulled her water-stained wallet from her jeans pocket and started counting bills.

Frank grinned at her. "Top or bottom?"

She returned the smile, suffusing it with a fair portion of naughtiness. "You know I always pick top, Frank."

He stretched onto his tiptoes, reaching for the top shelf liquor. "It's a good thing for you I'm married, Sera. Otherwise, I'd be forced to show you what you're missing, and I'd ruin you for all other men."

Sera kept the smile on her face, but something about it

felt forced. She was going through the motions, flirting the way Frank would expect, but her heart wasn't in it. "Then I'd just have to move on to women, wouldn't I?"

His laugh was big and boisterous, conceding that round of their game to Sera. She tilted her head in silent acknowledgement, then grabbed the bottle and returned to me. "I assume you were here to learn who Brian was hanging out with. You get what you need?"

"Yeah, I'm done. You know I don't like tequila, right?"

She looked at the bottle of silver Patron in her hand. "You're not drinking anymore. This is for me. I really don't want to have this conversation, and neither do you. And, for that reason, you are going to stay sober and in control for the foreseeable future, understand?"

I did understand, and her nervousness triggered my own. Whatever she was about to tell me, I knew it was going to be bad news.

I had no idea.

CHAPTER 19

T he snow was still lightly falling, and we walked through it in companionable silence. We headed toward the water, both obeying an unspoken desire to wait as long as possible before having this conversation. It was cold, but it didn't matter. We were elementals, and if we were going to have a difficult conversation, it would happen outside, in nature.

With the change in weather, the lake was mostly empty but for what looked like a few local hippies. When Sera pulled out the tequila, one of them gave her a thumbs up and looked like he might be considering joining us, at least until he caught Sera's expression. Her eyes were as hard and dark as iron. He scooted quickly away, leaving us alone.

"Put your feet in the water," she instructed me.

"What the hell's going on? Vivian's okay, right?" I'd just checked on her. I'd been told not to visit her, and I'd listened.

"Viv's fine. Feet, Ade."

Sera was completely and utterly freaking me out. "Simon?"

"Still by her bedside. Remove your fucking shoes or I will just throw you into the lake fully dressed." She wasn't joking. Whatever she had to tell me, this wasn't the time to push her.

"Like to see you try," I muttered, untying my laces. "You

do know you're the size of an Oompah Loompah, right?" The quips came out of habit, even as my brain was churning through options. Vivian was okay. Simon was okay. Sera was sitting right here. That only left one person. "No." I whispered the word, not even sure what I was denying.

Sera was done waiting for me. She yanked the boots off my feet and pulled off my socks, even as I continued to repeat, "No, no," over and over. She roughly rolled my jeans to my knee and thrust my feet into the water, letting the lake lap up to my calves.

"Reach out to it, damn it. I need you to connect your magic to the water. Only water, got it? That's the only magic you possess."

I nodded dumbly.

"Damn it, Aidan! No going catatonic right now. Repeat what I just said. Say it."

"The water is the only magic I possess." The words were dull, but as I spoke them, I felt the magic in my core reaching out, wrapping itself around the pure water of the lake. There was peace here, and my magic knew better than I did what I needed. It reached for that peace and delivered it to me, dulling the worst edges of my fear and paranoia. I was still terrified, and I couldn't decide if I wanted Sera to tell me what she knew or if I wanted to treasure these last few moments of ignorance, but at least I was in control of myself.

I knew that's why she brought me to the lake. More than anything, that told me something had gone very wrong. Sera had been watching me closely, ever since Oregon, but she'd never coddled me before.

"I'm okay." I stretched my legs out before me and burrowed my toes into the lake bottom, letting her see just how connected I was to the water. "Really. You need to tell me now, before I go insane from the waiting. And wouldn't that be ironic?" I managed a weak smile, which she didn't return.

"If you twitch in the slightest, if you even think about removing yourself from the lake, I will tackle you. Do not doubt that."

"Sera, I get it. You have sufficiently built suspense. Now will you just fucking tell me what happened?"

She took several deep breaths, followed by several long swigs from the bottle. Eventually, she met my eyes and held my gaze tightly, building a small, safe space where only the two of us existed. "Mac's missing."

"What?" I knew what she was saying, but my brain refused to construct a logical narrative from her words. "How do you know?"

"What I said in the note was true. I couldn't sleep. I had a question for him, so I knocked on his trailer early this morning. Normally, I'd just let a sleeping bear lie. I don't know why I chose this morning to visit him. But the trailer was empty. I waited, and he never showed."

"He could have been out running. He sometimes shifts in the mornings, I think. There are lots of other explanations. Maybe some hunter shot him. He could be hurt, Sera, and we're just sitting by the lake, drinking tequila? What the hell?"

I began to stand, and Sera lay a restraining hand on my arm. "What do you think I've been doing all morning, Aidan? I called Will first thing, and he'd scented the cabin before you even woke up. We've been tromping through the trees for hours, looking for any sign he was there. There's nothing. Ade, we have to assume Mac's been taken."

Thought completely abandoned me. All I felt was the warm, hungry power stirring to life, wanting an outlet. It wanted something to destroy.

I gave it more freedom than I ever should have. I let the

power stir through me, let the fiery magic expand through my body, reaching all the way through my fingers, stretching to my toes. It tingled and writhed, gleefully announcing its presence, and I felt the water struggle for dominance.

It wasn't an easy battle, and if I hadn't been in contact with the water, it was one I would have lost. Only the close proximity to the element I knew so well saved me—that, and the panicked look on Sera's face as I struggled against the violent instincts of the fire. They were instincts she knew well, and loved for her own sake, but she dreaded what they meant for me. We both knew that madness lay at the end of that path, and so, with a tremendous effort, I pulled myself back. I sought balance again.

It was not without cost. I felt my entire body shaking, the unrelenting shudders of someone fighting off hypothermia, wondering if they'd ever be warm again. The tremors ran from the top of my head to my feet, racking my entire body. My strength was depleting faster than I could recharge.

I submerged myself fully in the lake. When I got out, I'd feel the cold, but I was a long way from caring about that. I was just trying to get through each moment, one second at a time, and the only way I could do that was with the water's help.

I broke the surface and shook the water from my hair and face. "Is there a chance it was something else?" My voice was calm and deliberate. I actually didn't sound like a woman on the brink of going insane.

"There's always a chance," Sera said, but her doubtful tone let me know she didn't believe it. I didn't either. "He's not a child like the others."

"No, but he is a first-born." I lowered my head to the water until it brushed against my chin, then gave her an especially baleful look. "And you thought I wouldn't need a drink after hearing this news?"

She hesitantly held the tequila out to me. I wasn't sure she believed I was stable. I wasn't sure I believed it, either, but I supposed we had to work with the evidence in hand. For the moment, I was coping. Even so, I grabbed the bottle and took a swig, my grimace letting her know exactly what I thought of her choice of beverages.

"He was kidnapped."

She nodded. "It looks like, though I can't imagine who in this world is capable of taking down Mac. We've got to look on the bright side, though."

"When the hell did you become the Pollyanna of the bunch?"

"They've all been returned," she said. "They've all come back to us."

"With their brains scrambled, their memories missing, and unable to shift. You can be Pollyanna if you want, but it really doesn't suit you. I need to find him before he forgets I ever existed, and I know where to start. You with me?"

"Always." Sera grabbed the bottle back from me and replaced the cork, then stood slowly. "Lead the way, H2O. Let's find those mofos."

I walked out of the lake. With each step I took, snow clung to my wet clothes and skin, bringing a chill with it. It was welcome. I needed to be cold. I needed to be frozen, an emotional block of ice. Anything to keep me focused on our task, to avoid the bursts of pure rage that hovered at the edges of my consciousness. I had to be a bundle of absolute, deliberate will, and I had to direct that toward the search for the one man I thought I might love someday.

Because if I didn't find Mac, I feared I'd remain frozen forever.

FORTUNATELY, A FIRE only has to remain drunk as long as they want to. The moment she needed her brain to function at full capacity, she simply burned off the alcohol still in her system, leaving her completely sober and able to drive us back to Reno.

She offered to do the same for me, knowing my fire side would protect me from any burns, but I declined. I had a fast metabolism and another hour to sober up, and I'd prefer to spend that hour as numb as possible.

This time, we didn't climb the roof. We didn't even bother to ring the doorbell. We marched up the driveway and walked directly into the house. When Diane met us with that fucking shotgun in hand, I simply strode up to her and grabbed the barrel with both hands, yanking it from her.

She let it fall, quickly reassessing my threat potential and seeing that I was, in fact, more than some incompetent investigator. I was a pissed-off incompetent investigator, and that could make all the difference.

"I think we need to talk." Despite our dramatic entrance, Sera's words were calm and even, something I never expected from any fire and even less from her. She was going against her very nature, trying to keep the situation under control, or, more specifically, to keep me under control. She never forgot what I could become.

It was a noble effort. I rewarded her by not smacking Diane upside the head with her own gun, choosing instead to walk back to the door and prop it carefully in the hall closet. I felt considerably better having the shotgun removed from play, as a shell capable of blowing off a large chunk of our heads was one of the few things that no amount of magic could repair. Its absence quite firmly gave us the upper hand.

To prove that point, I gathered a large ball of water and let it hover near Diane's head. Sera rolled her eyes at my refusal to play calm and rational, but she also looked

relieved at how easily I summoned the water. If I was connected to my water side, the fire was fully in check. She
shrugged and called a fireball of her own, letting Diane
know exactly what she was dealing with.

"Isn't there a phrase appropriate to this situation, Aidan?"

I coolly surveyed the new scene. "I believe it's known as
turning the tables, Sera."

"I was thinking more that we were giving her a taste of
her own medicine."

"That works, too. I'm almost tempted to get the gun out
of the closet, just so I can point it at her and say she's been
hoisted by her own petard."

"You really want a valid excuse to use the word petard,
don't you?"

"Damn straight. There just aren't enough reasons to
refer to one's petard, are there?"

While we ran through our routine, Diane's face slowly
shifted. She was still wary, but the nerves she'd displayed
when we first threatened her with our elements evolved
into impatient exasperation. Sera and I did have that effect
on others.

"Just to be clear, are you here to kill me, threaten me,
or annoy me until I tell you whatever the hell you want to
know?"

"Still deciding." Whatever levity I'd managed to fake
while talking to Sera vanished the moment I spoke to
Diane directly. So long as there was any chance this woman
was involved in Mac's disappearance, I could not view her
as anything but my enemy, and my hard tone reflected that
belief. When she looked at me, her impatience morphed
back into unease, and I smiled to see it.

"Perhaps we should sit down," said Sera. "I'm sure we
can at least attempt to discuss this rationally."

It was Sera's voice, but the words coming out belonged

to someone else altogether. Sera was many things, but she was not cautious or restrained. For my benefit, for my safety, she was suppressing her natural instincts. For me, she was denying who she was. I wondered how long this had been happening without me even noticing.

In the midst of my panic about Mac, I felt a rush of pure, absolute love for my best friend. She was willing to lose a part of herself, the impulsive, outspoken, badass I knew and loved, if doing so would keep me sane a bit longer.

It wasn't a sacrifice I was willing to accept.

I took any rage I still felt and locked it tightly away. I was becoming worryingly good at compartmentalization, but so long as it allowed me to get through the day without setting anyone on fire, I would continue to do so. The occasional bout of emotional disconnection sure beat the alternative.

I joined the other two on the sofas, even as I continued to hold on to the water. So long as it hung in the air, it was a reminder that I was doing just fine, thank you very much. If I was visibly in control, Sera would have one less thing to worry about.

Especially since we really should be worrying about the woman sitting in front of us, her expression nervous and confused but not even a little bit guilty.

Since we were basically there to accuse her of being a nurse, perhaps she had good reason to look innocent. I opted for a direct approach. "You have access to medical supplies and other equipment," I stated.

She nodded, her expression cautious. She appeared to have no idea where I was going with this. "I'm a nurse, yes."

"So if, for example, shifters were being kidnapped and altered in some way—some medical way—you might be capable of providing the materials necessary for that to happen."

Her caution disappeared, replaced quickly by equal parts anger and exasperation. "I thought I'd cleared myself in your eyes. Is your short term memory really that bad?"

"That was before I saw your shoes."

She nodded, pretending to take my concern seriously. "Ah, yes, the smoking gun. Many a killer has been unmasked due to their choice of sensible footwear. If only I'd switched to sneakers, like so many nurses have, I'd have gotten away with it, too!" She ended her fake confession with an eye roll that would have done a teenager proud.

"It's not the shoes. It's the occupation. Whoever's doing this has access to medical equipment, and considering you work at the local hospital, that moves you to the top of our suspect list. So, if you want to keep us from harassing you on a daily basis, I suggest you explain exactly why you can't possibly be involved, and be really, really convincing."

She sat up and met our eyes directly, looking at Sera and me in turn. "The kidnapper messed with the brains, right? That's neuro. That's years of schooling, and no nurse would be able to do that. I'm an orthopedic nurse. I help set bones. I wouldn't even know where to begin with the other. And finally, I have no magic, no understanding of how your magic works, and no freaking motive. I have no idea why you two have become so fixated on me, but it's time to get a new hobby. I'm not the one."

I didn't bother to respond to her annoyingly logical defense. "Tell us about your meetings with Brian."

She looked between us, wanting more information. "Who?"

Her eyes didn't offer even a hint of recognition. She'd need to be a sociopath to lie so convincingly, and while that option wasn't off the table, I found myself, against my will, believing her.

I so desperately wanted her to have information, anything that would point us toward Mac, but her words made sense, and there was no hint of deception in her voice.

A family connection and a pair of white shoes weren't enough to indict her, even if it was more than anyone else seemed to have. She wasn't the only woman in Tahoe with red hair, and even brunettes and blondes had access to wig shops. Our lack of other options didn't automatically signal her guilt, and I feared she was right. We'd become fixated because she was all we had.

"Do you know of anyone else?" I asked, unable to just let it go. "Maybe someone who does work in neuro? They don't even need to be a doctor or nurse. It could just be someone who wanted access to the equipment, maybe for another person."

She began to shake her head. "No, the equipment is locked down pretty tight, so that seems unlikely. And I don't know—" She stopped speaking mid-sentence, her mind drifting somewhere unexpected. Sera met my gaze, certain Diane had just remembered something we really wanted to know.

"Tell us," she said, returning her black gaze to Diane's face, looking for any sign of prevarication or avoidance.

Before Diane could answer, my phone rang. I dug it out of my purse and saw Will's number on the screen. I could only think of one reason he'd be calling me, and I felt a surge of hope. I indicated to Sera that I needed to take it and left the room, knowing she wouldn't let Diane off the hook.

"We need you over here, Aidan," he said in greeting.

"Is he there?"

He paused, just for a moment, but that was enough. I felt my hope stutter and die, and something dark crawled into its place. The new feeling was hot and sharp, a panic that teetered on the edge of far more dangerous emotions. It was every emotion I'd been trying to avoid since Sera and I entered Diane's home, everything I didn't want Sera to see. I forced myself to listen to Will's words and pretended I didn't notice the heat creeping through my body.

"I just got a call from Celeste. It's your mother," he said. "Fiona was working with James, trying to find the barrier that's stopping him from shifting, to see if it was different from Pamela's. Something happened. She passed out. They can't revive her, Aidan. She's completely unresponsive."

"I'm on my way." The words were terse and direct, and I hung up the phone without noticing what I was doing. My mind was already several steps ahead, considering the many things that were going wrong and what they all had in common.

Shifters were being kidnapped, their memories erased and their magic blocked. A full-blooded elemental tried to fix it and now seemed to be in some sort of magic-induced coma. Confused teens and innocent children, my mother and the man at whose side I wanted to spend every cold night for the foreseeable future were all being affected, and the only leads I had were a dead former friend with access to drugs that blocked magic, his regular meetings with a redheaded woman, and a vague thought I'd just seen cross Diane's face.

At least I didn't need to wait to pursue one of those leads.

I knew the cost was high, but I didn't care. Mac was still missing, and now my mother was unconscious. Some things are worth the cost.

I sat directly before Diane, holding her gaze, and I let the fire loose. I knew that my grey eyes constantly shifted, as alive as the water that flowed through me, and they told every thought that crossed my mind. Now, I found the emotional core within and hardened it, turning my eyes to slate. I let my water side slip away without a fight and called on the fire to burn away all sympathy and kindness that might show in my eyes. At that moment, I didn't care how dangerous it was.

"You just remembered something." It was a statement of fact. I gave her no room to argue with me. Even so, she hesitated. "I'll make this simple. We're not playing that game where you pretend you don't know what I'm talking about, and eventually I find some threat or promise that convinces you to tell me what you know. Shifters are in danger. Something is wrong with my mother. You will do the right thing and tell us what you know, or I'll assume you're guilty and will have no compunction about slowly burning this house down. Perhaps I'll use your body as kindling."

Diane looked over my shoulder at Sera, perhaps hoping to see a bit more control on the face of the fire elemental. She assumed Sera would do the actual burning. She had no idea I could incinerate this entire block if I was so inclined. Right then, I felt very inclined.

"Ade." Sera spoke my name quietly, an attempt to ground me. She was still sacrificing herself, giving up her own anger to control mine. It was wrong. I knew I shouldn't let that happen, but I saw no solution. I couldn't stop the fire crawling through me. I didn't want to.

Sera rested one hand on my shoulder, trying to remind me of our connection, of my need for calm. Her words were even. "I can do this. Let it go. You don't need to do this to yourself." Diane looked between us quickly. Perhaps she was drawing conclusions no one should ever make. I found I didn't really care.

"And let you have all the fun? Hardly." I spoke the words with a small smile on my face. If one was going to become unhinged, one ought to do so in style. There aren't many times one has an excuse to play the villain.

Sera said my name again and placed herself at my side. I knew she was trying to distract me, but I refused to let her. I kept my eyes locked on Diane, watching the array of emotions that crossed her face when confronted with an unstable elemental.

Finally, she made the wise choice. "There's one thing, but I don't know what it means. I'm sure she's innocent, and there's no way I'm siccing the two of you on her until I've had a chance to talk to her. And for all that you're surprisingly good at this whole threatening thing, we both know that if you burn me, you'll never learn what I know. I need an hour. Two, tops."

I pretended to consider her offer. If I hadn't been lighting a houseplant on fire at the same time, I might have been more convincing. "No," I told her, my voice eerily calm. "This isn't a negotiation. Tell me what you know."

Sera pulled the fire to her, leaving the ficus burnt but unlit. "Aidan!" This time, she put the entire force of her personality into that single word, leaving behind the subdued, calm impostor I'd seen a moment ago. It was too late for calm.

Full-strength Sera was impossible to ignore, much as I might wish to. I whipped my head toward her, a snarl on my lips and a fireball already in my hands.

I flung the fire at her, a pointless exercise. If I'd been thinking logically, even a little bit, I'd have known that.

If I'd been thinking logically, I wouldn't have tried to burn my best friend.

But logic had already lost this battle. Diane needed to answer our questions, and nothing else mattered.

The fire hit Sera's body and was instantly absorbed, leaving nothing but a warm glow on her skin. "Stop this." The words were a command. Her black eyes tried to pull me into her, to hold me in her grasp and remind me who I was. She stared at me and tried to return my sanity through pure force of will.

She still saw the same woman she'd known for years, a water elemental and her best friend. The woman I was, most of the time.

Right now, I was not that woman. If I went looking for her, I imagined I could pull her to the surface and let her have control again, but that wasn't what I wanted. I wanted this power. I wanted this certainty. I wanted things to burn.

"I'll stop when she tells what she knows," I told her. It seemed a fair bargain. "So, you can help, or you can delay me and watch me set the room on fire. Your call."

Sera didn't show emotion the way other people did. Most of the time, she kept her vaguely sardonic mask firmly in place. A small twist of the mouth or a raised eyebrow spoke volumes.

At that moment, she was unable or unwilling to hide what roiled below the surface. Her normally impenetrable black eyes burned, lit by fierce emotions desperate for release. Her bronze skin glowed and her fire magic reached outwards, seeking an outlet.

I grinned, recognizing it. I stretched my own towards hers and let them mingle, her magic against mine. They were the same.

"I'm doing this because I need you to come back, Aidan. That is the only reason, and this discussion isn't even close to over." She didn't wait for me to reply, flinging a fireball of her own toward the ottoman.

It was a modern fabric, the kind that's been coated in flame retardant, and it was frustratingly slow to light. Sera focused all her energy on that flame, feeding life and magic into it. I joined my magic to hers, and the small flame instantly exploded toward the high ceiling, sizzling and crackling with eager life.

"How's your homeowner's insurance, Diane?" It was an idle question, the same way I'd ask her which cable provider she used. Perhaps unsurprisingly, she wasn't as calm.

"You insane... what are you doing?" I glanced toward her with raised eyebrows, feigning confusion, then lit the end table on fire. The wood was instantly alight. "Stop! Please, stop. I'll tell you."

"So, speak," I said, watching the bonfire on the ottoman swoop and dance through the large living room.

"Put it out first," Diane said, a desperate attempt to assert control.

I laughed, and eased the flames closer to the drapes. I used extravagant gestures, making sure Diane knew I was controlling it and was therefore the one she needed to satisfy.

"Fine. Look, if you hurt her, I will kill you both. I don't care how powerful you are. You'll still fall as easily as a deer."

"Is this the part where you're appeasing me, Diane? Because you may want to work on that a bit."

She dropped her head, ashamed. Not of her knowledge, but of her cowardice. Of fearing for her own safety enough that she was willing to share what she knew, despite its cost. "It's Dana, okay? She was asking a lot of questions about the hospital. She said she was interested in becoming a nurse, and I told her whatever she wanted to know."

I felt Sera instantly withdraw her magic. I grasped at it as it slid away, reluctant to let it go. It was so warm, so sustaining. Without it, everything seemed a little flatter, a two-dimensional painting in a three-dimensional world—a representation of reality, rather than the rich, vibrant truth.

"You too, Ade," she told me. I made a face at her, but some distant part of me knew I needed to keep my part of the bargain. It was still Sera, and while I would do anything for my mother and Mac, I would also do anything for her.

I slowly extinguished the fires. "I think you need to put them out," Sera said, her face fixed on mine.

"I did. The fire's out." I played dumb, not wanting to do what she asked. An embarrassing pout formed on my lips.

"You know how fire can hide in upholstery. Put it out, Ade." She kept using my name, insisting over and over again that I was still that same woman. I was Aidan. Aidan Brook. The daughter of an old one, possessor of one of the original surnames. I felt that woman within me, stirring. She was worn and battered, and more worried than I ever wanted to be, but she was in there.

Holding Sera's gaze, I finally freed her and let her float back to the surface. She stretched through my entire body, reaching to my fingertips and down through my legs, fitting herself back into each cell. The water magic gasped with relief, finding itself back in charge, and with almost no effort I was able to pull water from the air. The fire had eaten plenty of the water molecules, but the clouds outside hung heavy and low. The water came to me willingly.

I drenched the ottoman and the end table, and then I simply sat for a long minute, feeling the madness fade, much as a nightmare vanishes in the light of day. It may be gone, but a vague memory remains, a reminder of what lurks in the darkest depths of the subconscious.

Sera and Diane watched me the entire time, their eyes wary. I surprised them both by being almost reasonable. "Thank you. I'm sorry we had to do it this way, but we need to know everything that might help us. I promise, we won't burn Dana to a crisp or terrorize her too much. And if she's innocent—if you're both innocent—we'll replace your furniture. Ethan Allan okay?"

Diane nodded mutely, obviously not trusting the words of a walking, talking emotional roller coaster. I couldn't really blame her.

I stood slowly and headed toward the door, Sera directly

behind me. I knew she was studying me closely, looking for any sign I hadn't entirely returned, that part of my sanity had burned up along with Diane's living room set, and I knew I needed to find a solution to her worry before my best friend became my caretaker.

I had no idea what Sera saw. I felt like myself again, but that didn't mean I felt whole.

I turned in the doorway to look at Diane. She was hunched over, fear and grief on her face. She didn't want to be the sort of woman who'd rat out her niece. "We'll let you know what we learn," I told her, as gently as I could. "And after that, if all goes well, you'll never see us again."

She raised her face, and something new crossed it, something more than her fear and concern. It was calculating, and it held more than a bit of anger. Sera tensed beside me. She'd seen it, too.

"You controlled that fire," Diane said. "And the water. You have two elements."

There it was, the secret that could cost my life, spoken by a gun-crazy suburban deer hunter. She was not someone I'd have chosen to hold my life in her hands. "I suggest you keep it to yourself," I said. I could hear the exhaustion in my voice. "No one would believe you, anyway."

"Plus," added Sera, "if anyone finds out, I'll handcuff you inside your own gun cabinet and see how flammable your bullets are, one at a time. Look at me, and tell me if you think I'm lying."

Diane stared at Sera for a long time, looking for any sign that she didn't mean every word. Though I couldn't believe she would actually do what she was suggesting, Sera's face was cold and hard, as immoveable as I'd ever seen it. Finally, defeated, Diane looked away with a single nod. "Go," she said. "And never come back."

We went.

CHAPTER 20

Sera drove us west on 80, and for once we didn't argue about music. Without a word, she turned the dial to the Americana station I favored, apparently believing Alison Krauss would be more soothing than the Sex Pistols.

I tried to lose myself in the bluegrass, letting the fiddles wrap themselves around my agitated mind. Genuine peace might elude me, but I needed to find some approximation of that emotion. I closed my eyes and focused all my attention on the sound of a bow sliding across strings, blocking out thoughts of my mother, Mac, and my own actions at Diane's house.

There would be a price to pay. I knew that. I could already feel something within me shifting, the various parts of my magic repositioning themselves. Whatever I'd started, it wasn't over—but it wasn't time to face that. Not yet.

As we neared Truckee, Sera turned to me, face stoic and voice quiet. "Where are we going?"

I heard the question underneath. The shifters, including Mac, needed us to visit Dana first. I still couldn't believe she was our criminal mastermind, but it seemed likely she knew the person who was. I knew talking to Dana was our highest priority, if we considered the big picture.

But I couldn't see the big picture. All I saw, every time I closed my eyes, was an elegant woman with pale gold hair and eyes the same as mine, lying broken and damaged.

"I need to see her. I need to know she's..." My words drifted off, because nothing sounded quite right. I knew my mother wasn't okay. I doubted I'd instantly spot a way to save her. I wasn't sure I could do much of anything, other than be there, but I still had to do that one small thing.

Sera took the turnoff for Will's house without another word.

The only car in the driveway was Eleanor's Jeep. No one answered when we knocked, so we let ourselves in. The house was eerily silent. The downstairs was empty. The only sound was the stairs creaking as we headed to the second floor.

James's door was open a few inches, and we peeked inside. He was sleeping, but no aura of peace surrounded him. His breathing was ragged and uneven, and his feet twitched frantically. I'd seen animals do that many times during chase dreams. Wherever James's mind was, it wasn't anywhere human.

Celeste sat in the corner, watching every movement her son made. When I opened the door slightly she met my eyes, and tilted her head slightly to indicate the room next door. Though her eyes were dull and bleary, a more volatile expression lurked just below the surface, one loaded with anger and despair and several other emotions too complicated for a single word. It was the face of a mother in pain.

I nodded silently, acknowledging her presence and her grief, and left the room, closing the door behind me.

The guest room was next, and that door was wide open. I stepped inside, though Sera remained in the hallway, allowing me a moment of privacy. My mother slept in the queen-sized bed, a soft pillow beneath her head and a cheery yellow comforter pulled up to her shoulders.

Sleep was the wrong word. Sleep implied peacefulness

and rest, a temporary state from which one could easily emerge. Sleep left your spirit intact, and my mother was no longer whole. Her cheeks, a delicate pink even in the depths of winter, were now pale and waxy, frozen in a lax expression. Her fingers did not twitch, nor her eyelids flutter. I was used to her economy of movement—my mother was not prone to large, exuberant gestures—but even when she was still, life flowed from every pore. The woman before me had the same features as my mother, and yet I barely recognized her.

Tentatively, I sent my water magic looking for hers and was shocked to find nothing but empty space. It wasn't just that her magic was weaker, or hard to recognize. It didn't exist. The magic I so identified with my mother that I could use it to find her in a darkened room had simply vanished. She might as well have been human.

She must have found whatever was blocking James. If her magic had touched it, if she'd wrapped it around the blockage and tried to pull it toward herself in an effort to heal the boy, that could have been enough to steal her own power.

I had no idea what happened to elementals who lost their magic. I'd never heard of it happening before. As far as I knew, it wasn't even possible, no more than it was possible for shifters to lose theirs.

Brian hadn't known it, but he might have invented a weapon capable of destroying the magical races—and we still had no idea who controlled it.

I stared at her, fighting the sudden panic that rushed through me. I had absolutely no idea what to do.

For most of my life—the first fifty years of it, in fact—this had been the woman who fixed things. She was the one that held the family together, the rock among her flightier sisters. She could be demanding and manipulative, but find me an old one who wasn't that way on occasion. Most of the time, she'd simply been my mother, the woman whose quiet, competent presence gave me hope that everything would be okay.

I'd been so angry at her for one error of judgment that I'd forgotten all the rest. And while it may have been one whopping error in judgment, I knew she'd done it for the reason she'd done everything else over the course of my life: to protect me. She was my mommy, after all, and without her here to tell me what I should do, I had absolutely no idea how to make this better. I didn't know how to fix a single damn thing.

"She's stable." I looked up sharply, surprised to hear another voice. Eleanor sat by my mother's side, holding her hand lightly. I'd been so fixed on my mother when I entered the room that I hadn't even seen her. "Will's meeting with a shifter doctor at the hospital, arranging for another IV and respirator, just in case she doesn't come out in a day or two."

I nodded my head, acknowledging that I heard, though there seemed to be no response I could make. I wasn't sure how to deal with the wave of panic coursing through me, and I thought shutting down might be the best option.

From the doorway, Sera asked, "What happened?"

Things like that still mattered, didn't they? I had places to go, people to save. I had to delay my nervous breakdown for a more convenient time. I thought of my mother, the most emotionally controlled full water I'd ever met, and knew that's what she would do. That's how she'd begin fixing things.

It took a colossal effort of will, but I drew myself back from the brink. I still felt the panic and desperation creeping around the edges of my mind, calling to me. Those emotions weren't going anywhere, not while my mother was in this state and Mac was missing, but I erected a firm barrier, letting them know they weren't welcome right now.

I suspected that if I couldn't save my mom and Mac, I'd be letting those feelings in for a very long party, but I wasn't there yet.

With that, my focus returned, laser sharp and determined. I'd missed the first part of Eleanor's explanation, but snapped to attention for the rest. "Based on what she'd learned from Pamela, she wanted to see if James had the same altered neurology. No one was in the room with her, so we don't know what happened. Celeste and I were downstairs, and the first we knew something was wrong was when we heard her body hit the floor. She's been out ever since. That's all I know." She looked at me, apologetic, but I had no interest. If she wasn't of use to me, if she wasn't able to help, she might as well not exist. Laser focus may not be the way to make friends, but it damn sure got the job done.

"How long was she with James?"

"An hour, tops." Eleanor's tone suggested that wasn't long, but I knew better. If she'd been replicating the procedure she'd done on Pamela and Carmen, she should have been in and out in ten minutes. The earlier procedure had barely taken twenty, and she'd known what she was looking for the second time. Something had gone wrong.

"And no one was with her?" I heard my own voice, sharp and accusatory, but I couldn't be bothered to temper my anger.

"It's not like we could help," she said. "We had no idea what she was doing."

"He's your nephew. Celeste's son." I bit the words off. "I thought you might be interested in seeing if she was successful." No, I definitely wasn't making friends this day.

She didn't fight me, but neither did she meet my eyes. I

realized that, for all her efforts to escape her life and build a new one, Eleanor was weak. I'd been around so many strong-willed people lately that I'd forgotten that many people preferred for others to be in charge. My mother had told her she could handle it, and the two women had let her. End of story, almost. "Where was Will?"

She continued to stare at a spot on the bed, and I had the distinct sense she was eager for this conversation to end. "He wasn't here. I don't know where he was, honestly. It was something to do with Mac. He only showed up a few minutes after..." Her voice slipped away, unwilling to finish that sentence. After my mother had slipped into a coma.

"Will you call me if anything changes?"

Eleanor nodded. "Of course. Leave your number with me."

We only stayed for a few more minutes. There was nothing I could do. Three more times, I reached out to my mother, looking for even the smallest residue of magic, but each time I found nothing. She looked so still, so piti-fully small and weak. I brushed her hair back and tucked it behind her delicate ears, then kissed her forehead. I held the kiss for a long time, feeling her unnaturally cool skin beneath my lips.

"You better come back," I told her. "You always wanted the best for me, and while I don't always agree with your methods, forcing me to live thousands of years without the chance to forgive you doesn't qualify as 'best.' So don't you dare think of calling it quits."

I walked out of the room and down the stairs without a backwards glance. I heard Sera behind me, walking quickly to keep up as I headed directly to the front door. Will was just turning off his engine, and I shook my head at him. "Don't even unbuckle the seat belt." I spoke loud enough to be heard through the glass. "You're driving us to Carmen's."

He and Sera both looked surprised, but they didn't argue. I swung myself into the passenger seat of the Explorer as Sera crawled into the back. Earlier, I'd planned on talking to Dana in a calm, thoughtful manner, the sort of conversation that wouldn't trigger any pyromaniac impulses.

That was before I'd seen my mother and realized everything awful right now was the fault of one person we desperately needed to find. Pamela and James's inability to shift. The kidnapped shifter children. Mac going missing. And now my mother, in a coma and missing the very magic that defined her. I was done messing around, and Dana was our only link to this bastard.

I smiled. "Let's go terrorize a teenager."

By the time we arrived, full night had fallen over Tahoe, the stars still obscured by the clouds coating the night sky. The snow had ceased falling, though a quiet stillness lingered over the neighborhood, a sense of people curled up in their warm living rooms, enjoying this last wintry night before spring reasserted itself.

Carmen's house was silent. No cars sat in the driveway, and there was no visible movement in any of the front rooms. The illusion of stillness was shattered the moment we rang the doorbell and the resident canine sounded the alarm, letting everyone know he was ready and willing to defend his people, even if his people did have the poor sense to turn into cats.

The voice urging the dog to shush was gentle and soft. Not Carmen, then. The door opened slowly, and Dana's face stared out at us. She took in the three of us, and her eyes grew round and scared when she saw Will standing behind us. She knew Will, and she should have known she had nothing to fear from him if she was entirely innocent.

Something else caused that look of panic.

Surprisingly, her expression quickly gave way to relief.

"I know why you're here," she said, opening the door wider. We stepped inside, causing the corgi to shake and sneeze with joy at the possible new playmates. He dashed from the room and returned with a toy clenched firmly in his jaws. The poor thing really couldn't read the mood of the room. "Or maybe you're here for something else. It doesn't matter. There's something you need to know."

"I don't understand, Dana." She met my gaze directly. Tears hovered on her lashes, but they remained unshed. She wasn't about to descend into useless sobbing or otherwise avoid my questions. I felt my first glimmer of hope that we might actually get our answers without sending a teenage girl into years of therapy. "If you knew something, anything, why didn't you speak up?"

When I'd first met Dana, I'd seen the woman she would someday become, once she settled into her adult skin and found the barest measure of confidence. Now, I saw the child she'd once been. Her emotions caused her cheeks to turn pinker, and her lips were soft and loose. Whatever she'd done, I couldn't believe it had been malicious.

"I did it. It's my fault." Then again, I'd been wrong before.

I knew Will would be happy to dismember whoever had hurt his son, but he looked at Dana with more confusion than actual rage. He took her elbow and led her to the living room, urging her onto the sofa. She didn't fight him, but sank deeply into the overstuffed couch, as if happy to drown herself in the yards of brown leather. The small dog sat quietly at her feet, having reluctantly admitted we weren't there to play with him, though still hopeful we'd change our minds at some point.

This was my second time in Carmen's living room, but

I hadn't paid close attention before. When I took a second look, I saw no evidence of Carmen's personality or history anywhere in the room. No throw pillows or well-maintained family heirlooms, no crocheted afghans or framed family photos. Rather, it looked like she'd walked into a mid-range furniture store during their President's Day sale and bought whatever set would fit in the room. It was bland and forgettable, the furniture of someone who really didn't care what her home looked like. I recognized the decorative artwork and various knick-knacks from a recent trip to a big box store, seemingly bought to fill an empty wall rather than imbue the house with a sense of its owner's personality.

"This isn't her home," said Dana, following my train of thought. Her voice was matter of fact and utterly lacking in self-pity. "Not really. She stays here most nights, but her home is out there." She waved one hand toward the window, where the lush greenery of the Tahoe National Forest was visible, the thick growth of trees extending for miles.

I wasn't sure how to respond to a daughter admitting that her mother lived a completely separate life. I had plenty of issues with my own mother, but lack of attention had never been one of them. Hell, I'd needed to move a thousand miles away to get some freedom. I suspected Dana rarely had to go further than her own bedroom.

I tried to hide my pity, but wasn't successful. "It's not that bad," she said. "Mom and Pamela have their thing, but I'm daddy's girl. I still get to see him most weekends." I didn't think she was trying to convince me. It sounded like she needed to convince herself.

Sera studied a small cat figurine sitting on the mantle. "Where's Carmen now?" She walked around the room, excess energy pouring from her. She casually picked up one object after another, setting them all down in a slightly different place. Candles, remote controls, magazines, all found themselves moved a couple inches for absolutely no reason other than Sera's inability to sit still.

"She's with Pamela. She's hoping that being in the forest will remind her who she is and convince her to shift." The words were layered, filled with a depth of emotion I struggled to identify. Concern dominated, but threaded through her fear was resentment and guilt.

It was a volatile emotional stew, and it reminded me that despite her seeming softness and gentle spirit, this was a teenage girl sitting before me. I might have spent my own teen years on an isolated island, but if pop culture and its slew of teen movies had taught me anything, it was that teen girls were capable of just about anything.

Sera seemed to have the same thought. She stopped pacing directly in front of Dana, her jittery movements ceasing immediately.

Dana recognized the moment the getting-to-know-you portion of the proceedings ended. "What do you need to know?"

Will sat beside her, effectively blocking her in, but somehow his large, warm presence calmed the girl, offering comfort and security. I wondered if that gene ran in the family. Mac always had the same effect on me.

"Just tell us what you did, Dana. It's okay. We've all made mistakes." He even had the same warm, gentle voice. If this was a family trait, maybe there was hope for Brandon yet.

Dana met his eyes. Hers were also brown, though not the golden tone of her mother and sister. They were a dark brown, nearly the same shade as Will's, and they latched onto his eagerly.

As she spoke, she watched Will carefully, looking for any sign of anger or recrimination. He offered neither, but he also didn't offer forgiveness. Once I heard her story, I wasn't sure she deserved it.

"I didn't know, not at first. She said she wanted to go back to work, and she was interested in a local nursing program, so I should ask Aunt Diane about the hospital where she works. Just general stuff, you know. What it was like, how busy, how crowded, that sort of thing. I told her I could introduce her, and she could ask the questions herself, but she said she didn't want to be a bother."

None of us missed her consistent use of vague pronouns. Sera raised one sharp eyebrow. "Nothing about that seemed odd to you? An adult asking a teenager to do her research for her?"

Dana's eyes slid toward Sera, hearing the dubious tone in her voice. "Maybe. I don't know. It just felt good to be useful. To be wanted for something." Again, she spoke in that direct, even tone, like her belief in her mother's neglect was a fact of life rather than a wound that cut to her core.

"Go on," urged Will. He brought her gaze back to his. Sera flopped down on one of the armchairs, expelling her breath in a heavy sigh. This interrogation obviously wasn't moving fast enough for her.

"Patience, grasshopper," I muttered, a quiet aside, and was rewarded by one expressive finger. It might have been completely inappropriate to rib each other at that moment, but sometimes it seemed such behavior was coded in our DNA.

"Aunt Diane gave me all the information. I think she was just happy someone in the family was interested. She's kind of like me. More guns, sure, but she grew up like I did."

"You mean she was human in a family of shifters," I clarified.

She nodded. "She gets it. Maybe she thought I wanted

to follow in her footsteps or something. Make a career of being useful, of being wanted." That time a note of bitterness definitely crept in.

I thought back to Carmen's intense protective instincts. It might be easier for Carmen to relate to her shifter child, but I couldn't believe she loved Dana any less. I suspected this family was in desperate need of some family counseling—not that anyone in the Brook-Blais clan was in any position to offer advice on family drama.

I tried to let Dana tell the story in her own way, giving her the time to explain her actions, if not justify them, but she seemed in no hurry to get to the point. I was beginning to feel every bit as antsy as Sera and knew I needed to speed things up. I couldn't have a repeat of what happened in Reno. "When did the questions turn to medical techniques for scrambling shifters' brains, Dana?"

"Nice. Can I brag to Carmichael about your top-notch interrogation skills?" Without taking my eyes off Dana, I returned Sera's earlier finger to her.

Of course, when Dana immediately tensed and started babbling nonsensically, I had to admit Sera might have a point. "It wasn't like that! I didn't know that's what would happen. If I'd had any idea, I never would have... I just wouldn't. I love my sister, I do, and James is—" She abruptly stopped speaking, and I knew my original instincts had been correct. Whether he knew it or not, she saw James as something other than her sister's boyfriend.

Will cast a single, exasperated look my way, then turned back to Dana. He didn't pursue the comment about James, letting the unspoken words hang in the air. "We want to understand. Tell us what it was like."

"She said she just needed information. Where to get certain equipment, some medications. She said it wouldn't hurt them."

"Did you know what she was planning on using the equipment for, Dana?" Will's voice was still warm and calm, but I saw his hand clench into a fist and press hard against his thigh. He was fighting for his own control.

Despite the tension that coiled through the room, I think we all expected her to shake her head, to claim innocence of her unknown partner's motives. We'd never truly believed Dana was anything other than an unwitting patsy, and our chief goal was to find out who this mysterious "she" was. And so, when Dana nodded, slowly but deliberately, and finally let the tears she'd been holding fall, we were all too shocked to speak.

"I knew. I asked her why she wanted this stuff, because by now I knew it had nothing to do with a nursing program. And she told me. She thought she'd found a way to reverse the gene, but it wasn't the kind of experiment where you can apply for a grant or run it through some corporation's lab. She needed to learn where the hospital kept the equipment she couldn't just order directly. So I visited a couple times with Aunt Diane, and I paid attention to the security measures, and I told her what to do. How to get in the hospital and get what she needed."

She stopped speaking, her tears already drying up.

"Why would you do such a thing, little cat?"

Her eyes flared, the dark brown instantly alive, full of emotions she rarely spoke. "Cause I'm not a cat, am I? Never have been, and they'll never let me forget it. All their late nights in the woods. Hunting, they say. Can't have helpless little Dana along. And dad off in the city, selling stupid pharmaceuticals to support some big corporation, and forgetting I need support seven days a week, not just the two that he feels like showing up. Sometimes, I'm not sure they even know I exist."

My heart ached at the depths of her loneliness and her

absolute certainty of her isolation. I wasn't sure it was as terrible as she thought it was—there's something about being a teenager that amplifies every alienated feeling one could possibly have—but it was clear she believed her words were absolutely, painfully true. She thought she was alone and unloved. She'd attempted to change that state, and those actions had led to an unspeakable series of events.

I knew guilt weighed heavily on her. As she continued to speak, her words contained both self-loathing for her actions and the desperate longing that had led her to them.

"She said she wouldn't hurt them, but she needed subjects to see how the drugs worked. She said that, worst case scenario, the shifter metabolism would just power through them and they'd be fine in a couple days. No harm, no foul. But if everything worked the way she thought it would, they'd be human. They wouldn't be shifters anymore."

"And this was a choice you thought to make for them?" This time, Will's voice definitely lacked the warm and comforting tone he'd used earlier. As I watched, a small trickle of blood escaped from his clenched fist. He was doing his best to hide it, but he was fighting the shift, his claws starting to elongate.

Dana shook her head, miserable. "I thought then Pamela would be like me. She wouldn't be mom's favorite anymore. We'd all just be equal. And maybe, if we were all human, me and Pamela and James, things would be different."

She didn't specify just how things would be different, but I crept inside the head of a lonely, insecure fourteen-year-old, and I thought I understood. As long as she was human and Pamela was a shifter, he'd always choose Pamela. Maybe, if Pamela was just another girl, he'd finally see all Dana's human charms that he'd previously overlooked.

It was the sort of dramatic, impossible fantasy many

people told themselves but rarely acted upon. Somehow, Dana had come to believe the problem with her life was her humanity, and once she evened the playing field, all her problems would resolve themselves.

She wouldn't look at any of us. She fixed her eyes on her knee, showing through a small tear in her jeans. She plucked at the torn threads, a pointless distraction that, for just a moment, delayed the need to face what she'd done.

Her actions were horrible, her logic more so. And someone, I was certain, had helped her get there. Someone had fed her fears, adding kindling to the fire that always burned deep within, that certainty that she was second best in her mom's heart, invisible to boys, unimportant, unnecessary. The fire that said Pamela ruined everything, and everything would be better if she were more like Dana.

Someone convinced Dana not to come forward when blood had been found outside her window, told her that Pamela was just fine, and to wait. And when Pamela and James had been returned, their minds and magic ruined, someone told Dana that it was too late to speak up, and if she did, she'd be blamed. She'd lose the little bit of love she could still claim as her own.

And because Dana was still just fourteen, and scared, and lonely, she'd agreed to stay quiet.

"Who was it, Dana? Who did this?" She met my gaze for the first time since she began telling her story.

Her eyes were clear and dry, and for once they were devoid of uncertainty. I think she knew this was the only way she could start making things right again, or maybe she just didn't care who knew anymore. She rested her hand lightly on the dog's neck, seeking comfort in its warmth and unchanging adoration.

Quietly, unable to meet Will's eyes, Dana spoke a single name.

CHAPTER 21

Sera didn't even speak. She simply held her hand out, and Will dropped the keys in her palm. I guessed he'd heard about her driving skills from Mac. Will's house wasn't far, but at this point teleportation wouldn't have been fast enough. Besides, Will still looked shellshocked, too lost in his own thoughts to see the road directly in front of him.

"Who do we tell?" I asked from the back seat, phone already in hand.

Will didn't answer. His own phone was pressed to his ear, and by his conversation I gathered it was Carmen on the other end.

"We're going to need whatever help we can get," I insisted. "So, Josiah and the agents?"

"So they can both meet us? At the same place?" Her tone suggested my earlier adventures in fire-starting really had damaged my sanity. "I thought you liked the agents."

I took a moment to picture how Josiah might react to the two humans who knew too much about our world. Every scenario I ran through ended with an FBI agent bonfire. I had to give this one to Sera.

"Which one, then?"

Sera took a turn at a speed that would cause a Formula One driver to blanch and still responded in a conversational tone. "The agents could actually be useful. If they can handle bears and mountain lions, they can handle shifters. They carry those guns for a reason right? And they have access to lots of information." It all sounded reasonable, but there was still a note of doubt in her voice. "But our father is, well, he's Josiah."

I knew exactly what she meant, and though it pained me to admit it, our father was the better choice. The agents would be hampered by such pesky considerations as the law and morality, two qualities Josiah was happy to redefine on a case-by-case basis. He was the sort of man you wanted on your side, just because having him on someone else's team was too terrifying to contemplate.

Reluctantly, I keyed in his number—I stubbornly refused to add it to my contact list, but that hadn't kept my subconscious mind from memorizing it—and told him to meet us at Will's. I avoided all small talk and explanations, but he still sounded pleased to hear from me. He hadn't given up on me yet, or at least not on his plans for me.

The Explorer drew to a sudden stop in Will's driveway. I don't remember unbuckling the belt or opening the car door, but a moment later I was flying up the porch.

My mother still slept, in the exact position I'd left her. She was alone.

The breath expelled from my lungs in a long, slow hiss, relief battling with a delayed anger I was only now allowing myself to feel. She might not be in immediate danger, but she was by no means safe. On a hunch, I examined her neck, looking for the same small wound I'd seen on Pamela's. It was tiny but obvious, once I knew what to look for. It wasn't her work on James that had knocked her out. It was a needle.

On my way back downstairs, I peeked in on James. He still slept, and he still dreamed.

Nothing had changed, and yet it was completely different. Now, I knew who needed to pay.

"All clear. No one's home," I called, stepping onto the porch.

Will was already dialing. "She's not answering." He clenched his fist tightly around the cell phone, as if he longed to crush it into pieces, then deliberately returned it to his pocket. "Celeste isn't answering."

"Is she with Eleanor?"

"She isn't answering, either."

"Are they together? Just running errands or something? Celeste doesn't know what Dana told us, so why would she leave now?"

"Dana could have warned her." Will didn't seem to believe his own words. When we'd left Dana, she'd looked horrified by her actions, but she also looked relieved to finally be free of the secret. I couldn't believe she'd let herself be drawn back into Celeste's treachery.

"You didn't tell her or Eleanor you were visiting Dana, right?"

Sera and I shook our heads simultaneously. "No way," I said. "Everyone's on a need to know basis. I have trust issues these days."

"So she's probably out for groceries or something and will be back in a bit." Will sounded doubtful, not believing his own words.

Sera ignored him and strode to the Explorer, dropping to the cold ground and examining the wheel well. I knew exactly what she'd find, and a moment later a GPS tracker sailed through the air, landing with a loud thud on the porch.

"She knew exactly where we were," I told Will as Sera rejoined us. "She's been tracking us all along. All of us. She knew whenever we got close. She blew out our tire when Pamela returned, probably so I couldn't read the clothes. My mother ended up doing it, but it was delayed. She said the clothes seemed like they'd just been washed. With the crash, Celeste had time to do that. Anyone who'd commit attempted murder on a carload of people just to prevent me from catching a hint of her essence on a t-shirt isn't going to think twice about threatening a fourteen-year-old girl. She tracked us, and she knows we were with Dana."

Will stared at the GPS with rage, the small electronic a surrogate for the woman who put it there. She was his wife, and he might still love her, but I thought he might also hate her at that moment.

A dark sedan pulled into the driveway, and for a moment I hoped it was the agents, after all. They might be less prepared to deal with magical conflicts, but I was a lot more prepared to deal with them than with my father.

Unfortunately, the black car drawing to a slow stop was a luxury model rather than a Crown Vic, and it was driven by a familiar lackey. Jonathan put the car in park and watched our group with barely hidden curiosity as Josiah walked toward us.

Before he reached us, I pointed at the Explorer. "You should check your car for explosives, Will. If she put one on the Bronco, she might do the same to you."

Without another word, Will studied each of the SUV's tires, then popped the hood and examined the motor's components. He worked in silence, his brow knit so tightly I swore he was creating three new forehead wrinkles just for the occasion.

"He won't find anything." Josiah chose to ignore the complete lack of greeting he received and dropped himself directly into our conversation. "He's not her target."

"Maybe not before," said Sera. "But now he knows. He could be a threat to her."

"She always intended for others to know eventually." Josiah spoke simply, as if to a child. Of course, given our age disparity, maybe we always would be children to him.

I studied him, trying to follow the direction of his thoughts. I failed. So, apparently, did Sera. "That makes no sense."

I nodded. "Why would Celeste want others to know? If the families found out, well, enraged, grieving shifters functioning outside the law would lead to one dead kidnapper damn fast."

"Unless she gives them a reason to keep her alive," he noted, waiting for the light bulb to go on with exaggerated patience.

Sera and I stared at him with dropped jaws at the exact same moment, both of us finally grasping his meaning.

"The first-borns," she muttered. "From all the local shifter clans."

"If she controls the children, she controls the entire family. No one will hurt her so long as she holds their children's lives in her hands." I finished her thought. "Which means—"

"There needs to be a way to reverse the effects. She has no leverage if all the children are permanently mad. And if Fiona figured out how to undo the effects, Celeste would also lose that leverage."

I thought of my mother upstairs and the small mark on her neck. "Which explains why she was given a needle full of drugs when she was close to finding the answer."

Sera and I stared at each other, feeling excitement build as the pieces finally fell into place. For the first time, these kidnappings almost made sense.

Josiah nodded. If one can look both condescending and proud, he did at the moment. "It's only a theory, of course. She may just be the shifter version of a mad scientist."

"No," I shook my head. "We're right." I didn't know to what extent my certainty was due to the actual facts of the case and how much to my need for Mac to be safe, but either way, I was running with it. "Which means we need to find her lab, wherever she's doing this. Mad scientist or not, she working somewhere. If there's a way to reverse the procedure, it'll most likely be there."

Sera grabbed my phone out of my hand and pressed several buttons before stopping abruptly, her face tight. "Fuck." The single word contained an entire universe of frustration. "That's the sort of thing Vivian does for us. Real estate records, tracking the money. But she's not here."

"I may not be up to your earth friend's standards, but even I can find out if Celeste bought or rented a medical facility lately." Josiah rolled his eyes at Sera, and for the first time ever I saw myself in his face. That was my expression. My mother would never be so uncouth as to roll her eyes.

Unsettled, I found the compartment I used for all my conflicting feelings about my father and shoved that thought deep inside, then locked the box securely. This wasn't the time. I wasn't sure if it would ever be the time, and I was okay with that.

"It doesn't need to be a dedicated facility," I clarified. "She got the equipment from the hospital, at least most of it. Can we track her recent purchases, see if she sent them to another address?" I doubted she'd helped us by ordering large quantities of cotton swabs and rubbing alcohol on Amazon, but one could always hope.

Josiah nodded, already sending a note to one of his minions. "How big are we looking for? How many shifters does she have at this point?"

"I don't know. Mac, for sure, and at least one bobcat child. Mac was going to check with some other shifter families this morning, but I don't know what he learned."

I stopped speaking and only just resisted the urge to smack myself in the head. All the shifters had been taken near water, to quickly disperse their scent and throw any pursuers off the trail. If Mac had managed to speak to them before he was abducted, they might have still been around—and seen where he was taken, or at least in which direction. It was their river, after all.

"Otters," I announced, already considering how to lure the shy creatures out of hiding. "They'll know what to do."

They both nodded, and Sera offered a tiny smile, the first I'd seen in hours. "You know we're just pretending you don't sound nuts, right?"

"It doesn't matter. Josiah, just look for a building big enough for several shifters, a boatload of medical equipment, and one crazy woman living on borrowed time."

He looked highly amused by my attempts to order him around, but he also started making phone calls, wandering to a quiet spot on the porch.

Sera spoke quietly, glancing toward both Josiah and Will. "Even if he finds the building, it's not enough. We can't infiltrate anything with these guys."

She was right. Between a growling, seven-foot-tall bear and an elemental happy to incinerate anything that interfered with his plans, we weren't dealing with a particularly stealthy crew. "Even Carmen's too large. We need Simon."

She smiled at me again, a little wider than before. "Get the band back together?"

"Damn straight. I don't care what Vivian says. We need her, and apparently lack of respect for someone's stated boundaries is a family trait. It's time to see how good she is when doped up on painkillers. Grab the laptop from the cabin, and don't take no for an answer."

"Have I ever?"

If Sera listened when people said no, I'd never have come home. I'd never have been a part of this world, a part of these people's lives. Some days it wasn't easy. Some days I felt my entire world crumbling around my ears, but I would never regret saying yes to Sera.

This was what she did. She brought people together, and she kept them there. It was time for her to work her magic again.

We didn't say a word to the men, knowing any explanation would lead to a long argument that would delay our work. We just got in the car and started driving, windows up and Iggy Pop's "The Passenger" blaring too loudly for us to hear Will or Josiah protest as we drove away.

I STOOD ALONE at the river's edge, the cabin behind me. No sign remained of the earlier snow, but the night air was still needle sharp, the chill pricking my exposed ears and throat. Through the trees, the gleam of distant homes beckoned, their lights a welcome glow against the dark pines. Tomorrow, I vowed, I'd be safe inside my own warm home, and I'd have Mac at my side.

Tonight, there was still much to do.

I watched the river flow past, simply taking the time to say hello. It had been a long, exhausting day, and there was little sign it would end soon. I knew the situation was urgent, that each moment I wasted put Mac and others in danger, but I also knew better than to rush into a dangerous situation with half a plan and little control. So I sat easily on the bank, legs crossed, and let the river fill me, giving me the energy and peace I needed to make it through whatever the night had planned.

When I felt whole and rested, I reached out to the water, sending my magic gently through the stream. I found all the expected creatures, the trout and frogs, a few birds tucked away in the protective plants that drifted along the banks, and, not far away, a larger, warm-blooded creature hovered in the water, watching me. It was familiar, and I knew it had watched me before. It seemed to be drawn to my quiet moments, to my communion with the water. Maybe it sensed that, in our own ways, we were both creatures of the river.

Of course, I had no idea if that particular animal was a shifter or just a plain old river otter. One way to find out. "Good evening." I felt a slight stirring at the sound of my voice, a definite awareness of my words. Shifter, then. "I don't mean to startle you. Please don't go." I kept my words low and even, though I longed to speed through my explanations and learn what they knew.

A moment later, others joined the first, quietly positioning themselves in the river to better hear my words. "I want to know if you spoke to a man this morning. A bear shifter named Mac. He's missing, and I hoped you witnessed someone take him."

I waited, feeling the distress that fed through the water, a deep concern among the otters. They seemed to be arguing.

"Please. If you know anything, this will help not just one man, but shifters throughout the area. They're in danger. I know that sounds melodramatic and all, but it's the truth."

The first otter, the most curious one, made its decision and started swimming toward my spot on the bank. Before I could even exhale a sigh of relief, the others had surrounded it, chirping madly, trying to direct the animal away from me. The river easily told the story of their struggle. While the first one was stronger and more determined, the others were scared.

Calm and gentle was quickly losing its appeal. I gathered the water toward me, tugging the otters insistently to the bank. They all fought against it, even the bravest one, but my magic was too strong. They never stood a chance. When they were only a foot or two from me, I smiled, trying to show that I meant no harm, even if I was turning them into my own furry puppets.

"Let's try this again. I need to speak to you. It won't take long. I won't hurt you in any way, but if you swim away again, I will pull you back. I need to find the man you spoke to this morning, and there's no point telling me you didn't see him. I may not speak otter, but I'm guessing all that chirping meant you know something. So, your call. We can go back and forth all night, or you can shift and we can have a civilized conversation. Well, some approximation thereof." I didn't want to set their expectations too high, after all.

This time, the chirping was lower pitched, and I guessed I was hearing the sound of an otter muttering. A moment later, a naked woman strolled from the water. She was as comfortable in her nudity as Simon was, though she lacked his lean lines. She was a robust pear shape, with a thin layer of firm fat plumping the skin across her entire body. Insulation, I realized, against the freezing river. She didn't look unhealthy with the extra fat. She looked downright lush.

I wanted to treat her with the respect she was due, rather than squealing about the super cute otter, but that was hard to do when I saw her face. She was, in a word, adorable. Small ears, enormous, melting brown eyes, round cheeks, and a tiny button nose. I wanted to take her home and feed her and love her and pet her and call her George. Instead, I had to parlay like a reasonable adult. Life really wasn't fair.

"What the fuck do you want?"

I blinked, then blinked again, certain this paragon of sweetness hadn't just hollered at me while cursing like a sailor. Sure, I had a filthy mouth on occasion, but I wasn't a bundle of cute wrapped in an adorable candy coating.

I recovered, scrambling quickly to my feet. I didn't think I needed to worry about appearing unthreatening to this woman. She didn't seem to suffer from any crisis of confidence about her ability to handle herself. Several small brown heads poked out of the water, interested in seeing how this conversation developed. If I didn't get this woman on board, I would learn nothing from the others.

"I already told you. I need to know whatever you know about Mac, the shifter who lives here."

She shrugged. Even though she was naked, I had a sudden image of her wearing a leather jacket and steel-toed boots. Clothed or not, she was an all-American badass, and she knew it.

"I'm sorry I dragged you over here. I don't really have a lot of time or options right now, but I didn't mean to get off on the wrong foot. I'm Aidan."

I received a nod. She was happy to acknowledge that I had a name, even if she was disinclined to offer her own.

"And you are...?" I pressed. "I'd prefer to call you something other than Adorable Naked Chick."

She looked pained. She'd probably have been perfectly fine with being Naked Chick, but the other adjective was unacceptable. "Miriam."

"That's pretty." The words were out a second before my brain kicked in, telling me this woman might not want to have a pretty name. "I mean, that's really... butch?"

To my surprise, she smiled, revealing small white teeth. "It's fine. It's just a fucking name. Beats Naked Chick, right?"

"I don't know. If I looked as good naked as you do, I might consider changing my name."

She patted her curvy ass. "It's all the swimming. Very good exercise, you know."

"Look, I'm good with the other profanity, but can you avoid the e-word, please?" I couldn't help it. I knew we were short on time, and there were more pressing matters to attend to, but I sort of wanted to be her friend.

Miriam reminded me of the most awesome woman in a dive bar on a Saturday night—brash and brassy, the kind of woman who knew how to have a good time and wanted everyone else to join in. That kind of woman was also genetically incapable of taking anyone's shit, and I needed that kind of attitude. Right now, outspoken easily beat shy and retiring.

Her smile turned into a grin. "Yeah, I saw your attempts at yoga. If I was that uncoordinated while working out, I'd avoid it, too." I swore the otters watching from the river giggled.

I made a face at her, but I couldn't say she was wrong. "You watch us?"

She tilted her head to the side and held out her hands, a posture that loudly said "Duh." She had an eloquent face and body, prone to large, broad gestures and expressions, and she didn't need words to communicate. Fortunately, she was just as eloquent with her words, even if half of them were f-bombs.

"Of course we watch you. We watch all you fuckers living along our river. Need to know what you're up to, especially when the most powerful water we've seen in decades ends up living in our backyard. We don't want no more fucking surprises like before."

I feared she was referring to the time I'd temporarily moved the river through our living room to put out a fire. It had been necessary at the time, but it definitely didn't meet existing standards for environmental protection.

"Speaking of surprises, I'm sure you don't want to wake up one day and find your kids have been stolen." That's me, queen of the ultra-smooth segue.

"We take care of ours. We know the river. We're safe as hell out here. No one's touching us."

"Current evidence to the contrary."

Her eyes narrowed. She wasn't mad at me, exactly, but she didn't like being reminded she'd been at my mercy.

In truth, the only waters I knew strong enough to pull several otters through the rushing spring water of the Truckee River were my family members and one nutty hippie in Nevada City. The otters really weren't at risk, but I'd become pretty good at forming arguments only loosely based on reality. Sera had taught me well.

"Look, Pamela is fast and has sharp claws, and she still managed to get taken. James and Mac are freaking bears, which is damn near the top of the food chain around these parts, and Mac is careful. It wasn't enough." I neglected to mention they'd all known their abductor, which made it easy for her to get close enough to drug them. I'd fess up to my lies of omission later, when Mac and the others were safe. For now, I just needed her to help me.

She laughed, big and full-throated. "You aren't telling me the whole story, are you? I heard him call to her. Aunt, he said. Look, I'll make you a deal. We'll help you however we can, because even if the otters are okay—and trust me, the otters are always okay—we care about those other shifters, especially the babies. In return, you stop trying to bullshit me. Deal?"

I nodded, relieved, and felt hope stir. She'd seen them this morning. She'd seen Mac get taken.

"Good. Now, here's what I know. That woman was here early this morning. She had an inflatable raft, you know, one of those strong ones the tourist companies rent out to large groups, but this one had a motor strapped to it. It was more than strong enough for a bear and his auntie. She put it in the river, and she called to him."

"And he just came over?" That didn't sound right. Mac was cautious, and as much as he cared for his extended family, he had his own trust issues. With everything going on lately, it would have seemed more than a little odd for Celeste to be hanging out by the river at daybreak.

"He hung back at first. But then she gets this panicked tone in her voice, tells him that a blond woman is in the water, her foot trapped in the rocks." She gave me a telling look. There was no doubt who that blond woman was supposed to be.

"She used me." The words came out in a hiss, more animal than human. "She used me against Mac."

"Yeah. That crazy bitch must have known you were the one thing he wouldn't be rational about. Don't you hate it when evil is smart, too? Doesn't seem right. Anyway, she said she'd seen you fall in and called for him right away."

It wasn't a particularly smart strategy. Celeste must not know I couldn't possibly drown. Or maybe she did, and she also knew that Mac would forget that key detail in his concern for my life, just as he had when I'd been trapped in the Bronco after the crash.

It's hard for non-elementals to remember that, for the strong ones, our elements simply can't hurt us. It goes completely against everything they know. In their logical world, if someone is trapped in the river, they're going to drown. Despite knowing better, that must have been Mac's first impulse, and he'd walked right up to Celeste.

"I'm guessing she drugged him somehow," I said, my voice flat.

"Yep. He leaned over to look in the river and found a needle in his neck. A second later, he was laying on his stomach in the raft, taking one hell of a nap. Never even got a chance to fight."

For some reason, that angered me more than anything. It was bad enough to kidnap children, mess with their memories, and risk permanent mental damage, but to be so sneaky about it? To not even give her prey a sporting chance? The woman was a monster.

"And then she started up the motor and took off, heading that way." She pointed downriver, then looked at me. Waiting.

"I thought you said no more bullshit, Miriam."

She grinned. "Just want to see if you're paying attention."

"I know there's no way you'd let some crazy woman with access to pharmaceuticals that can fell a bear use your river without wanting to know a little more about her. Like you said, you gotta know what we're up to."

She nodded, pleased I wasn't an idiot. "Damn straight. And this woman, she's up to a lot, in a lovely office building northeast of here."

"Where is it?" I pulled out my notepad, ready to scrawl the address among my various musings and ramblings.

"We don't exactly get a good look at street numbers from this side. Besides, I thought you were in a hurry." She jerked her head toward the river, where the three otters started bobbing excitedly in the water. "Let's see how powerful you really are, water girl."

CHAPTER 22

In my life, I'd traveled by car, boat, plane, helicopter, and, on one memorable date, motorcycle. I could safely say, however, that this was the first time I'd traveled by otter.

Miriam and her three comrades surrounded me, two on either side. I only had one job, to speed the river's flow from the cabin to the office building where the shifters were being held. It wasn't easy work and required too much concentration to also worry about such pesky details as navigation or staying afloat, so I soon found myself carried along on the backs of four brown, furry pontoons who knew every inch of the river. They easily avoided the branches and jutting rocks that would have left me scratched and bleeding, and with my magic pushing the water to unnatural speeds, we arrived at our destination much sooner than I ever would have in the Chevy.

The otters led me to an office building just east of Truckee in a small industrial park home to a mix of shipping companies, mixed martial arts studios, and a couple of questionable chiropractors who favored low rent over a respectable location. The park held several identical buildings separated by a sprawling parking lot, nearly empty at this time of night. The buildings were squat and two-storied and looked to have been built sometime in the 80s. They were composed entirely of sharp geometric lines and large windows, many of them lit by bleak fluorescent lights.

They flickered uneasily, too worn to provide steady light.

During the day, it would look like a somewhat rundown but perfectly safe location. When the buildings' ominous silhouettes rested against the midnight sky, it was the setting for a horror movie. I felt the heavy weight of deja vu.

Though these buildings were better maintained and presumably occupied, they still reminded me overmuch of the warehouse where Sera and I had long ago tried to stop a killer, and where we only succeeded in bringing death. Even now, after so much had happened, I had nightmares about that night, still pictured the flames devouring everything in sight while I stood by, helpless.

Here I was again, preparing to enter another dark building on the outskirts of Truckee on another cold night, pursuing someone whose awful motives and actions I didn't understand. As on that night, my powers were proving erratic, even dangerous. Only hours ago, I'd allowed myself to set Diane's living room alight. I knew I wasn't in control, not really, but it didn't matter. So long as Mac needed my help, I had no other choice.

I stood on the bank where the otters dropped me, shivering in the night sky and yet unable to move. I simply stared at the building and fought the dread that rose within me, the inexplicable certainty that more nightmares waited inside.

"You know, you'll have better luck tonight if you're not dying of hypothermia." Miriam's voice jolted me back to the present, and my sense of foreboding dissipated under the strength of her cheery voice.

Miriam held the zipped nylon bag the otters wrapped around themselves when swimming. It held their cell phones and wallets in case they needed them, and that night it also held a dry change of clothes.

I wasn't cold while in the water, but now I felt the bite

in the air. I stood on the river bank in nothing but a wet t-shirt and underwear. It was quite daring for me, though the otters had snickered when I insisted on remaining partly clothed. After spending so much time with shifters, I was starting to wonder why Tahoe wasn't crawling with nudist camps.

The remaining three otters crawled out of the water and returned to their human forms. Each one was more adorable than the last, and once again I showed a superhuman restraint by not patting a single one on the head. There were two boys and a girl, ranging in ages from twelve to about eighteen. They all grinned at me shyly, and I thought the girl looked familiar.

Miriam offered each a pointed stare that reminded them they ought to give me some privacy. They turned to face the river, except for Miriam. She cheerfully kept talking while we both pulled on dry clothes.

"My sister's kids," she explained. "She's breeding again this year, so I end up with a whole lot of babysitting time. The woman really can't seem to keep it in her pants." I glanced at the backs of the other otters, but they didn't stiffen in the slightest. I guessed they'd heard this before. "But they're good kids, more or less. Mary there, she was the only one small enough to get into the building's crawl spaces and snoop around a bit, so she can tell you more than the rest of us."

Of course. I looked at the neat cap of brown hair and remembered a shy teenage girl lurking in the woods with Brandon and his friends. I approved of her current company far more.

I finished pulling on a worn, clean pair of dark jeans and a long-sleeved top. It was forest green and the darkest one I owned. I didn't have a single item of black clothing, suggesting that my future as a ninja would have to wait until I had a wardrobe upgrade. These were the stealthiest items I owned. I wrapped my blond hair in a knot at the nape of my neck and covered it with a dark blue knit cap. I had no idea what to expect inside the building, but I could at least pretend I knew what I was doing.

When dressed, I called Mary to me. She walked with more purpose than she'd shown at school, comfortable among her own kind. She smiled, and I was glad to see she remembered me and was eager to help.

"What did you see?" I asked. "Anything you know will help."

She made a face, wrinkling her nose and raising her lip in what I thought was supposed to be a sneer, though she was too damned cute to pull it off. "See that building there, away from the others? I think she has the whole building. I haven't seen or smelled anyone else, though it would be hard to pick up anything over that stench. The place smells awful. Just follow your nose and you can't miss where the animals are kept."

"You saw them?" The words burst forth, fast and desperate.

She shook her head. "Not saw, no. Smelled and heard them. Hissing and growling, and human sounds, too. Crying."

"Would a non-shifter smell and hear them?" I asked. Though the building was at least two hundred feet from its closest neighbors, there were still humans in the area during the day, and it seemed like none had noticed anything unusual.

"Doesn't matter," said Miriam. "You'll have a shifter with you." She lifted her chin, letting me know she was volunteering. This was news to me, but I was in no position to turn down help.

"Did you recognize any of the prisoners? What kind of

animal, at least?"

She furrowed her brow, trying to remember. "I think so. There was definitely a cat. Bobcats reek. They always pee in the water, you know, so no other animals smell them, and that just means we end up swimming in their toilet. So not cool."

While I could sympathize with her frustration over the bobcats' lack of manners, I really needed Mary to focus. "What else?"

"I think there was a wolverine, too. No mistaking that noise. No idea what the human was. And a bear, I think. Something big and mad was growling."

If he was mad, that meant he was still Mac. He still remembered, and wasn't yet the frozen-eyed zombie that James and Pamela had become after their time with Celeste. I wasn't too late. I had to believe I wasn't too late.

"Thanks. Now, for those of us who can't fit into the building's crawl spaces, where should I go?"

She pointed. "See that door on the left of the building?" I did. "Don't use that one. It goes to an office or something. Just a desk and filing cabinet. No shifters. The door's locked, too. There's a bathroom window in the back with a broken latch, but it would require some acrobatics to reach it. I guess you could break one of the big windows, but that would pretty much announce you're here."

I thanked her and sent her back to her siblings, then turned to Miriam. "This is stupid. What about me suggests I could succeed as a stealth infiltrator?"

"Absolutely nothing. So, what's the backup plan?"

"Under development." I pulled my phone from my jeans pocket and emailed Sera, quickly outlining the situation. Hopefully, she already had Vivian typing away on the laptop and would receive it instantly.

Will was next, and he knew the building I described. He

assured me he was capable of ditching Josiah, then hung up.

It wasn't that I didn't want to see my father—I didn't, but that wasn't my primary reason for avoiding him. Given his agenda, it was simply too dangerous. The man had one priority these days: protecting me, no matter the cost. He would interfere without sparing a single thought for the shifters' lives. Maybe helping the shifters wasn't the safest choice I could make, but that didn't mean it was the wrong one.

I stared at the phone for several seconds, until Miriam vocalized my thoughts. "You calling the agents in or what?" Her face held nothing but a vague curiosity.

"What? I mean... what?" For the first time, it occurred to me that these furry river spies had paid attention to things other than my workout regimen.

She shrugged. "I give the FBI info sometimes. I was glad to hear they're gonna be here permanently, too. I mean, otters can handle anything in the river, but we need help if one of those sharp-clawed assholes starts causing trouble. And I thought the agents might call you and your friend in."

A question I'd completely forgotten was answered. Miriam was the agents' anonymous source.

"Wait, you wanted us working on this?" After hearing from the other shifters that our work put us squarely at the intersection of bungling and incompetent, I hadn't expected the vote of confidence.

"I saw how you worked together with your friends to stop that earth bastard from killing people. You lot can handle yourselves." She spoke in a matter of fact tone, but I couldn't help puffing up at the praise.

Still grinning, I dialed. Carmichael picked up on the first

ring.

"Is this an update? Is this an honest to god call in which you remember what your job is?"

"Sarcasm is the lowest form of comedy, Carmichael."

"Yes, I know. That's why you and Sera are never as funny as you think you are."

"That's just mean. We're hilarious. Anyway, yes, I have news. You know how last time, we completely ignored you and went off and stopped the bad guy ourselves, not telling you anything about it?"

A long, very pregnant pause. Yeah, he remembered. "Yes." Just a single, terse word. I didn't need to see him to know his teeth were clenched, that square jaw of his just a little more chiseled.

"This time, you're invited, but there are rules."

"Remind me, Aidan. Who works for whom here?"

"Don't bother me with technicalities. But nice grammar. They teach you that in the FBI?" Okay, now I was just killing time until Will and Sera arrived.

Carmichael stopped arguing. This time, the debate had lasted less than a minute. Soon, he might give up after a mere fifteen seconds of conversing with me. "Tell me what we need to know."

"First, don't shoot the animals. That's second and third, actually. Unless it's a bear. And then only if it's the bad bear, not the good bear. You with me?"

"A professor in linguistics wouldn't be with you. I need more information, Aidan."

"I wish I had more. All I know at this point is there's a building full of shifters that need rescuing, and a woman responsible for putting them there. Bullets will kill any of them, so use them sparingly."

"And the woman is...?"

"Celeste. She'll either be a tall and muscular woman or a

six-foot bear who could rip your heart out. We're all hoping she's not in the mood to shift tonight, but I wouldn't count on it."

To his credit, he didn't ask any questions. His training in the ways of the Tahoe magical population really was coming along.

I gave him the address and begged him to be cautious. This was their job now, but that didn't mean they were ready for it. Even as we hung up, I was unsure if I'd made the right decision calling them in. I was sending two men with powerful firearms into a situation they only barely understood. I'd say the potential for disaster was high.

I stared at the building ahead of me and felt tension rise, nerves and fear and anger, all rolled into one, and I knew exactly how dangerous such an emotional cocktail could be. I took a slow breath and released it carefully, then repeated it. Miriam watched curiously. "Does that help control the fire?"

With that, any shred of control vanished. "What?" I sputtered.

"Does it help with the fire? Oh, don't deny it. I know what you are. I told you, we watch."

I looked frantically toward the three little heads several feet away. It was bad enough that one person knew. It seemed far more dangerous for a fourteen-year-old to have that knowledge. As we'd recently discovered, fourteen-year-old girls could inadvertently cause all kinds of trouble.

"Oh, they can't hear. Still, better safe than killed by your own kind, right? Off you go, little ones. Straight to your mother, no fucking around. I'll know if you stop anywhere, you know I will."

Nodding obediently, they slipped into the water and were quickly out of sight.

"What, exactly, do you think you know?" I asked.

"Enough. Don't worry, I don't tell tales. I don't often see the need to help people to their deaths, and I've yet to feel any such desire with you. Though call me adorable one more time, and we'll see if I don't change my mind."

It took a massive leap of faith to trust Vivian, Simon, and Mac with my secret, considering what a short time I'd known them. I'd never planned to trust strangers with my life, and now a foul-mouthed otter shifter and a gun-crazy Reno suburbanite knew what I was. I'd had better days.

And yet, there was nothing I could do. Somehow, I had to trust these two women. I'd visit Diane and make peace, and explain just why my abilities needed to remain unknown. It was either that or wire her mouth shut.

But that was later, and there was still much to do that night. "I guess I have to trust you, Miriam. You're not giving me a lot of other choices."

She grinned easily, then started walking toward the building. She didn't wait for me to follow, but I did hear her call over her shoulder. "You should. I'm damned trustworthy," she said, just before she was out of earshot.

She knew the one thing that could cost me my life, and she was about to back me on a blind assault on our resident mad scientist's laboratory. She damned sure better be.

We moved quietly toward the building. I let Miriam take point, figuring her keen senses would be more attuned to possible threats. While she was more capable than me when it came to the five senses, I was amused to see she didn't move easily through the trees the way Simon would have. She avoided stepping on dry branches or anything else that might give us away, but by shifter standards, she was damn near clumsy.

About a hundred feet away, we paused. Miriam sniffed the wind, then nodded, satisfied. "They're still in there."

She spoke quietly, the barest whisper. We were downwind from the building, disguising our own approach, but caution was still necessary. "Now what?"

It was a good question. We'd made faster time than I'd expected. Sera and the agents were making their way from the other end of the lake, and it could be more than an hour before they arrived. But Will wasn't far, and he ought to get there soon. I itched to simply attack, to burn the building and the woman inside, but that wasn't an option. I was allowed to risk my sanity, but not shifter lives.

"We wait," I finally said, trying to infuse the words with a certainty I didn't feel.

Minutes crept by, long seconds during which I imagined all the things that might be happening a hundred feet from my current spot. She could be working on Mac at this moment. While we waited, he might be forgetting I ever existed.

"Down girl," muttered Miriam. "I don't know much about what you are, but that can't be good."

I followed her gaze to my fingers, where tiny sparks flew impotently into the wind, seeking something to burn. "No, it's really not." I closed my eyes and pictured Lake Tahoe in winter, a still, cold source of energy and peace. I felt myself calm, and when I looked again, my fingers weren't doing their best impersonation of Roman candles. Vivian would be so proud of me.

The fire was too close to the surface. Even now, I could feel it snaking through my body, probing and testing, looking for weak spots. We had to hope our incursion into the building went quickly and smoothly, because at the moment I felt like a lit match, and any conflict or danger would be the kerosene that destroyed my control.

Miriam and I waited several long minutes in silence, studying the building, hoping for any new information.

Nothing moved.

We had no warning anyone was near until Will simply stepped from the trees behind us. No large man should ever be able to move as quietly as he did, but he seemed to control the ground and trees, and they obeyed his command to remain silent. Carmen stalked behind him, eyes alert. They only briefly acknowledged me, too intent on scanning the area for any potential threats. I was glad to see Josiah wasn't with them. That would have been one complication too many.

"You found her, little water," Will said, moving toward me and giving me a half hug with his right arm. It only lasted a moment, but I took that second to lean into him, to find comfort in his warmth and strength.

I thought Will might need comfort of his own. Strain showed across his face, and I suspected that, much like me, tomorrow he'd be dealing with a hefty emotional fallout. For now, though, he seemed willing to pretend the woman inside the building was a stranger. That was a delusion I was happy to share with him.

I introduced the various shifters. "You've helped more than you signed up for, Miriam. I won't hold it against you if you want to leave now that the cavalry's arrived." A bear, a mountain lion, and a dual magic elemental. Yeah, I thought we could handle this, particularly with Sera and the agents bound to arrive soon after.

Miriam didn't care. "You're telling me I got to be your guide, but I'm supposed to miss the fun part? Screw that. Just point me toward someone I can beat up."

Carmen looked at Miriam with undeniable respect.

"Word is the back window is our best bet, if we're feeling limber." I sized up Will. "Though I'm not sure that'll work for you. If Carmen and I can slip inside, maybe one of us can open the locked door."

Will was already stripping, and I averted my eyes in an effort to not see the uncle of my intended future boyfriend buck naked. There was a slight ripple in the air, and a moment later a large black bear watched me carefully, waiting for his chance to act.

"You ready to prove elementals aren't completely useless, Aidan?" Carmen asked, then shifted herself. I'd never seen a mountain lion up close, and she was stunning. Far smaller than the bears, and yet I wouldn't have bet against her in a fight. It wasn't just the claws and teeth, either. There was a hunger in her eyes, a readiness in her coiled muscles, that spoke to the purest predatory impulse. When Simon was a cat, he might occasionally hunt a bird or bug, but he could easily be distracted by a warm heater vent or tuna sandwich. I doubted Carmen's focus ever wavered from her prey.

There was no more reason to delay, and we moved rapidly toward the building. The window was high above me, but Will nudged me gently with his head, boosting me enough to reach it. Unfortunately, I lacked the arm strength required to pull myself up, and after dangling helplessly for a moment, was forced to drop down.

"Plan B, then," I muttered, resolutely not meeting anyone's eyes.

I stepped around the side of the building, finding one of the slightly larger windows Mary had mentioned. The window wasn't intended to be opened, and there was no locking mechanism. Fortunately, a large rock can unlock plenty of things, and after heaving it against the window a couple of times, the glass cracked. We were in.

Stealth was overrated, anyway.

I was inside a second later, my eyes adjusting to the gloom. Carmen and Miriam followed, but it was still too small an opening for the bear. Will left to wait by the locked door.

We'd landed in an empty room. Celeste had rented the whole building for secrecy, but she hadn't needed the entire space.

The room led to a hallway that opened in three separate directions. "Stick together or split up?" asked Miriam.

I grimaced. "This isn't a horror movie. We stay together." Carmen growled, though I had no idea if that meant she agreed.

If I'd been alone, I'd have needed to open one door after another and peer into every dark room, terrified each time that something would leap out at me. Fortunately, I wasn't alone.

"What are your noses telling you?"

I hadn't finished the sentence before Carmen padded down the hallway to our right, nails muffled against the thin carpet. She walked with certainty, tail low. We followed her through the dark building, only stopping long enough to unlock the door and let in an immense bear.

Carmen led us directly to a closed door under which a thin band of light emerged. She nodded at me, impatient. My nose might be useless, but at least I had opposable thumbs. I wrapped my hand around the doorknob and twisted, surprised to find it unlocked. Celeste knew we were here and wasn't attempting to keep us out. That should have been our first warning.

We entered the room, blinking rapidly, willing our eyes to adjust to the sudden brightness.

Once we could see again, our eyes fixed on a single, terrifying tableau.

We froze, processing two things at once. First, I saw Mac stretched out on a narrow hospital bed, a long needle held casually to his throat. Second, it wasn't Celeste holding that needle.

"How nice," Eleanor smiled. "We get to chat."

I stared at her. We all did. We needed the time to process the new situation, to weigh the new threat. Will growled, loudly, and I thought he had fewer reservations about mauling his sister-in-law than he did about harming his own wife. Carmen crouched low, ears back and fangs exposed, and a slow hiss built in her throat.

Part of my brain, a cold, detached section that barely felt like it belonged to me, worked quickly, piecing these new bits of information together. Diane told Dana. Dana told Celeste. Celeste told Eleanor. We'd been so close, but we'd missed one key fact, one all important detail.

Celeste was a mother bear, and every bit as protective as any mama bear in the wild. She'd been in agony watching her son suffer. Some things, I thought, could not be faked. She'd never intended to hurt her own son. Either something had gone wrong, or someone else had caused that pain. Maybe both.

Of course, the other part of my brain saw Mac dormant and helpless beneath her needle and wanted to start setting things on fire.

As ever, I fought it back, but it was slow to retreat. It knew this was just a temporary solution, and I'd be calling it back soon enough. If Eleanor hurt Mac, she would need to burn.

I stretched my water magic toward the syringe, seeking to control the liquid inside. My efforts were futile. The syringe was air tight, my magic was unable to push past the pipette blocking the needle.

But first, I needed to at least attempt a solution that didn't open the door to further insanity. Miriam and I were the only ones still in human form, and she was mainly along for the opportunity to smack someone. It looked like the burden of diplomacy fell on me. As with so many things lately, that could have been planned better.

"What do you want?" I bit out the words, making no attempt to hide my hatred.

"I want you to go away and pretend you never saw me, at least for a couple more weeks, but we rarely get what we want in life." Her voice was even and reasonable.

Her eyes, however, were anything but reasonable. They were bright and frantic, scanning the entire room. She knew there were more of us. Sera, Simon, Josiah, she'd met them all, and she had no way of knowing they weren't with us. I didn't wear a watch, but I knew it would be at least another half hour till they appeared.

Fortunately, if there was one thing I did really well, it was stall and babble and distract. With luck, I could convince her to use the full thirty minutes to share her diabolical plan.

Then Sera could set her on fire for me.

Behind me, I heard a desperate, pained growl. Will stared, not at his nephew, but at a woman stretched out on another bed. Celeste. She was on one of several beds, with the others occupied by children and teenagers, all sound asleep. They lined the walls of this room, white beds against white walls. The dull fluorescents and worn linoleum floor stopped the room from looking pure and clean. It might be sterile, but it felt dirty and ugly.

Eleanor followed his gaze. "Oh, calm down, Will. I'd never hurt my sister. She's on tranquilizers, just enough to sleep for a bit."

She didn't specify whether those tranquilizers were self-administered or if Eleanor had helped her sister to dreamland.

"Why is she here?" I asked, trying to put the final pieces of this puzzle together.

"She came with me willingly, you know." The words were defensive, but I heard truth in her words. She hadn't abducted her own sister. Celeste had known where her sister was, and what she'd been doing—and we knew she'd fed her information from Dana. She was still far from innocent, regardless of whether she'd intended for James to be hurt.

Though she spoke easily, even conversationally, Eleanor never moved, and the needle did not waver from Mac's neck. "Celeste can be naive, and she hadn't expected things to turn out the way they did. She told me things were out of control. I told her the only thing out of control was her Xanax addiction and, well, you know how sisters fight." She shrugged, unconcerned.

"What 'things,' exactly?"

She stared at me with the absolute focus of the beast that lurked within her. At that moment, I knew with utter certainty that everything else—the occasional appearance of weakness, the bright, mad eyes, the graduate student full of hard-won wisdom—were just acts, reflections of humanity she'd picked up over the years. The truth of who she was lay in the predator's gaze now fixed on me, the gaze that weighed every strength and weakness I might possess and judged my threat potential accordingly.

She wasn't ready to dismiss me yet, and I'd never be so foolish as to dismiss her. We were at a standoff.

"Don't play stupid, Aidan. You're many things, but that isn't one of them. The car crash, for instance. Celeste thought it was unnecessary. Your mother. Her son's poor mental state."

The reminder was too much for Will. He stood on his hind legs, bellowing his anger, then dropped and took several steps forward. Eleanor pricked Mac's neck with the needle, her thumb on the plunger.

"No!" I shouted, not even certain who I yelled at. "Stop, please." Will snarled, but he remained in place, and Eleanor slowly removed her thumb, though she kept the needle in his neck. Mac's eyes were fluttering, the noise and the pain drawing him to wakefulness. I was both thrilled to see signs of life and terrified he'd do something really stupid in an attempt to help.

"See, I said you were smart. Without even being told what's in this syringe, you knew you didn't want me to inject it. You're right, of course. If I give him this, Mac won't remember much of anything."

She cast her eyes toward Will, still staring at Eleanor with her death in his eyes. She was unconcerned. Her absolute confidence set off all my warning bells. The threat to Mac was the only card she had to play, and she couldn't keep an unpressed needle in his neck indefinitely.

As much as I might wish otherwise, I didn't think Eleanor was stupid, either. We'd guessed earlier that she had a plan. Control the children, control the families. We still didn't know the whole story.

Keep her talking. Keep her talking till Simon could drop down on her ugly, deceptive mug and claw her to bits. Keep her talking till Sera could show up and incinerate her. It was damn hard to press a needle while on fire, I was sure. And if Sera never made it, I could do it in her place. It might be signing my death warrant to do it in front of so many people, but I only had to look at Mac and the beds of the other shifter children to know the risk was worth it.

Yeah, I had a plan, too.

"Why?" I asked. Nice and open-ended, letting her share whatever she felt was important. Whatever might inspire her to keep talking.

"Why children? Why Celeste? Or why the drugs? You're going to have to be more specific than that, Aidan."

For once, I had the basic sense to keep my mouth shut. Eleanor was proud. I thought the beast inside might be proud, too. She wanted someone to know how she'd outsmarted everyone. My silence might just give her enough rope with which to hang herself.

"It actually didn't start with me. Growl at me all you want, Will, but it was your wife who put this in motion. Celeste loves James, but he wasn't ever going to be a doctor or lawyer when he fought the need to shift every time he smelled blood or got angry. He'd be trapped here, in this small town, for the rest of his life—just like the rest of us. We all know there's no escape. She wanted human children. Brandon will get to do whatever he wants in life. She wanted the same for her other son. James is supposed to go to college next year. She wanted him to go far away, and to go as a human, though she knew it wasn't possible."

"But you'd talked to Brian." The words brought a heavy weight to my chest. Even dead, I wasn't free of my former friend's crimes and betrayals.

"It's amazing what truths come out over a bottle of vodka, especially when you think you have common goals. He wasn't much a fan of shifters." No, he hadn't been. He'd made my father look like a paragon of tolerance when he spoke of them.

"So he gave you the serum, and I'm guessing you wore a red wig to every meeting, making it just a little harder for anyone to connect you to the drugs. But I still don't get why you did this. If you were just trying to help Celeste, why the other children? Why all the side effects?"

She studied me for a second, considering what to tell me. In the end, she seemed to decide it didn't matter what I knew. "Why would I go to all this trouble for one boy? I told Brian I'd use it to rid the world of shifters. He was an arrogant man, and he never believed anyone could outsmart him. He didn't give me shifter deaths. He gave me control over every shifter in Tahoe. That is why I did this."

Without another word, she shoved the contents of the plunger deep into Mac's neck.

CHAPTER 23

The response was instantaneous. Without the threat of the needle holding him back, Will leapt forward, knocking Eleanor to the ground. She landed flat on her back, her head cracking against the hard linoleum floor. He held one threatening paw above her face, claws extended and razor sharp.

I heard someone screaming and distantly knew it was me, begging him to spare her at least long enough to learn about the antidote. Despite his rage, I didn't need to remind him. Even as Will menaced Eleanor, his son was never far from his mind. Once she was immobile, he was content to hold her hostage, willing to wait for a more appropriate time to disembowel his sister-in-law.

Miriam observed the sudden rush of movement and considered her best move. Finally, she walked up to Eleanor, currently plotting her next action with a pissed off bear pinning her to the floor. From a crouched position, the otter shifter drew back her arm and delivered a right hook worthy of an Olympic boxer. Eleanor's head rocked backwards, and she groaned. Miriam had, quite truly, wiped the smug expression off her face.

With Will looming above her, Carmen watching carefully from the side, and Miriam bouncing on her toes, looking for any excuse to show off her left hook, Eleanor was, quite simply, screwed.

I crouched beside her snarling face, much closer than was altogether sensible, but I wanted to enjoy gaining the upper hand. "Need some help?" I asked.

While I was too busy gloating to be of any use, Carmen was thinking ahead. She shifted back to her human form and started sorting through the supplies at the bedside, finding several plastic tubes she began braiding with neat, efficient movements.

"It makes them harder to break," she said, in response to my questioning look. "You know bears are strong, right?" She tied Eleanor's left wrist to a leg of Mac's hospital bed, then repeated the motion on the other side. Will slowly backed away, dark eyes watching for the smallest unauthorized movement.

Carmen nudged her roughly in the ribs. "Talk."

Eleanor should have looked at least a little nervous. She was restrained and surrounded by a bunch of people who could, individually, send her to the hospital. Collectively, they could rip her into tiny pieces and spread them throughout the greater Tahoe basin. She had no advantage I could see. And yet, she was smiling.

Nerves crept along my spine, calling to my magic. Be ready, they whispered. She isn't done with you yet.

"Sure. I'll talk." Eleanor turned to me. "I told you I was a permanent student, remember? It's a funny thing. You spend enough time in school and people stop caring what degrees you're even bothering to get. They stop asking, particularly if they think you're just wasting your life and the family money. For the record, Will, the last one was a PhD in pharmacology & toxicology from UC Davis."

My breath caught, the nerves intensifying. I wasn't going to like what she said next. "You know Brian stumbled across a mix of drugs that controls the magic. It's a basic opiate/tranquilizer combo, with a couple of inhibitors that affect the central nervous system. Basically, it tires you out and makes sure your thoughts don't ever reach the magic. Simple stuff that wears off fast, and I'm a little embarrassed I didn't think of it first. But I did put my stamp on his creation, once he gave it to me. A few tweaks here and there, mix it with the right technology, and you've got a slow release system."

My blank face didn't offer the response she was looking for. Her words were full of scorn, but she continued her explanations. "You lot spend so much time obsessed with your magic that you forget science is just as powerful. A tranquilizer got them here, then an experimental amnesia drug made sure they had no memory of their time with me, at least for a while. That one's not mine, I'm sorry to say. They've been working on that for years at Harvard, and I just borrowed it. With James, I only wanted him to forget a couple days, not his entire family. I confess, with Pamela, I was curious what a larger dose would do."

Carmen didn't say a word, but I watched her claws slowly extend, and her slitted eyes narrowed on Eleanor's jugular. Will placed a paw on her upper arm. For restraint or comfort, I didn't know.

"Oh, calm down, Carmen. It should eventually wear off. I mean, it is still experimental, so I can't make any guarantees, but she'll probably remember you, some day."

My eyes went straight to Mac, wondering how large a dose he'd received. He was asleep, his body processing whatever mix she'd just given him. "Everyone in here's been given a nice, hefty dose. That's the thing with scientists. They always want to push just a little bit more, don't they?"

"Just the mad ones," I said. She looked amused. I might have complimented her, for all I knew. "And then you gave them Brian's adapted cocktail."

"Oh, no." She shook her head, happily continuing her story. We weren't intimidating her into telling the truth. She wanted us to know. Josiah was right—she'd always planned on this moment. She might have wished to tell us on her terms, rather than while tied to the legs of a hospital bed, but she was adaptable.

"Then I implanted the drug. Doesn't a verb make such a difference? If I just gave it to them, it would wear off in the time it took to work its way through the body. Even slow release wouldn't last more than 24 hours. But a single, tiny drop, released once a day, and my patients won't be able to shift for the next five years."

More than enough time to turn them completely into beasts.

Her eyes flicked over my shoulder. I followed her glance and saw a large digital wall clock. Any minute now, our backup should arrive.

Unfortunately, I doubted that's why she wanted to know the time.

"What have you done?" I backed away from her. I didn't know what I was protecting myself from, but I was certain I needed distance from something.

"It would have been irresponsible of me to implant a magic suppression without also implanting its antidote, wouldn't it? Microchip controlled, of course. Those things are so handy. You can even set a timer on them, did you know?"

Behind me, I heard a snarl. It was loud and unmistakable. Only one animal made that sound—a brave, vicious animal. "Wolverine," said Carmen, and the word sounded like a curse. Wolverines were considerably smaller than mountain lions and bears, but their ferocity was legendary. They were basically the honey badger of the mountains.

"Well, I know I'm staying in human form," said Miriam.

I thought that was a damned good decision.

All around us, teenagers and children were returning to their animal form, gratefully shifting after days or weeks of being denied what their bodies craved. I saw a coyote, a badger, a bobcat, and a beaver, all slipping easily from their beds. A moment later, they were shrieking, forced to turn back into humans. It hadn't been long enough, the shift. They needed more. Around the lab, I watched young shifters fall to the ground, scared and dejected, many of them sobbing in desperation. It was heart-wrenching.

"Don't you see?" Eleanor asked. "I had more than enough time to program their implants when I heard that window break. They'll shift when I decide, and only then. And if you don't allow me access to my equipment—all carefully password protected, of course—your children will be lost to you."

"Why?" I repeated my question from earlier, not sure I was any closer to understanding. "Why is it so important to control shifters?"

"Isn't it obvious?" She glanced at Will and Carmen. They both stood several feet back from Eleanor, but despite the pure hate that sharpened their features and set their eyes blazing, they could do nothing. They could not harm this woman so long as she held their children's future in her psychotic hands. They wouldn't stop trying to find a cure, but in the meantime, some of the most powerful shifters in the area were under her command.

She spoke as though her reasoning was self-evident. All I saw was a power-mad woman. However, I also knew that those who craved power for its own sake were the most inclined to abuse it, so it seemed a safe bet she wasn't going to use her newfound power to implement a shifter family game night.

She snorted. "You really have no idea, do you? Even

you, surrounded by Josiah and your mother and raised by the old ones? You know exactly what they say about us. How they hate us. How they deny we exist. How, no matter where I went in the world, they were there first, claiming what should belong to us." Her voice evolved into a snarl, the beast adding its voice to her words. "We were born from the same magic as you. We are not lesser. We are more. We are human and animal and magic. We are life, and you do not get to look down your nose at us. You do not," she repeated, the words bitten off one at a time.

She stopped, fighting for control. I saw her own claws extend and recede. She was unwilling to give the beast free rein, not while there was still work to do.

When she spoke again, her voice was calm, almost conversational. "Do you know there are at least five times as many shifters as elementals? Unlike you, our blood does not weaken through our matings with humans. We are strong. And yet, we let you make all the calls. What the humans know or don't know. You think we wanted a bunch of FBI agents sniffing around? But you lot get involved, and then I get to worry every day that I'm going to end up being experimented on in some government lab."

She seemed completely unaware of the irony. Or that it was a shifter who'd involved the FBI. I suspected such pesky facts wouldn't make a dent in her version of reality.

"So, what, you think if you control the shifter families, they'll take power from the elementals?"

"I think if I control the shifters, they'll do whatever I want, and I want the elementals dead." She smiled at the thought. "I'm sure most shifters wouldn't need much encouragement. We've been wanting an excuse to give you what you deserve for years. You are not better than us. You are not superior. Tahoe belongs to us, and family is all, Aidan. It is the strongest power in this world. We will do anything to protect our own."

"The way you protected James?" Perhaps I shouldn't bait her, but she'd just detailed her role as the architect of an elemental-free utopia. It was safe to say she started it.

She snarled. I could call her a crazy bitch all I wanted, but the minute I questioned her family loyalty, I'd crossed a line. "They are safe. They're all safe. I was going to announce myself in another week, anyway, and the children all would have made it that long. So long as their families don't fight me, the children will be able to shift as normal."

She still spoke in present tense, certain that despite being found out, she retained the upper hand. In many ways, it really was a diabolical plan, impressive in its scope and its high ranking on the evil mastermind scale.

Of course, I had an ace up my sleeve, one Eleanor had never met. I had Vivian. Eleanor might as well have a password of "12345" for all the good it was about to do her. Ten minutes on Eleanor's computer, and we'd control the implants.

Once we controlled the implants, we'd control Eleanor.

Unfortunately, that was still in the future, and Eleanor was in the mood to demonstrate how much power she still possessed. She looked over my shoulder again, eyes on the clock, and the beast grinned.

"How do you think a bunch of predators with no memory of their family, friends, or even being human might behave?" She looked at each of us, dangerously pleased with herself. "Let's find out."

Again, the shifts began, and the room rang with the howls and cries of frightened animals. This time, however, she allowed them to stay in their animal forms. Confused, scared, and desperate, the animals scanned the room, their fight or flight impulses reaching a decision. One by one, I saw them decide we were the threats, and those that didn't turn on each other turned on us, stalking slowly toward our group.

Above me, Mac rose, an enormous, growling bear. Madness was in his eyes.

The slow tension that had filled the room since we entered exploded into manic action as one animal after another began its attack.

Miriam dove for the beaver, struggling to subdue the panicked creature. Beavers might normally be peaceful creatures, but after several days of being Eleanor's personal lab rat, all bets were off. Miriam was cursing and muttering to herself, but the frustration was due to her unwillingness to hurt the small animal whose sharp teeth kept snapping dangerously close to her skin.

Elsewhere, Carmen reverted to her cat form and bounded after the bobcat. It only took a short chase before her muzzle was wrapped firmly around the neck of the small bobcat, who hissed and spat impotently while she carried him about the room.

Will was having far less luck restoring order. He'd found himself backed into a corner by both the wolverine and the coyote, who seemed to be overlooking their natural impulses to attack each other in the face of far more impressive prey. A quick swipe of his paw would have been enough to eliminate the threat but, like Miriam, he was too aware he was battling confused, innocent children.

All this happened in a matter of seconds, the same time it took for Mac to rip through the restraints tying him to the table and move unsteadily to the ground. The entire time, he emitted noises from deep in his throat. I couldn't even call them growls. They were suppressed screams, steeped in desperation and uncertainty. He rose on his hind legs, seven feet of well-muscled rage and confusion.

He bellowed, and all movement around me ceased

instantly. The beaver stopped fighting, the bobcat stopped squirming, and even the wolverine paused in its attempt to sink teeth into Will's forearm.

Mac hadn't even been here twenty-four hours. He couldn't be as deranged as those that had been here for days. I told myself that, even as I met dark eyes that held no knowledge of his surroundings, of me, or of himself.

The beast I'd glimpsed in his eyes several times, that hint of the animal that shared flesh with the man I knew, that was what stood before me now, unhindered by the human impulses and emotions and logic that normally restrained it.

This was the pure beast, an animal large enough to decimate any threats and, stripped of his memory, Mac saw nothing but threats surrounding him.

He dropped to all four legs and began a lumbering run directly toward me. In my peripheral vision, I could see Will shaking off the smaller animals still pestering him. It didn't matter. I was less than ten feet from Mac. Will would never reach me before Mac did.

I had mere seconds to make a decision. I consulted my magic, looking for my water, but where I expected to find fear of the enormous creature rushing toward me, I found anger instead. This wasn't some accident. This had been done to him, cruelly forced on him by that smirking bitch still sitting on the floor, convinced she'd bested us all.

I had access to fire, but that could never be an option. It was Mac, and there was no way on this earth or any other I would set him on fire.

I took the anger and forced it deep inside, refusing to even acknowledge its existence. It wasn't there. I was calm, so calm. I was a leaf on the fucking wind. For just one moment, I believed that, and in that moment I grabbed every bit of water I could find in the air and flung it directly at Mac, forcing it far enough into his nose and lungs that he'd be forced to stop for a single second. I only needed to buy myself that tiny fraction of time, just long enough for Will to reach us and subdue him.

It worked. It worked perfectly. He stopped mere feet from me, his face damn near comical in its confusion. He coughed several times, clearing the water from his lungs.

And then it all went wrong.

It happened so quickly, and yet I knew that years in the future I'd be able to describe that moment with perfect recall. Mac shook off the water and moved toward me, just a single step. He was close enough that I could see the individual hairs, the way his fur shimmered with so many different shades of brown. Some were darker now, coated with water that continued to drip from his face and chest.

There was noise, so much noise, then the room dropped into absolute silence.

I felt the heavy exhalation of air through Mac's nostrils, warm on my skin. And then, with no warning, he crumpled to the ground, a single whimper escaping his throat.

It made no sense. I stared at the darkening fur of his chest. I held a small globe of water in one hand, but I hadn't thrown it. There was no reason for Mac to be growing wetter. Then the water dripped, slowly dripped onto the floor, and I saw that it was red.

There was no thought. There was no planning, no consideration, no doubt. There was only the largest fireball I could conjure in a single heartbeat. I turned on my heel and threw it unerringly toward Carmichael, still standing in the doorway with a gun in his hand.

It flew toward him, too fast for him to grasp the threat and move in time. It was only Sera, standing just behind him, that saved his life. She grabbed the fire and pulled it to her without hesitation, extinguishing it.

Carmichael and Johnson stared at me as if I was a stranger, which I supposed I was. It was almost funny, the blank stares they both turned on me, and I stifled a giggle that sought to escape. Distantly, I knew such a reaction was inappropriate considering the situation, and not one others should witness. They might think I was having problems with my sanity. They'd probably be right.

Simon was the last one through the door, and his sharp eyes instantly took in the scene. He'd shifted with Mac many times, and he immediately recognized his friend, fallen on the floor. He ran to him and knelt at his side, determining the extent of the injury as best he could.

I felt a twinge, a vague sense I should be doing the same thing, that I was needed elsewhere, but such an act would require calm. I never wanted to be calm again.

Instead, I turned to Carmichael, who stared alternately between me and his gun, wearing that same stupefied expression that had covered his face the day I told him elementals existed. He looked like a target.

"I said to only shoot the bad bear!" The words came out in a harsh scream that belied the ridiculous statement. The anger made sense, much more sense than the laughter. I'd felt such pure clarity once before, while I watched my own house burn, and I welcomed its return.

"He was about to attack you!" Carmichael insisted.

"That's the bad bear," I shouted, pointing. "Shoot her!"

I turned back to the others, all of whom were staring at me in various degrees of shock. Even Eleanor appeared a bit uncertain. She hadn't counted on this. I grinned and sent a fireball directly to her. "Still feeling pleased with yourself, Ellie?"

Sera ran toward us and grabbed that fire too. I glared at her, then doubled up my attack, trying to produce more fire than she could control. She was always one step ahead, my half-blooded fire no match for her stronger blood.

"Aidan." I stopped, feigning a vast patience I did not feel. "We've got this. Mac needs you."

It took a moment for the words to penetrate. Mac was fine. No, Mac was full of drugs. And then I remembered, the one thing I should never have forgotten. Mac was lying on the ground, his breathing rapid and uneven, while I stood above him, toying with the people who'd done this to him. The rage dissipated instantly, replaced by shame and grief and desperation.

I dropped to my knees, speaking nonsense words I barely heard to a bear who didn't understand me. I begged him to stay with me. I swore we'd get help. I told him I hadn't meant to forget about him, any more than he'd meant to forget me. His eyes flickered open, long enough to focus on me. I saw no recognition in their depths, only pain.

Around me, I heard order slowly being reestablished. The animals were separated from each other, and Sera set large rings of fire around each one, just enough to trap them until we could either shift them back or at least drug them into unconsciousness again. I heard her voice, a one-sided conversation, and through my fog I heard the words password and server. Vivian was on the job. We'd have control over the drug implants within the hour. Eleanor had no power, not any longer. We'd won.

It didn't feel like a victory. Mac was fading before my eyes, his breathing growing shallower by the minute. I heard myself sobbing, but my body was numb, unable to feel itself fall apart. Simon kept pressure on the wound, his neat hands lost amidst the bloodstained fur.

"Is it his heart?" I asked. I'd studied basic human anatomy, but never thought I'd need to know the structure of a bear's internal organs. It couldn't be that different, right? The wound was directly in the center of the chest, a bit to the right of where a human heart would be.

He shook his head. "Just to the side." Mac sighed, a long exhalation, and several seconds passed before he breathed in again. "But it hit something, Aidan. A lung, maybe, or an artery." He sounded uncertain, speaking words whose meaning he barely knew. Simon was, after all, a theatre major. Science and medicine were hardly his forte.

"I can't do anything," he said, confirming my thoughts. "We need to get him to a hospital."

Sera joined us when she got off the phone. One look told her we didn't have much time. "We won't make it." I felt my own internal organs rearranging, my heart falling heavily toward my stomach. My body was turning to stone. "You'll have to do it, Ade."

I stared at her, knowing she was suggesting utter insanity. "I've never done anything like this. Not on humans, and definitely not on bears. I have no idea what I'm doing. I'll kill him."

Sera was quiet, waiting for me to admit what we both knew. If I didn't help him, he was dead regardless.

"Your mother could do it. Why can't you?" Simon's eyes never left Mac's face.

"She's full-blooded. And old. And well-trained. And not, you know, prone to loss of control at key moments." They were all good reasons I wouldn't be successful, and they weren't even the full story. Even calm, I could feel the fire dancing within me. No matter how I might wish to pretend, I wasn't pure water, and my body was done pretending it was. If the fire interfered at any point in the process, if it interrupted the water magic, Mac would die at my hands.

Even as I protested, I knew those reasons didn't matter. It was Mac's only chance, and I would take it.

"If I kill him..." I began. I didn't know how to finish that sentence. Don't let me go insane? Don't despise me? Don't keep me from joining him?

"No way." Sera answered just the second question, a tiny, forced smile making its way to her face. "We'll blame Carmichael."

My eyes went to the agent, hovering nervously in the concerned circle that had formed around Mac's prone body. He looked horrified, and I didn't care. "Get him out of here." Steel hardened my voice.

No one moved. "You heard her," Sera insisted, eyes black and flat.

Johnson lightly grabbed Carmichael's upper arm, moving him toward the door. I didn't watch them leave, but before they made it more than a foot, Simon stopped them. "I strongly recommend you submit no reports to your superiors until Sera or Aidan have approved them." He let his claws elongate, the threat obvious. A moment later, he relaxed, and I knew they had silently acquiesced.

Mac's eyes fluttered open, moving over each face now gathered around him. Miriam was supervising the children, making sure no one caught fire from their cages, but everyone else was there. His eyes roamed over Will, Carmen, Simon, and Sera, and the expression did not vary from face to face. Everyone was unfamiliar. I received the same questioning look as everyone else, and it broke my heart into tiny pieces. He'd said he would always know me, and it seemed I'd believed him.

But after he looked at everyone else, his eyes returned to me and stayed there, and I knew I would do whatever it took to keep him alive.

I pressed my lips to his forehead and spoke quiet words just for him, using the name he'd whispered in my ear the night we kissed. "Go to sleep, Connor. Close your eyes and let me fix you." I sent a desperate plea to the fire to remain quiescent, and then I reached my magic deep inside Mac's body just as he breathed his final breath. At the moment my magic grasped his life source, it was extinguished, and he died.

CHAPTER 24

I heard sobbing, but this time it wasn't me. It was Will, his deep voice accompanied by Celeste's gentle cries. During all the chaos, I hadn't noticed her waking up. She stood apart from our group, knowing she wouldn't be welcome, but she still wept as her nephew died before her.

I stared at her, at her pathetic snivels. "Don't you dare. You don't get to grieve. You started this. You do not get to cry for this man." She blanched under my stare, and I knew my eyes were gunmetal grey daggers. Her fear wasn't enough, and I felt little satisfaction. I wanted to hurt her. I wanted to hurt Eleanor, still tied to the bed, truly beaten this time.

The fire leapt at the chance.

It wasn't alone this time. For the first time ever, the fire didn't extinguish the water through the force of my anger. I'd worked too hard to secure my water side, to keep Mac safe no matter what treacherous emotions flowed through me, and this time it refused to be consumed by the fire. Instead, the fire swirled around my water half. The two magics joined together, and at last I understood what it was to be a dual magic. I wasn't one or the other, some fractured and broken elemental.

I was both, and this time, when the fire sang to me, madness did not beckon. I felt complete, and a pure, certain knowledge filled me. It was familiar and sure, a knowledge that had lived within me my entire life, so much that I wondered how I'd never heard it before. It spoke to me of absolute truths, of the purest magic of life and creation that existed at the dawn of time, and I knew exactly what I needed to do.

I'd helped my mother with enough healing to know the basics. You fed the magic in slowly, letting it attach to the body's water supply. You asked the water to find the impurities and invaders, to tell you of any irregularities it encountered, and you attempted to separate them from the body. You could use the water to move blood through the body, to inflate the lungs and urge the heart to beat. It was slow, detail-oriented work, and a single mistake would cost a life. It would require the utmost concentration and patience to bring Mac back from death.

I had the concentration but not the patience. Mac wasn't breathing, and I had no time to spare. I grabbed the fire, so active and demanding, and let it propel the magic through my body, through my fingers, and into Mac's pores. It reached deep within his body, into the bear that lay dead before me. It was indiscriminate, and it looked for any place to land.

What I sent into his body wasn't water magic, and it wasn't fire magic. It was the core of both, the pure magic of creation the first elementals were born from, the heart of the magic that lived within each of us. It was the magic of life. And the full-blooded ones, like me, we had a whole lot of it. It was the magical core that kept us alive through disastrous car crashes, that kept us from aging through the years, that kept us connected to the earth and water, the glaciers and volcanoes, the beaches and deserts. It was our very essence, and with the fire magic as propellant, I sent it rushing to Mac's bullet wound. Long-lived might not be the same as immortal, but this time it would be. I'd make sure of it.

It only took seconds. His body expelled the bullet and the flesh knit together, the wound closing instantly. I felt the internal organs repairing themselves, and with one insistent beat, his heart exploded back to life, eagerly pushing the blood throughout his body, carrying the magic to every inch of his body, repairing every damaged cell.

It wasn't enough. He was alive, but he wasn't yet Mac. I sent the magic exploring, consciously looking for the implants. They were hidden above the massive muscles of his forelegs, and the magic wrapped around them and filled them anew, devouring the unwanted drug. It turned out anti-magic medicine had its limits, and being confronted by the purest magic in the world was one of them. As I watched, Mac's fur slowly receded, his teeth shrank, his muscles reformed, and the man returned, his breathing weak but steady.

There was more to be done. The magic was eager to finish the job, but my absolute certainty in my task was wavering. I had no idea what such power would do when it touched his neural pathways, and though I desperately wanted Mac's memory to return, the risk was too great. He was alive. That had to be enough.

Reluctantly, I withdrew the magic, but it resisted, my own magic treating me like a stranger.

I'd asked it to do something unknown, maybe even unnatural, and it wouldn't return smoothly. It fought me at first, wanting to linger in the new warm body it had just discovered. At last, with great effort, one thread at a time slid back to me, back to my core, and it recognized its home. It called to the rest, and it all returned with increasing eagerness, fire and water, the very magic of life filling me up again, defining me.

It was more than I'd ever done, and I felt an exhaustion

that ran bone deep, my mind and the magic and my human body all depleted. I began to convulse from the effort, and without considering the medical wisdom of my action, I looked for the safest place in the room. It was right below me, and I lowered my shaking body onto Mac's chest. There was a haven in his warmth and solidity, and I drew it to me, letting it repair my pain and invisible wounds as I'd done for him.

I lay for a long time, feeling the shaking slowly stop. I could hear the others moving, speaking softly and beginning the horrible process of dismantling the lab. A blanket settled over me and Mac, and I felt myself begin to drift, the warmth and absolute fatigue conspiring to draw me toward unconsciousness.

In that last moment before sleep claimed me, I felt Mac's arm wind around my waist, and he pulled me closer.

HE SLEPT FOR days. At the end of the first day, I worried. By the third, I panicked. With Will's help, we returned him to his trailer. Someone was with him at all times. Every night I crawled in next to him, hoping my presence would remind him there was something worth coming back for.

I only left the cabin once, to visit my mother. Eleanor hadn't been able to insert an implant in her arm, so once the drug wore off, she awoke and we learned the full story. My mother had been working on James, trying to discover what was interfering with the magic, and she found the blockage to his memories instead. Unfortunately, Eleanor had been in the room with her at the time, and she was disinclined to allow my mother to unblock him. One long syringe with a crippling dose of the anti-magic cocktail found its way to her neck, and she'd passed out.

"We are magic," she told me from Will's guest bed. She was awake, but to say she was recovered would be optimistic. "We are never meant to exist without it. It would be like asking a human to exist without several vital organs. I shut down completely. There was nothing you could do until the drug wore off."

"But you're okay now?"

She grimaced, just a tiny bit, then allowed her face to smooth into its usual elegant mask. "I'll be fine, darling."

My mother, the martyr. "Come on. Let's go."

With Will's help, I got her to the car. I headed straight for Tahoe City, at the top of the lake, and let her lean on me as we made our way to the water. It was slowly getting more crowded. Though the lake was still cold, summer was nearly upon us, and it looked like several people were determined to get a jump on the worst of the vacation crowds. They thought nothing of the two blond women that looked like sisters standing knee deep in the water, one supporting the other.

She closed her eyes and fed hungrily on the lake's energy. "Ah, that is nice," she said. "Not quite the Pacific, but nice nonetheless."

I resisted the urge to defend Lake Tahoe. I might have grown up surrounded by the same ocean she loved, but this was my water now. My home was the lake and the river, not the island where I'd been raised.

"Better?" I asked instead. I knew she was. After a few minutes, she didn't need to lean on me any more.

She nodded. We stood in silence for a long time. "You have no plans to return with me, do you?"

"You know I don't."

"Will told me I needed to let my cub go, let her form her own sleuth. I believe that's what he said." She spoke carefully, the idea unfamiliar.

I smiled. "That's what a group of bears are called. Hey, have you heard about Wikipedia yet?"

She nodded absently. There really wasn't anyone who shared my enthusiasm for that site. "I did the only thing I could think to do to protect you. I believed it was the right choice until I heard you say otherwise. I thought that, so long as you remained a pure water and remained on the island, I'd saved you. Of course, look at poor Celeste. She did the opposite. She attempted to set her son free of his magical heritage, to give him the world, and she destroyed one life after another. Perhaps there is no correct answer."

I swished my foot through the water. "You did what you thought was right. It wasn't right—let's be clear about that—but I know you were trying."

It wasn't complete forgiveness, but it was a start.

She paused, uncertain how to approach the next topic. "I was told you used fire, Aidan."

"It wasn't planned."

"I'm sure not. How do you feel now? Mentally?"

"Surprisingly good." I almost stopped there. I didn't want to worry her with the small changes I'd felt since the lab, but keeping them to myself would be the same thing I'd accused her of doing—protecting a loved one from the truth. "Though I feel different. Sharper, somehow. Like I just got a new pair of glasses, and the blurred edges of the world are now clear and defined. I don't feel insane, though I'm not sure any insane person would feel that way. I'm mostly worried that this morning, for almost five seconds, I considered going for a jog."

She forced a laugh, though I didn't see the humor. That brief thought had horrified me.

"No desire to kill anyone yet?"

"Not so far, though I probably shouldn't be left alone in a room with Eleanor or Celeste anytime soon."

"The shifters will take care of their own. Will is a loyal man, and he hates to deprive his sons of their mother, no matter how misguided she was. If you remain in Mac's life, you will cross paths with Celeste."

"I'll be ready." I paused for a long time, trying to think of the best way to phrase an idea I doubted my mother wanted to hear. "In a strange way, I understand why Eleanor acted the way she did. Not the way she went about it, or the high levels of crazy she devoted to her master plan, but her reasons for hating us... she wasn't wrong. Elementals can't keep treating shifters the way we do and just expect them to take it."

She stared off into the distance, and I thought her mind was already back on the island, with its full-blooded waters who'd been determinedly set in their ways since the Renaissance. "Perhaps," she said vaguely. "I'm certain, however, that we at least won't need to worry about Eleanor attacking us—or anyone else—again. The shifters will see to that."

I nodded, unable to conjure any tears for a woman who'd had no qualms about hurting children and sought the death of all local elementals, myself and Sera included. I might understand the anger that motivated her, but I could still hate her for the way that anger had manifested.

Once, I despised death as a solution, but I was less certain these days. I knew I would never mourn the loss of Eleanor, no more than I mourned Brian. Sometimes, the world was just better off without certain people. Maybe it was my fire side hardening me, tempering me into a lean, mean, elemental machine. Or maybe I would hurt anyone who came after my family. Not the one I'd been born to, but the one I chose. It was growing every day.

And once again, I chose to include my mother in it. "If anything changes, if I feel myself becoming violent, I'll call you. I've told Sera to call you, if she notices anything. I won't disappear again. I promise."

She wasn't a demonstrative woman, but she wrapped her arms around me in a quick, fierce hug. "Good. However, I fear you'll be visiting the island sooner than expected."

That didn't sound promising.

"The council would like to see you. They're convening on the island next week." No, that wasn't promising at all.

"They don't know?" I asked, feeling the panic rise. Sure, I was often a neurotic, babbling mess, but I really liked being alive. I had no desire for the council to alter that state.

"No, they don't," she said firmly. "They're more concerned about the way you shared our existence with two FBI agents and then followed up by tilting Lake Tahoe about twenty degrees toward Emerald Bay."

"Oh. That." With everything that had happened, that day had somehow slipped my mind.

"Yes, that. I expect they will vote to ostracize you from the elemental world."

I considered that for a moment, thinking about what I could lose. The home I'd grown up on. My nutty aunts. I faced the possibility of centuries of solitude, cut off from many of my own people. But I also thought of what they couldn't take. Sera and Mac. Simon and Vivian. My mother. No matter what the council said, they weren't going anywhere, and they were my true people.

"You know, I'm okay with that." I felt a grin split my face, the same energy that was healing my mother filling me up, bringing a peace and joy I hadn't known in weeks. "I'm really okay with that."

AFTER I RETURNED her to Will's, I had one more stop to make. I phoned the cabin quickly, to make sure there'd been no change with Mac, and told them I'd return in a couple of hours. Then I climbed into my beat-up old

Chevy and made my way toward a certain Reno suburb. There was a long overdue apology I needed to make.

When I pulled up outside Diane's house, I didn't feel apprehensive, despite our previously antagonistic relationship. An hour of country music, the kind that insisted you sing along, had me smiling, and if that wasn't enough, there was the certainty I was doing the right thing. I'd harassed this woman time after time, and while she'd played a small role in the abductions, it had been entirely unintentional. She was innocent, and she deserved to hear me acknowledge that.

My good feeling lasted only until I saw the black sedan, a familiar lackey waiting patiently in the driver's seat.

I barely remembered exiting my car and running up the walkway. Even through the thick walls of the house, I could feel waves of magic rolling toward me.

I knew I was already too late, but I threw the door open and ran through the house in a panic, heading toward the source of the magic. It was strong, stronger than anything I'd ever felt in myself or Sera, and it left an unmistakable trail.

Josiah stood in the living room, and the fire Sera and I had wielded in that room was child's play compared to the blazes he controlled. One hand created fire, pushing it in nonstop streams toward its target, while the other withdrew the flames, maintaining the fire within a small radius and ensuring no neighbors saw a raging house fire and dialed 911. He'd placed her body on the hearth, and the smoke eagerly escaped up the chimney. To anyone watching, Diane had simply built herself an unseasonal fire in her living room fireplace.

"Stop." The word was somewhere between a scream and a plea, and I was already reaching out with my own powers, trying to quench the flames. I'd never done that before.

I'd always created fire in my anger. I'd never attempted to extinguish it, and I had about as much success as one would expect of a novice pitted against a master. Josiah glanced at me once and nodded, a simple acknowledgement of my presence, then returned to his work.

He stoked the fire hotter and hotter. I could have tried to stop him again, found some other way to distract him, but there was no point. Diane was already dead. Her much-loved shotgun lay fallen at her side, a useless threat against my father. I saw a large wound in the center of her chest. He must have borrowed her gun just long enough to kill her, so at least he hadn't burnt her alive. It was all the mercy he was capable of showing.

Diane's skin was charred and black, cracking to reveal the white bones beneath. Her hair and clothes had already been incinerated, and now Josiah cremated her. He was a one man murder squad and body disposal service.

That man was my father. The thought was nearly as nauseating as the smell of burning flesh that crept through the room.

I wouldn't leave to find fresher air. I owed it to Diane to watch this death I'd caused. Someone needed to bear witness. As I watched the bones crumble to dust beneath the unrelenting onslaught of Josiah's fires, I knew, no matter how many centuries passed, that I'd remember this moment. I wouldn't forget her death, and I'd never forget what my father truly was. I would not let myself.

Eventually, there was nothing left to burn. I'd sunk onto a white couch at some point, though I had no memory of doing so.

"Aidan," he said, smiling. "I didn't expect to see you today." Apparently, in Josiah's world, social calls were often accompanied by immolated bodies. Hell, maybe they were. I had no idea what the man's hobbies were.

"Why did you do this?" My words contained an obvious horror that Josiah completely ignored.

He stepped out of the room, and his words floated back to me. "You know why." He returned a minute later with a dustpan and broom and began to sweep up the mess. I felt hysteria bubble within me at the sight of my millennia-old father doing housework. Perhaps he didn't have a specific assistant for the cleanup and removal of human remains.

"She was innocent. She wasn't involved with the kidnapped shifters, not really."

He rounded on me, his face so fierce that I found myself shrinking into the stuffed sofa. "Why would I care about some shifter cubs? She could attempt a shifter genocide, and I'd probably buy her a bottle of champagne. That means nothing to me."

"Then why?" I asked. I wanted to hear him speak the words aloud, though I already knew.

"Because she saw you," he said, confirming my worst fears. "She knew what you are, and no one can know that. No one can possess information that would cost my daughter's life."

"I'm not your daughter," I said dully, watching him push a small, unburnt chunk of bone into the dustpan. "I didn't want to be your daughter before, and I just officially disowned you."

"Regardless," he said, the fierceness vanishing easily into sardonic amusement, seemingly at my expense. "I am still your father, and I will not allow such threats to your life to exist."

At that moment, breathing felt like an unfamiliar exercise. "How did you know?"

"They filed an insurance claim for fire damage. I knew you had visited her that day."

"You're stalking me." Outrage, yes. That was better than

numb.

He waved his hand, as unconcerned as ever about privacy concerns. "Always so dramatic. I can't believe you still think you don't act like a fire. I'm simply concerned, Aidan, as I ought to be."

"It could have been Sera," I protested. "You didn't know it was my fire."

He laughed outright. How nice that I amused him so. "Sera is my daughter, Aidan. She knows how to control her powers. The only time she's been unable to do so is in your presence." He waved at the ragged burn marks that scored the furniture. "This is not Sera's work."

"You can't just kill anyone who knows what I am."

"Of course I can. I know you told your sister, and I understand that, but you know how important it is to keep your dual nature secret, to tell no one else." His gaze focused on my horrified face. "You haven't told anyone else, correct?"

I begged my emotions to numb and found the part of myself that felt nothing, wanted nothing. I shook my head, willing the riot of emotions that still swirled beneath the surface to stay hidden for another minute, just long enough to fool Josiah. He nodded, satisfied, and I had to believe I'd managed to hide the truth from him. For now.

I was some alternate universe version of King Midas, except everything I touched turned to dead. I was already surrounded by enough ghosts to haunt me for the rest of my days. I couldn't bear any more. Simon, Mac, and Vivian had been risky enough, but they knew the stakes. They knew to remain quiet. Now I'd drawn Will, Carmen, Miriam, even Johnson and Carmichael into my secret. All it would take was a small slip, a casual comment, an indiscreet report, and they'd be dead. One after another, I could lose the world I'd built for myself.

I stood unsteadily and met my father's eyes. His were

the black of the fire elementals, the black of charcoal and ash. They were the same color as Sera's, but where hers offered comfort and humor, his were barely connected to this world. He did not see what the rest of us saw. He was one of the most powerful beings in existence, and I no longer cared. He would not take my world from me. It was mine, and I would fight for it.

I walked slowly over to the shotgun and hefted it onto my shoulder. I'd never fired one before, and it took me a minute to figure out the safety. Josiah patiently watched my movements, only vaguely curious. He didn't expect me to pull the trigger and send a blast directly into his right shoulder, and the pure shock that crossed his face when I did made me smile. He thought he knew me. He was wrong.

I didn't hit the heart. He would live. For several long seconds, I considered firing again. I couldn't imagine the world would be a worse place without Josiah Blais.

But I wasn't ready to be that person, not yet. One shot was enough to deliver the message.

"I am not your daughter." I repeated my earlier words, this time holding his gaze, and whatever he saw there caused him to waver. For just a moment, Josiah Blais looked uncertain. "Do not follow me, do not track me, and do not contact me again. I am done with you." Before he could recover, I walked from the room, leaving him with only ashes for company.

CHAPTER 25

Days passed, and while my shock and grief didn't fade, I found my recent habit of compartmentalizing my anger was useful. It turned out I had a special compartment reserved just for my father, and I placed everything inside it. He was out of my life.

It was time to move on with the people still in it.

Unfortunately, some of them were also moving on.

I stood on the ladder, watching Simon putter around in the loft space. "Sera just called. They'll be here any minute." He nodded, letting me know he'd heard, and continued to move around the loft, gathering a few final items.

I watched him and thought of at least twenty different arguments for why he couldn't leave. Carmen would be a terrible roommate. Living with two teenage girls would be hell. The corgi would chase him. Each thought crossed my mind, and each one I dismissed. Simon deserved better than my selfish desire to keep my friends close.

Instead, I forced a grin and focused on the good news. "So you've decided to give up the siren call of the stage, after all?"

"It turns out I missed auditions while tromping all over Tahoe with you lot. Besides, they were doing *A Midsummer Night's Dream* this year. Why that play is considered a classic is beyond me. I mean, fairies and spells? How ludicrous."

It was a plausible excuse. I didn't believe it for a minute.

"Of course. The part where the man turns into a donkey is particularly far-fetched."

He didn't smile, but neither did I. Without warning, sincerity sprouted through the facade of good humor I was trying to maintain. "We'll miss you. I'll miss you. I'm glad you're at least staying in the state."

He rolled his eyes. "You do know I will be fifteen minutes away, yes?" The words were caustic, but he smiled and quickly rubbed his cheek against my shoulder.

Outside, we heard the unmistakable growl of Sera's Mustang. Simon shifted and flew out the window, leaving me to carry his discarded clothes and bag downstairs.

By the time I joined him outside, he was hugging Vivian. She didn't seem to mind that he was doing so completely naked. She was thin and pale, but she was wearing a Star Fleet Academy t-shirt and smiling. That was the Vivian I knew, and I rushed for her as soon as Simon let go. She felt fragile, and I thought if I wrapped my arms too tightly about her, she would break. I released her after a quick hug, unwilling to push her too far. She'd helped us break Eleanor's password and gave us control of the implants, but she wasn't back, not yet.

Olivia, waiting impatiently in the driver's seat, was proof enough of that.

"Did you thank your mom for me?" she asked. I nodded. Once my mother had recovered her energy in the lake, she'd promptly expended it by healing the shifters' memories. As a group, we'd discussed whether to leave the block that prevented them from remembering their time in the lab. Two voices had come out strongly against that plan, and somehow my mother and I had convinced a bunch of shifters to follow the advice of a couple of elementals. The children's abductions were now part of who they were. There was no protecting them from that.

There was only one person she'd been unable to help. Whatever I'd done to him, it had altered him too much. She had no idea where to even begin undoing the changes I'd caused.

Vivian had been next on my mother's list. She'd healed my friend in two hours. The doctors were, of course, mystified, but we figured we'd just given them at least one new journal article.

Sera stepped onto the porch, Vivian's bag in hand. She gripped it tightly, and I knew she was debating whether to actually hand it over. "You don't have to do this, you know. This is still the woman who ignored you for weeks. Also, I have it on good authority she watches a lot of reality TV."

Vivian shrugged. "She loves me."

Sera was unimpressed. "There are different kinds of love, Vivian, and some last longer than others. Just remember that your room will still be here when you get sick of watching repeats of *The Biggest Loser*, okay?" She carried the bag to Olivia's car and threw it in the trunk, avoiding eye contact with the woman inside the car. I don't know if Olivia could hear Sera's words, but she didn't look happy.

I wasn't ready to say good-bye, not yet. So long as they remained at the cabin, there was a chance they'd change their minds. They might stay.

Denial, it seemed, had all sorts of uses.

"There are some people here that want to thank you for deactivating the implants. Can't you stay?" I tried to keep the pleading tone from my voice. I failed.

"I can't," she whispered. "I need to be away from all this for a while. Please understand."

I couldn't argue. I knew exactly why she had to leave. Our lives had been one disaster after another for months on end, and I couldn't promise her that wouldn't continue. Too many questions were still unanswered, too many problems still needed to be faced. I might want her at my side, but I couldn't demand she stay there. It wouldn't be fair.

This whole maturity thing kind of sucked sometimes.

"Do what you have to do," I said, to both Vivian and Simon. I felt something tight release with the words, a sense of letting go of something I'd not known I was holding. Fear that they wouldn't come back, perhaps.

Simon climbed in the back seat, still naked. Olivia attempted a straight face, but I could see the shock she was trying to hide. Somehow, that cheered me up immeasurably. If she was going to steal Vivian from us, at least Simon was making her work for it.

Vivian struggled back into the passenger seat, her movements stiff. Her recovery wasn't complete.

She closed the door, and the car reversed slowly down the drive. We raised our hands in silent farewell, watching until they were out of sight.

"This doesn't feel right," I told Sera.

"Damn straight it doesn't." Her face was expressionless, as it always was when she felt strong emotions.

"They might be happy, though." I didn't mean to sound as doubtful as I did.

"For a while, they will. Then Simon will tire of eating raw deer instead of canned tuna, and he'll find his way back. And those two? They're doomed." Her tone left no room for argument.

"What makes you so sure?"

"Seriously? Their names are Olivia and Vivian. Liv and Viv. That is way too twee to last. Two months, tops."

"So we just let them go." I knew that's exactly what we had to do, but I needed to hear someone else say it.

"Well, you know. Free will and all that."

"Then what happens?"

She turned to me, and finally a smile cracked her face.

"Then we put the band back together."

I nodded, accepting the truth of her words. It wasn't much of a plan, but it was a start.

We walked through the house, needing to break the news to our visitors that the guest of honor wouldn't be joining the party. The shifters had all set up camp on our back porch the moment they heard Vivian was being released that day. Ever since she'd saved their children from Eleanor's implants, our earth friend had become something of a folk hero to the shifters. If asked, I thought Will and Carmen might compose a song in her honor.

It gave me hope for the future of elemental-shifter relations.

Through the sliding glass door, I watched our guests. Will and Carmen stood at the railing overlooking the river. They weren't talking, but peace hung over them, and I thought James and Pamela would find fewer obstacles to their future happiness, at least from their families.

Miriam sat in a corner with a half-drained bottle of booze, teaching Brandon and Mary how to play quarters and winning handily, despite playing two sober opponents. When she saw me, she winked, then sent another coin soaring into the cup.

And standing at the grill, where salmon cooked on one side and pancakes lay neatly across the griddle on the other half, was the reason I got out of bed each morning. I stood at the door, not quite ready to join everyone's celebration.

Mac knew I was there instantly, and his eyes met mine. He smiled, and for that moment my sadness over Simon and Vivian disappeared. Mac was safe, and alive, and he knew me. Nothing else mattered.

"Dude, watch the fire," Brandon muttered, unimpressed by our display.

Our eyes dropped to where the unattended fire had

seized its chance, eagerly seeking freedom through the iron bars of the grill. Without a second thought, I grabbed a quick ball of water and dropped it, killing the fire with a sharp sizzle. At least I managed to save the pancakes.

I pulled the magic back toward me, but it came unwillingly. It wanted to play. It wanted to dance with the other magic it found, the familiar power that lingered just a few feet away. That small hint of elemental magic that hadn't returned to me the night Mac died.

Several uninvited drops of water slithered down the back of my shirt. They played against my skin, drawing circles across my shoulder blades. I met Mac's gaze again, and again he smiled, this time with more than a hint of devilry.

No one else noticed. No one else knew, and we had no plans to change that anytime soon.

We weren't together. We couldn't be, not with so many questions still unanswered. But we weren't apart, either.

I wrenched my eyes away from his and looked at each face in turn.

In theory, everything was terrible. I wasn't sure if I'd put the agents on probation or they'd done so to me, but the end result was the same: I had no job. I was about to receive a banishment sentence from the council. My father was a murderous psychopath whose existence threatened the lives of everyone I loved. My own magic was slowly shifting, pushing me closer to a mental state I still didn't understand. Two of my best friends had just left, off to explore new lives. And just for good measure, I may have turned Mac into a magical freak of nature.

My world was getting stranger and less predictable by the day, full of new people and new puzzles. I thought that might be a good thing.

Balance, I decided, was a myth. It implied stagnation. It was something we told ourselves when we needed to believe we had a semblance of control over our own lives. Things changed, constantly. People entered and left our lives, sometimes several times. We adapted and grew, or we didn't and shriveled. It was our choice to make.

I made my choice. I stepped onto the porch, and I let my world get a little bit bigger.

Acknowledgments

At times, this book felt like something of a beast (pun totally intended)—a lumbering, uncontrollable creature determined to have its way. These are the people who helped me tame it, and I am beyond grateful for all their hard work.

My editor, Kaari Busick, continues to be my greatest champion, and her love for the Elements series helps keep me excited about writing it, even on those days when it feels like I'd have better luck bench-pressing grizzly bears than meeting my word count.

Sarah Goshman, publicist extraordinaire, has done an amazing job helping readers discover the Elements series, and I cannot thank her enough for her work.

Carrie Stewart has helped in so many ways, both big and little, that I can't even begin to list them all. Suffice it to say this book would not have been published without her.

Special thanks to my tireless betas, Jessica, Rachel, and Shelly, who assured me I hadn't taken the series completely off the rails while also pointing out an embarrassing number of plot holes and unclear motivations. Thanks as well to Carol, for generously volunteering her time to review the final draft, and to Cynthia Fliege, for creating another fabulous cover.

Lake Tahoe Wildlife Care were the source of my improved knowledge about the local wildlife population and the reason I now know bears adore watermelon and bobcats only pee in water—important information to possess, I'm sure you'll agree. They have an open house every

August, and if you're visiting Tahoe, it's definitely worth the trip.

Thanks to the citizens of Truckee for not screaming too loudly about the way I frequently install buildings where none exist and insist on raising the town's crime rate.

Finally, thanks to the readers who have become invested in the Elements world. It still amazes me that others are connecting with these characters and places I love, and I am thrilled to share them with you.

About the Author

Mia Marshall has always been obsessed with stories. When younger, her version of cleaning her room involved neatly organizing her books, then ignoring all other messes in favor of re-reading *The Wizard of Oz* series just one more time. As an adult, she earned an unnecessary number of degrees in literature, education, and film. She planned to spend the rest of her life teaching stories to others, but she became distracted and started writing those stories herself.

Mia has lived all over the US west coast and throughout the UK. These days, she lives somewhere in the Sierra Nevada mountains, where she is hard at work on the next Elements book.

www.ingramcontent.com/pod-product-compliance
Lightning Source LLC
Chambersburg PA
CBHW020244200626
46816CB00001BA/120